Quest of Eight Addendum: The Other Side of the Boravak

Richard Reda

I0525876

Quest of Eight Addendum: The Other Side of the Boravak

Richard Reda

The Quest of Eight

Addendum: The Other Side of the Boravak

Quest of Eight Addendum: The Other Side of the Boravak

Richard Reda

The Quest of Eight

Addendum: The Other Side of the Boravak

By

Richard Reda

Published 2013

ISBN-13:
978-0-9912728-0-8
ISBN-10:
0991272803

This book is dedicated to our first eight Grandchildren

Summer

Lochen

Solveig

Sean

Natalie

Stella

Quinn

Liam

And to two more who may only exit in our imagination. A special thanks to my wife, Karren, for her support and her editing.

Quest of Eight Addendum: The Other Side of the Boravak

Richard Reda

Quest of Eight Addendum: The Other Side of the Boravak

Richard Reda

Quest of Eight Addendum: The Other Side of the Boravak

Richard Reda

The Quest of Eight

Addendum: The Other Side of the Boravak

Chapter one

He discovered a small opening; so small he almost missed it. No wonder the others never found it, he thought. He considered trying to squeeze through it, but was worried. What was on the other side didn't trouble him. It was the uncertainty of what he'd find when – and if – he came back through to this side. He was somewhat convinced that he knew where he'd reappear; it was when he would reappear that unsettled him. He has been warned about crossing to the other side. But desperate times call for desperate measures, he told himself. And these were desperate times.

Aitch was a Phynnodderee. He and his people lived in the woods that grew along the shore of the sea. They had been there for generations – long after the Great War. He didn't know much about the Great War, other than the stories that were told by the village rectors. These were the spiritual and temporal rulers of the Phynnodderees. Aitch's father was not one of the village rectors and had little regard for them. Still, it was not wise to run too far afoul of their direction.

The Phynnodderees had been endowed with some limited mystical powers – some more limited than others, and many different from one another. No one knew for certain where these powers originated, or why certain powers were bestowed on certain people. Aitch's father could sing so beautifully, he could communicate with the birds – even understand them. His mother could make potions and elixirs from almost anything. His sister, Emm, was still very young and her powers hadn't yet manifest themselves. As for Aitch, he was unique. He was the only Phynnodderee who could change shapes.

He could shape-shift into almost anything he wanted. The only problem was that, being green himself, everything he shifted into was also green. This was good if he wanted to turn into grass, but not so helpful if he turned himself into snow.

As a very young boy, before this ability developed, Aitch disappeared from his village. He was gone for three days. His father had searched far and wide for him, enlisting the help of every feathered creature for miles around. But he was nowhere to be found. When he returned, he had aged by more than two years, although he had been gone only three days. He assured his family that he had been safe. He told them he had gone to the other side and been trained in the magical arts, not the least of which was his ability to shape-shift.

After getting over her relief at his return, Aitch's mother berated him for wandering off, demanding to know where he had been. She was even angrier to hear that he had gone to the other side. That was forbidden, she had shouted at him.

"We're supposed to search for weaknesses," she shrieked. "Openings; to make sure they can't be breached; not to go through them! Have you learned nothing?"

"I went with..." he started to say, but then stopped, suddenly worried about what she would say if he told her he left with some stranger.

"With?" she asked, her voice climbing in equal proportion to her blood pressure. "You went with someone? Who? Tell me this instant!"

It was too late now, he realized, cowering in the face of her rage. He debated about changing shape into something that would allow him to escape, but quickly reconsidered. He'd have to come back sooner or later and if he disappeared again, he was worried his mother's wrath would only increase exponentially.

"An old man," he started to say.

"What?" both his parents shouted at once.

"What old man?" his father demanded. "Who? Where is he now?"

"He said he was an Alchemist," Aitch said in a voice barely above a whisper.

He knew there was no way for him to present this information in a positive light. As the words were coming out of his mouth, they sounded bad – even to him. He lowered his head, waiting for the inevitable; bracing himself for the worst. Instead, he was met with silence. He raised his eyes slowly upward. The look on the faces of his parents raised his anxiety level more than the admonishment he expected to receive.

"What?" he asked.

"Have you spoken of this to anyone?" his father asked.

"N-n-no," Aitch stammered. "I came directly home. I haven't seen or spoken to anyone else."

His parents looked at one another and Aitch could see some sort of silent communication pass between them. Then a look of resignation came over his mother's face and she turned away. Her knees seemed to weaken and she bent over as she reached for the nearest chair, slowly lowering herself to sit. She looked up at her husband and appeared to have suddenly aged in Aitch's eyes.

"You better go see the rector," she said in a thin voice.

Aitch's father clenched his jaw, thinking about what she said. He then slowly shook his head, resigning himself to what appeared to be some kind of distasteful task.

"Come with me," his father snapped.

Aitch had to run to keep up. He wanted to ask why they were headed to see one of the rectors, but he didn't want to tempt fate and figured he'd find out soon enough. They skirted around the outer edge of the village and then arrived at the home of the oldest of the rectors. Aitch was wide-eyed. He had never been here before and knew how little regard his father had for the rectors.

This particular rector lived in a small, low cottage made of field stone with a moss roof. There was an old wooden door in the center at the front, but no windows. Aitch's father looked around and then softly rapped on the door. A few seconds later, it creaked open and a pair of eyes peered at them from the darkness.

"I need to speak with you," Aitch's father murmured. "It's urgent."

The figure on the other side of the door nodded and stepped back. Aitch's father looked around once more and then pulled him by the collar into the cottage. It took several seconds for his eyes to adjust to the darkness. The interior looked bigger than he expected. There was a small central room with a fireplace on the opposite side; an opening off to the left and a similar one to the right. Aitch guessed that one led to a kitchen and the other to the sleeping quarters. It was very much like his own home, only smaller.

The rector motioned to a padded bench on one side of the fireplace while he sat in a chair on the other side. Aitch's father sat down and pulled Aitch down next to him. The rector raised an eyebrow, waiting for an explanation.

"He says he's been with the Alchemist," Aitch's father said without any introduction.

The rector showed no change in his expression; his dark eyes shifted from Aitch's father to Aitch and back again. The silence hung there for several seconds. To Aitch it seemed to be endless.

"And you believe him," said the rector – more of a statement than a question.

"Yes," Aitch's father said after some thought.

"Are you certain?" the rector finally asked.

"Look at him," Aitch's father shot back. "He's aged far more than the three days he's been gone. And watch his eyes."

His father turned to Aitch and said, "Who have you been with?"

Aitch looked from his father to the rector and back again, uncertain as to what was expected of him.

"Answer," his father demanded.

"The Alchemist," Aitch whispered, and then clarified, "a man who said he was the Alchemist."

"Tell him," his father said, motioning to the rector.

Aitch repeated the answer, facing the rector, who studied him closely.

"See?" asked Aitch's father. "There's no change in his eyes. He's telling the truth."

Phynnodderees were unable to lie without the pupils of their eyes fluttering and the irises changing color slightly.

"He's telling the truth as he knows it," replied the rector dismissively. "That doesn't make it the truth."

Aitch's father wrinkled his face in frustration. He knew it was the truth. He could feel it. He was certain the rector knew it was the truth, too, but was refusing to acknowledge it. He took a deep breath in an effort to control his anger.

"What did he teach you?" Aitch's father asked him. "What power did you learn?"

Aitch looked from his father to the rector and back again. He looked around the room and then down at the bench on which they were seated. Without saying anything he closed his eyes and concentrated. Within seconds he began to change shape and took the form of a cat. His father jumped back and the rector jumped to his feet. Aitch quickly changed back.

"All right, Madjer," the rector said to Aitch's father, the color drained from his face. "I believe you."

"You should have believed me from the start," Madjer snapped. "You're my own uncle."

Uncle, thought Aitch. He's my father's uncle? And I'm learning this only now? How is that possible? He wanted to ask dozens of questions, but knew he should keep quiet.

"Yes," answered the rector. "I should have."

He looked from Madjer to Aitch and ran his fingers through his hair, scratching his head. He slowly sat down again, his eyes fixed on Aitch.

"You've been to the other side?" he finally asked.

"I think so," Aitch answered. "I don't know for sure."

"How can you not know for sure?" his father shouted.

"Don't be so harsh with the boy," interjected the rector. "This is the Alchemist we're talking about, after all. He probably met with you at some point and erased it from your memory."

Madjer turned towards the rector and glared at him, but kept silent. He searched his memory for any indication that this might have happened. He could recall nothing, but knew that his memory could not be trusted – at least not in this matter.

"Start from the beginning," the rector instructed Aitch. "Start from when you first met him."

Aitch explained that a few days ago – or was it years – shortly after his morning meal, he had been in the forest, not far from the village. He was gathering herbs for his mother when a strange light appeared. At first he thought it was a reflection of the sun, but he couldn't see its source. He walked towards it, going deeper and deeper into the woods.

The light seemed to dance. It bounced from one tree to another, and then into the foliage to disappear. Seconds later, it reappeared, but slightly further away. He looked around to keep his bearings. Certain of where he was, he continued on, following the light. As he approached a stream, the light once more disappeared. As Aitch crested a small rise near the bank of the stream, he came upon an old man.

The man was sitting on a large rock at the edge of the stream. He had long white hair and a long white beard. His skin looked like parchment and his eyes looked like they were filled with milk. He's blind, Aitch thought. As this came into his mind, the old man turned directly towards him and smiled.

"Hello, Aitch," the old man said. "How are you this fine day?"

"How do you know my name?" Aitch asked, immediately wary.

"I know all about you," the old man replied. "I know all about you, your sister, your parents, and your village."

"You've told me what you know," replied Aitch, keeping his distance. "But you didn't answer my question: how do you know my name?"

"That's right," the old man laughed. "I didn't. Actually, I'm not sure how to answer that. I've known since before you were born. Your father told me, although I'm certain he doesn't recall telling me – or even that he recalls meeting me."

"Who are you?" demanded Aitch.

"Ah. That's easier," he answered. "I'm the person who is referred to as the Alchemist. Perhaps you've heard of me."

He had. For as long as he could remember, the stories that had been handed down for ages among his people included a reference to the Alchemist. He had been a figure that played prominently in the Great War and events that occurred long before that. A group of very powerful sorcerers and enchantresses called Kelpies had banded together in an alliance. They were unstoppable; wreaking havoc throughout the land. They had been released from ancient prisons, amassed an army of followers and threatened to destroy everyone and everything that would not pay homage to them.

An unlikely group of heroes had taken them on with the help of an Alchemist and trapped them inside a structure called a Boravak. The Boravak was the world in which Aitch and the Phynnodderees lived. They were among several of the peoples responsible for protecting their environment: ensuring the well-being of the Boravak. The Kelpies eventually turned on one another in what had been referred to as the Great War. This conflict lasted a very long time and very few places were safe. In the end, one by one the Kelpies destroyed themselves and many of their minions; but not completely. Two survived. Two sorcerers, who were not of the original Kelpies.

The two survivors called a truce and divided the Boravak between them. Over time, a normalcy returned to the land and peaceful villages sprang up. But as time passed, the Boravak began to change. Weaknesses began to appear. The Alchemist would return periodically to repair the weaknesses and relied on the local people to help him maintain the well-being and security of the Boravak.

The primary people to whom this was entrusted were the Phynnodderees. Over the years, the Alchemist watched them closely. He discovered that in every other generation there was one or two of them who were special in some way. He soon realized that there was a thread of mystical ability that ran through them and was becoming more prominent as time passed. He believed that this ability stemmed from a link with the eight ancient leaders of the peoples of the world, whose descendants had fought the Kelpies and secured the Boravak.

When Aitch was born, the Alchemist could sense a tremendous power had arrived. This power resided in the new-born baby. The Alchemist knew that as the child grew older his powers would need to be properly developed. He also knew that any display or use of an untrained power would be viewed as dangerous by those around the child.

One afternoon, while Aitch's father was hunting in a distant part of the forest, the Alchemist appeared to him. At first Madjer was frightened by the sudden burst of light. Then he became curious and crept carefully towards the flickering beams. He came upon an old man sitting on a log. The Alchemist introduced himself and in the conversation that followed, he quietly cast a spell on Madjer.

In the spell he instilled the ability on Madjer to contain and hide Aitch's powers until the boy was old enough to be schooled by the Alchemist. The spell also made it so that Madjer wouldn't be aware of doing this or have any recollection of meeting the Alchemist. When the spell had been cast, the Alchemist disappeared. Madjer blinked his eyes and wondered why he was standing where he was; dismissed the lapse in his memory as a sign he was getting older; and quickly forgot about it.

A few years later, the Alchemist once again appeared. This time he met with Aitch on an afternoon when the young boy had been gathering herbs for his mother. The same strange light Aitch's father had seen several years earlier now appeared to Aitch.

"Hello, Aitch," the Alchemist said when the boy was close enough to hear him. "How are you this fine day?"

"How do you know my name?" Aitch asked.

And so began their first meeting. The Alchemist talked to him at length, telling him about the history of the time before the Great War – long before the Phynnodderees ever existed; long before they settled where they now lived and grew to populate the forest. He told Aitch about the powers with which he had been born – powers Aitch felt he had, but which he never thought to display or develop.

"Ah, yes," replied the Alchemist. "Your awareness of your capabilities, as well as your lack of any desire to display them. I have to admit that the later was my doing – with a little help from your father."

"But why?" asked Aitch.

"Because you weren't old enough to understand the implications of having that power," the Alchemist answered.

"What does that mean?"

"It means that there are forces in your world that would feel threatened by you and would do you great harm if they found out about your powers before they could be developed enough to be cloaked and to enable you to protect yourself," the Alchemist told him.

"Who would want to hurt me?" Aitch asked, nervously.

"Right now, that's not important," said the Alchemist.

"Not important?" interrupted Aitch. "Maybe not to you, but I think it's important to me."

The boy has spirit, the Alchemist thought. He considered the best way to approach this subject and decided that he needed to begin at the beginning. Before he started, he waved his hand and enveloped the two of them in a thin mist.

"What did you do that for?" asked Aitch.

"It's a simple spell," said the Alchemist. "It will slow down time around us and hide us from anyone who happens to wander in our direction. This is going to take some time."

He then explained the initial rise of the Kelpies and their war against the leaders of the different peoples of the world. In their attempt to control the land, they destroyed the leaders and terrorized the people. He told him how he and the Enchantress, Meri Hocto, had separated and imprisoned the Kelpies, keeping them hidden for several centuries. He told him about Tebaga and Ena Ray, pupils of the Enchantress, who turned against her, causing the destruction of her magical pendant, and how the things they set in motion almost resulted in her death. He explained how the Rebbercands became a force for evil and he described the destruction they caused wherever they went.

He explained how B'nair and Bacham had discovered long lost pieces of the pendant and the power it bestowed on them. At the same time the unusual alignment of the planets was beginning and would have a significant effect on the resurgence of the Kelpies. Fortunately, the descendants of the ancient leaders came together and were able to challenge and defeat the Kelpies, entrapping them on this side of the Boravak as they made their escape to the other side. In the aftermath, the Kelpies turned on each other in what was known as the Great War, and destroyed themselves.

All that remained were two sorcerers – Ena Ray and Tebaga, who rose from the ashes. They were both extremely dangerous and manipulative, but without the power of the pendant, their abilities were limited. They agreed to divide the Boravak in half and maintained an uneasy peace over the years that followed. Ena Ray chose to rule the goblins, and lived in the north, and Tebaga ruled the Rebbercands, living in the south.

Once this tentative peace fell over the Boravak, the Alchemist helped the scattered peoples who remained rebuild their villages and societies. He needed them to be the caretakers of the Boravak. Each had a different role, but chief among these people were the Phynnodderees. As time has passed, the peaceful residents of the Boravak had prospered and grown. However, the descendants of Ena Ray and Tebaga had also grown. Grown in number and become restless.

The north was presently ruled by Walipreen – a cruel and vicious tyrant, and the descendant of Ena Ray. He was the result of cross breeding among the goblins. The kingdom over which he presided had initially been comprised of these creatures. As time passed, this population divided and faded. Now it was comprised of several different types of creatures, most predominantly the Phookas. Phookas were relatively small, goat-like people. They had long, narrow faces; small, beady, and close-set eyes; and long horns. They lived in caves and underground tunnels, much like their goblin cousins. They were notorious thieves.

Walipreen was a Phooka, or at least mostly a Phooka, but he was distinct from them. His genes still included those of Ena Ray, so he was much bigger, much smarter, and much more devious that the Phookas he ruled.

The south was ruled by the twins Rampool and Prine, both of whom were highly paranoid, easily manipulated and very dangerous. They were the descendants of Tebaga. Their kingdom was made up of the Rebbercands; however, they no longer wandered as nomads. Instead, they created a string of villages comprised of poorly made mud huts. They separated themselves from all other societies, became entrenched in their narrow-minded views, regressing instead of progressing over time.

Although there had been no outright attacks on the peaceful citizens, there had been secretive attempts to disrupt the peace and turn the people against one another. The Phookas were especially known for being devious and ruthless. The Rebbercands, for the most part, were foolish and ignorant, fearful of change or anything different than they. Walipreen saw this as an opportunity to attack and control them, stealing them away from the twins and making them his slaves. But he also knew he would be much more powerful if he had the pendant in his possession: the pendant that was on the other side of the Boravak. In order to find a way to the other side of the Boravak, he needed to control the primary keepers – the Phynnodderees. The twins were also aware of the existence of the pendant, but lacked the imagination of Walipreen.

"And that is why you are in danger," explained the Alchemist.

"That doesn't explain anything," argued Aitch. "I don't know how to get to the other side of the Boravak, so why would they be interested in me?"

"Perhaps not," said the Alchemist. "But you know where the weak spots are, or at least how to find them. And sooner or later, those weak spots will become openings that can be breached. That must not happen."

"That still doesn't explain why I'm in danger. I can't get through to the other side, even if I knew where the weak spots were. And I don't know where this pendant thing is."

"You have a power, as yet untapped, that could open up a door to them that must remain closed," the Alchemist explained.

"I still don't know what you're talking about," Aitch replied, somewhat frustrated.

"Not yet," answered the Alchemist. "And that's why I'm here and why you are coming with me."

"With you?" asked Aitch. "Where?"

"To the other side of the Boravak," answered the Alchemist.

"NO!" shouted Aitch. "I can't. That's forbidden."

"I know it's forbidden," the Alchemist replied. "I'm the one that forbad it. So, I suppose I can be the one to now allow it; don't you think?"

"I suppose," answered Aitch uncertainly. "But why do we have to do that? Can't you do whatever you're going to do right here?"

"I'm afraid not," the Alchemist said. "This will take some considerable time, and it's not safe here."

"How much time?"

"Depending on how adept a student you are," the Alchemist told him, "it could take as much as two or three years."

"WHAT?" shouted Aitch. "That's impossible. I can't be gone that long. What about my parents? They'll go ballistic if I'm gone that long. Shouldn't I at least tell them?"

"It won't be that long for them," the Alchemist assured him. "I grant they may get a little worried, but that won't last long. And it's far better that they are anxious over your disappearance for a short period of time, than the alternative they – you; all of you – would face if you don't come with me."

"I don't understand," Aitch complained. "How can me being gone for two years…"

"Possibly longer," interjected the Alchemist.

"Yeah, yeah," Aitch shot back. "Whatever. How can it be longer for me than them? That doesn't make any sense."

"Because the Boravak is not only a different place," explained the Alchemist, "it's a different time. Time here does not pass at the same speed as on the other side. That's one reason why crossing over has been forbidden."

As he was speaking, the Alchemist had risen to his feet and walked slowly up to Aitch. It had been so casual that Aitch hadn't noticed. As they were conversing, the Alchemist made a twirling motion with one finger and the thin mist that had surrounded them grew thicker. With a snap of his fingers, the mist disappeared. Aitch spun around, examining the surroundings. They were still in the woods.

"What did you just do?" he demanded.

"We're safe now," replied the Alchemist.

"That doesn't answer my question," snapped Aitch. "What's with you? Do you always not answer questions?"

The Alchemist wrinkled his brow, considering Aitch's question.

"I've never given it much thought," he answered. "I merely assumed that the comments I've made are sufficient. No one has ever complained before. Well, except, perhaps, the Enchantress. She's very clever and very inquisitive, you know. Oh, no. You don't know, do you?"

"You're stalling," Aitch cut him off. "I want an answer, and I want it now. What did you just do?"

"I've moved us to the other side," he answered, a wry smile on his face.

Aitch looked around once more and studied the trees more closely. They didn't look any different, but when he tried to find the path he had taken when he first discovered the old man, it was gone. The realization that he was in a different forest slowly sank in.

"The other side?" he asked, his voice cracking; his throat suddenly dry. "That's not possible."

A sensation of panic swept over him. He felt dizzy. Was this some kind of spell? Was this really the Alchemist, or was it some other sorcerer? Was he in trouble?

"It's entirely possible," the Alchemist said. "Because it's true. You'll be fine. Trust me."

He turned and started to walk through the forest. Aitch stood there and watched him go. After a few steps, the old man turned back and motioned to him.

"Come on," he said. "You'll not learn anything standing there, and we have a lot to do."

Aitch ran after him, the sensation of panic slowly evaporating. After about a hundred yards, the forest ended and a wide grassy field opened up ahead of them. Not far to their front was a small fortress of some kind. Why didn't I know this was here, Aitch asked himself. Because you're on the other side of the Boravak, you dope, he answered.

The fortress was larger than it had first appeared. In fact, it was a castle on the edge of a cliff overlooking a vast sea. The water was a brilliant blue, blending into the blue of the sky on the distant horizon. As they approached the castle, a large door opened, seemingly by itself, and closed as they walked through.

"This is where you'll be living for the next few years," the Alchemist informed him.

At the mention of the time he would be here, Aitch felt a sadness overcome him. He wouldn't be seeing his parents, his sister or his friends for such a long time. The Alchemist turned towards him and appeared to read his mind.

"I know this is difficult for you," he said. "But try to remember. When you go back, only a few days will have passed for them. You won't have missed much in the time you're gone, but what you will learn will be immense."

Aitch thought that they would have something to eat, that he would be shown around the castle, taken to his room and that they would start tomorrow on whatever it was he was supposed to do. He was mistaken. The Alchemist took him into a large room and sat down on an old chair.

"Let's begin," he announced.

"With what?" asked Aitch.

"If you could do anything you wanted," the Alchemist asked, "what would it be?"

"Go home?"

The Alchemist rolled his eyes, took a deep breath and said, "Besides that."

"I don't know," replied Aitch. "I've never thought about it."

"Well, think about it now. What would you like to be able to do?"

Aitch scratched his head and looked around the room, as if searching for an idea. His mind was a blank. Fly, he asked himself. Maybe. Run really fast, he asked. That was a possibility. Become invisible? That would be a good one, he thought. All the while the Alchemist sat silently, watching him. Aitch sighed, self-conscious that the Alchemist watching him. You'd think he'd have some idea, he said to himself.

"My ideas would do you no good," the old man said.

Oh, poop, Aitch thought. Can he read my mind?

"Can you read my mind?" he asked out loud.

"No," answered the Alchemist. "It's fairly obvious what you're thinking, though. The powers you have are deep seated. They've been buried since your birth. They will, however, rise up and tell you what they are. All you need to do is concentrate."

"Right," answered Aitch, nodding in agreement, but not believing him.

Fly, run, disappear, he thought. All of them. I'd like to be able to do all of them.

"Change shape," he suddenly blurted out.

His comment surprised even him.

"No," he said. "Wait. That's not what I was thinking. Why would I say that? Did you make me say that? I was thinking about flying, or running, or hiding. I never thought of changing shape. Is this some kind of trick?"

"Slow down," murmured the Alchemist. "I did nothing. The suggestion was all your own. I told you the power would manifest itself."

"I don't understand."

"In all likelihood," the Alchemist explained, "you have several abilities. The one you just mentioned, though, is most probably the strongest."

"Changing shape?" Aitch asked, incredulously.

"Shape-shifting," answered the Alchemist. "Yes. A most valuable talent, by the way."

"Can you do it?"

"No, I can't."

"If it's so valuable a talent, then why can't you do it?" Aitch asked.

"It doesn't work that way," the Alchemist tried to explain. "I have other talents."

"But what if I don't want this one?"

"It's not a matter of whether you want it or not. That's like saying you don't want to be a Phynnodderee. You don't really have any choice in the matter. Of course, you don't have to use it, I suppose. But that would be a terrible waste."

"So, how do I do it?" Aitch wanted to know. "I've never done it before. What do I do?"

"I'll teach you," replied the Alchemist.

"How are you going to teach me," Aitch challenged him, "if you don't know how to do it yourself?"

"That's just one of my many talents," smiled the Alchemist.

And so began their first lesson. It took more than three months before Aitch was able to actually change his shape, and when he did, he changed into a girl.

"Wonderful," he complained. "I can turn into my sister – just what every guy wants to do."

"Patience," demanded the Alchemist. "This is an excellent first step. The next will be easier and will come faster."

He was right. Within another week, Aitch was able to shape-shift into a number of different animals. Then he learned to change into inanimate objects. By the time six months had passed, he was changing into almost anything he could think of and doing it with ease.

"This is great," he announced. "And it didn't take nearly as long as you thought it would."

"Well," said the Alchemist, "we're not exactly done."

"What do you mean?" asked Aitch. "I can shape-shift easily and turn back whenever I want. I can turn into anything I like. What more do I need to learn?"

"Sorcery," the Alchemist answered.

"What? You never mentioned anything about sorcery."

"I never mentioned anything about shape-shifting, either," the old man replied. "Shape-shifting is only one of your abilities. You have others that need to be developed."

"All right," said Aitch. "Still, it can't take as long as learning how to change shapes."

"Shape-shifting is your predominant skill," explained the Alchemist. "It was the easiest for you to learn. The others will be harder and take longer, I'm afraid."

"Others?" wailed Aitch. "You mean there's more than one?"

"Oh, yes," answered the Alchemist. "And it's important that you develop them all to the fullest. I fear the time is coming when you will need them."

He didn't explain what he meant, and Aitch didn't pursue it. He resigned himself to more lessons and dedicated every possible minute to learning what he needed to learn in order to get home as quickly as he could. The Alchemist had been fairly close in his prediction. Aitch was his student for two years and eight months.

When his lessons were over, the Alchemist escorted him from the castle and into the woods. As they walked Aitch thanked him for all he had done. He said he was actually going to miss the time they had spent together. He was excited to be going home, but he was sad that he would no longer be spending every day with the Alchemist.

"I know this sounds hard to believe," he said as he walked a few steps ahead of the Alchemist. "I think I'm going to miss being with you."

When there was no answer he thought, the old man is too choked up to speak. He waited for the Alchemist to say something, listening closely for any sound. When he realized he couldn't even hear footsteps behind him, he began to turn. A rush of wind threw leaves up into the air, momentarily blocking his view. When they cleared, he saw he was alone.

"Where did he go?" Aitch asked, and then he shouted, "Where are you?"

He ran back the way he had come, but there seemed to be no end to the trees. The path to the fortress was gone; the field was gone; the castle was gone. He slowly realized that he was back on the inside of the Boravak; back home.

He ran back to the village and back to his home.

"And that was when I found you," he told his father. "And then you brought me here to the rector."

The rector and his father had listened to his story in silence the whole time. Now they could only look at each other, speechless.

Chapter two

itch looked at the opening, debating about whether this was the right thing to do or not. He had run out of options. He needed the help of the Alchemist and everything he had tried to conjure up the presence of the old man had failed. Now his sister was in danger and he would do anything to save her.

Several years earlier, at the time of Aitch's birth, the surge of power that had accompanied this event had been felt by the Alchemist. He knew something special had happened, and began to watch the Phynnodderees more closely. Unfortunately, he wasn't the only one who felt this burst of energy.

Far to the north, Walipreen also sensed that something had changed. He would have been unable to describe it if asked to put it into words. It was a feeling more than anything – a tightening around his chest, a shortness of breath, a sudden and inexplicable sense of danger. He had long ago moved as far away from the wars as he could – back to the ice fields in which his ancestor, Ena Ray, had been held prisoner for so long. He felt there was a certain irony in the comfort he felt so near the place that Ena Ray had detested.

When Ena Ray and Tebaga discovered that they were the lone survivors of the Great War, they agreed that continued conflict between them was pointless. In reality, the Kelpies had not actually been destroyed. Evil never dies. The two sorcerers had absorbed the powers of the defeated Kelpies and with that the evil that permeated their souls. Both Ena Ray and Tebaga were immensely powerful and equally villainous. However, having been tutored by the Enchantress at the same time, they had a healthy, if begrudging, respect for one another. In spite of whatever past animosity they bore, they realized that neither of them would win if they persisted in trying to conquer one another.

Ena Ray took the remaining goblins with him to the north. He could not bring himself to return to the Crystal Citadel and, instead, wandered the ice fields as a nomad. Walipreen, however, had no such aversion to the cavern that had been Ena Ray's prison. It afforded him a level of security that he craved. Any attacks from the armies of the twins would be long known before it could ever reach him. He would have more than enough time to implement counter-measures.

He had resided in the Crystal Citadel for several years, allowing his power to fade; his skills to rust. The surge of energy he felt at the birth of Aitch served as a reminder of what he once had been — of what he was in jeopardy of losing forever: total domination of the Boravak.

He had no idea what the source of the burst of power was, but he knew it hadn't come from him or his people; nor did it come from the twins or the miserable Rebbercands over which they ruled. Something told him it was centered among the Phynnodderees. He pondered the situation for weeks, trying to determine the best way to approach this. He didn't want to alert the twins to anything, assuming they were as dull-witted as they had always been.

He decided to send the Phookas out to spy on the Phynnodderees. He would need someone he could trust, but immediately dismissed that thought. He trusted no one, least of all the Phookas. He would have to find one of them with half a brain; one who could follow instructions. He summoned one he thought might fulfill his need; one named Chardon.

"I want you to take a small party and spy on the Phynnodderees," he instructed the Phooka.

The Phooka smiled, or at least the grimace he made Walipreen took for a smile. It was hard to tell. His thin gray lips stretched over a row of small, yellow teeth. His eyes squinted and his nose wrinkled. He could just as easily have been in pain. When it came down to it, Walipreen considered, he didn't really care if the creature was smiling or in pain. The goblins had been ugly creatures, but the Phookas were worse.

"But you are not to steal anything," he added.

Whatever had passed for a smile seemed to fade. The lips stopped stretching, the nose stopped wrinkling and the eyes stopped squinting. It was a smile after all, Walipreen decided.

"What are we to look for?" Chardon asked.

"I don't really know," replied Walipreen. "Anything unusual."

Chardon's face seemed to compress in on itself, apparently confused.

"Everything about them is unusual," he finally said. "How will I be able to tell?"

"Look for anything that seems to be unusual to them," Walipreen tried to explain.

He knew he would not be able to describe what he had felt in any terms Chardon would understand.

"Just watch them and then report back to me," he added.

The Phooka did as he was instructed. He took a party of five with him. They spent six months hidden in various locations around the main Phynnodderee village and watched them. They could discover nothing out of the ordinary, made the journey back and reported this to Walipreen. At first he was angered, but then dismissed this and considered that perhaps he had only imagined the feelings. A few years later, he felt another surge.

He thought about sending the team of spies out again and then was struck with the thought that the sudden burst that he felt may be coinciding with the birth of someone imbued with an extraordinary level of power: a sorcerer or an enchantress. If that were the case, then the use of this power would not be manifested for a number of years. This might explain why the Phookas hadn't noticed anything unusual. That, and their lack of any imaginative capability.

Still, he thought, it might be good to keep eyes on the Phynnodderees. So, he instructed Chardon to keep a small group near the village and to have them report back at regular intervals. Several years passed, over which he felt a few additional, unexplained sensations. These were not like the others. He could tell they were somehow connected, but he knew they were different.

One day, one of the Phookas observed something unusual. Chardon escorted him in to see Walipreen and report. At the sight of his leader, the Phooka was suddenly not so sure of what he had seen.

"Out with it," Walipreen demanded. "I'll be the judge of its importance."

"I was in the forest outside of the village," the Phooka began. "I wasn't even on duty, actually. But this boy came walking towards me. I knew I wasn't to be seen, so I burrowed."

He nodded and grinned as if he had done something noteworthy. Walipreen waited for him to go on.

"And that's all?" he asked when the Phooka remained silent.

"Oh, no," he stammered, realizing he had more to tell. "He walked past me."

Walipreen waited. Even Chardon knew there was more to report and cuffed the Phooka across the back of the head.

"Spit it out," he shouted. "All of it, you dimwit."

"Yes, yes," he sputtered. "Sorry. Well, he walked past me, and didn't see me at all. So I followed him. He went out of sight over a small rise. I crept through the brush to see where he went, and there was this fog. But there shouldn't a been no fog – weren't no reason for fog to be there; come out a nowhere, it did. I tried to go into it, but I couldn't. It just moved. Then there was this flash of light and the fog was gone – real sudden-like. And so was the boy. He was nowhere."

"Tell him the rest," Chardon urged him, ready to cuff him once more.

"Oh, yeah," the Phooka added. "I looked all around. I followed the footprints which just ended – like he was raised up into the sky; cept he wasn't. I'd a seen that. I stayed there looking for him for three days. I was about to give up, but as sudden-like as he vanished, he un-vanished."

"What do you mean, he 'un-vanished?'" demanded Walipreen.

The Phooka cowered, worried that he had said or done something wrong.

"I mean he just showed up again, walking through the woods from the same place he vanished from. He was talking to himself."

"What was he saying?" Walipreen asked.

"Something about it being good to be home, but he'd miss someone, cept there weren't no one there and I didn't see him throw anything at anyone, so's he couldn't a missed no one."

"He didn't throw anything," Walipreen interrupted. "He didn't miss someone with something he threw, he missed them...never mind. You wouldn't understand. Is that all?"

"No," the Phooka added. "He looked...different."

"Different? How?"

"I don't really know," the Phooka answered nervously. "All them Phynnodderees look...different, but this boy – he changed some way. Maybe older? I guess."

He left the Boravak, Walipreen thought. He crossed over. But how? The Alchemist. That was the only answer.

"How much older?" he nearly shouted.

"I don't know," the Phooka muttered. "I'm not even sure that was it, exactly. He looked a little bigger and walked different. I don't know. He was different. That's all – just different."

Walipreen was silent for several minutes. Chardon and the other Phooka stood there waiting.

"Am I in trouble?" the Phooka whispered to Chardon.

"No," Walipreen announced. "You're not in trouble at all. In fact, you've done quite well. You can leave me now."

The Phooka smiled broadly and stood there until Chardon gave him a push and the two of them left Walipreen to his thoughts. What did this mean, Walipreen wondered. He was sure the Alchemist had taken the boy to the other side of the Boravak, but why?

He called on Chardon once more.

"There is a source of tremendous power somewhere among the Phynnodderees," he said. "I think it might involve this boy."

Chardon listened in silence, his expression still a mystery to Walipreen. He couldn't tell if the Phooka was concentrating or in gastric pain. He tried to describe what he had felt, but when he finished he wasn't convinced Chardon understood what to look for.

"Send another party to observe the Phynnodderees," he directed.

"Can we steal this time?" the Phooka asked.

No, thought Walipreen. He still doesn't know what to look for — thick as a brick. And what was worse was that Chardon was probably among the smarter Phookas.

"What, exactly, would you like to steal?" he asked.

The question seemed to confuse the Phooka even more than he was already confused. His face twisted as he thought about an answer.

"I don't know," he finally said. "Stuff."

Walipreen could have strangled him then and there, and would have if there was anyone else he thought he could send.

"Study them first," he ordered. "Then you can steal. Just make sure you don't get caught and that you come back to me with some useful information."

Chardon made another face; one that Walipreen was fairly certain was a smile. He then left without another word. Once more his small team studied the Phynnodderees, and once more they really couldn't detect anything out of the ordinary. No one disappeared. No one looked different. The boy didn't seem to change much while they watched him. And worse, they also could not detect anything much worth stealing. Disheartened, they prepared to leave.

"What a waste," one of them complained. "All this time and nothing to show for it."

"We have to take something," another one said. "If we go back with nothing we will look like fools."

They crept closer to the village. It was near dusk. Many of the Phynnodderees were settling in for the evening. There was one, however, who was near the edge of the forest. It was a small one and it seemed to be alone. The Phookas burrowed into the ground and crept closer. Very slowly and very quietly, they surrounded the Phynnodderee. When the Phookas had it completely encircled, they sprang.

In the blink of an eye, they grabbed the small creature, covered its mouth and dragged it under ground. Within minutes they were far away from the village, their plunder tucked tightly in their arms, bound and gagged.

When they returned, Chardon reported to Walipreen that they had seen nothing unusual, as before. He questioned the Phooka at length, but in the end he was no further ahead than he was before. He was about to dismiss the Phooka when he thought to ask.

"Did you steal anything?"

The Phooka shrunk slightly as if he had been caught doing something wrong. His eyes darted left and right before he answered.

"Yes," he admitted.

His curious behavior piqued Walipreen's interest.

"What?" he demanded to know.

Chardon lowered his head and shifted his feet. He wasn't sure what Walipreen's reaction would be, and he wished now that they hadn't stolen anything.

"Out with it," Walipreen shouted.

"One of the Phynnodderee," Chardon blurted out.

"Show me."

Chardon left the chamber and returned a few minutes later. He had the Phynnodderee in tow with a rope tied around its neck, its hands bound behind its back and a gag tied around its mouth. Walipreen was amused at the precautions Chardon had taken. What was he afraid of, he wondered. As they moved closer, Walipreen was shocked at what he saw.

"That's just a child," he said.

"Yes," replied Chardon. "But they're treacherous when they're young."

Walipreen walked up to the Phynnodderee and removed the gag from its mouth. Before he could do or say anything else, the child snapped at him, trying to bite his hand. He moved it away quickly and took a step back.

"I tried to tell you," warned Chardon. "They're small, but they're dangerous."

The Phynnodderee glared at Walipreen in silence. Even though only a child, it didn't seem to be in the least bit frightened. Instead, it seemed highly irritated, and, as Chardon had pointed out, very treacherous. He was about to send them away so that Chardon could do as he pleased with his prize, but then felt a tingling similar to the feeling he had that caused him to send the Phookas out to spy in the first place.

He walked around the Phynnodderee, studying it from every angle. The child turned its head only, continuously glaring at Walipreen. He kept a safe distance, not wanting to get bitten. When he stopped, he noted that the sensation was still present. He knew nothing more about its source or meaning; only that it was still there – and somehow still significant.

"Leave the creature with me," he finally ordered.

"What?" complained Chardon. "It's mine. I found it; I captured it; I brought it back."

"And now you can leave it with me," Walipreen answered.

"NO!" Chardon confronted him. "You said we could steal."

"Yes, I did," replied Walipreen with a withering gaze. "But I never said you could keep. Leave it with me or you'll be joining it in whatever condition I choose."

Chardon made a face that looked like a grimace, although as far as Walipreen could tell, he could just have easily been smiling. Then he tossed the rope that ended in the noose around the Phynnodderee's neck. Walipreen made no effort to catch it, letting it fall to the floor. Chardon made some low, odd growling sound, turned and slunk out of the room. Walipreen watched in silence as the Phooka departed.

When he turned back, he noticed the Phynnodderee looking around the room, apparently for an avenue of escape. He bent down, picked up the rope and gave it a slight jerk. Instead of being intimidated and submitting to his control, the Phynnodderee snarled and ran at him attempting to bite him. He yanked the rope, pulling his captive to the floor face down. Then he quickly put a foot in the middle of its back to secure it while he repositioned the gag.

"Chardon was right," he said, not really expecting a reply. "You are treacherous."

He spun the length of rope around its body, securing it even more tightly and then sat down to consider what he was going to do with spoils of Chardon's theft. What secrets do you hold, he wondered. He tentatively extended his hand and placed it on the Phynnodderee's head.   It pulled its head away, but Walipreen grabbed a handful of hair and held it in place. The sensation of power that emanated from the small creature pulsated through his hand.

Still, he couldn't discern what this meant. The more he thought about it, the more he considered that he would need to reach out to the twins to see if they had felt the same surge of power and if they had any idea what it meant. He had to be careful, though. He didn't want to alert them to anything. They were both very greedy and very suspicious. They might try to steal the Phynnodderee for themselves. He would have to arrange a meeting for something completely different.

And, he couldn't go to their kingdom to meet. That would look suspicious. He would send an emissary to them: an offer that they should meet. But what reason could he give, he wondered. What would make them come out of their hole? What would entice them? The pendant! That would be the bait: news of the pendant. No, he thought. They wouldn't fall for that. They'd know he would never share the pendant. Then he had a better idea: revenge on the Alchemist. He would tell them he had discovered an opening in the Boravak, but not big enough to break through. However, if they worked together, they might be able to entice the Alchemist to return, if only to fix it. That would do it.

And he would have the Phynnodderee somewhere nearby so he could see if they reacted the same way he had. If they didn't, then no harm. He knew they would never reach agreement on a strategy to break the Boravak and would return home. On the other hand, if they sensed the same thing, he'd figure out what to do when that time came. Who should he send? Then it came to him.

He settled on someone he could trust and who the twins would be obligated to accept. Nelluc. Nelluc was actually a Rebbercand. He had been given to Walipreen by the twins shortly after his birth. He was a direct descendant of Tebaga and was offered as a guarantee of peace. In exchange, Walipreen had sent Dekene to the twins. Similar to Nelluc, Dekene was a direct descendant of Ena Ray. The gesture on the part of both parties had been based on the assumption that by sending each other someone who was a part of their "family," someone very important to them, to live in the realm of who would otherwise be considered an enemy, would ensure that peace was maintained.

This assumption, however, was false. The twins had no feelings of love or fealty towards Nelluc, any more than Walipreen did for Dekene. In spite of this, the exchange seemed to work. The two boys were raised in opposing domains as if they had originated and belonged there; and a delicate peace had remained intact. He sent for Nelluc.

The Rebbercand arrived and noticed the Phynnodderee bound and gagged off to one side. He glanced over once, but made no comment, waiting for Walipreen to tell him what was expected of him.

"I am about to send you on a journey," Walipreen announced to Nelluc.

"As you wish, Uncle." Nelluc asked. "Might I ask where?"

Walipreen was not really Nelluc's uncle, but he had given himself that title when the boy had been sent to him by the twins. It was as good as any, he felt.

"To see Rampool and Prine," he answered.

Nelluc's face revealed nothing of what he felt about going home. He had no recollection of them, other than what Walipreen had told him, which wasn't much. He had no recollections of anything other than his time in the north. Walipreen could have said he was sending him to the Cerulean Sea and it would have had no different impact.

"When?" was his only reply.

"Soon," Walipreen answered. "I have to prepare the message I want you to deliver first."

"Will I be going alone?"

"No," said Walipreen. "It's a long journey and there will be some areas that may be less than safe. I will arrange for a company of Phookas to accompany you."

48

"I look forward to it," Nelluc answered.

He lies as easily as the twins, Walipreen thought. Or maybe he doesn't want to disappoint me. He wasn't sure. The problem with being deceitful was that Walipreen believed everyone was as untrustworthy as himself. He let the silence linger, wondering if Nelluc was going to ask about the Phynnodderee. When he didn't, Walipreen broke the silence.

"Did you notice what Chardon brought back from his recent exploration?" he asked.

"Yes, I did," he answered. "A Phynnodderee. A child if I'm not mistaken. He's quite the warrior. It must have taken considerable daring to capture so formidable an opponent."

The sarcasm in Nelluc's comment was not lost on Walipreen. He knew the two did not get along and that Nelluc had little regard for the Phookas.

"I want you to watch over it," Walipreen said.

His decision was spur-of-the-moment. He really hadn't thought about it before and wasn't sure why he made it. The look of surprise on Nelluc's face, though, was worth it.

"Me?" he asked. "What am I to do with it?"

"See if you can get any useful information from it," Walipreen said.

"I thought I was going on a journey," Nelluc pointed out.

"You are; but not immediately. I have to set the stage first. Once that's done, I will send you out. In the meantime, you can apply yourself to this task."

49

Nelluc stared at the Phynnodderee. He didn't really want to be bothered with it. Besides, once Chardon discovered it was now in his possession that would only infuriate the Phooka. A faint smile crept across his face. The thought of something that would irritate Chardon gave him a hint of pleasure.

"As you wish, Uncle," he said.

"Use whatever techniques you feel appropriate to find out what it knows," Walipreen instructed, "but don't kill it."

He didn't think Nelluc would be so cruel, but he wanted to scare the Phynnodderee. He watched the small creature as he said those words, but could see no reaction at all. He wondered if it might be deaf. He clapped his hands suddenly, and the child turned towards the sound. It could hear, all right; but the threat of harm or even death seemed to have no effect. Interesting, he thought.

Nelluc walked over to the Phynnodderee and loosened the bonds from its feet so that it could walk.

"There is no place for you to run," he told it. "So there's no use in trying. Follow me."

He turned back towards Walipreen and gave a slight bow.

"If I may be excused, Uncle," he said.

Walipreen nodded approval. Nelluc turned and without looking to see if the Phynnodderee was following him, left the room. The child watched him for a few seconds, during which Walipreen wondered if some less than gentle prodding would be necessary. Then, without any further coaxing, it shuffled after Nelluc, the ropes still tied around its knees inhibiting its movement only slightly. Walipreen felt the tingling sensation fade as the Phynnodderee departed. Yes, he thought, this strange power is in some way connected to that creature.

Nelluc led the way through a series of winding and confusing hallways – tunnels, actually. When Walipreen established residence in the Crystal Citadel, he had set the goblins to work making it more habitable than it had been when it was his ancestor's prison. Still, though, it was eerily cavernous, and the winding, intersecting passageways were indistinguishable from one another. Having grown up here, however, Nelluc knew them with a great degree of intimacy.

At one end of the Citadel there was a small grotto that was separated from the rest of the tunnels by a large chasm. Early on, Walipreen learned to avoid this area, having seen a number of the goblins try to cross the gap, only to be immediately sucked into the void. This had been the specific part of the Citadel where Ena Ray had been banished for so long. Walipreen had the passageway leading to this spot blockaded, and made sure none of the other passageways could access it.

He created a large room in another area which led to his own, personal quarters. This was the room in which he had received Chardon and the Phynnodderee. He created pockets in which the goblins lived, barracks-style. These were in strategic locations between his quarters and the entry to the Citadel. He had prepared for the attack that never came – or at least it hadn't so far.

The reconstruction of the tunnels and the creation of living quarters inside the Citadel had taken decades. Over that time Walipreen's self-inflicted sequestration had been a key factor in the diminishing of his powers and in making him more vulnerable. He often wondered if the same thing had happened to the twins. The extent to which his powers had faded became evident to him when he felt the first surge of energy.

He had tried to summon images – something he had once been able to do with ease. Nothing was forthcoming. He tried casting spells on the Phookas who had the misfortune to be present when his ability to summon the images had failed him. They did not turn out as he had expected and he was unable to reverse those that he had cast. That was when he sent the first expedition to spy on the Phynnodderees.

The despair and depression that followed the news that the spies had discovered nothing had lasted for quite some time. He separated himself from almost everyone, including Nelluc. When Nelluc pressed him for the reason for his long period of darkness, he became suspicious of Nelluc's intention. His paranoia served to galvanize him. When the second surge of energy was felt, he knew he had to find its source and regain his former power – whatever the cost.

He knew the Phynnodderee that Chardon had fortuitously captured was key; he just couldn't make the connection. He decided to allow Nelluc to try to learn what he could about this strange creature. He wanted to glean as much information as he could before he engaged the twins. Whatever Nelluc could find out would also help frame the message he would have Nelluc carry to them. He watched in silence as Nelluc left the great hall and the Phynnodderee slowly tagged after him.

The Phynnodderee quickly realized it would be lost if it didn't keep up with the Rebbercand. As the two quickly walked through the corridors, strange objects in the walls provided a glowing light to illuminate the way. These objects seemed to sparkle a little more brightly as the Phynnodderee passed them by. This was not lost on Nelluc, but he made no comment.

Finally, they reached a larger opening and arrived at what appeared to the Phynnodderee to be some kind of living space. It was Nelluc's quarters. There was no door or other means of closing this area off from the passageways – no way to ensure any privacy. But long ago, Nelluc had made it clear that no one was to approach without invitation.

He studied the Phynnodderee for a few seconds and then removed the rope from around the child's body, untied its hands and removed the gag. He then motioned to a stone bench that had been carved out of one of the walls. He, himself, sat down on what looked like a stump. It was clearly made of wood, but the roots had been truncated and it looked far from comfortable.

The Phynnodderee sat down and stole quick glances at the surroundings while, at the same time, keeping a careful eye on Nelluc. After a few minutes, Nelluc rose and disappeared around a corner. The Phynnodderee watched in disbelief at being left unguarded by the Rebbercand or anyone else. But Nelluc had been right. There was no place to which to escape. Any thoughts about such an attempt came to an abrupt end when Nelluc returned with a cup and a plate of food.

"I'm sure you must be hungry and thirsty," he said, placing the cup and plate on the bench next to his captive.

The Phynnodderee looked at the food and then at Nelluc, but didn't make any movement.

"It's not poisoned," Nelluc said, retaking his seat. "If that's what you're worried about."

They stared at each other for several more seconds.

"Eat or don't eat," Nelluc said. "It makes no difference to me."

Slowly, the Phynnodderee reached for the cup and took a sip. Realizing that it was only water, it reached for the plate and poked a finger at the various morsels, moving them around, studying them to determine what they were. Finally, it picked one piece up and tentatively bit into it. Nelluc watched in silence as the Phynnodderee ate almost everything on the plate and then finished the water.

"Do you feel better?" he asked.

He didn't really care if the Phynnodderee felt better or not. He only wanted to get the small creature to relax and start talking. He waited for an answer that clearly wasn't coming. He realized he knew very little about Phynnodderees. How old did they have to be before they began talking? Maybe this one was younger than he thought. Maybe it hadn't yet developed the ability to speak.

"Do you understand what I'm saying to you?" he asked.

Again he was met with a blank stare. It was as if the small figure was contemplating some complex issue. He was about to give up when the Phynnodderee slowly nodded.

"Ah," commented Nelluc. "A glimmer of intelligence after all. Will wonders never cease? So now that we've established that you can understand me, can you speak?"

The Phynnodderee slowly nodded, but kept silent.

"Wonderful," replied Nelluc.

They studied each other intently for a few more seconds. Nelluc was thinking about what kind of information this child could have and how to obtain it. He didn't want to resort to violence, although he had no personal objections to this method. He simply didn't think it was really effective. He decided on a more roundabout approach.

"Have you been harmed?" he asked.

The Phynnodderee seemed to scowl at him.

"I mean aside from being taken from your home by force," he explained. "Did Chardon injure you in any way? The Phooka? Chardon is the name of the Phooka who captured you, tied you up and brought you here. Did he injure you?"

After a few seconds the Phynnodderee shook its head, and gave what looked to Nelluc as a slight sneer as if to say that it would take much more than what Chardon had done to cause injury. There was a certain air of defiance that he detected in the Phynnodderee.

He knew little about these people. Since he had been born and raised in the Citadel, he had never been in contact with them before. He had heard stories about them – them and their magical abilities. But these stories came from the Phookas, and in addition to being notorious thieves, they were also notorious liars. He wasn't sure what he could believe.

"That's good to know," he said. "What's your name?"

The Phynnodderee merely stared at him. This was going to take some time, he thought.

"My name is Nelluc," he said. "As you can probably tell, I'm NOT a Phooka. I'm a Rebbercand. Do you know what a Rebbercand is?"

Nothing. There was no response or even any acknowledgement that he had asked a question, let alone that what he asked was understood. He might as well have been talking to the wall.

"Look," he said. "I understand you are probably frightened."

This was met with a slight snort. If this child was at all frightened it provided no such indication. It was either incredibly brave or had no clue whatsoever of the danger it was in.

"I mean you no harm," Nelluc continued. "I don't expect us to become friends, and I'm not going to make any promises, but if you talk to me, I may be able to convince the Phookas to return you to your home."

It was a lie, but he hoped that, even if the Phynnodderee knew it was a lie, a kernel of hope might exist that the child would believe it. Nelluc waited to let this sink in before he continued.

"I'm not going to tie you up again," he went on. "As I told you before, and as you may have already discovered for yourself, there is no escape from this place. Even if you got outside, you don't know where you are or how far away from your home you are. While you are here, you will be under my protection. The Phookas will leave you alone. That is, of course, unless you displease me. Do you understand?"

He waited for some kind of response. Instead the Phynnodderee continued to glare at him.

"I'll take your silence as a sign that you do understand," he said. "And to be perfectly clear on this, your continued refusal to speak is beginning to displease me."

He hadn't raised his voice, and that was probably more ominous than if he had been yelling.

"I can be a patient person, but even my patience has its limits," he continued. "I have offered you a certain degree of freedom, as well as my protection. If this is not satisfactory to you, I am more than willing to give you back to Chardon to do with as he pleases. Trust me; that will be far less enjoyable for you than any time you might spend with me."

When the Phynnodderee didn't respond, Nelluc sighed deeply and then got to his feet.

"Very well," he said. "Let's go find Chardon. I'm sure he'll be thrilled to get you back."

"What do you want me to tell you," the Phynnodderee said. "I won't tell you anything that will put my people in danger."

Nelluc was less shocked by what was being said than he was by the sound of the voice speaking the words.

"You're a girl!" he said, sitting back down.

"And you're not as stupid as you look," she replied.

"I've never met a Phynnodderee," he said once he regained his composure. "I wouldn't have been able to tell just by looking at you. How old are you?"

She wrinkled her brow, not really understanding his question. Phynnodderees didn't measure time the way others did. They did not mark their aging by any specific passage of time. Therefore, the question had no relevance to her.

"I don't know what you mean," she said.

"What I mean is, how long ago were you born?"

Thinking this might be a trick question, she tried to guess the hidden meaning. She didn't want to make any reference to her family or her village that would give him any information that might be used against them. In her village, the seasons were almost all the same, so counting such things as summers or winters didn't apply. She really had no idea how old she was. She was old enough to be as old as she was.

"I don't know," she finally replied. "We don't think about things like that."

Nelluc wondered if she was lying. What he didn't know, and wouldn't be able to understand even if he did know, was that Phynnodderees almost never lie. They know how their eyes react when they do. Consequently, they see no purpose in trying to do anything but tell the truth.

"How do I know if you're telling the truth?" he asked, unable to just dismiss her response.

"How should I know?" she shot back. "And what's more, why should I care?"

"You should care because if I think you're lying to me, I would be greatly displeased. And I've already told you what would happen if you displeased me."

"Whatever," she said, still defiant. "Anyway, I'm not lying."

"Fine," Nelluc answered.

"Emm," she said, after a few seconds.

"What?" he asked. "What's emm?"

"You asked me what my name was," she answered. "My name is Emm."

Chapter three

But desperate times call for desperate measures, Aitch told himself. And these were desperate times. His sister, Emm, had been kidnapped by the Phookas. That was more than a week ago. Search parties had scoured the area. The only way anyone was able to conclude that the Phookas had been involved was that Aitch's father had discovered holes in the ground, up through which they had likely come. His father had summoned the birds which confirmed his suspicions, but none of them could point to which direction they had taken Emm.

His parents were in such anguish, he felt guilty about the few days he had been gone when studying with the Alchemist. Recalling this time, he thought that if anyone could help, it would be the Alchemist. Aitch returned to the part of the forest where he had seen the old man several years before, hoping that the birds that had spoken to his father had been wrong; hoping that, instead, the Alchemist had taken her in the same manner he had taken Aitch. But he could find no sign of the Alchemist or his sister.

He came to the only conclusion left: she had been taken by the Phookas. He knew that the longer she was gone the more likely it was that they'd never see her again. He had to find the Alchemist. He concentrated on the stories the old man had told, trying to think of where he might be able to find him. Then he recalled the final scene. That was why he was now back in the cavern. It was also here where he sensed the weakest part of the wall – the wall no one could see; the wall almost no one else knew about.

He had climbed down the ancient ledge. The images that had been carved into the sides of the walls were greatly faded. Still, they looked ominous and far too life-like. In spite of his fear, he reached out and touched the face of one of them. Kythauls. That's what they were called. He didn't know how he knew this, but he did. He didn't think the Alchemist had told him their name; only that the Kelpies had brought them to life. No, he thought. It was only one of them that could do that: Akmen Milzu – the Mountain Kelpie; one of the three leaders. The Alchemist had told him about the three leaders.

He backed away from the half gargoyle, half goblin figure and scanned the others, identical to this one, which were imbedded in the stone walls. He also saw dried up roots that had long ago pushed their way through the ground into the chamber. They now hung limp and withered. Still, he thought it wise to keep his distance.

He climbed along the ledge until he came to a section that had broken away. He looked beyond the break, further down into the chasm and could see a ledge on the opposite side of a wide, deep breech. He imagined himself as a bird and immediately changed his shape, becoming a large, green hawk. Might as well be something that could easily defend itself, he thought.

He spread his wings widely and floated in tight, descending circles to the lower level. As he was landing, he shifted back to his natural shape. Ahead of him he saw what might have once looked like doors. Now it was only gouges in the stone in the shapes of doors. In the center he saw where the handles had been and a circle that encompassed the handles. In the middle of all this, he saw something caught in the stonework. It was a blond hair. That was when he found the hole.

He had never known that this place existed, even though it was not far from his home – less than a day's journey. Well, it was a day's journey while in the shape of an eagle; probably longer if he had walked. In the time he had spend with the Alchemist, part of his lessons included very detailed accounts of the rise and fall of the Kelpies; their imprisonment for nearly two thousand years; the alignment of the planets and the return of the Fury, which coincided with the rise of the sorcerers Ena Ray and Tebaga; and then the eight descendants of the ancient leaders all came together to defeat the Kelpies and secure them in the Boravak. The Alchemist told him of the final battle in which two of the eight were almost left behind, except one of the others did the unthinkable – he dove back into the Boravak to rescue them.

He had been stuck – half in and half out. Since the Boravak is not only a different place, it's a different time, the part of him that was stuck inside returned to a time several years before the battle occurred. He couldn't escape and was locked in place until the events that first brought him to this place, happened again. To make things even more confusing, the period of time that passed for the half of him that was stuck outside the Boravak was only a minute or so. As the Alchemist described all this to Aitch, trying to sort it all out gave him a headache.

He shifted into the shape of a hummingbird and hovered before the wall, staring at the thin strand of blond hair. It was caught and imbedded in the rock. He picked up the end in his long, narrow beak and gently fluttered backwards, pulling the hair free. It stopped suddenly and the end snapped off. No, he shouted to himself.

He looked closer. There was little more than an inch protruding from the stone. He moved closer and pinched the strand as close to the wall as he could and tugged gently and slowly. This time the hair held and he was able to pull it completely free of the stone, revealing a tiny hole. It was so small, even with the hair removed, it was almost impossible to see. He wondered how he would be able to fit through it. He thought about widening it somehow, but dismissed that idea. He couldn't leave an opening behind that would be accessible to anyone or anything else.

He returned to his natural shape and suddenly panicked. He couldn't see where the hole was. He quickly returned to the hummingbird and hovered up and down and from side to side, searching intently for the opening. It took several minutes before he felt a minute change in the air pressure and a thin glimmer of light. Now what, he thought. He had never tried to shift from one unnatural shape to another, but he knew he couldn't go back to his own body and risk losing sight of the opening.

On the other hand, he couldn't continue to hover. Sooner or later something was going to come along and hear or see him, and in this size, he was too much of an easy target.

"There's barely enough room in that hole for air to get through," he hummed.

That's it, he thought. He knew he couldn't change himself into air, but he could transform into the next best thing – smoke. The trick would be to make this change from his current shape as a hummingbird. He was beginning to realize he should have paid more attention to the Alchemist's lessons. Too late to be worrying about that now. He closed his eyes and concentrated on shifting. Not only had he never shifted from one unnatural shape to another, he had never shifted to something so lacking in form. He hoped he'd be able to get back to his own shape once this was over.

Slowly the bird began to dissolve. His head started to blur and expand, and then to break apart into smaller and smaller pieces. If Aitch had been able to watch himself transform, he would have said it reminded him of some of the potions his mother made. She would add a powder that had hardened into a lump to a broth that was heating over the fire. The lump would slowly break apart into individual crystals and then dissolve into the liquid.

In a similar manner, the hummingbird gradually turned into a giant wisp of green smoke. When the transformation was complete, Aitch discovered that he had no sight. He hadn't thought about that. What was he supposed to do now? He was about to transform back into the bird when he felt the slight difference in air pressure. As a bird it was barely noticeable. As smoke, it felt like a strong wind.

He moved towards the source of the difference. He could feel the rough surface of the stone and slid up and down and left and right until he discovered the tiny gap. He pushed himself into the opening, the rest of the cloud following behind. He had expected to travel through several feet of rock, and hoped the tiny gap didn't abruptly end. Instead, he felt like he had passed through nothing more than a sheet of parchment.

He felt something press against him and he wiggled to one side and the resistance disappeared. He thought that he might have just come to a turn or a twist in the stone, but then he remembered that the stone had very quickly ended. He felt like he was oozing to one side. Suddenly, he felt a strange warmth. He could no longer feel the shape of the stone that surrounded the thin aperture or whatever it was that had been blocking his way. He could sense that his cloud-like shape had no boundaries, but he still couldn't see anything. He tried to back up slightly and felt something rough behind him, but it wasn't stone.

He pushed his form upward and then from side to side, feeling the shape and the texture of what he had passed through. It feels like a tree, he thought in amazement. OK, he said to himself. Now let's see if I can shift back. He concentrated on returning to his natural shape. Slowly he could feel himself lowering to the ground.

Within seconds he could feel the dirt and grass under his feet. He could feel the warm sun on his body. He reached a hand back and could feel the tree behind him, but he still couldn't see. He realized his eyes were clamped shut. He took a deep breath and opened one eye and then another. As his vision came into focus, he found himself looking at another boy, just about his size, who was staring at him open-mouthed with a slingshot dangling from one hand.

Sean had been wandering through the airy forest at the bottom of the glen that bordered on a crystal blue body of water and a pristine shore. He had been looking for herbs and berries. He spotted a large grasshopper and recalled the first time he met his friend, Summer. She had been riding one that had tossed her off. He had been so surprised to see her that he had forgotten the taboos of his people which demanded that the forest creatures avoid contact with the faeries. Likewise, she had been so surprised by his sudden appearance, she, too, had forgotten the warnings of her people.

It was the beginning of a long and very close friendship – one that had seen them through many unusual circumstances. As Sean reached the end of the glen, he looked up the long, low hill at the tree that sat at the top. It was a very large and very old tree and its limbs stretched out in a nearly perfect circle and high into the sky.

It wasn't an ordinary tree. Not long ago, Sean and his friends were inside it. Actually, they were in a Boravak – a world within a world. This Boravak was inside that tree. He had been inside and knew what was there, but it was still hard for him to imagine it. He was a Dozor – a guardian – of his people. Even though he hadn't been officially appointed, he knew he was also a guardian of the Boravak.

He came back to this tree on a regular basis to make sure it was strong; to make sure that nothing else came through. What he knew to be on the other side was too dangerous – too unimaginable. After he and his friends had come through, the opening that led from the inside to the outside quickly closed, turning into a knot low and in the center of the enormous trunk.

When he made his regular visits, he studied that knot closely. It was a knot unlike any other. In the center was the very end of a long blond hair. He remembered how it got there. He remembered how he and Liam had held onto Quinn's legs trying to keep him from crossing back over; how the trunk seemed to close in on him; how they struggled until he popped out followed immediately by Lochen and Stella. He remembered, too, how much Quinn had aged in the seconds he was half in and half out.

Stella had worked her magic and transformed his too-soon aged face back to what it had been before. She hadn't been completely successful, though. There was a streak of white at his left temple that had never returned to its original blond. When the opening closed completely, a single strand of his blond hair was caught between the worlds.

On this particular day, Sean made a leisurely climb up the knoll to the tree. He studied its wide branches and massive trunk. He ran his hand along the rough bark as his eyes slowly lowered to the knot. Something wasn't quite right. He bent down closer. The hair! It was gone. He pressed both hands against the tree and pushed his face as close as he could. There was no sign of the blond hair.

"What the..." he muttered.

Before he could finish his sentence, a strange green smoke began to seep from the thin hole where the hair had once been.

"No," Sean shouted. "NO! Wait a minute."

He pressed his finger against the bark, trying to stop the smoke from coming through. At first he thought he had been successful, but then the smoke seeped around his fingertip to one side. He looked around for something to plug the opening. The dirt was too dry and he was too far away from a stream of any kind. Besides, sooner or later, the mud would dry and fall away. He looked for a stone or a piece of a branch.

"No, you dope," he chastised himself. "Those are too big. You need something like a pine needle."

He looked around for a pine tree. Nothing.

"Where's a pine tree when you need one," he shouted in vain.

When he turned back to the tree, the cloud of green smoke was much larger and seemed to be pressing itself against the bark. He pulled out his slingshot, but there was nothing to shoot at. He knew any stone would just pass through the smoke. What was happening? He could only watch in horror. What if one of the Kelpies figured out a way through? Whoever it was, he would be ready for it. But he wasn't ready for what happened next.

The smoke began to change shape, forming into a person. Then it seemed to solidify and within seconds Sean was staring at a boy who was just about the same size as him. Except this boy was green – and completely naked. The slingshot dangled from his hand and his mouth dropped wide open.

"Can you see me?" the boy asked Sean. "I mean you no harm."

"Dude," Sean finally replied. "Painting yourself green and running around naked isn't much of a disguise. And I don't think you'll be doing much harm to anyone like that."

The boy's eyes widened. He looked down at himself in shock.

"That's never happened before," he said.

He then quickly covered himself up and looked imploringly at Sean.

"Uh, can you, ah, give me...I need...is there..." he stammered.

Sean just looked at him, not sure what he should do.

"Come on," Aitch shouted in frustration. "Give me something to cover up with."

Sean looked around. Seeing nothing, he held out his slingshot.

"A slingshot?" bellowed Aitch. "Are you kidding? That's your idea of cover?"

"It's better than nothing," replied Sean.

He looked at the slingshot and then back at Aitch.

"Maybe not," he agreed. "Wait here." He ran down the knoll to the nearest gathering of trees.

"No," Aitch shouted after him. "I thought I'd go for a stroll to the nearest village."

Sean found some large leaves and several honeysuckle vine runners. He yanked them up and ran back up the knoll.

"Here," he thrust them out towards Aitch and then turned away.

Aitch took the larger leaves and covered the essential parts, tying them in place with the thin strings of honeysuckle.

Everything was way too small, and no matter what he did, he was still far too exposed.

"I hope you're not allergic to poison ivy," said Sean over his shoulder.

"What?" shouted Aitch.

"Just kidding," answered Sean. "Are you decent now?"

He turned to look.

"Not really," he said appraising the poor job Aitch was able to do in covering up. "But it'll have to do until we find something better. By the way, who are you and where did you come from?"

Sean raised his slingshot as casually as he could, readying it in case the answer was something he felt might present a threat. The motion was not lost on Aitch, and he prepared himself to shift his shape at the first sign of danger.

"My name is Aitch," he answered, his eyes bouncing back and forth between Sean's face and the slingshot. "I'm a Phynnodderee."

"You're a knotty tree?" Sean asked, not sure he heard him correctly.

"A Phynnodderee," Aitch repeated slowly.

"Uh-huh," Sean replied, taking a couple of steps back. "And where did you come from?"

"Uhhh – the other side...from inside that..." Aitch wasn't sure what to tell this person, not knowing if he was friend of foe.

He tried to casually look over his shoulder at the tree. In the corner of his eye, he could see Sean raising the sling shot. He closed his eyes and concentrated. At the instant Sean pulled the sling back and fired, Aitch shifted his shape into a large, green armadillo. The stone struck the hard outer shell and bounced off.

"Ouch," shouted Aitch. "Hey, that hurt. What are you doing? I said I wasn't here to harm you."

"How did you do that?" shouted Sean, as he readied another stone.

"I'm a shape shifter," Aitch shouted back. "Will you put that thing away?"

"You better not try any funny business," Sean challenged as he lowered the slingshot.

"You're the one with the weapon," said Aitch, defensively.

He raised his head and looked up at Sean. Seeing that the slingshot was down, he uncurled his armored body and shifted back into himself.

"Aw, dude," moaned Sean. "You're naked again."

Aitch quickly gathered up the leaves and the vines and reapplied his cover.

"I wouldn't have been if you hadn't tried to shoot me," he answered, indignantly.

"Yeah, well if you had seen what I've seen, you wouldn't be so trusting, either," Sean muttered. "So finish telling me. Where did you come from?"

Aitch looked back at the tree. He wasn't sure he'd believe what he was about to say, himself.

"Inside that tree, I guess," he said. "I know it sounds weird…"

"No," said Sean. "That's the problem. It doesn't sound weird."

Aitch slowly turned back and looked again at Sean. A realization of who this person was began to sink in on him.

"You're one of them, aren't you?" he asked. "One of the ones who left the Boravak. You're one of the ones the Alchemist told me about."

"You've met the Alchemist?" Sean asked.

"Yes. He trained me."

"To do what?"

"Shape shift," answered Aitch. "Among other things."

"What sort of things?" Sean pressed.

"Mystical things," Aitch answered vaguely.

He still wasn't sure he could trust Sean, although if this was one of the eight descendants of the ancient leaders, he would probably know how to find the Alchemist.

"That's not important now,' Aitch continued. "I need to find him."

"Why?"

"I don't have time to explain," Aitch shouted in frustration.

"Make time," demanded Sean as he slowly raised the slingshot.

"All right. All right! I think the Phookas stole my sister. She disappeared and we looked all over for her, but we can't find her. They are the henchmen of Walipreen, but he hasn't been seen outside the Citadel in who knows how long, and besides, what would he want with her; I would think he'd rather want to steal me; but they might have sold her to the twins, although that doesn't make much sense, except they're not known for doing anything that makes sense. The problem is that we don't have enough power to go into Walipreen's territory or the twins' territory, either, and if we did, that might be enough for them to join forces again and that would be a real mess..."

"Wait, wait, wait, wait," Sean held up his hand. "I don't understand anything you're talking about. What are hookies; who is wall paper and what twins are you talking about?"

"Phookas," answered Aitch. "Not hookies. They're underworld creatures."

"Like goblins?"

"Sort of, only worse," Aitch told him. "Besides, goblins don't exist anymore."

"Since when?" asked Sean, incredulously.

"Seriously? Like almost forever. And it's Walipreen, not wall paper. He's the sorcerer of the north. The twins, Rampool and Prine are the twins – the sorcerers of the south. Look, if you're really one of the ones who came through that Boravak and locked up the Kelpies, then you know the Alchemist. I really need to find him. Will you please help?"

Sean studied the green boy for a while and thought about what he had described. Nothing he said made any sense. He knew about the Kelpies, but it seemed he only knew that they existed. He didn't say anything about them being a threat or a power. Instead he talked about this Walipreen and some twins that Sean had never heard of. This was all too weird.

He looked past Aitch at the tree and decided there was nothing he could do about any opening. He figured that either Lochen or Stella could patch up any hole. He'd need to find them first.

"OK," he said. "I'll help you."

"Thanks," Aitch replied. "Thanks a lot."

"Don't get too excited," Sean cautioned. "I haven't seen the Alchemist in a long time."

"He lives in a castle," Aitch offered. "It's at the edge of a large field that leads to a forest and it overlooks this really bright blue sea."

"Oh?" Sean replied. "Is that so? That's really helpful. It only describes more than half of this world."

"The castle, too?" asked Aitch.

"No, but knowing the Alchemist, the castle either moves or was just an illusion."

"Ohhh, this is a nightmare," wailed Aitch. "I should have never left."

"Let's find some of my friends," Sean said. "One of them may know where the Alchemist is, and even if they don't, they may be able to help."

74

Aitch looked back at the tree, and then to Sean. The hope that had been there earlier had faded. Now Sean only saw defeat and despair.

"Come on," he tried to be upbeat. "Things will be all right."

He headed down the hill and turned to the north instead of heading back to his Lodge. He would pick Summer up along the way.

"We're walking?" asked Aitch. "Wouldn't it be faster to fly?"

"Yeah, it would," answered Sean. "At least for part of the way."

"I can shift into a large bird and carry you," Aitch offered.

"And will your leaves turn into a bird, too?" asked Sean.

Aitch thought about it for a second or two.

"Probably not," he said, looking down at his makeshift wardrobe. "Maybe. I don't know. I'm not sure what happened."

"You mean you don't run around naked in wherever it is you come from?" Sean asked.

"Of course not," Aitch replied, somewhat indignantly. "What do you think we are, a pack of savages?"

"Hey," said Sean, "I'm not the one wearing a bunch of leaves."

"I don't understand," moaned Aitch. "My clothes have always changed when I've changed."

"Just the same," continued Sean, "it probably wouldn't be a good idea for you to be switching back and forth until you get this little wardrobe malfunction thing sorted out. We can walk. Our first stop isn't that far."

Aitch soon discovered that his concept of "far" was completely different than Sean's. They seemed to have walked for hours, first across a wide field and then into a forest. Aitch had always been adept at finding his way in strange places, but in this place he was completely lost. He was certain they had been going in circles, and finally said so to Sean.

"Well," Sean admitted, "you're half right. We're not exactly going in circles. It's more like spirals."

"What's the difference?"

"Circles are circles, obviously," Sean replied. "Spirals are more like...well...spirals."

"Oh, that clears things up."

"OK. If we were walking in circles, we'd always end up in the same place. We're not doing that. We're walking in spirals, which is circles that sort of move."

"And why are we doing this?" asked Aitch.

"To avoid the pixies," answered Sean.

"And what are pixies?"

"Are you for real?" questioned Sean. "They're nasty little flying things that can cast hexes. They're like a bad rash that you can't get rid of for months. They're your worst nightmare. Well, maybe not your <u>worst</u> nightmare, but they're pretty bad. You must have seen them before."

"No," replied Aitch. "I think I'd remember something like that."

"Where exactly do you live?" Sean asked.

"In a forest. I don't know how else to describe it."

He went on, though, to tell Sean about his village and the surrounding area. Some of it sounded familiar, but other parts didn't. For a moment, it sounded like he was describing the same forest where Sean's Lodge had been when he and his family had lived inside the Boravak. This thought made him wonder if they had, in fact, actually been living inside a Boravak, or if that had been created at some point in their journeys. But when? And how did they end up inside in the first place? It was all too confusing.

"I don't know," he said when Aitch had finished. "It seems to me that the area you were talking about is right near where a whole bunch of pixies live. You should have seen them at some time or other."

"Little flying things?" Aitch asked. "I'm sure of it – never seen them. And you say they can cast hexes?"

"That's about all they do," Sean answered. "They're really nasty. If you see one, get away as quickly as you can. I'll try to hold them off with a few shots from my sling."

Aitch looked carefully around him, peering through the trees and shrubs for any sign of trouble. Eventually the tall trees gave way to large flowering bushes, and the spiraling pattern they had been following eased into a more straightforward path.

"We're almost there," Sean said.

"Good," said Aitch. "Where's 'there?'"

"Summer," Sean called out, ignoring Aitch's question. "Summer. Where are you?"

Seemingly out of nowhere, Summer appeared, fluttering her wings and diving from above in a straight line towards Sean. Her sudden appearance and rapid motion startled Aitch, who didn't know what a summer was. He reacted instinctively. He took a deep breath and concentrated.

In the blink of an eye, he transformed himself into a giant bullfrog. Immediately after the shift was complete, his enormous tongue darted out, stuck itself to Summer and snapped her and it back into his mouth.

She had spotted Sean even before he called her name. She had heard him and the strange looking person with him coming through the woods. She blended into the background, hovering high in the trees until she saw who it was that had been making so much noise. Her eyes were first attracted to Sean's traveling companion: a boy about the same size and appearance except that he was dressed in leaves and was almost the same shade of green. How peculiar, she thought.

As she made herself visible, she dropped downward headfirst. She fluttered her wings to slow her descent and that was when the green boy spotted her. Her eyes flickered from him to Sean in the instant he disappeared and was replaced by an enormous frog. Summer didn't have time to register the change and before she knew what was happening something flew out of the frog's mouth, hit her with a jarring crash and then yanked her into sudden darkness.

"What are you doing?" shouted Sean in complete shock. "Spit her out. NOW! Spit her out."

Aitch did as Sean asked, opening his mouth and ejecting his tongue with Summer still stuck to it. He gave the tongue a snap, flinging Summer off, and retracted it into his mouth. She flew through the air, covered in frog spit and landed unceremoniously on her butt, skidding across the ground.

"Oh, yuck," she shouted. "I'm covered with goop. What just happened?"

"Are you crazy?" Sean shouted at Aitch. "What were you thinking?"

Aitch started to respond, but before he could, Sean raised his hand, cutting him off.

"Sean!" shouted Summer. "Where did that frog come from and where is that guy who was here just a second ago. Is this some kind of trick? Is this your idea of a joke? I'm all sticky...and I stink!"

"This isn't my fault," Sean pleaded. "I found this guy..."

He turned to see that Aitch was still in the form of the bullfrog.

"Change back," he shouted. "Or whatever it is you do. Go back to the way you were – the way you're supposed to be."

Summer wasn't sure she heard Sean correctly. What was he talking about? Change back to the way you were? He's probably been out in the sun too long, she thought. Or eating things he shouldn't be eating. He was talking crazy. She rolled over onto her hands and knees, trying to get to her feet, but there was some kind of sticky substance all over her.

Aitch transformed back into his original shape.

"I'm sorry," he said, frantically. "I thought it was a pixie. You kept talking about pixies and how nasty they were and then this thing comes out of nowhere and dive-bombs us. How was I supposed to know?"

"Pixie?" shouted Summer indignantly. "You thought I was a pixie? Are you blind? Do I look red? Do I..."

She was still stuck to the grass, trying unsuccessfully to get to her feet. She managed to peel one hand away from the ground. She was staring in disgust and amazement at the long string of goo that ran from the hand to the grass. She raised her hand as high as she could until the thread finally snapped and her arm was free.

She tried to brush her hair out of her face, but the substance that was still covering her hand became smeared into the hair, further obscuring her vision. She tried to kneel upright, but she couldn't extract her other hand. She could feel her wings sticking together as well.

"What is this stuff?" she demanded.

Sean turned to face Aitch.

"Get that glop, or whatever it is, off of her," he ordered.

"Oh, yes," he said. "Of course. Sorry. It's only...never mind. I don't think you want to know."

He waived his hand and a tiny cloud formed about a foot over Summer's head. Sean watched, too puzzled to say anything. A second or two later, the small cloud turned dark and emptied a miniature rain storm, depositing a substantial amount of water all over Summer's body. The sudden downpour flattened her to the ground. While it rinsed away the sticky substance, it also created a small puddle of mud in which she now found her face planted.

"Enough," she sputtered, lifting her face from the mud. "Stop. Please."

"Have you gone completely mental?" shouted Sean. "Or have you always been like this?"

"Sorry," answered Aitch.

He waved his hand again and as quickly as the cloud and rain had appeared, it vanished.

"It was the quickest way I could think of to clean it off," he said.

"IT?" shouted Summer. "It? You're calling me an it?"

She pushed herself up to her knees, shook the mud off of one hand and then the other. Then she wiped the hair out of her face, pulling it back behind her head.

"IT?" she repeated. "I'll have you know..."

She stopped in mid-sentence, getting her first clear glimpse of Aitch.

"Why are you naked?" she asked.

Chapter four

Walipreen had decided to wait a while before sending Nelluc out on his diplomatic mission. He thought it would be better for the Rebbercand to glean whatever information he could from the captured Phynnodderee first. In the meantime, he decided it was time for him to hone his sorcery skills. He had gone too long without using them and they had grown dull.

At the same time, he thought it would be good to delve more deeply into the ancient legends about the Alchemist, the Enchantress and the Kelpies. He now regretted not having paid closer attention to his mentor, Lingram, when his former instructor had been trying to teach him in his youth. Lingram had spent what Walipreen felt had been agonizing hours talking about the powers of the Kelpies and how they were the source of Walipreen's own power.

He had told Walipreen that the Kelpies had been foolish; fighting with each other and wasting the strength their unity once had held.   If they had banded together as they had originally planned, they could have defeated the Alchemist and his partner, the Enchantress Meri Hocto. Instead, they had allowed the Alchemist to divide them and then to pit them against each other. As a result, they had lost everything.

They and all who followed after them were trapped inside the Boravak. It was like a blanket, covering them and keeping them from growing, expanding, and controlling.   The Kelpies had known they had been duped when, in the final battle in the cavern near the edge of what had once been the Venomous Swamp, they watched the descendants of the ancient leaders disappear through an opening where doors to the gargoyles' kingdom had once led.

Those doors had been sealed shut by the band that held the stone that was the source of the Enchantress's power. The band had once been in the possession of his ancestor, Ena Ray. It had been stolen from him by eight misfits, and then transported to the doors of the gargoyles' kingdom. This act had shut down the return of an enormous force called The Fury, which Ena Ray had been able to control from his prison in the Crystal Citadel. It had been a temporary measure, though.

The band and the stone it held were parts of a pendant worn by the Enchantress. When the band had been separated from the stone, the stone itself had been shattered into four pieces and scattered to the far reaches of the world. Over a long period of time, one by one the pieces were located and the stone was re-joined; this time in the possession of another Enchantress. Once the stone and the band were reunited, the possessor of both would hold unimaginable power.

The Kelpies had allowed this power to slip through their hands. They watched in frustration as an opening appeared in the once sealed doors and one by one, the eight interfering busybodies slipped through, taking the pendant with them. It was at that instant that the Kelpies understood that they had been trapped inside the Boravak.

In the struggle to locate the pieces of the pendant and to release the Kelpies from the prisons in which they had been held for centuries, these intruders had destroyed a number of their foes. But power such as this can never be destroyed. Those that fell victim to the attacks by these eight perpetrators only went dormant for a period of time. Gradually they were restored and rejoined the remaining Kelpies. But by then it was too late. There had been eight Kelpies, and their number had been added to by the ancestors of the two current forces. Ena Ray and Tebaga had been protégés of Meri Hocto. She had foolishly thought that she could guide them to follow her own path.

They had turned against her and taken sides with the Kelpies, bringing their force to ten: ten of them against the Alchemist and the Enchantress. When they should have been able to make the most of this dominance, they had not. Instead, they allowed the eight descendants of the ancient leaders to come together and become a united force. While the eight descendants gathered the pieces of the pendant and kept the Kelpies divided, the Alchemist created the Boravak. He moved the homes and villages and all of the people associated with these eight to the other side of the Boravak. And when he was done, the eight discovered the opening and escaped, leaving the Kelpies and their minions behind.

Still, instead of uniting their forces and finding a way to break through the Boravak, the Kelpies fought among themselves in what became known as the Great Wars. Battle by battle, they expended their power, wasting it away until it was next to nothing. Ena Ray and Tebaga were wise enough to stand on the sidelines and watch the devastation.

Weakened and defeated, the Kelpies returned to the only homes they had known: the prisons in which they had been held for centuries before. This time, though, their exile was of their own choosing. In the aftermath, Ena Ray and Tebaga became the dominant powers. They had enough sense, though, to declare a truce, uneasy though it may have been. They divided the world between them and took their followers to their respective realms.

As time passed, and without any challenges to their authority, their powers dwindled – weakened and diminished through lack of use. Over the years there had been small flare ups: little more than heated exchanges, empty threats and blustering, and at most, brief and isolated battles. When Walipreen and the twins, Rampool and Prine, eventually became leaders of their respective peoples, they agreed to trade "emissaries" as a show of trust, which was how Nelluc came to live and grow up with Walipreen and Dekene had been sent to the twins.

Walipreen recalled the lessons of his mentor and how, at the time, he had dismissed them as the wandering and pointless reminiscences of an old man. Now he realized that he had too easily dismissed information that would now enhance and bolster his far too weakened powers. He would need those powers as an advantage over the twins in the event that things did not go as he planned. He needed to find the Kelpies.

He knew that half of them were in the north. Those he would find first and then he would tempt fate and travel into the realm of the twins seeking out the other four. He was uncertain if the twins had the same thoughts that he had. In his limited contact with them, he had always dismissed them as being rather stupid, but it could all have been an act.

He struggled to recall the lessons of his former mentor, but managed to dredge up an image of an ice lake where one of the Kelpies resided – a place not too far from his own domain. He assembled a small team to accompany him; a team which included Chardon – a small reward for bringing him the Phynnodderee.

"How long will you be gone?" Nelluc asked when he was informed of Walipreen's vaguely outlined plans.

"That's hard to say," Walipreen replied. "I have a number of places to stop and I don't know as yet how long I'll be staying in each one."

He had only told Nelluc that he was going out exploring. He didn't reveal his destination or his intentions. He wasn't sure how much he could trust the Rebbercand and decided to exercise caution. He didn't normally keep secrets from him, but the stakes were much higher now; at least he believed they were. He had no idea how long his journey would end up being or the changes that would take place while he was gone.

"But where are you going, Uncle?" Nelluc persisted.

"Where my interests take me," Walipreen said.

"And I'm to remain here?"

"Yes," Walipreen answered. "Until I return. I need you to protect that Phynnodderee and to get as much information out of it as possible."

"I see," said Nelluc. "Of course."

"Don't pout. It doesn't become you."

"I'm not pouting," Nelluc whined. "I was only hoping for some time away from all these Phookas. The smell is unbearable. I need some fresh air."

"Ha!" laughed Walipreen. "That's what they say about you. But now you have a Phynnodderee to keep you occupied. See if it smells any better."

Before Nelluc could raise any further objections, Walipreen cut him off, gathered his entourage and left. Nelluc stood at the entryway to the Citadel and watched as Walipreen moved south and then slightly westward. Walipreen hadn't bothered to disguise where he was headed. He hadn't mentioned any particular location to Nelluc or anyone else. He expected to make a quick trip and return shortly. He was wrong. He had taken a large force with him, which required extensive supplies. The supplies, exhaustive as they were, would be insufficient.

Nelluc watched until the travelers disappeared over the horizon. He could tell in which direction they were moving and wondered what would draw them that way. And why now? He returned to his quarters and consulted some ancient maps he had discovered in the ruins of a settlement several miles to the west of the Citadel.

He could determine that on his current route, Walipreen would come to the edge of the Ice Kingdom and an expansive cliff overlooking a large inlet. There was nothing after that he could reach without benefit of something that floated on the sea. However, just short of that cliff there was a frozen lake.

"Saldeti," gasped Nelluc. "He's looking for the Kelpie."

Unlike Walipreen who had been bored by his mentor when forced to study history, Nelluc absorbed the information like a sponge. He was very knowledgeable about the history of the Kelpies, their original uprising, their imprisonment, their escape, and the subsequent Great Wars.

"Curious," he said to himself. "What can he hope to obtain from Saldeti?"

It should have taken Walipreen only three days to reach his destination; but the size of the force he brought with him required almost three weeks. He was afraid that the Twins were making similar plans and feared an attack. Eventually, though, they reached the lake – or what had once been a lake. Now it looked more like a frozen crater. A large gaping hole that had been created by another Kelpie marred the pristine beauty of the area. It was as if something had been yanked out of the ground leaving behind an ugly aftermath.

Walipreen approached cautiously. There were boulders and snow drifts around the edges of the lake that he negotiated to reach the opening. As he moved by one of the large drifts, he brushed against it and the lighter layers of powder fell off revealing a figure beneath. Captivated, he brushed more of the snow away and discovered a large misshapen creature in a block of ice.

No, he thought. The creature isn't IN the ice; the creature is made of ice. It resembled a tiger of some kind, but had been distorted in some way, melting partially and then refreezing.

"What went on here?" he muttered.

"Perhaps we should leave this place," growled Chardon. "We're no match for whatever did that."

"Silence," Walipreen commanded. "When I want your opinion, I'll tell you what it is. In the mean time, you and your army stay here. Don't touch anything and try not to cause any trouble."

He didn't wait for an answer or any other acknowledgement. He turned away from the mound of ice and moved towards the center of the lake – towards the hole. When he reached the edge, he could see what appeared to be steps leading downward into the darkness. He bit back his fear and began his descent.

Before he was half way down, the sounds of the wind above him faded to nothing. All he could hear were the sounds of his own footsteps as he carefully moved from one tier to the next. The ice was scarred and rough. He could even see what looked like scorch marks in some places. How could ice burn? What could cause this?

The lower he went the darker it became. He was beginning to doubt that he was in the right place. He had remembered parts of his mentor's lessons and the description of the ice lake. This had to be it, but there was no sign anyone was here any longer. He was near the bottom and the light had faded considerably. He was about to give up and return to the surface when he heard a voice.

"Who is there?"

The sound was barely audible; almost a whisper. Walipreen stopped moving. His eyes scanned the darkness searching for the source. Was he only hearing things? He took a tentative step in the direction from which he believed the sound came. He was so far down that the sounds from the surface above were completely absent. He could hear the pounding of his heart and the intake of his breath. So could whoever – or whatever – was down here with him.

"Who is there?" the voice repeated.

The words were spoken more strongly this time. Walipreen could sense the speaker was either very old or very frail. In spite of that there was no indication of any fear in what he heard.

"My name is Walipreen," he answered.

"That means nothing to me," came the response.

"I...uh...my..." Walipreen was confused by the statement and wasn't sure how to reply. "I'm the Sorcerer of the North," he finally declared.

"North of what?"

"Wh...I...er..." he stammered.

This is ridiculous, he thought. He took a deep breath and started again.

"I am Walipreen, descendant of Ena Ray, Sorcerer of the northern hemisphere. I am in search of the Kelpie called Saldeti. Where can I find him?"

"Ooohhh, descendant of Ena Ray, Sorcerer of the northern hemisphere, are you? I supposed I should be impressed with such a grandiose title. Do I bow in your presence? Should I tremble?"

"I would rather you simply answer my question," Walipreen snapped back, angrily.

He took a step closer to the voice and was immediately met with a blast of intensely freezing air. Before he could react, he found himself frozen in place, coated in a thick layer of ice and unable to move. A tiny light appeared above and in front of him and it slowly grew more intense, illuminating his surroundings.

Out of the darkness stepped a stooped, wrinkled old man, squinting at him like a mole that had just poked its head up through the earth. Walipreen had never seen anyone who looked as old as this person. He was dressed completely in a tattered black robe and hood with only his face exposed – his face and one boney, wrinkled hand that was raised in the air, palm out and fingers splayed.

He cast some kind of spell on me, Walipreen realized. He struggled against the coating of ice, but could move nothing.

"Relax," replied the old man. "You won't be going anywhere until I decide to release you. And that's not going to happen until I'm satisfied as to who you are and what you want."

"I told you who I am," Walipreen said. "And I told you what I want. I'm looking for the Kelpie known as Saldeti."

"I know what you said," the old man answered. "Because you say it doesn't make it so. What do you want with Saldeti?"

91

Walipreen was reluctant to say too much to this stranger, but he didn't see that he had much alternative. Once he was free, he would crush this ancient troublemaker.

"Do you know of the Boravak?" he asked.

"You are wasting my time," the old man said. "I am not the one to submit to questioning."

He slowly began to close his hand and Walipreen could feel the ice becoming much colder and harder. It seemed to be squeezing against him. It felt like his body was being pierced by thousands of needles.

"I believe the Boravak has weakened," he gasped. "I think it is somehow connected to the Phynnodderees. I believe that the Kelpies hold the key to breaking through to the other side."

The freezing sensation lessened, as did the crushing grip of the ice.

"And what key would that be?" asked the old man.

"I don't know," Walipreen answered.

"You're lying," snarled the old man.

The intense cold once again began to seep into Walipreen's body.

"I'm not," he pleaded. "One of my subjects captured a Phynnodderee and is interrogating her now. But I need to speak with as many of the Kelpies as I can to learn more. Only then will I know what the key is."

"And what have you learned from the other Kelpies?"

"I haven't spoken to them," Walipreen answered. "I have only started out. My home is in the Ice Kingdom – in the Crystal Citadel. I sought out Saldeti because he is the closest."

The old man seemed to be considering what Walipreen had said. He lowered his hand and the ice faded away, releasing Walipreen.

"You've found him," replied the old man.

"You're Saldeti?" Walipreen asked, trying to hide the disbelief in his voice.

"Yes," the old man said. "I am Saldeti, the Ice Kelpie. Not what you expected, am I?"

"No...I...that's not..." Walipreen stuttered. "I didn't know what to expect."

"After we discovered that the Alchemist and those eight....intruders had escaped and had taken the Enchantress' pendant with them the recriminations began to fly. When we later discovered the extent to which we had been duped, things only got worse. Instead of uniting and strengthening our power, we began to fight amongst ourselves. Sides were drawn, which quickly changed and shifted like the sands of the desert or the snows on the ice plains.

"Ena Ray and Tebaga seem to have been the only ones of us who kept their heads. They stood back and watched as we battled each other...and for what? There was nothing left. In the end we squandered whatever powers we had, and drifted off to a self-inflicted solitary confinement."

The Kelpie, already old to begin with, seemed to age even more before Walipreen's very eyes. The admission of the folly of the Great Wars appeared to settle over him like a blanket. He looked exhausted.

"I'm afraid I have nothing I can offer you," he said, clearly defeated.

Walipreen looked at the figure before him and took a step forward. He slowly reached out his hand; a look on his face that Saldeti couldn't decide was one of compassion or pity. When he was close enough to touch the Kelpie, Walipreen shot one hand towards the old man's head, grasping it tightly, and clenched his other hand out to his side, holding the tired old body immobile.

"I think you underestimate your value," muttered Walipreen.

He began to pull Saldeti's remaining powers – his very essence – from the Kelpie's mind and body. Flashes of memories flew into Walipreen, becoming one with his own memories. Everything that had made Saldeti who he was, now merged with the fibers of Walipreen's make-up.

When he had stolen all there was to steal, he dropped the shell that remained. The substance that was Saldeti was now absorbed into Walipreen: all the evil that had accumulated in his lifetime, all the experiences that made him who he was, all the knowledge and all the power now belonged to Walipreen. He threw what remained to the ground and headed out of the tomb, back to the surface.

When he emerged from the pit, he found Chardon and the others waiting for him. They had managed to follow his instructions for once and kept out of trouble. Chardon gave him an odd look.

"What is it?" he demanded.

"Nothing," replied Chardon as lowered his head. "It's just that you were down there so long; it was difficult to follow your order and remain here. What if you had been injured?"

"What are you talking about?" snapped Walipreen. "I've been gone less than an hour."

Chardon looked at him in amazement. The Phooka thought he noticed a change in his master. It was only fleeting, but he was certain there was a darkness that hadn't been there before. Walipreen was not pleasant to look upon at any time, but something about him now looked more threatening – more evil. It sent a shiver of fear through the Phooka.

"Master," he said, fearful of incurring his wrath, "you've been gone more than a week."

"That's impossible," barked Walipreen.

He looked at the army spread out on the ice. They had set up an encampment and guard stations. It was apparent they had been there for some time – much longer than the hour he felt he had been gone. What had happened, he asked himself.

"Did you find what you were seeking," he asked.

He wasn't really interested, but it was the only thing he could think of to deflect attention from his reaction to Walipreen's odd behavior and his appearance. Chardon had lowered his eyes as he asked the question, but now found the urge to look again too strong to resist. He raised his glance tentatively. It was still there, but he forced himself not to display anything.

"Not completely," Walipreen slowly replied.

He was trying to reconcile what he was seeing with what he remembered. How could so much time have elapsed? He considered returning to the Ice Kingdom, but something in the memories of Saldeti overruled that urge.

"We should head west from here," he said. "Towards the mountains and volcanoes."

"As you wish," Chardon replied.

Before they left, Walipreen turned back to the gaping hole in the center of the lake from which he had just emerged. He raised his hands into the air, then spread them out to his sides, and then brought them together with a loud clap. The hole began to close until it was sealed completely, burying Saldeti once again beneath hundreds of feet of ice.

Chardon watched in amazement; started to say something, but then thought better of it. Without a word, Walipreen stepped back from the hole as it closed and then turned and headed west. Chardon gathered the others and followed quickly.

"What just happened?" whispered one of the Phookas.

"Quiet," snapped Chardon. "I don't know and I'm not sure I want to know. Just do what you're told."

"Where are we going now?"

"West," Chardon answered. "That's all you need to know," he added, cutting off any further discussion.

They made their way across the far reaches of the Ice Kingdom, creeping at a snail's pace, and burning through their supplies at an alarming rate. They passed a nesting of Strelkas. The Phookas knew about these creatures, but none of them had ever seen one before. Walipreen didn't allow any time for them to study or tamper with the nests. He knew how dangerous the birds could be.

Eventually, they reached the mountains, and the army began the climb to the crest. The winds were especially brutal, as if they were purposely trying to prevent any progress. Walipreen pressed onward. The Phookas were not used to such extreme weather and gradually were becoming more vocal in their objections.

"Walipreen," Chardon called.

He was several yards ahead, and the other Phookas were strung out behind; the gap between them all growing wider with each step.

"Please," Chardon called. "We need to rest."

Walipreen stopped and spun around. He took a few menacing steps towards Chardon.

"You can rest when you're dead," he shouted.

"That will be sooner rather than later," Chardon responded.

Both were surprised by the comment. Chardon had never confronted his master. As soon as the words were out of his mouth, he realized he had gone too far. He lowered his head in supplication, waiting for whatever punishment Walipreen would dispense. But there was only the sound of the roaring winds. He looked up into a face filled with rage.

"Sir," he added quickly. "I only meant that if we don't rest, we won't last much longer and we can be of no service to you."

Chardon had been with Walipreen for as long as either of them could remember. In all their years, the Phooka had never stood up to the sorcerer. He had often grumbled a minor complaint, but only under his breath and never seriously. This time, Walipreen could sense something difference: a note of defiance, perhaps. His anger was diffused by the Phooka's comment.

He looked beyond the speaker at the others strung out behind to a point beyond where his vision ended. They were clearly exhausted. They were excellent burrowers and diggers, but the cold, the wind and the deepening snow were conditions they had never before encountered. They were taking their toll. Chardon was right. If they didn't stop, Walipreen would quickly find himself alone. He was not yet ready for that. The fact that they had been marching close to six months was lost on him. He had lost his concept of time.

Without speaking, he raised one arm. Chardon lowered his head even further, waiting to be crushed. He thought about trying to avoid the blow, but was too weary and cold. He knew any reaction would only delay the inevitable, rather than avoid it.

Walipreen felt a strange power course through his body. It was like a wave of ice that began deep in his chest and surged through his upraised arm. He stretched his hand out over the snow and a clear sheet of ice began to form. It spread from his hand outward and downward, forming a large dome.

"Get inside," he ordered.

Chardon looked up at the dome and then at Walipreen. As the realization that he was not being beaten sunk in, he looked back at the other Phookas, and motioned them to follow him. They trudged through the deepening snow into the dome, leaving the supply wagons outside. Once they were all inside, Walipreen followed, closing the shell, except for a small opening at one end.

When they were all inside, he made a fist and then opened it quickly. A burst of heat radiated throughout the dome. He looked up at the top, expecting the heat to melt the ice, but nothing happened. He understood that these must have been some of the powers he had drained from Saldeti.

The Phookas huddled together until the radiated heat eased their tired muscles and they could relax. One by one, they opened small pouches tied to their waistbands and pulled out small rectangular objects that they bit into and chewed. Walipreen had never given any thought to what Phookas ate.

"What is that they're eating?" he asked Chardon.

The pieces were a dull gray color and looked to have the texture of leather. The Phookas' very sharp teeth separated small chunks of the substance, which they seemed to wad in their cheeks – one on each side; taking no more than that and placing the remainder in their pouches.

"Grubmeal," Chardon answered. "Would you like some? It is very potent."

"I think not," Walipreen said. "But I appreciate your offer."

He noticed that he did not feel the least bit tired or hungry. He wondered why. Normally after such a climb and so long since his last meal, he would be ravenous. Instead, he had no interest or need for food. Or rest, for that matter. Perhaps later, he thought.

It didn't take long for the Phooka's strength to revive. Even Walipreen could see the change in their appearance. He would have to remember to give them time to rest in the future. Although he didn't feel the need to stop, he knew he wasn't ready to continue on this venture without them.

"Are you rested?" he asked them.

"Yes," Chardon replied on their behalf. "Thank you. We will try not to cause you any further delay."

"No," Walipreen answered. "You were right to let me know. I won't let that happen again."

Chardon had never heard his master speak like this before. It was almost an apology. He was uncertain how to react. He wondered what happened in the ice cave when Walipreen had descended into the darkness alone. He also wondered if whatever caused this change was a good thing or a bad thing.

Walipreen snapped his fingers, and the dome disappeared. The sudden cold and the exposure to the powerful winds were unexpected. The Phookas were blown to the ground and sprawled in the drifts of snow, Chardon included. Walipreen stood where his was, his hair and clothing whipped by the wind.

Without another word, he turned and continued up the mountainside. The Phookas scrambled to their feet and quickly followed after. A few hours later, they came to the top. As they crested the summit, they came upon a vast crater.

"What manner of place is this?" Chardon gasped.

"An ancient volcano," Walipreen told him.

He glanced down at the nearby Phooka and saw the look of fear on his face.

"Long extinct," he added.

Before them was a wide chasm with a ledge around a part of the opening, several feet below them. There were remnants of what looked like anchoring for a bridge of some kind, but no sign of the bridge itself. A large section of the ledge off to one side had crumbled and sloped down into a heap of rubble.

On the opposite side was a lower level comprised of a larger, flat expanse, leading to what looked like a cave. Walipreen had no idea what had happened here, but he could sense that some sort of battle had taken place. Heat from the central crater rose up into the air, but quickly dissipated in the frigid, howling wind.

They walked along the ledge in the only direction available to them, towards the lower level and the cave. Once below the crest of the mountain, the wind left them alone and the heat from the depths of the volcano warmed the air. Chardon understood that Walipreen had said this volcano was extinct, but he could hear the rumbling of the lava far below them, and feel and see the waves of heat floating upward.

He was not convinced this volcano was, in fact, extinct. He didn't recall seeing any evidence of recent eruptions as they made their way up the outside, but he wasn't sure that was proof, one way or the other. He knew better, though, than to question Walipreen. He could only hope that the sorcerer was right.

They made their way around the mouth of the opening until they came to the end of the ledge. They were nearly thirty feet above the lower level and there seemed to be no way down to it. Chardon looked back the way they had come and could see that the ledge ended just short of the opposite side – where an apparent landslide had taken place. There was no way across or down from there. They seemed to be at an impasse.

"Wait here," Walipreen ordered.

"But..." Chardon began to object.

Where was he going, the Phooka wondered. He watched as Walipreen stepped to the edge and jumped off. Chardon scrambled after him in a vain attempt to stop him. Instead of crashing down on the rocks below, the sorcerer almost floated out and over, landing safely on the flat part of the lower ledge.

Without looking back, he turned to his right and disappeared into the cave. Chardon moved back from the edge in stunned silence.

"Where has he gone?" asked one of the Phookas. "Have we been deserted?" asked another. "We need to get out of here," said a third. "There is evil in this place."

"Quiet! All of you," shouted Chardon.

He leaned back over the edge and looked down towards the cave opening. He was also looking for a way down that was a little safer. He wanted to know what Walipreen was searching for and what was in that cave. He craned his neck as if that would help him see and hear more than he already could. The noise of the wind was less inside the caldera, but it was still blocking out anything that might be coming from the cave.

Before he knew what happened, Walipreen appeared at the opening. He emerged so suddenly that Chardon jerked back in shock. Then he slowly crept back and peered over the edge once more.

When Walipreen had initially entered the cave, he knew immediately that this was where the Kelpie known as Neraka Ferr had been entombed. He couldn't explain how he knew this and eventually realized that this knowledge must have come from the memories he absorbed from Saldeti. He was amazed at how clear and real they were – as if they had been his own.

He knew the crypt was at the back of the cave and that the ceiling was covered with bats – or had been at one time. He looked up and saw nothing but the ceiling of the cave overhead. He dismissed this as another of Saldeti's inherited memories. When he reached the end, he could see where the Fire Kelpie had been buried, but there was no sign of him.

Could I have recalled something wrong, he asked himself. The Kelpie should be here, but it's evident that nothing has been here for ages. He searched the small cavern. When he was convinced that there was no other place the Kelpie could be, he turned back to the opening and walked out.

He strode out of the cave onto the ledge to the rim of the crater. He knew Chardon had been watching for him and that his sudden appearance had startled the Phooka. He gave no thought to how he would know that. His thoughts were preoccupied by a sudden sensation that was coming over him.

The heat from the volcano was rising. Ash and smoke began to pour over the edge. Walipreen took a few steps back as the black clouds seeped over the rim of the crater and spread across the floor of the ledge on which he was standing. Through the smoke he saw two large hands, molten red, grasp the edge of the outcrop, followed by a head and then a body.

The creature pulled itself up from the magma and climbed to the surface. He stood face to face with Walipreen, the heat pouring off his body. As the air around him began to cool him off, he shrunk in stature. Within seconds the imposing body of fire had been reduced to a smoldering mass, hunched and feeble looking. Even the intense heat had abated to nearly nothing of note.

"Who are you?" the figure rasped.

His voice, Walipreen could tell, was once dominating and threatening. Now it was as wispy as the smoke that curled around the creature's feet, fading into cold ash.

"I am Walipreen," he answered. "And who are you?"

"I am the Fire Kelpie," the creature answered. "Neraka Ferr."

Chapter five

itch was speechless. He couldn't understand what was happening. When he came through the Boravak and met Sean, he was naked. Somehow, his clothing didn't transform with him or it had somehow been prevented from moving from one side of the Boravak to the other. But now, he had no explanation for why he was once again naked. He had shape shifted into a bull frog and then back again. Every other time he had shape-shifted, he was clothed in the same garb he had worn before making the change.

That wasn't happening now. Maybe it has something to do with this place, he thought. He turned to look at Sean for help.

"Why is this happening?" he blurted out. "Help me."

He dropped to the ground and curled up, covering himself as much as he could.

"And don't offer me your slingshot," he said before Sean could do anything.

"Your slingshot?" Summer asked.

"And you," Aitch shouted at Summer, "whatever you are; don't look."

"Summer," Sean said. "Can you find some big leaves?"

"Only if you ask nicely," she snapped.

"And nothing poisonous, if you don't mind," Sean shouted as she flew off.

"Poisonous?" whined Aitch. "Seriously? He...uh, she... would do that?"

"Probably not, but I would," Sean replied. "What were you thinking?"

"I already told you," Aitch answered defensively. "You were going on about pixies and all of a sudden this thing...this...it, I mean she...came out of nowhere. I just reacted."

"It's a she," said Sean. "And furthermore, she's a faerie, not a pixie, and, if that's not enough, she's a faerie princess. Do they have princesses where you come from?"

"No, they don't, but I get the idea," said Aitch.

Before they could go any further in their conversation, Summer returned with a fistful of large leaves, which she dropped on top of Aitch.

"Here," she said. "Please cover yourself up."

"Thanks," he replied, arranging them strategically. "I'm really sorry. I'm new here and I didn't know who or what you were. Honest. If I had known," he glared at Sean, "I would never have reacted that way."

Summer thought it over for a few seconds before speaking.

"All right," she declared. "You're forgiven. This time. And only because it was probably Sean's fault in the first place."

"MINE?" complained Sean. "Why was it MY fault?"

"The source of all misinformation?" Summer asked. "Are you kidding? Stop. I'm not listening to you. Save it for another time."

Sean folded his arms and clamped his mouth shut, a frown furrowing his brow. Summer turned back to Aitch.

"Who are you, by the way?" she asked.

Aitch explained, telling Summer about his sister and the Alchemist; how he came through the Boravak and that he needed help.

"We better find the others," she said when he was finished.

"That's what we were doing," said Sean. "We came to get you first."

"OK, then," she said. "You found me, so let's get going."

"Is she always this bossy?" Aitch asked in a whisper to Sean.

"Always," replied Sean. "And sometimes it's even worse than this."

"I can hear you," Summer called as she flitted away.

The two boys followed after her at a trot as she led the way further through the forest. Without any indication that the forest was coming to an end, it ended. Aitch was so startled by the sudden change and the view that he stopped in his tracks and stared, open-mouthed.

"Oh, wow," he exclaimed.

"What?" Sean asked as he stopped and looked back at Aitch.

"That's...I've never seen...I mean...wow," was all he could sputter.

They had come upon a wide expanse of brilliant white sand on either side of a wide shallow river that was cascading over hundreds of wide, flat rocks making a series of small waterfalls and pools that spanned the width of the river and ran at least a mile in length. The water was crystal clear and small palms and ferns sprouted up in various places along the course of the waterway. As they got closer, Aitch could see small figures splashing in the pools and sliding down from one rock pool to another on the crests of the falls.

"Natalie; Stella," Summer shouted and waved.

She swooped downward towards two figures near the top section of the falls. They were deep in conversation. The older one seemed to be only half-listening as she watched the others splash and float below her. The younger one was not dressed for the water and was sitting precariously on a nearby rock carrying on her side of the conversation. At the sound of Summer's voice, they both turned, stood and smiled, and waved back.

Their eyes shifted from Summer to Sean and they waved to him. Then they saw Aitch and their smiles faded and their hands dropped. As the two boys got closer, another figure rose from the pool immediately behind Natalie and Stella. This one was much taller and had long red hair. As she stood she pulled her hair back and broke into a wide smile as she caught sight of Summer.

"Solveig," Summer exclaimed. "You're here, too. That's great."

"What's a Solveig?" Aitch muttered to Sean.

"That's her name," Sean explained.

"Who are these people?" Aitch asked.

Sean explained the relationship of his friends and pointed out that there were three others they needed to find.

"Why do we need so many people?" Aitch asked. "And what about the Alchemist? That's who we really need."

Summer heard the comment, spun around and dove down to face him, inches from his nose.

"We need all these people, because that's how we do things," she snapped at him. "We have each others' back, and we're a team. We tried doing things split up and it didn't work out so well. If you need our help, especially if it means going back through the Boravak, then it's all of us or none of us."

"Geez," whined Aitch. "I was only asking. Besides," he added indignantly, "I didn't ask for your help. I only asked about finding the Alchemist."

"Oh, really?" Summer asked, fluttering backwards, putting her hands on her hips and giving him an appraising look. "Is that so? Well then, be on your way. Go find the Alchemist. Don't let us stop you."

Aitch clenched his jaw and glared at Summer. He stared at her for a few seconds, and thought about summoning another storm cloud over her head. He looked past her to the three who were sitting on the rocks in the stream and then turned towards Sean. Before he could say anything, Sean intervened.

"Summer," he said, "you need to dial it back a notch. He doesn't know anything about us. He came through the Boravak without knowing what he would find and ends up in a place that's very different from what he left looking for someone none of us has seen for quite a while. He needs our help, even if he doesn't know that himself."

She cocked her head to one side, taking Sean in with a look that could have frozen fire. Before she could speak, Natalie walked past her and up to Aitch, with her hand extended.

"I'm Natalie," she said. "I'm the princess of the water sprites." She motioned to Stella and Solveig and added, "That's Stella. She's an Enchantress, and the other one is Solveig, who is princess of the mountain people. The others that Summer mentioned are Liam, a Pathfinder, Solveig's brother, Lochen, who is a sorcerer, and Quinn, a Guardian of the Ice Kingdom."

"The Ice Kingdom?" Aitch echoed. "That's where Walipreen is."

He started backing away, jerking his hand from Natalie's. His eyes darted from one to another, the fear visible on his face.

110

"Are you subjects of Walipreen? Are you friends of the Phookas? What have I done?" He looked for an escape route, but Sean cut him off.

"Hold on," he said. "We don't know who this Wally Bean person is or what these futons are."

"Walipreen," Aitch corrected. "And Phookas. That's who took my sister."

He took a deep breath and immediately changed shape into a Blue Falcon. Summer gasped in fright and darted away from him behind the nearest bushes and blended into the background, making herself as invisible as she could. Stella moved in front of Natalie and was ready to cast a spell.

"Wait," shouted Sean. "Everybody stop! Aitch, please change back. You're not in danger here. Trust me. If anyone meant to do you harm, that would have happened by now. We are friends of the Alchemist. If he's your friend, too, then that makes you our friend. We'll do whatever we can to help you."

Aitch hovered for a few seconds before lowering to the ground and changing back to his original form.

"That was neat," exclaimed Solveig. "How did you do that? But more importantly, why are you naked?"

Aitch looked down and saw she was right.

"Not again," he wailed, scooping up the leaves that had fallen at the moment he converted to the Falcon shape. "Why is this happening?"

"You mean that's not normal?" Solveig asked.

"Of course not," he shot back, embarrassed as he adjusted the leaves and regained his composure. "Do you think I enjoy running around naked?"

"I was only asking," said Solveig. "Still, it was pretty neat."

"It's not so neat when he covers you with slime," muttered Summer as she reappeared and moved away from the shrubs.

"The Alchemist taught me how to do it," Aitch answered, still a little wary.

"And when he taught you that little trick, didn't he teach you how to keep your clothes on?" asked Sean.

"Yeah," said Aitch. "This hasn't been a problem before – only since I've been here."

"My brother is a sorcerer," Solveig continued, "and he can do all sorts of thing, but he can't do that. Can you do that?" she asked Stella.

"No," Stella answered. "He's a shape shifter. None of us is a shape shifter. I've heard about them, but that Kelpie who made herself look like Summer is the only other one I've met. How do we know you're not the one who's here to do us harm?"

"It's kind of hard to be a threat when you're naked," Sean answered for Aitch.

"Enough, please, with the naked stuff," pleaded Aitch. "I'm not here to harm anyone. I'm here to find the Alchemist. I need help to find my sister who was taken by the Phookas. If you don't trust me, I understand. Just let me be on my way and I'll find the Alchemist by myself."

"Who's looking for the Alchemist," said a voice from the other side of the stream.

Aitch turned to the sound and felt his knees weaken. Standing on the other side, much too close for his comfort, was a giant dressed all in white. He had never seen anyone so big, although it was rumored that Walipreen was enormous. He had never seen Walipreen, so he assumed the stories of his size were myths.

Quinn took a large step into the middle of the stream and crossed it in one more. As he did, another figure appeared – one that had been hidden from view: Liam. Liam jumped from one rock to another as if he was dancing on air and landed on the opposite shore next to Quinn. Quinn was a few feet in front of Aitch, who was looking up, dumbstruck.

"And who's this little green guy?" Quinn asked, bending down to get a better look.

In a completely reflexive action, Aitch transformed into a puff of smoke. Quinn jumped back, waving his arms.

"Whoa," he shouted. "What just happened? Where'd the little green guy go?"

"Aitch," Sean shouted. "Come back. This is Quinn. He won't hurt you. I promise. He's with us. You're safe."

The wisp of smoke swirled and reformed into a tighter cloud. In a matter of seconds, Aitch had resumed his original shape.

"Oh, dude," shouted Liam. "You're naked. What's that all about?"

"Why does this keep happening?" wailed Aitch as he gathered up the fallen leaves and quickly covered himself.

"I don't know," said Sean. "But either you have to stop changing shapes or we need to figure something else out."

"Why didn't that happen when he changed into the Falcon?" asked Natalie.

"You changed into a FALCON?" Quinn boomed. "Oh, wow, I wish I had seen that. Can you do it again?"

"Maybe later," muttered Aitch as he continued to adjust the leaves.

"Yeah," said Sean. "He still has some things to work on before he entertains you."

Sean took a few minutes while Aitch continued to adjust his leaves to explain to Quinn and Liam where Aitch had come from, what had transpired to this point, and what should be done next.

"I haven't seen the Alchemist since...I don't know," said Quinn. "Since not long after we moved to this side of the Boravak. How about anyone else?"

They were all in agreement. It had been some time since they escaped and none of them could recall any sign of the Alchemist much after that.

"Maybe Lochen knows," suggested Stella.

"That's possible," replied Solveig. "If any of would know, it would be Lochen."

"Where is he, by the way?" asked Sean.

Before anyone could speculate, there was a crack of thunder, a flash of light and something landed in the nearby water, sending up a tremendous splash of water. Everyone ducked and covered their heads, but no one was spared a good soaking. Aitch looked up to see where the source of the disturbance was only to be met with an enormous wall of water crashing down on him.

The force of the wave was so strong that it flattened him to the ground. When he sat up, he saw someone sitting on a glowing slab of stone that appeared to float on the water at least for a few seconds.

"What. Is. Wrong. With. This. Stupid. Thing?" the person shouted, one word at a time.

"Still having trouble with the transporter stone?" Stella asked.

Aitch's eyes darted from the person in the water to Stella and back, and then to Sean.

"I'll explain later," Sean said.

"YES!" Lochen shouted in frustration. "I'm using the same stupid control mechanisms as before, but nothing seems to work. Not only can I not steer the stupid thing, but I can't get the stupid thing out of the stupid atmosphere. It hops form one stupid place to another stupid place. It's...it's...it's..."

"Stupid?" Quinn offered.

"Exactly," Lochen replied. "It's stupid!"

He climbed off the stone as it began to sink below the surface and slipped on a rock, his foot sinking in the water to his knee.

He waved his arms to regain his balance, swung his other foot around too far and fell forward into the stream.

"Arrgghhhh!" he growled.

He rose up out of the water and awkwardly made his way to the shore. Once there he swung one hand from his head downward and his robe was instantly dry, although his hair was still dripping water. He shifted his eyes upward to see where the drips were coming from, wrinkled his brow and waved his hand over his head, drying his hair.

"That's better," he said.

He immediately focused on Aitch who was sitting in a puddle of water, gaping up at him.

"You're a Phynnodderee," Lochen declared. He took a few steps toward Aitch, who scrambled backwards trying to maintain a safe distance.

"How interesting," Lochen continued. "I've read about your people, but I've never...wait. They don't exist in this world...you're from...how you...what are you...did you come through...that's not..."

"Will you PLEASE finish at least ONE sentence?" shouted Solveig. "You do this all the time."

"What?" Lochen asked, turning to Solveig and then, immediately forgetting her question, turned back to Aitch and tried to step closer. But Aitch kept crab-walking away from him.

"Who are you?" Aitch stammered. "How do you know about me?"

"I'm the sorcerer to the mountain people," Lochen replied. "And I know nothing about you. Personally, that is, but I do know about the Phynnodderees. The strange thing is that they don't exist in this world. Which means you came through the Boravak; which means that there must be a breach of some kind. If that's true then we are in danger – all of us; everything. We need to find the Alchemist."

"Yes," shouted Aitch as he jumped up. "That's what I've been saying. Do you know where he is? Do you know him?"

Lochen's eyes widened. "How do you know the Alchemist?" he asked.

"He was my teacher," they both said at the same time.

Lochen looked more closely at Aitch. He noticed for the first time that Aitch was wearing nothing but a cluster of leaves. He looked closely at the leaves and then shot a glance at Summer, understanding immediately that she had provided them. Then he looked back at Aitch.

"You're a shape shifter, aren't you?" he asked. "That's how you got through the Boravak."

"How can you know that?" demanded Sean. "No one told you anything about that."

"That's not important now," Lochen dismissed the question. "There's something more, isn't there? Something dreadful has happened on the other side."

"Yes," answered Aitch. "The Phookas stole my sister."

"Phookas," repeated Lochen.

"That's right," said Aitch. "They're…"

"I know who and what they are," Lochen cut him off. "Tell me about your sister. Is she a shape shifter as well?"

"No," said Aitch. "At least I don't think so."

Lochen seemed to be thinking and everyone's eyes were focused on him, waiting. Aitch was about to ask him a question, but Sean signaled for him to remain quiet. The Lochen spun around to Stella.

"Can you cast a vision?" he asked, motioning to the pendant she wore around her neck.

"Not out here," she answered. "I need a sanctorum."

"Are we near yours?" he asked.

"Not unless you can get that to work," she answered motioning to the transporter stone that had settled to the bottom of the stream.

Lochen looked at the contraption he was not able to control as he had done before – before leaving what had been his home all his life, and coming to this side of the Boravak. He furrowed his brow in frustration.

"That doesn't seem to be a viable option," he muttered. "How far are we?"

"Several hours, I'm afraid," Stella told him.

"I think we are faced with a situation that demands a greater sense of urgency," he said.

"Does he always talk like that?" Aitch whispered to Sean.

"Usually it's worse than this," Sean whispered back. "The scary thing is, I actually understand him this time."

Lochen began twirling his hand in a circle, raising it higher and higher, above his head; widening the circle until his arm was stretched out as far as it could. Dust began to form into a cloud that grew thicker and wider, gradually transforming into rock and creating an enclosure around all of them.

"There," he said when he was done. "It's not much, but it will have to do. Can you make this work?"

He had created a small ring of stone that encircled them, providing a makeshift sanctorum. Stella turned completely around, as did the others, staring in disbelief.

"How did you do that?" she asked.

"I'm not quite sure," he replied. "Since being transplanted here, I have developed some unusual powers. I'm not sure of their origin; I only know that they exist." He glanced again at the transporter stone and added, "Other things don't seem to work quite the same way."

"If you haven't been able to get that transporter stone working right," said Solveig, "I hope you haven't been trying to visit the stars again."

"No," replied Lochen, as he looked up at the sky and a look almost of misery clouded his face. "That's another thing that's not quite right. It's all...different. But that's another discussion. Right now we need Stella to cast a vision."

She stood in the center of the stone circle, closed her eyes and raised her hands. Instantly images flashed on the walls. Aitch stared wide-eyed and open-mouthed as he saw pictures of the people who were with him in this strange circle. They seemed to be of varying ages and in different locations. He saw an enormous dragon, a troll, a gnome and several other strange and frightening creatures. He saw bridges collapsing, volcanoes erupting and ice shelves crashing into the sea.

The images seemed disjointed and overlapping. In some instances he saw the same people in different settings at the same time. In other instances there were hundreds or thousands of creatures and then they'd disappear as quickly as they had appeared. Suddenly, there was cloud that was so black it looked as if the stone wall itself was opening into the darkness. The black was growing larger and deeper, drawing the other images into it until it filled most of the wall. In a flash of brilliant light, it all disappeared – images, the blackness, the wall itself.

"That was freaky," said Natalie.

"Yeah," agreed Liam. "Even more than usual."

"What does it mean?" Lochen asked Stella.

"I can't tell," she replied. "I've never had a vision like this before."

"What can you tell us?" asked Natalie. "Anything?"

"Not much," said Stella.

"Was it because of me?" asked Aitch. "Did my presence make things...I don't know...messed up?"

"I didn't get that sense," said Stella. "But who knows. Everything on this side is, as Lochen said, different. Maybe I can't conjure visions anymore."

"Forget what you saw," said Lochen. "What did you feel?"

"Danger," she said almost immediately. "And a tremendous evil."

"Awwww. Not again," wailed Quinn. "Are you sure? Is it on this side? Maybe it's not. Maybe it's only on the other side."

"Yes, I'm sure," said Stella, "but I can't tell where."

"It can't be on this side," said Liam. "Can it? I thought the Boravak was keeping it contained on the other side."

"I did, too," said Lochen. "However, as evidenced by the presence of this Phynnodderee – a people that do not exist in our world – it is apparent that the Boravak can be breached. Whether or not it has, and by someone other than our friend here, has yet to be determined."

Lochen's reference to Aitch being their friend was not lost on him. He felt a sudden wave of relief and trust flow through him. He also felt a sudden and very strong kinship with them. He knew in that instant that they would do whatever was necessary to help him and that he would do the same for them.

"What do we do now?" asked Liam.

"I think we need to see where...what did you say your name is?" asked Lochen.

"Aitch," he replied. "My name is Aitch."

Lochen looked closely at him for several seconds. It seemed as if he was about to say something and then reconsidered.

"What?" asked Aitch. "Really. That's my name."

"Yes," said Lochen finally. "Of course it is."

He dismissed whatever it was he had been thinking of and turned to the others.

"We need to go to the place Aitch came through the Boravak," he said.

"We're not going back over there, are we?" asked Quinn.

He stepped backwards into the stream. Liam reached up and pushed on his back to keep from getting stepped on.

"Whoa, big guy," he said. "Don't tell me you're afraid."

"Hey!" Quinn shouted as he turned and looked at Liam. "Remember this?"

He pointed to the streak of white in his hair that Stella had never been able to change back to its original blond. It was all that remained to remind them all of how he had been locked between the two worlds. It had been only seconds for all of them, but it had been years for him; years with the top half of his body stuck in the opening of the Boravak. He dove back through to save Lochen and Stella, only to get trapped in a different time until they reappeared years later. Only seconds passed for Liam and Sean who had held his legs in an attempt to stop him.

As the opening closed around him, sealing him suspended between the two worlds – two places in two separate eras of

122

time – he could see that the battle he had fled only seconds before, had not yet happened; and wouldn't for several years.

Natalie stepped closer to Quinn and placed her hand on his arm. He had saved her life in another place and time. He had gone back to save Stella, her Enchantress – someone whose life was tied to hers. She could sense and understand his fear.

"We will not be separated this time," she said to him. "And no one doubts your courage."

"I didn't say I wouldn't go," he said after a few seconds. "I'm just not looking forward to it."

"I don't think any of us are," said Summer. "But we have to find out if the Boravak is weakening, and..."

She looked at Aitch. She had clearly heard Lochen's reference to him as a friend. Her initial encounter with the Phynnodderee had not been one on which strong friendships were usually built, but as soon as Lochen had called him friend, she knew he was right. There was something about the strange green boy that put all of what had happened initially behind her. She knew he could be trusted – with their lives if it came to that. He needed their help. Right now, that was all that mattered.

"...and," she continued, "we have to help Aitch and his sister."

"I agree," said Lochen. "I fear we have no time to waste."

"Wait," said Liam. "Don't we need supplies?"

"I don't believe we have the luxury of sufficient time to amass the extensive provisions you were accustomed to in the Swamp," said Lochen. "And beyond that, I really have no thought as to what we may need. The possibilities are endless. As Stella's vision was limited, we have no clue as to what we may expect. Provisioning for every likely event would most likely be counterproductive. And further, we don't know what, if any of those provisions, would pass through the Boravak."

"Couldn't he have just said no?" Aitch mumbled to Sean.

"Any one of us could have just said no, but I think one word answers are impossible for him – unless you really need a detailed explanation. Then you're lucky if you get any words at all," Sean replied. "Sometimes he just stares at you and nods. Oh, and if he asks you if you want to go on a little trip, don't. There's no telling where you'll end up."

Sean looked up at the darkening sky. The first stars were beginning to shine and he recalled a trip with Lochen on a transporter stone that was quite literally out of this world. He was right about something, though, this place was different.

"You guys are going to take some getting used to," said Aitch.

"You don't know the half of it," Summer said as she fluttered past him.

"It will be night soon," said Solveig. "Should we wait, or do you want to take a chance with your transporter stone.

Lochen looked back at the slab of stone that was at the bottom of the stream. It was still glowing slightly, but the silt and sand from higher up were slowly covering it. He committed this location to memory, so he would know where to find it if he ever came back this way, but he shook his head in response to Solveig's question.

"No," he said. "I think not. I'm still puzzled by the inherent inconsistencies in the stone's characteristics on this side of the Boravak. As time is of the essence, I think it a wiser course of action to forgo the potential expedience of a transporter stone due to the uncertainty of what destination it will take us."

Solveig was used to Lochen's elaborate commentary, but Aitch could only stand and stare in disbelief.

"I think Solveig's right," said Sean. "Those woods are inhabited by pixies. It will be hard enough to avoid them in the daytime. Going through at night is just asking for trouble."

"I'll take care of the pixies," said Lochen. "You just lead the way. Everyone stay close. That includes you, Summer."

They formed a tight group and followed closely behind Sean as he picked his way back through the woods. This time, though, he took a more direct route, avoiding the spiraling path he had led Aitch on earlier that day. Lochen snapped his fingers and a globe of light encompassed them all and sent out a short beacon, lighting the path ahead.

Taking the more direct route, they made much better time. Still it was well into the night by the time they reached the spot where Aitch had come through. There before them was the towering tree with the peculiar knot in the center of the trunk just a few feet from the ground.

"It doesn't look any different to me," said Natalie. "Did you really come through here?"

"Yes," he answered.

Quinn bent over and looked at the knot and then turned his head towards Aitch, a look of disbelief on his face.

"There's a tiny hole in the center of the knot," Aitch explained. "Although it's not a knot on the other side. Anyway I shifted into smoke and came through."

Quinn's eyes moved from Aitch to Sean.

"I saw it happen," said Sean. "He was smoke and he seeped through just like he said."

"Well he can get through," said Summer. "But what about the rest of us? I don't want anyone changing me into smoke."

"Nor would I recommend that," said Lochen. "Even if one of us had the capability to convert us, that ability may not exist to reverse the process on the other side."

"So what do we do?" asked Natalie.

"It appears that we have to trust that what is about to happen will not unleash the evil that has so far been successfully contained within," answered Lochen.

"What are you about to do?" asked Solveig nervously.

"Stay as close to one another as possible," directed Lochen. "I'm about to open the Boravak."

Chapter six

Shortly after Walipreen and his party left the Ice Kingdom, Nelluc made his way down into the lower levels of the keep. When the Kingdom had been occupied by Quinn's people, the rooms to which Nelluc was headed were used for long term storage. Now, though, they served as dungeons to hold those who Walipreen determined had failed to meet his expectations. This was where Emm was being held.

Even this far below the surface, the strange properties of the ice created a glow that provided enough light for Nelluc to find his way. He had ordered that Emm be placed down here, but had given no specific instructions as to how she was to be treated. He could see that this oversight had been a mistake.

He found himself in the lowest level where the rooms were very small – barely four feet square and not much higher. Emm, of course, was able to stand upright, and if she chose to sleep, would have enough room to stretch out. There was, however, nothing for her to sleep on and she had been manacled and chained to the walls, which prevented her from getting in a prone position. Instead, she sat with her legs crossed and her back straight, as if she was meditating.

The image of her in this pose – defiant and self-assured in spite of her surroundings and the potential danger she was in – left Nelluc somewhat disconcerted. He was also embarrassed that this mere child would be dealt with so severely.

"I apologize for the treatment you've received," he said to her once the door to her cell had been opened.

At first she refused to acknowledge him. She kept her eyes shut, her back erect, and her expression neutral. Nelluc was uncertain as to what to do or say. He realized that although she was the captive, right now it seemed as if she had the upper hand. This thought was unsettling to him. He turned to one of the two guards.

"Release her from those chains immediately," he ordered.

The guards entered the cell without a word and unlocked the chains. Emm lowered her arms and opened her eyes. She fixed her gaze on Nelluc, but kept silent. Nelluc had expected her to thank him or to say something – anything. Her silence was beginning to infuriate him.

"Bring her along," he ordered as he turned and left the cell.

He made his way back to the upper level to his own quarters. The guards followed with Emm between them. When he got to his room, he sat down and motioned her to another chair. He then dismissed the guards, telling them to wait outside.

"Would you like something to eat or drink?" he asked.

"No." she replied.

Nelluc studied her for a few seconds.

"Why did the Phookas gag you?" he asked, recalling that she had been bound and gagged when she was brought in to Walipreen.

"I bit one of them," she said.

"Really?" Nelluc laughed. "Their skin is like leather and extremely bitter. They also have a very high threshold for pain. I doubt your slight nip was cause for fear."

"You'd have to ask them," she answered.

"I would, but I doubt I'd get the truth from any one of them. I'd prefer to hear from you what really happened."

"I already told you," she said. "I bit one."

Nelluc could tell she was lying. He waited, but she offered nothing more. He stood and walked to the door. Opening it, he saw the two guards still posted outside.

"Who among the party that brought this creature back is still here?" he asked.

He knew that Walipreen had taken Chardon with him on whatever quest he was making. Chardon would have taken many of the Phookas who were on the earlier spying mission on this same quest. He was hoping that Chardon didn't take all of them. The two guards looked at each other and then looked blankly at Nelluc.

"Who did Chardon leave behind when he left with Walipreen?" he demanded. "Out with it, now or you'll both be in one of those cells below – together."

"Clartom," one of them blurted out.

The other one glared at his partner, but said nothing. The speaker only shrugged.

"Bring him here, at once," Nelluc ordered.

Nelluc returned to his seat and waited for the arrival of the Phooka. A few minutes later, there was a knock and the Phooka known as Clartom entered.

"You wanted to see me?" he asked.

"Yes," replied Nelluc. "Tell me what happened after you captured this child. Why was she gagged?"

Clartom looked from Nelluc to Emm and back, clearly uncomfortable. He shifted on his feet and lowered his eyes.

"She bit one of us," he said.

"Oh, really?" said Nelluc. "Which one?"

"What?" asked Clartom.

"Which one?" Nelluc repeated. "You said she bit one of you. I want to know which one."

"Uh...ah...I don't remember."

"Was it you?" demanded Nelluc.

"No."

"Was it Chardon?"

"No."

"Who else was on the raid?"

"I don't remember," answered Clartom.

Emm watched the exchange in silence, wondering what Nelluc was trying to discover.

"Move over next to the child," he ordered.

Clartom looked at Nelluc as if waiting for some explanation. Nelluc only raised his eyebrows, waiting for Clartom to comply. The Phooka looked at Emm and then back at Nelluc and shuffled sideways until he was standing next to her.

"Extend your arm," Nelluc ordered. "No, not towards me, you imbecile. Place it in front of her."

Clartom furrowed his brow in confusion and slowly did as instructed.

"Bite him," Nelluc ordered Emm.

"What?" she asked incredulously.

"Bite him," Nelluc repeated. "Just like you claimed you did before."

Emm hesitated, debating her options. Seeing none, she leaned forward, opened her mouth and bit down on the extended hand. Clartom stood motionless, watching. Almost immediately Emm spat in distaste. Clartom looked even more confused and turned to Nelluc.

"Is that the best you can do?" he asked. "Do it again, but this time like you mean it."

Emm looked worried, but did as she was ordered. She snapped at the extended hand, biting down as hard as she could. The bitter taste was so strong, she started to cough and gag. Her face puckered in disgust and she wiped her mouth and tongue with her hand. Clartom remained unphased.

"Just as I suspected," said Nelluc. "You're both lying. The question is why."

Nelluc watched the two of them. Emm kept her eyes on him, but the Phooka could not maintain contact. His eyes shifted downward, towards Emm, or up towards the ceiling, but he wouldn't look at Nelluc. He got up from his chair and moved in front of Clartom.

"I want the truth, or I shall be compelled to tell Walipreen upon his return that you have been disloyal."

"But I haven't," cried Clartom.

"Who do you think he will believe?" asked Nelluc. "You or me? I want the truth and I want it now."

"She wouldn't stop talking," blurted Clartom.

"That's all?" asked Nelluc.

"No!" Clartom almost shouted. "She was telling us to do things. At first we thought it was a joke, but then it was nearly impossible not to obey her. We had to do something, so we gagged her."

"What exactly did she tell you to do?"

"I don't remember," Clartom replied. "Even now, I don't remember why we did it, just that we felt we had to."

"Because what?" Nelluc asked in disbelief. "She told you all to do something that you don't remember? That's absurd."

"What did she tell you to do? It's a simple question."

"I can't remember," Clartom pleaded. "Honest. I just can't remember."

Nelluc thought this was so ridiculous that it was probably true. The Phookas weren't particularly smart, but he found it difficult to believe this little girl could talk them into doing anything.

"I don't believe you," Nelluc said, as he turned and walked away, resuming his seat.

Clartom was distraught. His fear of being reported as disloyal was monumental. Emm could sense that in this state, he was at his most vulnerable. His resistance would be minimal and she might not have an opportunity like this again. She decided to take a chance; it might be her only chance to escape. She glanced down at the long, thin dagger the Phooka wore at his belt and then leaned closer to him.

"Stab him," she said in a whisper she hoped Nelluc couldn't hear.

Clartom heard the words and a strange feeling came over him: a sense that this might be his only path to escape the wrath of Walipreen. He fidgeted, looking at Emm and then at Nelluc. He heard the words echo in his head and imagined they were his own thoughts.

"Stab him," she ordered again in a hiss.

Nelluc heard the noise, but couldn't make out the words. He could see the heightened level of anxiety in the Phooka's eyes. He assumed it was the fear of Walipreen.

"Do it now," demanded Emm. She turned slightly in his direction and repeated," Stab him."

Clartom could feel the thoughts rising from his own mind. Do it now, he told himself. Stab him, his inner self said. If he didn't act, he would be blamed for everything, although what he would be blamed for was unclear to him. The sense of urgency, however, was undeniable.

"What are you telling him?" asked Nelluc.

He could now see that she was saying something to Clartom, but he couldn't make out what she was saying. He stood up and walked towards the two of them. A strange feeling crept into the core of his consciousness — a sense of imminent danger. Emm could feel her chance slipping away.

"Stab him," she shouted.

"What?" Nelluc said.

He didn't trust what he heard. Clartom reached for the blade and began to withdraw it. At the same time Nelluc could see what was happening.

"Put that thing away," he ordered as calmly as he could.

"Stab him," Emm shouted once more.

Clartom pulled the blade from his belt and moved towards Nelluc. His face was twisted. Nelluc looked into his eyes and could see the conflict within. He could see that Clartom knew what he was about to do and what his fate would be afterwards, but he could also see that the Phooka was powerless to stop himself. He shot a glance at Emm, realizing that she was the source of the danger.

Clartom had the blade raised above his head and was within striking range. He brought it down in a swift, forceful motion. At the last second, Nelluc raised his own arm and deflected the blow. The dagger's point missed its target, but the blade cut into Nelluc's arm. Nelluc stepped aside and pushed the Phooka past him and down to the floor. The blade hit the stone and broke; Clartom's hand twisted as he fell and the broken end he still held turned upward, striking him in the ribs.

The sudden pain cleared his mind. He rolled over onto his back, the broken dagger in his hand, his ribs bleeding. He looked up at Nelluc, who was holding his arm where it had been cut, and then he turned his face towards Emm, and back to Nelluc.

"Please," he pleaded. "Forgive me. She made this happen. It was as I told you. She made us do things. She made me do this. I beg you. Forgive me."

"Get up," shouted Nelluc. "Get up!" he repeated when Clartom remained immobile on the floor.

"Get up and get out of here," he shouted again, kicking at the wounded Phooka.

Clartom scrambled to his feet and ran out the door. As he passed the guards, they could see the bleeding wound and ran into the room. Nelluc was holding his arm in an attempt to stop the bleeding. The guards looked from him to Emm and back out the door at the disappearing figure of Clartom.

"They were right," Nelluc hissed at Emm. "You are treacherous."

He turned to the guards and told them to find something to bind and gag her. They both rushed out of the room and he walked back to his seat.

"What exactly did you do?" he asked. "Not that I expect you'll tell me."

He studied her while he waited for the guards to return. His arm was throbbing and his shirt was soaked with blood. He thought about what happened and recalled the description that Clartom had provided about the party that had brought this child back to the Ice Kingdom. Clartom had told him that the Phynnodderee had bit him. The Phooka knew this wasn't true. Even Nelluc knew it wasn't true.

But Nelluc believed Clartom when he said he couldn't remember exactly what had happened. He was certain that the Phooka wouldn't recall what had happened in this very room. The child had somehow crept into the Phooka's mind and controlled his thoughts. One of them on that spying party had figured this out and had gagged her.

Nelluc felt exhaustion settle over him like a blanket. He began to feel strange. He tried to clear his head, but he had a compelling urge to sneak the Phynnodderee out of the Kingdom and take her home. He knew this was ridiculous, but the urge was almost overwhelming. It reminded him of standing on the edge of a cliff and having a similar urge to jump. He stood up and started walking towards the child, just as the guards returned.

All this time, Emm had been staring silently at Nelluc. When the guards entered the room, she lowered her eyes and a look of resignation clouded her face. In the same instant, the strange compulsion Nelluc had felt for helping her escape disappeared.

"Tie her securely," he ordered. "Make sure the gag is tied tightly and then return her to the dungeon. And chain her to the wall."

He waited until they left and then he went to have his wound tended to. When he entered the chamber of the shaman, he saw that Clartom was having his ribs tended to. The Phooka looked up at Nelluc.

"I don't know what happened," he said.

"Don't worry about it," Nelluc replied, assuming the Phooka was referring to his attempt at stabbing him.

"I can't help but worry about it," Clartom continued. "One minute I was with you and then the next minute I'm in some distant hallway bleeding from a wound I don't remember getting. How can this be?"

Nelluc stared at him, uncertain whether the Phooka was trying to pretend that he didn't recall the incident. Clartom seemed to notice for the first time that Nelluc was wounded as well. He jumped up, pushing the shaman's hands aside.

"You're wounded," he shouted. "Have we been invaded? How did this happen?"

The Phooka then turned to the shaman.

"See to him first," he demanded. "His wounds are more severe than mine."

He doesn't recall any of it, Nelluc realized. It dawned on him then that the Phynnodderee was more dangerous than he had originally thought. Without waiting to have his arm tended to, he rushed out of the chamber and ran down to the dungeons. He passed the guards who were returning from having delivered Emm.

"Is she secure?" Nelluc demanded.

"Yes," one of them answered. "We returned her to her cell as you ordered."

"Very good," Nelluc said.

He turned and headed back to the shaman, but was stopped when the other guard spoke up.

"We left the gag in her mouth, but we untied her hands as you instructed. I don't understand why you wanted her hands free. She'll only remove the gag herself."

"What?" shouted Nelluc. "Come with me. NOW!"

He made a dash to the cell and ordered them to open the door. Inside, Emm was standing in the center of the room, her hands free, and, as the guard had surmised, she had removed the gag from her mouth. Before she could react, Nelluc directed the guards to re-fix the gag and to secure her arms to the chains in the wall. He could feel her hatred burn into him as she glared at him.

When she was as secured as could be, he looked at the guards and realized that in a very short time, she had somehow convinced them to disregard his instructions to them. He also realized that keeping her here would be impossible. Sooner or later, she'd convince some unsuspecting guard to release her and probably to give her a weapon. The question was, where could she be kept?

When the cell door was locked, Nelluc ordered the guards to keep the entire hall leading to this cell guarded at all times. No one was to enter or go anywhere near the cell or the hallway without his permission. He gave specific instructions on how meals were to be delivered to the prisoner, making sure that several Phookas were safely out of range of her control any time anyone else had to get close to her.

The problem as he saw it was that he had no idea how much distance was required to be safe or how many people she could control or influence. He had to come up with another place to hold her or to release her as she was demanding. That, however, was a decision for Walipreen, not him. Until Walipreen returned, Nelluc would have to take steps to safeguard the Kingdom. Otherwise, he was afraid, they could all be lost.

He returned to the shaman to have his arm bandaged. There was no sign of Clartom, not that he expected the Phooka to still be there, or to have suddenly recalled the reason they were both seeing the healer. While he sat and had his arm ministered to, his eyes wandered across the shelves of herbs and potions.

"Is there an elixir in your bag of tricks," Nelluc asked, "that would prevent someone from reading your mind?"

The old healer laughed, "No, I'm afraid nothing I have will do that."

Nelluc let his thoughts drift as the physician rambled on.

"There are very few places here in this land of ice where I can find the ingredients for the most basic potions and poultices. Of course, I travel with the master very little these days. But in my youth, I came across many unusual concoctions that did some very unusual things. But the need for those kinds of elixirs has diminished since the Great War and the peace that was made with the Twins."

The shaman rummaged around in a large pot and removed two large black leaves that he wrapped around the long, deep cut. Then he uncorked a bottle releasing a foul odor into the air. He poured the contents onto a strip of cloth and then squeezed the liquid over the leaves.

"This will sting a little," he said to Nelluc.

It stung a lot. As he wrapped the soaked leaves in a strip of cloth around Nelluc's arm, he continued talking and Nelluc continued to ignore him.

"Of course before the Great War there were several very skilled sorcerers and enchantresses that could create any number of potions. And spells; they could cast spells of an unimaginable variety. And, of course, there was the one they called the

Alchemist. But we don't talk about him; certainly not in the presence of the master."

He pulled the binding on the bandage tighter, causing Nelluc to wince. He motioned for Nelluc to stay put while he searched through a random collection of bottles for something he wasn't inclined to explain, talking all the time.

"And long before the Great War," he continued, "there was this ancient town. At one time it had been a thriving center for learning and trade, but then these..." he was careful about choosing the words to describe what he was about to say, "...town leaders, I suppose you could call them. They sealed off the town and planted poisonous bushes around the village walls to keep people out. Instead, the plants poisoned the water and the food the town relied upon. Before long, everyone inside was dead, while everyone outside...well, they were much better off."

"Thank you, healer," Nelluc cut him off. "That was very educational."

He had grown tired of the pointless rambling talk and was anxious to leave. He stood up and began to return to his room and attempt to find a solution to his problem. The shaman looked up in surprise.

"Oh, you're leaving," he said.

"Yes," Nelluc replied. "I'm afraid I have a serious problem to solve."

"Of course," said the shaman. "I just thought you wanted to know about how to keep someone from reading your mind."

Nelluc stopped in the entryway and turned back to the healer, biting back his frustration.

"And what would that be?" he asked acidly.

"The plants that surrounded the village walls," replied the shaman.

"What about them?"

"They have many properties," said the shaman. "Only one of them was the poison that the village elders thought would keep people out. Well there were the thorns, too, I suppose – very nasty; and dangerous. Well, fatal, really, if they broke the skin, but not if one only came in contact with them – or the leaves. Mere contact would only cause a long and painful illness. I imagine one would wish for death, but as far as I know just brushing up against them would not be fatal."

"How, exactly, does this prevent someone from reading your mind," Nelluc asked, trying to get the old man back on the subject.

"Oh, yes," he replied. "As I was saying, the poison was only one property. There are many others, but to your question, as they grew around the walls of the village, they created a barrier that warded off many spells. One such spell was the ability to read minds. It was said that the Alchemist could do this, although that may only be legend. I don't know if anyone ever witnessed firsthand his ability to read minds."

"Are you saying I would have to plant these...these...these poisonous plants around someone I wanted to keep from reading others' minds?"

"Of course not," said the shaman. "I'm not aware that these plants exist anymore. Besides to do so would be to invite ruin upon yourself. Wasn't I clear about what happened to the village around which these shrubs were planted?"

Nelluc could feel his anger rising.

"I don't understand," he said through clenched teeth. "If these plants are extinct then what was the purpose of your story?"

"The point is, that even in a state of decay, they have a tremendous effect on barring spells. The potency of their poison has worn off, but several of their other properties are still remarkably effective. Preventing the reading of minds is but one."

Nelluc waited for the healer to continue. "And?" he said when nothing more was forthcoming.

"And, all you need to do is go to this village. Once inside the walls, no one on the outside would be able to read your thoughts. Of course, once you left, then the power of the plants would no longer protect you."

"What if I put the person who could read minds inside this village?" Nelluc asked.

"I suppose that would work just as effectively," he answered.

"Where is this village?" Nelluc pressed.

"Well to the south," the shaman answered. "Of course, when you come to think of it, almost everything is to the south. Let me think."

"Come with me," Nelluc ordered, grabbing the healer by the arm.

He dragged the old man from the healing chambers down a long hall and two levels below to the map room. Inside this room were dozens of charts, maps and drawings. Many of them were very old and none of them had been updated in decades. Dust covered most of the room.

Nelluc pulled one scroll from a cabinet that was off to one side and opened it. Not seeing what he wanted, he tossed it aside and selected another. The shaman walked over to the discarded map and began to roll it back up.

"Leave it," demanded Nelluc. "No one has referred to these maps for years. No one is going to care if they're neatly arranged or not."

The healer looked dismayed. He stopped rolling the map, looked around the room and, for the first time, noticed the disarray that it was in. He looked back at Nelluc, down at the map in his hands, and then back around the room. He shrugged his shoulders and tossed the map on the floor.

When Nelluc found what he was looking for, he pushed the papers and other materials from a nearby table and spread the map out. He motioned for the shaman to join him.

"Show me on here where that village is," he ordered.

The shaman moved closer and looked down at the drawing. He wrinkled his brow and extended a finger towards the area designated as the Ice Kingdom. He ran his finger southward and then to the west, past an area identified as the Venomous

Swamp. He raised his finger and concentrated on the nearby markings. Then he found what he was looking for.

"There," he said. "The Village of the Thumpers."

"Where?" asked Nelluc. "I don't see any such label."

"Oh, it's not the actual name of the village, or the geographic area," replied the shaman. "That's just what it was called – a very long time ago."

"Thank you, healer," Nelluc said, rolling the map up. "You've been very helpful."

"It is my pleasure to serve you," he replied.

Nelluc turned and left the shaman standing in the map room. It took several seconds before he realized he was no longer needed and he made his way back to the healing chamber. In the meantime, Nelluc went in search of Clartom. It didn't take him long to find the Phooka.

"What happened to your arm?" Clartom asked when he saw Nelluc.

"Nothing of importance," Nelluc replied, unsure of Clartom's lapse of memory was one of reality or convenience.

Nelluc told him that he was taking the Phooka on a journey. He directed him to assemble ten of the most seasoned and trustworthy warriors he could find and to assemble enough provisions for at least three weeks.

"Have them ready in the armory and come find me when they and the supplies are gathered," he ordered.

He returned to the healing chamber and the shaman. He asked for a specific potion.

"Why would you ever want something like that?" the healer asked in shock.

"As a precautionary measure," Nelluc replied. "Do you have anything like that?"

"Well,,," he hesitated. "Yes, actually, I do. How much to you need?"

"Enough for eleven Phookas," he answered.

"Eleven?"

The shaman was dumbstruck. He had never been asked for anything like this before, and had this potion only in the event of some unknown emergency. He couldn't imagine really needing it, especially not for eleven people.

"You want to use this on Phookas?" he asked, not fully comprehending what was being asked of him.

"Yes. Is there a problem with that? Will it have any side effects?"

"No," replied the shaman. "At least I don't believe so. You must understand, I've never used this potion, so I can't predict exactly what will happen"

"Will it kill them?" Nelluc demanded.

"No," the shaman answered. "It won't kill them, but..."

"That's all I need to know."

He took the vial the shaman provided and went to the armory. By the time he arrived, Clartom and ten other Phookas were waiting for him. He was about to have them all drink from the vial, when something occurred to him.

"How many of you can read?" he asked.

"Read?" they asked.

"Yes, read."

"Read what," one of them asked.

"Anything!" Nelluc nearly shouted. "If I write you a note, how many of you can read it?"

All but two of them raised their hands. Nelluc told those two to leave. He wouldn't need them. Then he passed the vial around and told them all to drink from it. Once they were finished, he explained what was about to happen.

"The potion you just drank will eliminate your hearing," he said.

They looked at him in shock. Some of them began to grumble.

"It is necessary," he continued. "We are going on a journey that will be very dangerous. On this journey and even after we reach our destination, you would have heard things that would put your lives at risk. This was the only way to keep you safe."

He had to shout the last words. Even as he was speaking, their ear drums were turning to stone, and their ear canals were swelling shut and hardening. At first they could hear a ringing sound. Many of them covered their ears in a futile attempt to block out the ringing. Only then did they realize it was coming from within their own heads.

147

A sense of panic swept over them that Nelluc hadn't considered. They were all looking at him in a menacing manner. He pulled a small piece of parchment from his pocket and scratched out a note. It read, "This will not last forever. You will be greatly rewarded."

Both statements were lies, but he would deal with the repercussions when the time came. Within seconds all sound was nothing more than a memory for the nine Phookas. Nelluc saw that they were still angry but the false promises had tempered that anger.

"How long will this last?" Clartom shouted.

Nelluc wrote another message, telling him that he was shouting, which was not necessary. He added that it would wear off once their lives were no longer in danger, although he failed to indicate when, if ever, that might be. He told them to return to their quarters and to get some rest. They would leave at first light.

As the others left, he pulled Clartom by the arm, keeping him behind. Once the others were gone, he wrote another note: "I know I should have told you all before I gave you the potion. For that I apologize."

Clartom was taken aback by the words. No one had ever apologized to him. He looked down to see that Nelluc was writing some more: "You are in charge of the others. You must make sure that they are ever watchful. You must also keep an eye on me throughout this journey so you will know when I need to communicate with you."

Clartom nodded his understanding and read the last message: "In the morning, it will become clear to you why this had to be done." As an afterthought, Nelluc added, "Your reward will be even greater." Another lie.

Clartom grimaced, which Nelluc understood was a smile. He then dismissed the Phooka and went to his own quarters to make final preparations. He wrote a message for Walipreen in the event the sorcerer returned before he did, although he thought that was unlikely. When he was finished, he made his way back down to the dungeon.

He had the guard open the cell and he looked in on Emm. She was still bound and gagged and chained to the wall. She looked up at Nelluc and glared at him.

"Get some rest, child," he said. "We're going on a long journey tomorrow."

Chapter seven

Walipreen stared at the shell that was once a powerful and intimidating force – the Fire Kelpie. Now, though, he looked more like a burned out shell. When the figure first rose from the volcano, he looked much different than he did only seconds later.

"You seemed to have transformed," Walipreen commented. "Does the air up here not agree with you?"

Neraka Ferr noted the edge of sarcasm in the stranger's voice. He fought to regain his strength, but knew that his efforts were futile. He moved closer to Walipreen, but the younger man showed no signs of being alarmed. There was something about him that looked familiar. The Kelpie just couldn't identify what it was.

"Do I know you?" he finally asked.

"I don't believe you do," Walipreen answered. "We have never met."

"There is something about you that reminds me of someone I once knew," he said.

"Perhaps you recall one of my ancestors," Walipreen said, a curious smile creeping into his face.

"And who would that be?"

"A sorcerer by the name of Ena Ray,"

At the mention of the name, Neraka Ferr stepped back. He hadn't heard that name in years. He searched his memory for the last time he had seen Ena Ray. It had been during or near the end of the Great War. He and that other one – what was his name? Tebaga. That was it. The two of them had joined the Kelpies to complete the circle of eight, replacing Pantano Izaki and Ollos Foscos, the two Kelpies who had been dispatched by those miserable intruders.

It all seemed to have happened such a long time ago. He tried to think about how much time had passed and realized that it was, in fact, a long time ago. Whatever happened to those two – Ena Ray and Tebaga – he wondered. They had managed to avoid the frenzy that followed in the years after the disappearance of that sorcerer and the small Enchantress who had held off the onslaught of him and the other Kelpies.

"Yes," he said after a while. "I remember that pretender."

Walipreen refused to take the bait.

"You didn't answer my question," he said, instead.

"Which one was that," the Kelpie asked.

He knew what the question was. He also knew that this descendant of Ena Ray was treacherous. It had been a mistake to return to the surface. As long as he remained inside the volcano, his strength and power remained. However, when he came to the surface, it faded quickly. It was the result of the spells they had cast on each other when the in-fighting began. He had underestimated Saldetti. It was his spell that did the most damage.

"What is it that you are seeking?" Neraka Ferr asked, trying to change the subject.

"Information," Walipreen replied.

"About what?"

"The Boravak."

"What about it?"

"I want to know how to get through it," said Walipreen. "Or to break it down."

"That's not possible," answered Neraka Ferr. "We tried; all of us. Whatever spells the Alchemist used to create it could not be broken. What makes you think anything has changed?"

Walipreen wasn't sure it could be changed. It was just a sense he had; somehow related to the surges of energy he had experienced – twice now. He knew that something on the inside had happened. His inability to understand what that was or what it meant angered him. He knew he had to know more about all that had transpired in the time before the Great Wars.

He had often heard about this Alchemist, the Enchantress, and the eight misfits that defeated the Kelpies. He believed they were all connected in some way to each other, to the Boravak, the Kelpies, and to his own ancestor: Ena Ray. He needed to know what these connections were, and then, he thought, he would be able to unlock the key to the Boravak. Once that happened, then his powers would be limitless.

He was certain the answers, or at least most of them, resided with the Kelpies. He didn't think they would give up those answers willingly, even if they were aware they held them. When he had extracted the thoughts and memories from Saldetti, he could tell that the Ice Kelpie had only a fragment of the whole story. He could also tell that the Kelpie himself did not fully understand the full extent of what he knew.

Now, facing the Fire Kelpie, he could feel another piece was at hand. He stepped forward as casually as he could, but the Kelpie stepped back, closer to the edge of the volcano. If he returned to the fire below, Walipreen was convinced he would not be able to follow and would not then be able to draw him out again. He raised his hands in appeal.

"I need your help," he said. "I have felt unusual forces recently. I don't know the source or the explanation for these forces, but I believe they may indicate that the Boravak is weakening."

"How did you come to that conclusion?" Neraka Ferr asked, his guard still up.

Walipreen slumped his shoulders, lowered his head and shook it. He took a step back, almost turning away, but then looked back at the Kelpie and took a subtle step closer.

"I don't know. What I mean to say is that I can't explain why I believe this, only that it came upon me suddenly and with a tremendous intensity."

He spoke with all the sincerity he could, gesturing to emphasize his quandary; all the time inching his way closer; moving back and forth to disguise his closing the distance between them.

"And what do you expect from me?"

"As I said: information," he pleaded. Little was handed down from my ancestors, I'm afraid to say. As a result, I know little of this person called the Alchemist, the woman Meri Hocto or their minions."

At the mention of these enemies, Neraka Ferr dropped his guard. His concentration on not allowing this stranger to get too close and on keeping the safety of the volcano within easy reach all diminished. He had been duped by Walipreen's false display of vulnerability. He took one step away from the rim of the crater and growled.

"They escaped with the pendant," he snapped in anger.

Walipreen barely heard the words. He had noticed the lowering of the Kelpie's defenses and the step he took away from the safety of his volcano. It was now or never. He lunged forward and thrust his hand behind the Kelpie's head, pulling him close. He pressed the other hand against Neraka Ferr's forehead.

The Kelpie realized too late that he had been trapped. He struggled to generate a searing heat to burn his captor's hands. What he was able to summon went unnoticed by Walipreen. The Kelpie reached up to pull the hands away, but he could feel what little strength he had quickly evaporate. He could feel his legs going limp; his arms grew heavy and dropped to his sides.

Walipreen could feel the life energy drain from the Kelpie into his body. He could feel all the memories, all the knowledge, all the life experiences as they seeped from Neraka Ferr into him. In an instant he understood the reference to the pendant. He knew what it was, but still did not know of its significance. He also knew that among the Kelpies, half of them were sorcerers and half were enchantresses; but that Neraka Ferr was an extremely rare enchanter. He also knew in the same instant that he was still missing several key pieces and would have to seek out the remaining Kelpies – and, eventually, the twins, Rampool and Prine.

When the essence that had been Neraka Ferr now resided in Walipreen, the Kelpie dropped to the ground in a lifeless heap. Glassy eyes stared blankly up at Walipreen. The expression on Neraka Ferr's face betrayed the confusion he felt.

"Please," he pleaded, not even understanding what he was pleading for.

"I have what I need from you," Walipreen told him.

The sorcerer stepped up to the shell sprawled on the ground and nudged it with his foot. He was surprised at how little it weighed; at how little substance remained of the carcass. He pushed with his foot. Neraka Ferr extended his arms and tried to grab the leg closest to him. To Walipreen it felt like the light touch of feathers trying to grasp his ankle. He gave a final push and the body rolled over the side and back to the pool of lava below.

"Let's see if that restores any of your power, old man," murmured Walipreen. He then sat down as Neraka Ferr's memory became his. Not far above him, Chardon and several of the other Phookas had been watching as this drama unfolded. They could not hear any of the conversation, and could not tell what had passed between the two below them. They could not mistake, however, what their master had done to the other.

As Walipreen held the Kelpie's head between his hands, they saw subtle changes take place. The sorcerer seemed to grow slightly taller and became broader in the shoulders. The change was not radical, but to those who knew him closely, they were obvious.

When he had disposed of the Kelpie's body, they watched without understanding why he simply sat there, unmoving. Days later, he came out of the trance-like state in which he had been and turned to look at the observers, they could see a change in his eyes, as well. There was an intensity in them that had not been there before. His already dark irises now appeared such a dark black that they appeared more like deep wells falling to a void of unimaginable depth. They were rimmed with a thin deep red line.

Neraka Ferr's memories and knowledge blended with those of Saldetti's that Walipreen had absorbed not so long ago. They merged together, giving Walipreen a perspective of all that had gone on long before in the initial rise of the Kelpies, the battle with the Alchemist and the Enchantress – although some of those aspects were still unclear – the defeat at the hands of eight strangers, and the Great War.

As the fibers of these memories became imbedded in Walipreen's mind, they also merged with his own memories. At first he knew this was happening, but he ignored the sense of loss of his own identity. He soon forgot that these threads were the experiences of another's life and the separation between them and his own became blurred.

He climbed back to the crest of the caldera and once again saw that the army had made an encampment. He looked at Chardon and fought to keep from asking how long he had been inside the crater. He was certain it had been only minutes, but what he was seeing before him told a different story.

"Are your men rested?" he asked Chardon.

"Yes," the Phooka replied. "Would you like to eat something?"

"I..." he started to say he had no need for food, but reconsidered. He had no recollection of the last time he had eaten. He didn't feel hungry, but realized that to decline to eat would likely only create more suspicion and fear among the Phookas.

"I would, yes," he replied instead.

Chardon rummaged through the dwindling supplies and found something suitable. Walipreen accepted the offering – a slab of some kind of meat. He could tell it was beginning to spoil and concluded that they would need to search for something fresh as soon as they got off the mountain.

He looked around at all the eyes fixed on him and then thought it better to sit and finish his meal before ordering them to break camp. He forced himself to eat the entire slab and drank some water. As he was finishing, Chardon gave instructions to pack up the supplies and be prepared to leave at the master's bidding.

"When you are ready," he said to Walipreen. "And where will we be moving?"

Walipreen saw the look on the Phooka's face. He was anxious to return home. He would be disappointed. The sorcerer tried to calculate how long they had been gone, but couldn't. At their present location there was no apparent change in the seasons by which he could estimate the passage of time. On this side of the mountain, it was always winter.

"We need to replenish our supplies," he said. "As soon as we're down from this mountain, send out some hunting parties."

He had managed to avoid answering the question, but the Phooka understood that they would not be going home. Chardon turned away and made the necessary arrangements for the entourage to begin its long, slow movement off the mountain.

By the time they reached the base, their food supplies were gone. There had been several reports of desertion. Walipreen seemed to be immune to the complaints. He was making a direct line to the area that had at one time been known as the Venomous Swamp. In Walipreen's time, no one understood how this region had warranted that name.

While there were signs of several varieties of toxic plants and pools of highly acidic water, for the most part, the area was a lush garden. Lost in the history of the place were the efforts of its one time resident, a man known as The Pathfinder, who had worked tirelessly to convert the jungle of poison plants and nests of lethal reptiles and animals into a garden.

It had taken him several years and the help of his friends to accomplish. Over time, once the change had started, it continued on its own momentum. Under normal conditions the trek from the northern volcanoes to the western region of the Swamp would have taken a few weeks. That was not the case for Walipreen and his reluctant army. For them time dragged.

As the party made its way across open fields, more of the Phookas deserted, burrowing into the ground at night and tunneling away in different directions. In spite of the reductions in their numbers, their progress was slow. Several times hunting parties were sent out and the supplies were replenished. As the days rolled from one to another, the desertions eventually died down and the army, now about two thirds its original size, stabilized.

When they finally reached the Swamp, they found the first of several storage caves. Some of them were dug into the ground or the low hills, while others were constructed from logs and timbers. The mechanisms that locked the simple doors were easily opened and Walipreen had memories of gargoyles that had at one time traveled near here. They weren't his memories, but he could not make that distinction.

"What are these places?" Chardon once asked.

"They were supply holds," answered Walipreen. "They were built and filled by one called The Pathfinder so that he could travel throughout the Swamp and have ready access to equipment, supplies, or shelter and protection from the gargoyles that wandered mostly at night."

It was not an answer Chardon had expected. He knew Walipreen had little interest in history, and had never ventured this far south before. How could he know this?

"But these locks, surely, couldn't keep anyone out," the Phooka said.

"The gargoyles were unable to work even the simplest mechanisms," Walipreen answered. "These were more than sufficient."

"How do you know this, master," Chardon asked.

"I traveled here, and had a number of encounters with The Pathfinder," he replied.

"I never knew that," replied Chardon, knowing it was untrue.

"I..." Walipreen stopped.

His initial certainty that he had been here before and had battled The Pathfinder and his friends caused him to pause. When had that been, he asked himself. What had happened, he wondered. How could he know some of this, but not all of it?

"I..." he faltered. "I mean, I recall my mentor talking of it."

Chardon knew he was lying, but couldn't understand why he found it necessary. At the next storage building, the army made camp, and Chardon explored the contents. This stronghold was much bigger than the others they had come across. Inside was a strange contraption that looked like a boat of some kind, but it had wheels.

Chardon climbed up the side and could see what he guessed was a steering mechanism and a seat with pedals in front of it. What manner of mystic could conceive and build such a thing, he wondered. There were several blades of varying sizes, which he confiscated and distributed to his closest friends.

He discovered some minimal food supplies, rope, large quantities of material, and other items of which he could discern no use whatsoever. As he left the building and closed the doors, he could see gouges cut into the face around the lock. Was this evidence of the attempts by the gargoyles to break into this place? He had heard of these gargoyle creatures. It was told that they may have been the ancestors to the Phookas, but since his people kept no recorded histories, these stories were nothing more than just rumors.

The next morning, Walipreen told him to remain in camp, that he would proceed alone, since they were very near their destination.

"Do not venture close to the river," he warned. "There are creatures that inhabit those waters that are dangerous. If your men must forage, have them do so in the direction from which we have just come. No place here is safe for them."

He spoke with such authority that Chardon wondered if Walipreen had, in fact, been here before. He said nothing, though and watched as the sorcerer climbed through the thick vines and brush and disappeared from sight.

Not long after he was out of sight of the Phooka, Walipreen came upon several large pieces of cut stone near the edge of the river. He approached the opening and his senses were assaulted by memories of a fierce battle. This was the place where the Kelpies had been defeated. He could feel the rage of Neraka Ferr. He could see the burst of molten fire that he threw at a young sorcerer and the small Enchantress who was by his side.

He could feel the presence of the Swamp Kelpie, Pantano Izaki, but knew he had not taken part in this battle. Where had he been? He had no recollection. He pulled the overgrown vegetation out of the way and revealed an opening between the large stones. What he sought was down here, he knew.

He moved into the darkness and the air suddenly became stale. He waited for his eyes to adjust to the lack of light, not wanting to create any kind of illumination. At his feet a gray-green mist began to form. Up from the mist grew a figure. It was indistinguishable at first, but then began to take shape.

He could see a head become clear. It was covered with long matted hair that hung in thick strands. It was a dull gray and brittle. A long gaunt face appeared, the eyes closed, the skin dead and wrinkled like ancient parchment. As the body took shape, Walipreen could see it was as long and thin as the face atop it. The creature was clothed in a shroud that looked ancient and threadbare – more like strings of dead vines; the vines he had pulled from the entryway.

Hands that extended from long, boney arms looked skeletal. Walipreen wondered if the creature was alive or dead. As this thought came and went, the eyes opened and a wave of putrid air escaped from its mouth.

"Who dares to enter my tomb," the voice croaked.

"I am Walipreen," he responded. "I seek Pantano Izaki."

"You would be well advised to seek caution instead," the creature responded. "Finding what you seek may not be as pleasurable as the search."

"You are the Kelpie," Walipreen said.

It was a statement rather than a question. He knew he had found the Swamp Kelpie. Its eyes showed a flicker of light and then went flat again, but stayed fixed on the visitor. Walipreen studied the ancient sorcerer. In the dim light, it was hard for him to see much more than what appeared to be an apparition. He lacked the substance of the other two Kelpies he had encountered.

"Yes," Pantano Izaki replied. "I am the Kelpie."

He seemed to lack interest in whatever it was that brought Walipreen to him. The silence hung in the air for several seconds.

"There was a fierce battle here at one time," Walipreen said, breaking the silence.

The Kelpie said nothing.

"There is more below us in this cave," he continued.

Still the Kelpie remained silent.

Walipreen took a step towards the lower level, but the Kelpie cut him off. As ethereal as he appeared, the sorcerer could sense the substance behind the figure. In a flash of motion, Walipreen grasped the creature's head in his hands. It felt like holding a soft but solid form. The thin hands with cracked and blackened nails reached up to pull Walipreen's hands free, but his faded strength was no match. The once powerful Kelpie was too frail, too defeated to withstand the attack.

His eyes glimmered slightly and then he seemed to accept his fate and ceased his struggle. As the memories flowed from one entity to the other, the Kelpie faded to almost nothing. Any substance that had existed evaporated and sank to the ground joining the fog that covered the earth.

Once Walipreen had absorbed everything, he felt a sharp pain in the center of his chest. He knew instantly it was the stabbing sensation of a dragon's tooth that had pierced his heart in another life time. He staggered briefly with the recollection of the incident, an image of flowing red hair on a young woman wielding the tooth and driving it into his chest emblazoned in his mind.

He gasped a deep breath and saw another figure trapped under an odd looking structure – one very similar to that he and Chardon had seen in the stronghold they had come across further west. She was half buried in the sand of some distant desert, shielded by the odd looking structure from the battle that was raging not far away. He was standing over her, about to destroy her when the other one struck him in the heart with the tooth. He had been swallowed by the sand and remained dormant until she and the others had escaped.

Walipreen shook his head, trying futilely to erase the memory. He had touched the face of death and realized that evil never dies. But it had been well contained for a very long time – contained somehow by this very place. He knew there was something much more to this place than the cavern that it appeared to be.

He saw that the fog still hung on the floor of the cave and knew the lingering mist was the shell of the Kelpie whose life he had just stolen. Stepping through it, he moved deeper into the cave until he came upon a larger opening. He could see figures carved into the stone sides like pillars holding up the domed ceiling. He knew instantly that these were Kythauls; that they had come alive at the command of the Kelpies when they battled for the pendant. The roots that broke through the earth had also been called to life.

He looked down at the lowest level. He knew that was where the others had disappeared. That was the source of the Boravak. He knew that this entire world was held within a tree on the other side. It was another creation of the Alchemist. His frustration raged.

He clenched his fist and threw a bolt of intense heat at the small landing, knowing it would do nothing to break the barrier. He would remember this place. He vowed to return to it once he had amassed more power and he would break through to the other side. When he did, he would find the Alchemist, the Enchantress and those eight who had confined the Kelpies in this prison. They would know his anger; they would feel his retribution.

He turned and headed back to the surface. He brushed past the dead roots and took one final glance at the worn and lifeless Kythauls. He had not noticed, however, the small pile of clothing in a heap on the ground in front of a hole no bigger than a strand of hair.

When he returned to the surface, he saw that once again more time had passed than he had realized. A complete camp had been set up and there was evidence of extensive hunting and gathering of food supplies. When this had first happened, he had some concern about the lost time. Now he paid little attention to it.

When Chardon saw him approach, his face could not hide his shock. The changes in Walipreen's physical features were more pronounced. His face seemed slightly distorted: his lips pulled back in somewhat of a sneer; his eyes more deeply set and furtive. He appeared taller, but more hunched over. His back was broader but rounded and he walked in a sort of lurching motion.

"What is it?" he demanded when he was Chardon's reaction.

"Nothing, master," the Phooka replied. "It's just that I wasn't expecting you. I assume you were successful."

"What is that supposed to mean?" he snapped.

He was growing suspicious of Chardon. No; it wasn't just Chardon. He was suspicious of everyone. He jerked his head to the right and then to the left, looking to see who was listening. One unsuspecting Phooka happened to look in his direction. Walipreen took two quick steps in his direction and leaned over him.

"What are you looking at?" he shouted.

"Nothing, master," the Phooka stammered. "I was awaiting your command."

Walipreen ground his teeth, glancing back and forth between the Phooka and Chardon. He gave a slight shake and seemed to regain control of himself. He then turned away from the Phooka.

"We're moving," he announced. "Get your men ready."

With no further instructions or comment, he turned away and moved back towards the opening from which he had emerged. He raised both hands and lifted the enormous ancient slabs of stone that had once served as the tomb for Pantano Izaki. He raised them into the air, brought them together and planted them in the ground as if marking the spot once more.

He looked at the waterway that bordered the encampment. On the other side was a forest – the forest of the Navedis. He had heard stories of these people, but believed that they were now extinct. So much of this land had been populated before. Now many of the people were gone; but where, he wondered. He knew he would learn that soon. For now, he needed to find the next Kelpie.

"All is ready, master," Chardon said.

The Phooka had approached Walipreen from behind, making as much noise as he could to alert the sorcerer to his presence. Walipreen had been deep in thought, the memories of Pantano Izaki imbedding themselves within his own memories. He hadn't heard the Phooka until he spoke. The voice startled him and he jumped around to face it.

As he spun around, he raised his arm to cast a spell. The Phooka cowered before him, arms raised in a futile attempt to protect himself. Walipreen caught himself, stopping the blow from coming.

"What do you want?" he shouted.

"Nothing, master," Chardon replied. "I only came to tell you that all is ready whenever you wish to depart."

Walipreen seemed not to understand what was being said. He then looked beyond the Phooka to see the army assembled and ready to set out. The scene slowly registered and he lowered his arm.

"Very well," he said. "We will continue east."

"To the desert?" Chardon asked.

"Of course, to the desert," Walipreen answered.

The Phookas were burrowers and lived as much underground as they did above ground. Deserts, however, were impossible to burrow in. Phookas not only disliked deserts, they feared them. They felt exposed and vulnerable in areas where they could not seek refuge in the ground. They never journeyed out to sea, or along the rivers and streams, and they never traveled across the desert. Even the frozen wastes of the Ice Kingdom were preferable to the desert.

"But, master..." Chardon tried to explain.

"You will go where I order," Walipreen cut him off. "Is that clear?"

The Phooka expected the desertions would begin again and probably get worse once it was discovered where they were heading. He wanted to caution Walipreen against this decision, but he could tell that this was not the same person as the one with whom they had started this journey. He realized any discussion was pointless.

"Yes, master," he said. "Of course. As you wish."

He turned and moved back to the rest of the entourage and gave the instructions to begin moving. He refused to answer questions about where they were going. He knew it wouldn't take long for everyone to know where that was. He knew many would remain loyal – to a point, but he couldn't tell what that number would be.

He stood and watched as the line began to file slowly by. He considered his options, including desertion, but knew that was no real choice for him. His destiny was tied to Walipreen. He had no other options. He wondered where all this was going to end, and felt certain that he would not be there when that end came. He felt – no, he knew – his end would come sooner.

Walipreen watched the Phooka walk back towards the assembled army and then immediately dismissed any further thoughts of him or the others. He turned towards the east and began walking. His thoughts focused on the desert. He knew exactly where they had to go. He had been there before. He rubbed the phantom pain in the center of his chest.

No, he thought. I've never been there. That was the Kelpie's memory. As quickly as that realization came, it was gone. He remembered very vividly seeing the desert location – the place his friend, Angin Topan, was buried. How long had it been since he had seen his old friend? He couldn't recall; after all, he had been absorbed into the desert sand shortly after she had been released from her prison crypt.

As he walked, his body continued to change in subtle ways. Saldeti's eyes – the depths of death itself – were now Walipreen's eyes. The strength and power that had been Neraka Ferr now belonged to Walipreen and twisted his body, broadening his shoulders. With each step he took towards his next destination, his features continued to change.

His thin, wispy hair began to thicken and tangle. As it grew, it twisted and hung like moss from the trees in the Swamp where Pantano Izaki drew his essence. Walipreen was not only absorbing the knowledge and memories of the Kelpies, he was taking on their physical characteristics. He was losing himself piece by piece.

Chapter eight

Nelluc lead the small party of now deaf Phookas as they led Emm, still bound and gagged, from the Ice Kingdom. As an added safety measure, he had a hood tied over her head. He wasn't sure what other tricks she was capable of, but was taking no chances. He wanted to get her away and secured before Walipreen returned. He could deal with the sorcerer later on.

He viewed travel much more differently than Walipreen. The sorcerer preferred to walk and with a large company to ensure his security. He believed that by walking, he could see well in advance any potential traps.

Nelluc, on the other hand, had no fear of attack. The only source of any invasion would be from the Twins. As Nelluc was a Rebbercand, as they were, he was sure that he would come to no harm at their hands. He managed to find several sleds and dogs to pull them.

His teams raced across the ice fields and within a few days had reached the southwestern boundary. He had thought to leave one of the Phookas behind to guard the sleds. While he had no worries about being attacked by the Rebbercands, he was not as convinced that they wouldn't send parties into the north to steal. They were notorious thieves and liars.

He decided against leaving a guard, though, since the Phooka would end up returning with him to the Ice Kingdom only to discover that his loss of hearing was permanent. The shaman had nothing to cure the potion Nelluc had given to them. Besides, he would only need one of them for the return trip.

Once they parked the sleds and dogs, they set out across the open fields. He had come this way as a small child, but had no real recollection of the journey. He had been exchanged for Dekene somewhere near the range of mountains that divided the north from the south. From there, the remainder of the trip was in the company of Phookas. That was probably why he had no fondness for them to this day.

He had been hauled like a sack of vegetables and fed the disgusting things they called food. The journey took forever as they avoided one mythical "evil place" after another. Hadn't they realized that they were now living in the heart of evil, and had been for a long time?

After a few more days they could see a mound off in the distance. Amid the green of the fields, this place looked like a blister. It was a black hump on the horizon. Even the Blue Falcons, which flew where they pleased, avoided the space over this location.

As they travelers got closer, they could see the wall that enclosed the ancient village. It was covered with dead vines. The leaves had not decayed, but hung on dead stems from the dead trailers that rose from the contaminated ground and clung to the stone. Long, dangerous thorns still stuck out from the branches that criss-crossed the barricade that surrounded the village.

"NELLUC," Clartom shouted.

Nelluc motioned yet again, indicating that it was not necessary for him to yell. The Phooka was still not aware that he was, in fact, yelling, but mumbled an apology. Nelluc motioned for him to speak.

"Surely that is not the place you mean to take us," he said.

Nelluc scribbled out his response: It is perfectly safe as long as you avoid contact with the plants surrounding the village.

Clartom looked at him with skepticism. Nelluc wrote more: We will find a suitable prison cell for the Phynnodderee and then if you like, you and your men can establish your living quarters outside of the ruins. You'll only have to go in to feed her.

Clartom considered this and then nodded his understanding. The village was still more than a day away. Nelluc decided to get far enough before stopping for the night so that they could arrive early the next day. He didn't want to spend the night anywhere near this place. It was nearly dark by the time they stopped.

Even being this close made it difficult for him to sleep. He recalled the stories of this village. He was familiar with the history: about how the Thumpers sealed it off from the surrounding population and then planted the poisonous plants around the walls to further discourage any attempts to get in. He was certain anyone alive knew about that.

He also had heard from Walipreen's mentor that a piece of the mysterious pendant had been hidden here – the same pendant that his distant relation, B'nair, had nearly possessed. This place held all sorts of secrets, but Nelluc was interested in none of them. He only hoped that the shaman had been right, and that the residual spells cast on the dead vines would contain the Phynnodderee's ability to control the thoughts of others – at least until he could figure out a way to control her and use this ability to his own advantage.

He woke the Phookas up at first light to get an early start. Even so, it was nearly midday by the time they crossed the decrepit draw bridge and passed through the village gates. At first he wondered why the gates would be open, but then he realized that there was nothing to steal and no reason to enter this unholy place. He assumed they had been opened when the piece of the pendant had been either hidden or found. It really made no difference.

He led the way across the bridge and down the main road. The silence was eerie and he considered that this was at least one thing that would not spook the Phookas. Their entire world was silence, now.

Emm, however, was keenly aware of the change. For a while after the morning's start, she had heard birds warbling and feathered wings flapping; she had heard the tiny buzz of insects and the gentle rustling of the breeze. Eventually all of that faded into nothing. She didn't need to see where they were to know it was not a place that welcomed them.

She pulled against her restraints, but the Phookas yanked her along. She felt a coldness creep through her skin as she felt her feet crossing the wooden planking of the draw bridge. She sniffed the air and could detect death and decay – not overpowering, but pervasive. This was a place of unspeakable evil.

She fought even harder against her restraints until she felt her bound arms jerked sharply forward until she lost her balance and fell. She struggled to stand, but whoever had control of her leash only pulled harder and dragged her across the bridge and then the ground until she felt the cold of the stone and then the pulling stopped.

Once Nelluc was beyond the gates and close to the town center, he motioned for the Phookas to stop. He turned back to see that Emm had fallen and had been dragged into the village. She clumsily got to her feet and fought to remove the hood from her head. Her hands were tightly bound and the hood had been tied behind her neck. She wasn't going to be released until he decided to release her.

He motioned for the others to stay put and then signaled to Clartom to come with him. The Phooka looked back mournfully at his companions and then resigned himself to his duty and followed Nelluc deeper into the village.

Beyond a well in the center of the town and to the left Nelluc saw a large stone structure. He pushed aside a rotting wooden door and entered what he reasoned was a guard house of some kind. Towards the back of the main room was a stone staircase that spiraled downward. He sent Clartom back to the others to find materials to make a torch and waited.

Clartom had found an ancient oil pot and some rags. He wrapped the rags around a piece of wood he pulled from a heap of debris and soaked the rags in the oil. Once it was lit, he returned to the building to find Nelluc at the top of the staircase. He handed him the torch and followed h him downward.

When they reached the bottom of the staircase, Nelluc could see that his initial assessment of the building had been wrong. It was not a guard house. It had been a mill. The lower room was circular in shape. In the center at one time had been a large circular stone platform on which a wheel was turned to grind wheat. In the center of the platform was a place for the center post that rose up through the ceiling and the roof above.

It had probably been attached to some kind of windmill, Nelluc surmised. The wheel was long gone and the platform had been reduced to rubble, the larger pieces removed and only the smaller stones and dust remained. The post, too, was gone, leaving a hole through to the sky above. There was evidence that whatever rain fell, it left a small puddle in the middle of the room. It hadn't rained in a long time, but the water stains still marked the place it pooled.

There were no windows or doors; no exit other than the stairway. Nelluc decided this was perfect. He scribbled out a note to Clartom: We need to find where the forge was.

Clartom looked at him in confusion. Nelluc only pointed to the note again and motioned for the Phooka to follow him. They exited the mill and moved through the village, until they found the forge. Nelluc had some of the other Phookas find materials to light the fire and he located the necessary tools and materials. When they were done, he took them to the mill. There, he drove a long spike into the stone floor in the center of this room.

He fastened a chain to the loop at the end of the spike. Then he had Emm brought down. She staggered down the steps, the hood and the gag still in place and her hands still bound. She could smell the evil that had inhabited this place. She bit down on the gag to fight back her fear. She was shoved into the center of the room where she fell to her knees. She could feel hands holding her down, while an iron collar was fastened around her neck.

She could hear the rattling of the chain as it was linked to the collar. The sound of the hammer beating the link shut resounded in her ear. When the noise stopped, she could hear the sound of feet retreating up the steps and out of the mill. She remained motionless, waiting; her hands tied behind her, the gag tightly secured in her mouth and the hood still covering her head.

Were they going to leave her here alone, she wondered. She turned her head and could hear the chain attached to her neck rattle. She stood up, shook her head, feeling the weight of the chain and the tightness of the iron collar. Her scream was muffled by the gag, when the hood was suddenly pulled off her head.

She found herself face to face with Nelluc. Clartom was standing next to him. She turned and looked around, seeing a circular room of stone walls, a stone ceiling supported by wide, thick beams, some of which looked old and splintered. There was rubble on the floor, but nothing else, aside from a stone stairway to one side. She looked up and could see a round opening in the ceiling almost directly over her head and she could see the sky through the opening.

"Welcome to your new home," Nelluc said. "Only the best accommodations for our guest."

She glared at him and cursed him under her breath. He turned to Clartom and wrote something. The she watched as the Phooka nodded and left. Nelluc looked around the room and then back at Emm.

"I've instructed Clartom to find some straw and some bedding," he told her; "and a few other...essentials – to make you more comfortable."

She took a menacing step towards him. Even though he was much bigger than she was, he backed away.

"Now, now," he cautioned her. "I've told Clartom that once I'm gone, he can remove the gag and the bindings, but if you misbehave, I might change my mind."

She looked around the room again and back towards the stairway where Clartom had vanished. Nelluc could see the thoughts running through her mind.

"They're all deaf," he informed her. "You won't be able to say anything to them that will control what they do." He added with a chuckle, "Your pleas will fall on deaf ears. And even if you shout, your spells will not escape this village, no matter who may hear you."

Clartom returned with some of the other Phookas in tow. They were carrying piles of moldy straw, a pair of stained and ragged blankets, a pair of buckets, some candles and a few other odds and ends – whatever they could scrounge from the nearby buildings that they imagined Emm would need or use.

Nelluc wrote out the instructions to Clartom to remove the gag and the bindings once he was gone, as well as a schedule to minister to their guest. Clartom read the pages and then nodded his understanding.

"Don't worry, child," Nelluc told Emm. "You won't be here for very long. I expect Walipreen to return to the Ice Kingdom within the next few days. I will advise him of your special skills and see what he wants to do with you. In the meantime, I'll confer with the shaman about a potion that will counteract your little trick. If you cooperate, who knows? In a week or two, you may be released to go back to your home."

Emm lunged forward and kicked him. He grabbed his leg where she struck and staggered backwards. Clartom stepped between them and pushed her to one side, knocking her to the floor. She struggled to get to her feet, but the Phooka took two quick steps towards her and stepped on the chain, yanking her back to the floor.

"That is exactly the kind of behavior I warned you about," Nelluc said as he rubbed his shin. "I'll take that as a sign that you don't want me to stay and chat a while. As much as I would like to, though, I really must be going."

He nodded to Clartom and then climbed the stairs and left the village, beginning his return trip to the Ice Kingdom. Clartom watched him leave and then turned his eyes to Emm. He watched her in silence for several minutes. When he was certain that Nelluc was beyond the village walls, he pulled the dagger from his waistband.

Emm shrunk back away from him as far as the chain would allow; a look of fear in her eyes. The Phooka pushed her head down and in one quick motion sliced through the ropes around her wrists. Emm slowly moved her arms in front of her as the feeling slowly returned to her hands. She rubbed them together to warm them and to get the blood circulating as Clartom pulled the gag from her mouth.

He was still standing on the chain, so her head was still close to the floor. She thought about biting his leg, but recalled how tough and bitter tasting Phooka skin was and dismissed the idea. He took his foot from the chain and stepped back. She rolled from her knees to a sitting position and looked back at him.

"Release me," she ordered.

He looked at her blankly.

"Release me," she repeated. "You will release me."

He could see her lips moving and guessed what she was saying, but he only shook his head and pointed to his ear. Then he walked to the stairs, took one look back at her and grimaced. She assumed this was an attempt at a smile and she screamed at him.

"RELEASE ME!"

Her voice echoed off the stone walls and was followed by silence. She stood up and pulled the chain after her. There was enough length for her to come within a foot or so of the walls and only the bottom step of the staircase. She looked at the two buckets. One had water in it and the other was empty.

"What am I supposed to do with the other...oh," she suddenly realized. "That's supposed to be a toilet? I hope they don't get the buckets mixed up."

She looked at the other items the Phookas had brought: some parchment and a piece of charred wood. She thought these would allow her to write her requests to her guards. She wondered if she wrote, "release me," if they would. She doubted it.

She looked at the candles and saw that there were about a dozen of them, but there was nothing with which to light them. Wonderful, she thought. Not only are they deaf, but stupid as well. She heard a noise above her and moved to the hole in the ceiling to see if she could make out what it was. As she looked up, she saw something dropping down. She jumped out of the way as several logs and branches tumbled through the opening and bounced across the floor.

"Hey!" she yelled. "You almost hit me. What are you doing?"

A few second later one of the Phookas came down carrying a torch. He planted it in a holder in the wall near the base of the stairway and then left.

"Wait," she yelled.

She ran after him and was brought up short when she reached the limit of the chain. She pulled at the collar in a vain attempt to loosen it. Her brother was a shape shifter. Right now, she wished she had that skill. She looked around at her desolate surroundings and choked back tears. Then she sat down and waited.

Hours passed and there was no sound or sight of the Phookas. She was worried that they had all deserted her. She would starve to death in this pit. Just as she was giving up hope, she heard some shuffling on the floor above her.

"Help," she yelled. "Please."

Her pleas were met with a small sack being dropped through the hole. She ran to the center, dragging the chain along with her and looked up through the hole. Whoever had dropped the sack was gone. She reached down and opened the container. She found a small slab of gray meat. She looked at it in disgust.

"They have got to be kidding," she said. "Who eats this stuff?"

She rewrapped the meat and looked back up the opening waiting – hoping – for something else to be dropped through. Nothing seemed to be coming besides nightfall. She could feel the air getting cooler and thought she should probably make a fire.

She pulled the dried limbs and small branches into the center of the room so that the smoke from the fire would go up through the opening. When she was satisfied that the wood was ready she went to the torch. It was in the wall, beyond the length of her chain. She turned sideways and reached out as far as she could. She was barely able to grasp the middle of the torch with the tips of her fingers.

She worked it back and forth, loosening it from the holder and almost dropped it. Once it was free, she took it back to the fire and lit the wood. The kindling burst into flame and caught the larger pieces. Soon it was roaring and heated the entire room. In fact it was so hot that she had to move back to the far reaches of her chain. Even that was not enough. The heat reached out as if to grab her.

"I shouldn't have made it so big," she muttered.

She endured the heat until the fire abated and the temperature in the room became more comfortable. She still had the torch in her hand and was about to toss it on the fire when she realized she may need it again. But she had no place to put it, other than the holder, which would be hard to get to easily.

She decided to light one of the candles and then smothered the torch's fire with one of the blankets. She then sat at the outer edge of the fire, proud of herself for what she had worked out. After a while, her hunger grew overwhelming and she revisited the sack with the foul smelling meat. Hoping that burning it slightly might help, she stuck it on the end of one of the dried branches and inched her way closer to the fire, extending the branch with the meat on the end, over the blaze.

It was only slightly less disgusting, but she fought back her urge to spit it out, considering that she had to maintain her strength just in case an opportunity arose. Fed and warmed, she bunched up the straw and threw one of the blankets over it to make a bed. Eventually, she drifted off to sleep, only to be wakened in the middle of the night by the sound of thunder.

A storm had broken out and rain was now pouring in the hole over her fire. Within seconds, the water had put the fire out and the cold night air seeped into the stone walls and floor, and into her bones. She looked up at the hole in the ceiling and her earlier feeling of pride vanished.

She built another pyre close to the stairway, relit the torch from the candle and put the torch to the wood. In a few seconds, the fire was in full force, the smoke trailed up the staircase, and the cold of the stone dissipated. As she drifted back to sleep, she hoped she would not have to do this for very long.

------------------ *** ------------------

As Emm was learning to cope with her new surroundings, Nelluc raced back to the Ice Kingdom. Without the Phookas he was able to make better time across the open fields to the spot where he had left the dogs and the sleds. He moved the dogs to a single sled and left the others behind. With the larger team, he cut even more time off his return trip.

When he finally arrived, he went straight to the throne room where he expected to see Walipreen holding court. He was stunned to find the room empty. He then headed for the master's personal chambers, but they were still sealed.

"He's not returned," Nelluc uttered in surprise.

He couldn't understand why Walipreen was still gone. It had been weeks.

"Well," he said to no one. "What can I do to make the best of this time?"

He fell back into his normal routine, and quickly realized how much of that involved reacting to demands and needs of Walipreen. The more frequent and longer periods of inactivity wore on him. As the weeks melted into months and the sorcerer still had not returned, Nelluc considered sending out a search party.

The problem was, he had no idea where to look. He had assumed that Walipreen was traveling to the southern ice fields in search of the Kelpie known as Saldeti. After that, though, he had no inclination as to what direction his master would go. The only one he thought he could ask was Chardon, but that Phooka was with Walipreen.

More time passed and Nelluc's anxiety grew. He became worried about what would happen to him if Walipreen never returned. He was a Rebbercand in a world of Phookas. Even though he had lived here most of his life, he knew there was no love lost between the two peoples. He had no reason to believe the sorcerer would come to any harm, but his imagination began to run wild in all sorts of directions.

He frequently thought about the Phynnodderee he had left behind in the village of the Thumpers, but whenever he considered going back for her, he worried that Walipreen would return while he was gone. His indecision added to his level of stress.

One afternoon as he was deep in thought walking from his room towards the armory, he spied a Phooka he was certain had been in the forces Walipreen had taken with him. He followed the Phooka until he could pull him aside away from anyone who would overhear them.

"I know you," Nelluc said. "You were among the ones who left with Walipreen."

"No," replied the Phooka. "You have me mistaken with another."

Phookas were notorious liars, Nelluc thought; you would think they would be better at it.

"Don't lie to me!" he demanded.

He moved closer and stood over the Phooka trying to intimidate him.

"I...uh...that is..." the Phooka stammered. "Oh, you mean recently? Yes, I was a member of that transport."

"Then what are you doing here? And how long have you been back?"

The Phooka looked left and right, lowered his eyes, unable to face Nelluc.

"Answer my question!" Nelluc ordered.

"Which one?" the Phooka asked, stalling for time.

"Both of them, you idiot."

"I've been back about two months," he replied. "I'm in the guard rotation."

"I don't care what you're doing now," Nelluc snapped. "I want to know why you're not with Walipreen."

"But you asked me what I was doing here," he pleaded.

"Unless you want to face the master when he gets back, you had better start explaining."

"He's not coming back," the Phooka answered.

"What do you mean?"

"He disappeared in a volcano," the Phooka told him. "We waited for several days, but he didn't come out. No one survives a volcano. Many of us decided we should come back. Some stayed, but the others, the ones who were with him – we thought...we were sure they were lost, too."

His story was riddled with lies, but there were too many for Nelluc to sort out. The state of his own level of stress and indecision further compromised his ability to sort out the truth. He knew of a volcano far to the west of the Ice Kingdom. There were many stories of its volatility. If Walipreen had, in fact, gone there, and if he had attempted to descend into the volcano itself, it was possible that he had been lost.

"And this happened two months ago?" asked Nelluc.

"Longer," said the Phooka. "I've been back here more than two months. It took us almost a month to travel from the volcano back home."

Nelluc was so shocked by this news that he felt his legs weaken. Was it possible that so much time had passed? He thought back to when Walipreen first left and what had transpired in the interim. He needed time to think. He needed to be alone. He dismissed the Phooka and ordered him not to discuss this or the sorcerer with anyone.

Once the Phooka was out of sight and he was alone in the hallway, Nelluc slid to the floor, his senses reeling. Could it be true? Could Walipreen be dead? If so, how long before that word got out? He knew the Phooka wouldn't be able to keep that a secret for long. For now he had kept silent for no other reason than to save his own skin. Soon, that motivation would be overtaken by the urge to brag.

And then what, he wondered. What will become of me – a Rebbercand in an entire kingdom of Phookas? He wouldn't last through the end of the day. He indulged in several minutes of self-pity before pulling himself together. He pushed himself up from the floor and leaned against the wall, wiping the sweat from his brow.

Think, he ordered himself. You'll stay alive as long as they all think Walipreen is still coming back – or until you can either escape or secure your position of power. Escape is out of the question. He knew he couldn't leave the Ice Kingdom without accompaniment by at least a dozen Phookas. To attempt that would only draw unwanted attention.

That left the other two options: convincing them all that Walipreen was still alive or securing power. He knew he could keep up the lie of Walipreen's return for a while, but not long. So he was left with making himself the leader. How could he do that, he thought.

In his mental strategizing he was oblivious to the fact that he had accepted at face value the assumption that Walipreen was dead. The lie by the Phooka was more easily accepted than the truth, fed by his panic, deceit, and ego.

He decided he would have to make it clear that Walipreen was leaving while he took steps to bolster his position. He would get a team of the Phookas started on planning for the master's return – a celebration of sorts. That should keep them busy for a while.

That decided, he turned his focus on establishing himself as the new master. He realized he could not do this alone. He needed some outside force or event to catapult him into that position. Then it dawned on him: the Twins. He would send an emissary to the Twins. Walipreen had talked of doing this before he went off and got killed.

"Now I'll do it, instead," Nelluc announced to the halls.

I'll make them believe it was I who killed Walipreen. I can even offer up the captured Phynnodderee as a gift – won't they be surprised when they find out what she can do. I can get them to bring a force here to the Ice Kingdom to serve as my personal guard. Even a handful of battle-tested Rebbercands will instill enough fear into the Phookas to keep them in line.

Excited by the idea of a plan, he hurried back to his personal quarters to flesh it out. He considered the weak points of both prongs of his strategy and mitigated them to the extent possible. He knew that any such endeavor was not guaranteed of success, no matter the amount of planning. But in this case, the stakes were high – his life and future – so he wanted to reduce as much as he could what would be left to chance.

He spent the rest of the day and much of the night convincing himself that he had thought of all there was to think of. Early the next morning, he sent for his aide. When the Phooka arrived, Nelluc tried to be as nonchalant as possible.

"I've decided that we should prepare a celebration for the master when he returns," he said.

"Is he expected?" asked the aide.

The question caught Nelluc off guard. Had word already gotten out that Walipreen was dead? Had that foolish Phooka deliberately disobeyed his order to not speak of this?

"What do you mean?" Nelluc asked, playing for time to think.

"You said we should prepare a celebration for his return," said the aide. "I only asked if he was expected. Will he be home soon? How much time do we have to prepare?"

Nelluc breathed a sigh of relief.

"I have no set date as yet," he replied. "But as he has been gone so long, I would anticipate his return soon. And he should have a celebration befitting, don't you agree."

"As you wish," the aide replied.

Nelluc was not completely convinced the aide was as ignorant as he let on, but he couldn't delve any deeper without betraying what he knew. Instead, he launched into a summary of the activities he had in mind. He smiled inwardly at the thought that this celebration would more likely be for him when he made it clear that he was the new master of the Ice Kingdom. Then another thought struck him.

"I have another idea," he announced. "It has been too long since we have seen our allies to the south."

"Allies?" the aide asked.

"Yes," Nelluc continued, as if the idea of the Twins as allies was a long standing history. "The Twins. We should extend an invitation to them."

"But I thought..." the aide began.

"What?" Nelluc cut him off. "That they were not welcome here? The master's own nephew, Dekene, is their guest as I am here. The Twins are my uncles. How could they be anything other than welcome guests?"

"I...but...as you wish," the aide stammered.

"I know," Nelluc continued. "We'll send an emissary to them. In fact, I would like you to lead that emissary."

"But I thought I was to prepare the celebration," the aide replied.

He had no interest whatsoever in venturing to the south and facing the Twins. Panic had crept into his voice and did not go unnoticed by Nelluc.

"Ah," he said. "You're right. I suppose you can't do both, can you. Well, then. Who would you recommend to serve as emissary?"

By forcing the Phooka to offer up someone else – a fact that Nelluc would make sure the unlucky soul selected would know – he had ensured the aide's support in both the celebration façade and the invitation to the Twins. The Phooka was uncomfortable naming someone else, but did not have the wherewithal to understand the trap Nelluc had so quickly and so easily set.

"Uh…oh…I don't know," the aide hesitated, and then blurted out, "Galen."

Of course, Nelluc thought. Pick the most stupid individual known.

"Excellent choice," he said, instead. "Summon him now, while I prepare the invitation."

The aide's shoulders slumped, realizing what he had done, and that his part in this would be known throughout the Kingdom before the day was out. He left Nelluc's chambers in search of Galen. In the meantime, Nelluc drafted the note that would be sent to his uncles.

My Dearest Uncles, Rampool and Prine,
I have mixed tidings to bring to you. It seems
that Walipreen, sorcerer of the North is no
longer with us. I am left in his absence, alone
to rule the Phookas. I would benefit from
your sage guidance at the earliest possible
opportunity.
Your grateful nephew, Nelluc

He had to choose his words carefully. He had made sure to not say that Walipreen was dead, or that he was usurping his throne. He would secure the note in an envelope and seal it, but he couldn't trust that the Phookas would keep it that way. He wouldn't put it past them to open the letter and read it – assuming they could read – and tell the Twins that was the way it had been given to them.

Just as he was finishing the message, the aide returned with Galen. Nelluc made a show of folding the note, placing it in an envelope and sealing it closed before handing it to Galen.

"Your friend here," Nelluc motioned to the aide, "has recommended you for a very important task."

Galen cast a sideways glance at the aide. Although he did not yet know what this so-called important task was, he knew enough that he had been offered up as a sacrificial lamb. He would make sure word of this got around.

"I would like you to do me the honor of taking this invitation to my uncles in the south," he explained. "The twins, Rampool and Prine," he added when he saw the look of confusion on Galen's face.

191

Galen shot another glance at the aide, one that clearly communicated his anger. The aide refused to make eye contact.

"Take a small party with you," Nelluc continued. "No more than ten in all, and leave at first light. I expect you to be as quick as you can. There's no telling when our master will return and I would prefer that my uncles are here to greet him. Is that clear?"

Galen mumbled his understanding. He wouldn't have enough support to mount any defense if attacked, which meant he was likely walking into a trap. He expected it was likely he would not be returning to the Ice Kingdom. He considered just going into hiding, but knew that he would be found too easily and would suffer for failing to complete this task.

He could only hope that the contents of the letter pleased the Twins and they decided to let him live. He would leave instructions with his closest friends that if he failed to return, the aide would be made to suffer - long and painfully. Resigned to his fate, he took the offered letter and left without any further discussion.

"Well, now," said Nelluc, smiling. "Now that that's done, let's plan the celebration."

Chapter nine

Jochen moved to the knot in the tree and could see the tiny hole that had at one time been plugged with a strand of Quinn's hair. The thought of what might be on the other side concerned him greatly. He hesitated for a second and then turned to look at the stranger from the other side he had only just met. He couldn't explain it, but he trusted this person completely.

He took a deep breath and made one last check to see that all the others were bunched as closely as possible. He wondered if that was the right thing to do. If someone or something was waiting for them on the other side, it could capture them all at one moment – or worse. Sensing his dilemma, Stella tapped him on the arm.

"Wait," she said. "I have an idea."

Lochen sighed in relief and they all backed up a step or two as if there were invisible ropes binding them together.

"Natalie should be in front," she said.

"Oh, really?" asked Natalie.

"Of course," said Lochen.

Without explanation, he moved her to the front of the group. He nudged everyone forward again.

"Wait," said Summer. "Sean needs to be right next to her."

"What?" Sean protested.

"You're right," said Lochen.

Aitch watched, somewhat confused, while everyone shuffled and changed positions. On his own, he moved up next to Sean.

"No," said Stella. "That's my place. You need to move to the back."

"The back?" he objected. "Why? And why do these two have to be in front? I should go first. I'm from that side. I know what to expect."

"Oh, do you?" Quinn asked. "All right. What's on the inside of that tree? Right now? And how long has it been there?"

"Well," argued Aitch. "I don't know exactly what's on the other side..."

"Any more than any of us," Liam cut him off. "Look. We've been together for a while longer and we've faced some pretty scary things. Trust us."

"I don't think it's necessary to argue about who goes first," Solveig cut in. "Aren't we all going in at almost the exact same time? What difference does it make?"

"Natalie should be in the front and in the middle," explained Stella, "so that she can surround us with a bubble as soon as Lochen opens the passage."

"And Sean should be right next to her," added Summer, "with his slingshot ready..." She looked at Sean who was staring at her waiting for her to finish. "With his slingshot ready!" she repeated.

"Oh, yeah. Right," he said, taking the cue and arming his slingshot.

"And I should be next to Natalie, ready to cast a spell," said Stella.

"Then Lochen should be at the back, sort of like our last line of defense," said Liam.

"Oh, no," said Lochen. "If you are all in front of me, I won't be able to see the spot in which to open the Boravak."

"Oh, for crying out loud," moaned Aitch. "Do you guys have to debate everything? I'm going – with or without you."

At that he shifted shape into the puff of green smoke as he did when he passed through the first time. The wisp thinned itself out, bent towards the knot and started for the tiny hole.

"NO!" shouted Lochen.

He couldn't stop Aitch, so he pushed his way to the front, started swirling his finger and the speck of an opening immediately widened. Before them they could only see blackness. Lochen immediately began pushing them all through to the other side. As soon as they were through, he made a circular motion with his hand and quickly closed it into a fist. The aperture snapped shut. They were through.

"Don't anybody move," he hissed. "And stay close."

"How can we not move and stay close at the same time?" whispered Sean. "What if we're not close to begin with? Don't we have to move to get close?"

"Shhhh," seven voices hissed at him.

"I was just asking," whispered Sean.

"SHHHH!" seven voices hissed again.

As their eyes adjusted to the dim light, they could see where they were. It sent a shiver down their spines. They were standing on the ledge where they had been cornered by the advancing Kelpies. Their eyes were drawn to several places. Some looked at the roots that had extended from the dirt walls, reaching out to strike them, to grab them. Now they were broken and brittle. Most of them had broken off and dropped to the ledge or fallen into the cavern below.

They saw the Kythauls; the grotesque carvings in the stone that had come alive at the command of their attackers. Now they were once again dormant, covered in dust and cobwebs. Still an unpleasant sight, they seemed less threatening and somehow older and worn.

They looked to the higher ledges and the stairway where the Kelpies had launched their attack. They could see the passage that led to the surface, bits of light poking through the vegetation that had overgrown the opening.

Seeing that they were alone, Natalie spoke up. "It looks like we're down here by ourselves."

"It looks the same, but somehow different," said Quinn. "I still don't like it. Not one bit."

Lochen stepped forward and his foot struck something that had not been there before: a small pile of some kind of cloth. He looked around and saw that Aitch was still in the form of the cloud of smoke.

"I think it's safe for you to transform," he said.

The cloud swirled around, shifting from a horizontal shape to a vertical one and then solidified into the figure of Aitch. Lochen bent down and picked up the cloth.

"I believe these are yours," he said.

"Dude," said Quinn. "Where did your leaves go?"

Aitch was once again naked.

"Awwww," he wailed, turning and trying to cover himself. "This is really getting old."

"Tell me about it," mumbled Sean. "I've seen far too much of you."

Aitch hastily shook the dust out of the clothing and put it on.

"Yuk," he complained. "These don't feel right."

"Are you sure they're yours?" asked Solveig.

"Of course they're mine," he said. "Who else would they belong to?"

"Some mystery nudist?" asked Liam.

"Cute," Aitch shot back. "I'm not a nudist. I don't know why my cloths don't transform with me. They always have before."

"You said they didn't feel right," said Stella. "What's wrong with them?"

"Aside from being really dirty," Aitch answered, "they smell funny."

"Funny how?" asked Summer as she fluttered down and hovered over his shoulder sniffing the air. "Ugh," she added, "you're right. They're really musty. Did somebody bury them or something?"

"They're old," interjected Lochen.

"No, they're not," countered Aitch. "I've only had them for a few weeks, and they got left behind when I came over to the other side. I was there less than a day."

"You were on _our_ side less than a day," replied Lochen. "On this side it's been much longer. I would estimate close to fifteen years."

"What?" Aitch exclaimed. "That's not possible."

"That's why this place looks different," said Natalie. "It's been fifteen years since we were here."

"Not exactly," said Lochen.

"But you just said fifteen years on this side of the Boravak had passed," said Sean. "What? Are you changing your mind now?"

"No," answered Lochen. "Allow me to clarify. I said fifteen years had passed since Aitch was last here. It's been a bit longer since all of us were last here."

"Well that makes sense," said Solveig. "We crossed over, what...a year or so ago?"

"I don't know," said Quinn. "This place looks like we've been gone longer than that."

"We have," said Lochen. "By my estimates it's closer to two thousand years."

"There must be some weird echo in here," said Sean. "I thought I heard you say two thousand years. That's really crazy."

"Yes," said Lochen, "it is crazy, but true. Of course I may be off by a decade or two, but I don't believe so. I can see by the striations in the wall over here..."

"Back up a minute," interrupted Aitch. "Let's get back to that part about it being fifteen years since I was here. How is that possible?"

"Because the Boravak is not only a different place, it's a different time," Lochen explained. "I'm sure Quinn understands that perfectly."

"Don't remind me," he said.

"This is just nuts," argued Aitch. "There's no way it's been fifteen years."

"Give or take a few days," said Lochen.

"Like that makes a difference," Aitch mumbled. "What's happened to my sister, then? What about my family; my village?"

"I would be reluctant to speculate," said Lochen.

"What does that mean?" snapped Aitch.

"It means he doesn't want to guess," interjected Liam. "But I think we need to get out of here. I don't like being in a place I can't get out of."

"We need to be careful, though," said Solveig. "We don't know what's on the surface."

"You don't suppose those Kelpies are still around, do you?" asked Quinn.

"Aitch would probably know about that better than any of us," said Summer. "What about it, Aitch? Are the Kelpies still around?"

"No," he answered. "I mean, yes. They are, but they're not very powerful."

He explained about the Great Wars and all that transpired after that, including the rise of Ena Ray and Tebaga, and then their descendants – the current rulers of the north and south.

"Wow," said Liam. "I guess we <u>have</u> been gone a long time."

"And we can expect some of that has changed in the fifteen years Aitch has been gone," added Lochen.

"All the more reason we need to be cautious once we get to the surface," said Solveig.

"We need a sanctorum," said Lochen. "If Stella can project some images, we may have a better idea of where things are. Is this cavern suitable," he asked.

"No," she answered. "It's not really round, and with all that's gone on here, I'm not sure any visions would be clear."

"Looks like we need to go up," said Liam.

Lochen spotted a nearby carving of one of the Kythauls, struck a hand out in its direction, and curled his fingers as if grabbing it. The figure was wrenched free from its position in the wall and dropped across the crevice that separated the ledge they were on from the opposite side.

"What?" he asked when he saw the others looking at him. "We need a way across."

Without waiting for the others, he stepped on the statue and walked to the other side. One by one, the others followed. He then led them up the staircase, avoiding the broken steps, until he reached the level just inside of the opening.

"Hold on," said Aitch. "Let me go first."

He quickly changed shape into a bird and circled the small group.

"If someone or something is up there, I can see if they're dangerous before we all just show up."

"You mean you can still talk when you change shape?" asked Quinn.

"Only if I'm not an inanimate object, like smoke," Aitch replied.

"Summer," said Lochen. "Go with him."

"What?" asked Aitch. "You don't think I can do this by myself?"

"I'm sure you are quite capable," Lochen answered. "However, if there happen to be hunters above and they happen to be searching for birds, you may make a desirable target. It would be advisable to have a backup."

"Boy," muttered Aitch. "I'll bet you're a lot of fun at a party."

Lochen furrowed his brow in confusion. "I'm not entirely certain how my level of entertainment in a social gathering is at all relevant to our situation here."

"Right," replied Aitch as he turned towards Summer and said, "Let's go."

Aitch led the way through a gaping hole in the vines that had grown over the entry. He remembered the vines, but he was pretty certain that when he had come through here at the time he discovered the hole, the opening in the vines was barely noticeable. Someone else has been through here, he realized. When he passed the large stones, which he noted had also been moved, he took a quick look around and could see no sign of anyone else.

"Go get the others," he told Summer. "I'll keep looking around, but I don't think anyone's nearby."

She darted back down the cave and in a few seconds, the rest of the group arrived at the surface.

"Oh, wow," said Liam. He was stunned at the change in the surrounding landscape. "This used to be part of the Swamp."

"It's still called the Swamp," said Aitch. "Although I don't think anyone knows why any more. There are a few places where there are marshes and bogs, but for the most part this whole area is like a giant garden."

"I can't believe this," said Liam.

He was so surprised that he had to sit on a nearby rock. Everyone else looked around. This had not been their home, but they had been in the Swamp several times with Liam. There was nothing that was recognizable to them.

"You did this," said Summer.

"What?" he asked.

"This," she said, her arms spread out motioning to their surroundings. "This whole place. You planted the flowers and made the fresh water canals."

"I just got it started," he said. "I really hadn't done much. I certainly didn't do all this."

"I disagree," said Lochen. "You provided the foundation. Nature did the rest. Well done."

"Yeah," said Sean. "This is really great, but where are we, because none of this looks familiar. Can you still do you 'I can find anything' stuff?"

"I guess so," said Liam. "Where do you want to go?"

"I have to come up with everything?" asked Sean.

"We need to find a sanctorum," said Lochen.

"What's that?" asked Aitch.

"A circular building or enclosure of some kind," said Stella.

"I've never looked for something like that, so I probably wouldn't have noticed one even if I had seen it," he replied. "Sorry."

"I don't think we should stay here," said Quinn. "This place gives me the bejeebers."

"What's that?" asked Aitch. "Some kind of hex?"

"I'll explain later," said Sean. "It's nothing you really have to worry about."

"He's right," said Stella. "I can feel the evil in this place. I don't care which way we go, but we need to move."

"Do you know of a people called the Navedis?" Lochen asked Aitch. "They had a village at one time not far from here – or at least where I believe 'here' is."

"They don't sound familiar," said Aitch.

"They lived in a forest on the other side of this river and to the west," said Liam.

"If they still exist," said Aitch, "they don't live in that direction. That whole area was set on fire during the Great War."

"What about any other village?" asked Solveig. "Is there anything else nearby?"

"Yeah," he said. "Well, at least there was fifteen years ago. I can't be sure of anything anymore."

"That will have to do," said Lochen. "Which way?"

Aitch shifted back to his normal shape, surprised to find that his clothes had made the transition with him.

"Finally," he announced. "See? This is the way it's supposed to be."

"Interesting," said Lochen. "I imagine the ability for you to transform your clothing as well as yourself is affected by which side of the Boravak you are on."

As they headed west, Lochen thought about the implications if what he had just said. Solveig and Natalie had a few limited mystical powers. He and Stella had been more extensively trained. He thought about how much his abilities had been enhanced after crossing to the outside. He wondered if they would be altered or diminished now that he had returned. He had been able to move the carving of the Kythaul without any difficulty, but he wasn't sure if that was a true indication. Something to keep in mind, he thought.

A few hours later, they came over the top of a low hill and saw a small village spread out before them. There were a number of huts and other buildings scattered in a haphazard manner. The road they were on seemed to divide the town in half with no other roads or cross streets in evidence.

"Do you know the name of this town?" Lochen asked Aitch.

"I've never seen it before," he said. "The village I remember was still several miles further. This must have sprung up after I left."

"Summer," said Lochen. "Fly ahead and see what you can learn, but keep out of sight. We'll wait here."

"Wait," said Aitch. "I'll go with her."

"That won't be necessary," she said. "I can take care of myself."

"I'm sure you can," Aitch replied. "But this is my world. You may not know what you're looking at."

"He's right," said Lochen. "Go ahead; the both of you. But be careful."

Aitch closed his eyes and immediately transformed into a butterfly so that he and Summer were the same size, and then they darted off towards the village. A few minutes later, they were within eyesight of the outlying buildings.

"Rebbercands!" the both gasped.

"What are they doing this far north?" Aitch mumbled.

"We need to get closer," said Summer.

They rose higher into the air to be less conspicuous, keeping one eye above them on the lookout for predators and the other on the people below. A little further into the village they came upon another sight that startled them.

"Oh, my," exclaimed Summer. "What are those things?"

"Phookas," said Aitch. "They don't normally get along with Rebbercands. What happened?"

"We need to get back," Summer said.

They made a direct route back to the others and shared what they had seen. Aitch explained how the Rebbercands made up the army of the Twins and the Phookas were controlled by Walipreen. He further explained that while the two weren't necessarily enemies, Rebbercands and Phookas didn't exactly get along, either.

"Something has happened in the last fifteen years to have changed that, apparently," said Lochen.

"Aitch," said Natalie, "Can you change into either one of them?"

"I suppose," he said, "but why would I want to do that?"

"To mingle with them and figure out what's going on," inserted Liam, understanding where Natalie was going.

"Won't that be dangerous?" asked Sean. "Won't they get suspicious if one of their own needs a history lesson?"

"Not if he says he's been away for a long time," suggested Solveig.

"I'd have to have been on the other side of the planet to have not noticed something like this," said Aitch.

"Or at sea," said Stella.

"Rebbercands don't have boats," said Aitch.

"Maybe so," said Lochen. "But these villagers don't know that."

"And he could be transporting a couple of us – as prisoners or captives of some kind," said Natalie. "That would make his story more plausible."

"That might work," said Aitch. "But I can't be dragging all of you along."

"No," said Lochen. "Three should be sufficient – Liam, Sean and me."

"Wait a minute," objected Solveig. "Why you three?"

"Because Liam and Sean are both adept at the use of weapons, and I have magical powers," Lochen replied. "Besides, you, Solveig, are an excellent tactical strategist. If something happens to us, I have no doubt you will find some way to rescue us. Stella needs to keep that pendant out of the hands of anyone associated with these people. Natalie can protect you or at least defend you with a bubble. Summer is too small, and Quinn is too big."

"I hate it when you're right," Solveig finally acknowledged.

Lochen conjured bindings for the three of them while Liam hid his various blades, except for one that he gave to Aitch. Aitch made his transformation and asked how he looked. Before anyone could reply, he changed back.

"What happened?" Sean asked. "Can't you shift into a Rebbercand?"

"Yes, of course I can," Aitch replied. "It wasn't quite right, though. I don't think I was ugly enough."

"You looked pretty ugly to me," said Quinn. "I wouldn't want to be around you."

"Thanks," said Aitch, "but it wasn't as good as it could be."

He concentrated again and quickly made the shift. When he had transformed, he looked down at himself and frowned.

"Does anybody have a mirror?" he asked. "No? OK."

He quickly changed back to himself again.

"Now what?" asked Liam.

"It still wasn't right," he said. "I wasn't bulky enough."

"You're not a piece of art," said Solveig. "It doesn't have to be perfect. It's good enough."

"Well, you may be willing to settle for 'good enough,'" said Aitch, "but I need to get this right."

He closed his eyes, took a deep breath and shifted again. As soon as he changed, he changed back.

"We really don't have time for this," said Lochen.

"Just a minute," pleaded Aitch. "I've almost got it right. Once more."

He shook himself and made the shift. No sooner had he changed than he looked down, shook his head and changed back.

"Almost there," he said as the others watched him in disbelief.

"I can feel myself aging," mumbled Natalie.

"I can do this," said Aitch.

He blinked and shifted. As he looked down and gave signs that he was still not satisfied, Quinn grabbed his arm and pulled him aside.

"Dude," he said. "It's as good as it's going to get. Give it a rest."

"Ohhh!' moaned Aitch. "All right."

When they were finally ready, they began their way towards the village.

"What do we expect to find out?" Aitch asked along the way.

"I'm not certain," answered Lochen. "But any information should be useful."

As they entered the village, they became the focus of several intense stares. Lochen realized that they should have given some time to better prepare the cover story, and what they expected Aitch to do. He was leading them into the center of the village and had not as yet spoken to anyone. If he or the other two "prisoners" said anything, they would be immediately discovered as frauds.

Finally, they were stopped by one of the Rebbercands. He was much larger than Aitch and was carrying an axe that looked all too familiar to Lochen, Liam and Sean. The Rebbercand motioned for them to stop, but didn't say anything. Instead, he circled them, looking closely at the three captives before coming around to face Aitch. The three could not keep from staring at the axe. When the Rebbercand shifted it from one hand to the other, they tried to not show their relief.

"Who are you and <u>what</u> are they?" the Rebbercand demanded.

"And who, exactly, are you?" Aitch demanded back.

The Rebbercand puffed himself up and stepped close to Aitch, towering over him and staring down at him. Aitch looked up defiantly, putting his hand on the hilt of the blade Liam had given him.

"I am the village elder," he finally responded. "Now answer my question."

"I am..." Aitch hesitated. They hadn't decided on a name. He knew Aitch was not a normal Rebbercand name. "Um...er...uh..."

"And who are these creatures, Umeruh?" asked the Rebbercand.

It took Aitch a few seconds to realize that the elder had mistaken his stammering for a name. It was too late now to correct him. He stepped aside and gestured to the three tied behind him.

"They are prisoners," he said. "Captives from a raid."

"What kind of raid?" the elder asked. "I've never seen the likes of them before."

"Oh," Aitch stammered. "From far away. Way far away. Really, really far away." He had a worried look on his face. "The other side of the Sea," he added in a panic.

The Rebbercand looked hard at Aitch.

"You've been to the other side of the Cerulean Sea?" he asked in disbelief.

"Yes?" It was as much a question as an answer. "I've brought these captives back as a gift for the Twins," he added to fill the silence that followed.

"Quiet, brother," the elder hissed.

He raised his hand to motion silence as he looked around to see if Aitch had been overheard. When he was certain that no one was listening, he put his arm around Aitch's shoulder and pulled him in close.

"You must have been gone a long time," the elder said. "A lot has changed. The Twins are no longer in power. Those still in allegiance to them are hunted."

"Hunted?" asked Aitch.

"Yes," said the elder. "And never heard from again if they're captured. I'm sure I misunderstood you. I'm sure you said these prisoners are a gift for Walipreen. Isn't that right?"

"Of course," said Aitch. "That's what I meant to say."

"You have traveled far," said the elder, still looking around for any signs that their conversation had been overheard. "You look like you could use a rest. Your color seems a bit green."

"Yes," said Aitch. "You have no idea how far I've come. Rest would be good."

"Then come with me, Umeruh," the Rebbercand said. "I'll see that you get a good meal in you and a comfortable place to spend the night. That's an unusual name you have. How did you come by it?"

"A family name," Aitch replied, his mind racing. "On my...uh... mother's...uncle's side. It's a combination of both their names." Shut up, he told himself.

Shut up, Liam, Sean and Lochen said to themselves. Aitch began to walk off with the Rebbercand, letting the rope that held them drop from his hand. The three stood still, staring at each other and then at Aitch. Sean was about to call out, but Lochen raised his hand to signal him to be quiet. Instead, he let out a loud sneeze.

At the sudden and unexpected noise, Aitch and the Rebbercand spun around to see the three standing where they had been left, their hands still bound together.

"Oh," said Aitch. "I guess I shouldn't leave them behind. Do you have enough food and sleeping quarters for them, too?" he asked.

The Rebbercand looked at him strangely and Aitch realized his mistake. He put his hand on the hilt of the blade, ready to cut the bindings. He hoped he would be able to free his friends before the Rebbercand could cut him in half. Suddenly, the Rebbercand burst out laughing.

"What a sense of humor you have," he gasped between fits of laughter. "Food and sleeping quarters for them. I suppose being at sea for so long you have to be able to joke like that."

"Yeah," laughed Aitch. "We do that kind of stuff all the time. But I do need to keep them fed and rested. They won't make much of a gift if they're starved and worn out."

"Yes, yes, yes," said the Rebbercand, still laughing. "We have some scraps of food and some straw in the barn that will suit them just fine."

Aitch turned back to his friends and shrugged. Lochen nodded, Liam looked relieved, and Sean glared at him.

"Here," said the elder. "Let me get that."

He took the rope lead and gave it a jerk, pulling the three roughly along behind them.

"So tell me, Umeruh," he continued. "How long have you been away?"

"Oh, about fifteen years," Aitch replied.

"That is a long time," the elder said. "And yes, a lot has changed. You have much to learn about if you want to keep your head attached to your shoulders. Stick with me, my friend. I'll make sure you'll learn everything you need to know. And who knows? Maybe you'll see fit to leave me one of these strange creatures as a gift in exchange. After all, Walipreen would probably be as satisfied with two as he would with three."

Aitch looked back at Liam, Lochen and Sean as the Rebbercand put his arm around his shoulders and led him through the village. What had they gotten themselves into, he wondered.

Chapter ten

The Rebbercand led the way to a large building on the southern side of the village. He took the prisoners to an outbuilding that had been a barn at one time. The straw on the floor was filthy. He pushed the threesome into one of the stalls and closed them in, locking the door. The stall and the door were made of old, weathered slats, but were secure enough that they could not be pulled apart. That fact was of little concern, since Lochen was certain that if the need arose, he could easily pry them apart with a simple snap of his fingers.

"Could you at least conjure up some fresh straw?" complained Sean.

"No," Lochen replied. "We must do nothing to betray who we are."

"Just move it aside and find a patch of dirt," suggested Liam. "Might as well get comfortable. We may be here a while."

"I don't recall signing up for this," groused Sean.

"Quit whining," came a voice from a few feet above them.

They all jumped at the sound. As if appearing from nowhere, Summer floated down from the darkness, transforming from her near invisibility.

"What are you doing here?" demanded Lochen. "I thought I indicated you were to stay behind."

"I don't recall any such indication," she said. "Besides, I don't recall anyone appointing you as the one in charge. If I remember correctly, I'm a princess and you're what...a sorcerer. Sorcerers do not order princesses around."

Lochen clenched his jaw, took a deep breath and let it out slowly.

"Fine," he said. "Go where you like, but why are you here?"

"Someone had to look over you four," she said smugly. "And from the looks of things, it seems like you need looking over. It stinks in here."

"Where's Aitch?" asked Liam.

"He went into the main building with the Rebbercand," she said. "They're sitting in a courtyard having a nice meal and a conversation."

"Can you get close to them?" Lochen asked.

"Oh," she said in mock surprise. "Now you need me to do something? Little old me? Are you sure?"

"No," he snapped, "but as long as you're here, you might as well do something useful."

"I suppose," she said, still teasing. "What do you want me to do?"

"Listen to their conversation and share the information with us," Lochen said. "And keep a close eye on Aitch to make sure he doesn't get himself into trouble."

"And what if he does?" she asked.

"Get back here immediately," said Lochen. "We will have to forgo our disguise and rescue him. And then find a way to get out of here with our heads."

She did as he asked and fluttered over the roof of the building to the interior courtyard. It was late in the day, but there was still a lot of sunlight. Summer blended into the background of an overhanging tree, lowering herself as much as she could until she found a good hiding place where she could listen to them talk.

The Rebbercand had provided a lavish amount of food and had a jug of ale from which he was filling cups for Aitch and himself. Every time he took a long drink, Aitch would pour his cup out in the nearby plants. Good idea, she thought.

"You must have had a lot of adventures if you've been all the way to the other side of the Cerulean Sea," said the Rebbercand.

"Oh, yes," said Aitch. "A LOT of adventures. You can't imagine."

"Tell me," his host said.

"Uh...tell you what?" Aitch gulped.

"About your adventures."

"Oh, well...they...ah...Whew!   Yeah.   They...uh, they...they probably don't compare to anything like what's gone on here," Aitch tried desperately to steer the conversation in a different direction. "I mean, when I left, things were much different. Tell me about..." he looked around conspiratorially. "The Twins."

The Rebbercand choked on his ale, and gasped, "Shhh. I told you that's a dangerous topic to bring up."

"And one I need to know about if, as you say, I wish to keep my head attached to my shoulders."

"Hah!" the Rebbercand exploded. "You're right about that. All right, but then you have to tell me about the other side of the sea."

"It's a deal," Aitch replied.

Summer made herself as comfortable as she could while the Rebbercand told his story and drank his ale. All the while, Aitch listened attentively and continued to pour his drink into the plants.   The Rebbercand admitted that he didn't know everything, but based on what he did know, it seemed that about fifteen years ago, something big had happened – something that made Walipreen leave the Ice Kingdom and go in search of the ancient Kelpies.

Not long after he began his journey, his nephew, Nelluc, left the Kingdom with a small detail. Word of this had spread among the

Phookas because immediately prior to this, he had given a potion to the men selected for this assignment that deprived them of their hearing. Little was known of this journey because the Phookas who went never came back.

Further, the events that transpired after Nelluc returned caused this secret adventure to fade in importance. It was only by chance that any knowledge of this secret adventure survived to the present time.

"I'll explain more about that later," said the Rebbercand.

Nelluc had not been informed of Walipreen's destination or how long he would be gone. By the time he had made his own foray and come back, the Sorcerer of the North had been gone close to a year. There were rumors that he had been killed. Nelluc began to panic.

"If he was Walipreen's nephew," asked Aitch, "what reason did he have to panic?"

"He wasn't a true nephew," explained the Rebbercand.

He told about the trade of Nelluc for Dekene between Walipreen and the Twins – an insurance policy against further wars. As a Rebbercand, if Walipreen had, in fact, been killed, Nelluc was exceedingly vulnerable.

Nelluc sent a message to his true uncles, the Twins. The message was worded very carefully, but the Twins understood it completely. They were informed that the northern kingdom was theirs for the taking. Walipreen was gone and Nelluc was holding the fort for the time being.

Nelluc had expected the Twins would arrive with a moderate contingent of an army to support him and to install him as the ruler of the Ice Kingdom and the northern territories. After all, he was their own blood relation.

Instead, they arrived with a conquering army. They threw Nelluc into the dungeons. When he pleaded with them, they pointed out that he was more Phooka than Rebbercand, having lived among them nearly his entire life. He talked like them, he dressed like them, and he even smelled like them.

He begged them. He pointed out that it was they who had sent him to Walipreen; what did they expect he would do, if all he saw were Phookas? He asked them if Dekene was more Rebbercand than Phooka, since he had lived with them nearly his entire life. That was when Nelluc knew his fate was sealed. The Twins had disposed of Dekene shortly after he was traded to them.

"But why would they do that?" Aitch asked.

"They didn't want to be vulnerable," the Rebbercand explained.

They had to assume that Walipreen would do something similar to Nelluc, and even if he didn't, they did not want to be prevented from either launching an attack or taking a defensive stand because of the threat of what Walipreen might do to Nelluc. In their minds, he was already lost. They had no loyalty towards him.

Since he was of no value to them, they bound him from head to toe and took him to the edge of the cliff in the southeastern part of the Ice Kingdom and threw him into the bay hundreds of feet below. As they were hauling him to his fate, he begged for his life. He told them he had something they could use – a secret weapon.

And what was this secret weapon, they asked. He told them: it was a Phynnodderee. They laughed in his face. They told him there was no Phynnodderee warrior that could possibly be of any value to them. It wasn't a warrior, Nelluc tried to explain. It was a girl; a child.

A child? Do you take us for fools, they asked. He tried to explain that she had special powers, that she could control minds. She must be controlling yours, they taunted him. Where was she, they wanted to know. He said she was someplace safe; someplace where her powers were contained. She was under guard and in a place where the spells contained her. Those were his last words as he was flung into the sea.

At the mention of the child, Aitch grew anxious. He wanted to run out and search for her; he was sure it was Emm. He fought back his urge to ask questions about the Phynnodderee. He didn't want to alert the Rebbercand to his true interest. He let him continue his story. And he did.

As it turned out, Walipreen wasn't dead. He had been traveling to each of the ancient Kelpies. No one knew what he was doing with them but after each visit, he changed. At first, the changes were hardly noticeable. But soon they became more dramatic.

"What kind of changes?" asked Aitch.

"He was becoming more powerful, for one thing," the Rebbercand explained. "But there were rumors that he was changing physically, too."

"Rumors?" asked Aitch. "Couldn't anyone tell for sure?"

"Yes, rumors. Few Rebbercands had ever seen Walipreen before, so all we had to rely on were things the Phookas said. And you know you can't trust a Phooka. When he left the Ice Kingdom, he took an army with him. Over time, a lot of them deserted and a lot more...well, no one really knows what happened to them. Only a handful came back with him and there was something not right about any of them."

Aitch listened with rapt attention as the Rebbercand described Walipreen's transformation. According to the few Phookas who would talk about it, they found the hiding place of Saldeti first. Walipreen went down into the bowels of the Ice Lake by himself and was gone several days. When he came up, he sealed the Lake over as if nothing ever was there.

At first nothing seemed different. But then they traveled to the volcano on the western side of the Ice Kingdom. Once again, he went into the crater alone in search of Neraka Ferr. This time, though, the Kelpie found him instead of the other way around. A handful of Phookas were perched on the rim of the volcano and watched as Walipreen seemed to suck the life out of the Kelpie and then toss him into the cavern.

After that, he sat there for days, staring into the hole. None of the Phookas was willing to go down and see what was wrong with him. They just stayed put and stared at him. His skin began to look like it was blistering – not a lot; just in a few spots. But his shoulders looked like they grew wider and thicker. When he stood up, he hunched over a little. In spite of this, he looked taller somehow.

By now, several of the Phookas had deserted. Some just went underground, searching for small settlements in remote places where they hoped they could hide. Some were stupid enough to return to the Ice Kingdom.

Walipreen didn't appear to care about the desertions or maybe he didn't notice, although that doesn't seem likely. He was noticing everything. His senses were all working at a much higher level. Anyway, he hauled his remaining army to the southern edge of the swamp.

Aitch gulped at the reference to this location. He waited nervously as the Rebbercand described finding the hideout of the Kelpie, Pantano Izaki. Walipreen left the Phookas at the entrance to the cave where the Kelpie was found. The sorcerer was in there for days. When he surfaced, his skin had a greenish-black pallor, and face had an expression of wariness and suspicion.

But now something else had changed. He spoke of experiences he had that the Phookas had not known of before. He referred to the other Kelpies as his brothers and sisters. It was as if he, himself, had become a Kelpie. One of the Phookas made the mistake of questioning him about it. Walipreen never touched him, but by pure force, he crushed the Phooka. No one else questioned him again.

There were more desertions, especially when they discovered they were traveling to the desert in search of Angin Topan. The Phookas feared the desert, but they feared Walipreen even more. They had no way to discern which direction they were traveling, and were certain they were lost, when in the middle of nowhere, Walipreen stopped and conjured up the ruins of some ancient temple.

It rose from the sand, and the Kelpie came with it. This time there was no hiding what took place between Walipreen and

Angin Topan. He spoke to the Imp as if he had known her for centuries. She tried to cast a spell on him, but he brushed it aside and, striking like a snake, snatched her in his hand.

"What the Phookas described that happened next," said the Rebbercand "is beyond belief. Even all the lies ever told by all the Phookas across this land are nothing compared to the one told about Walipreen and Angin Topan."

"And yet you believe it, don't you?" asked Aitch.

The Rebbercand refilled his cup and drank deeply. His brow furrowed, deep in thought, considering Aitch's question. He slowly turned his head in the direction of his guest and nodded.

"Yes," he said. "In spite of everything, I do."

Aitch wanted to ask him why, but let the Rebbercand continue with his story. Walipreen held the Imp in his hand and then moved his thumb up to press against the Kelpie's head. All who were watching expected him to crush the Kelpie, but instead he held her there doing her no apparent harm.

They stood like that for three days, locked and frozen like statues, except that Walipreen's body began to slowly change. His back broadened even more. Ridges began to appear from his shoulder blades down to his hips. The ridges continued to protrude outward until they separated from his lower back, forming enormous leathery wings. As this was happening, Angin Topan changed as well. The only way her changes had been described was as if her soul was being pulled from her.

Her color drained, and the expression of defiance on her face shifted into a look of resignation. When Walipreen finally moved, he simply dropped her to the ground and then stepped on her as if squashing a bug. He drove her deep under the sand, turned and ordered the Phookas to prepare to travel to the mountains.

By now the size of the accompanying army had been so reduced that the great amounts of time it had taken to move from one location to another were reducing greatly. Walipreen was also stopping less frequently and the Phookas were forced to forage as they went instead of setting up camps and sending out hunting parties.

The foraging was made simple though, as Walipreen, with his heightened senses, could hear, smell and see the prey that the Phookas needed for food. He often instructed a small group of them to head off in one direction or another telling them where the sources were. The hunting parties would go out, gather only what was needed and return immediately.

Finding food was less of a concern for them, however, than their next destination. The mountain range that extended from the Cerulean See to the Viridian Ocean divided the lands in half, designating the realm of the north, which belonged to Walipreen and the realm of the south, which belonged to the Twins. The mountains were a neutral area that served as a buffer. Entering it was a sign of aggression.

As the ever decreasing army marched passed the purple rubble that had once been the kingdom of the mountain people, the Phookas realized they were entering an area that had been forbidden to cross. They also realized they were heading for the lair of Akmen Milzu, the Mountain Kelpie. What they couldn't know was that the Twins had already entered the Ice Kingdom, at the invitation of Nelluc.

When Walipreen confronted Akmen Milzu, the Kelpie did not submit as easily as her predecessors. She cast spell after spell, building walls and creating landslides as she backed away from the sorcerer. It was all in vain. Walipreen swatted everything aside as if he was swatting at flies. In the end, she was forced to submit to his power.

By now he no longer cared if the Phookas saw what was happening. It was clear even to the most naïve of them that the sorcerer was drawing all of the power from each of the Kelpies and absorbing it into his being. They could see that the result was not only an exponential growth in his strength, but both his mind and body were also changing.

The physical changes were immediately obvious. Walipreen was taller and more muscular than he had ever been. His face was becoming distorted; his lips thickened and were drawn back in a sneer that often looked more like a grimace. His eyes bulged beneath a broader, thicker brow, and his hands bore more of a resemblance to claws than fingers.

The changes to his mind, though, were more worrisome to the Phookas. It was clear that as he absorbed the memories, the power and the knowledge of the Kelpies, they were becoming so intertwined with his own, that he could no longer distinguish between them and his own.

Once he had finished with Akmen Milzu he traveled to the once thriving port city of Satamakau. The town was now deserted, the victim of extensive flooding. Even now, the smell of death pervaded the area. The Phookas knew of the disaster that had caught hundreds of their cousins in a tidal bore in the harbor. They were reluctant to go anywhere near the water.

Walipreen paid them no heed. Once he reached the shore he spread his colossal wings and took flight, going due west out over the ocean and out of sight. It was at this point that the greatest number of Phookas deserted, leaving behind less than half of the original army. A few of them knew what was out in the sea – the Kelpie, Ollos Foscos.

When Walipreen returned four days later, his mouth now extended forward almost beak-like and a large tail protruded from the base of his spine, splitting halfway down into two tentacles: evidence of his conquest of Ollos Foscos.

With only two Kelpies remaining, Walipreen decided to eliminate what he determined to be unnecessary. He pointed a finger at Chardon, lifting him into the air. He looked the Phooka in the eye without saying a word. It was as if he could read Chardon's thoughts. When he had finished, he lowered the Phooka to the ground and called out the names of ten others.

Chardon would recall later on that while he was held in the gaze of the sorcerer, he had an undeniable sensation to think of the ten Phookas he believed to be the most loyal and trustworthy. He hadn't mentioned their names; only seeing their faces in his mind's eye. Those were the ten names Walipreen called.

Once those ten had stepped to one side, Walipreen waved one taloned hand, made a circular motion with it and then clamped it shut. In that instant the rest of the army disappeared. At some later time Chardon made inquiries and sent out emissaries, but could never discover what had happened to them or where they went.

As soon as the other Phookas had disappeared and before it could register on the eleven that remained, Walipreen scooped them up in his arms, spread his wings and took to the air. They soared above the ghost town of Satamakau and southeast over the mountains and past the ancient five towers of Virkio. They could hear a screeching sound they thought might be dragons, but could see no sign of the beasts. They turned inland, flying over fields and woodlands. They landed late in the day in a deep, dark forest.

As dusk settled, they could hear the howling of wolves. The Phookas gathered as close to their master as they could, fearful of getting lost in the dark. Walipreen moved quickly, seemingly oblivious to any threat that surrounded them. He knew exactly where to go. The Phookas watched as he approached a large tree along the edge of a shallow stream. The tree was black with black leaves. Even in the darkness the tree seemed to absorb any light around it.

Walipreen strode purposefully to the tree, extending his arms out to the sides and then quickly bringing them together. A resounding crash split the air and the tree immediately transformed into the Kelpie, Rovek. There was no exchange of words; no time for the Kelpie to react or to defend himself. The sorcerer raised an arm and brought it down in a forceful blow, driving Rovek to the ground.

Standing over the fallen Kelpie, Walipreen pressed a hand to Rovek's head. His body went rigid and convulsed as Walipreen pulled all the essence from the Kelpie. When he was done, his eyes burned red, his face extended further than before, his nostrils flaring, and razor sharp teeth began to show over his leathery lips.

He spun around to the Phookas who could only lower their heads, avoiding any eye contact at all. He told them they had one more stop to make. Without waiting to rest; without waiting to absorb the memories of the Kelpie as he had needed to do earlier, he grabbed the Phookas in both hands and took to the air.

They flew through the night. Even the moon failed to illuminate the sky. Dark clouds had obscured everything above them. Walipreen fixed his vision to some unseen point on the far horizon and beat his wings. As Rovek's being became one with Walipreen's, the sorcerer would growl or moan, and mumble incantations in a language that was foreign to the Phookas, every one of whom now wished it had been he who had vanished.

In the early dawn, they approached a massive sea of holes that spread out as far as the eye could see. Chardon had heard about this place but had not believed it was real. His ancestors had fled this place when the Kelpie Scirios had been imprisoned by the Alchemist in one of the pits. He could not imagine how Walipreen would know which one the Kelpie was now in.

But Walipreen did know. He dove down to the ground and stood on the edge of one such hole. It was too narrow for his now enlarged body. He bellowed in anger, calling Scirios' name. Foolishly, the aged Kelpie rose to the surface in defiance, only to be met with the wrath of the sorcerer.

A giant claw grasped the Kelpie, lifting him in the air and holding him tight, while another claw cupped his head. The Phookas could smell the fear as it poured from Scirios' body. Within seconds, he fell limp, drained completely of all that made him who he was. Walipreen tossed the carcass into one of the pits as if discarding waste.

He spun around to face the Phookas. They cowered under his stare, but instead of destroying them he acknowledged their loyalty and told them they would soon be rewarded; but first, they would travel home – back to the Ice Kingdom.

On the return to the north, the consciousness of the eight Kelpies blended with his. All memories were now one; his own lost among them and no longer distinguishable. This was the price he had paid for knowing all there was to know – about the Kelpies, about the Alchemist, about the Enchantress and her pendant, and about the Boravak.

He would return home and then lead an army to the south to deal with the Twins. He would find out soon, though, that such a journey would not be necessary. They had already invaded and taken over the Ice Kingdom and were waiting for him – for the sorcerer that had been him. They could never imagine the foe they were about to face.

Walipreen's thoughts then turned to the Phynnodderee that had been captured. He understood that the kidnapping of this particular one had been merely chance, but that chance had been providential. She had the ability to lead him to the way through the Boravak. He would rule this world and the one on the other side. He would destroy the Alchemist and the Enchantress and take the pendant. He would be all powerful and immortal.

When he eventually reached the Ice Kingdom, he knew immediately that something had changed. He could see no sign of the Phooka guards or patrols. Instead, he saw signs of Rebbercands. They were a wasteful people, and slovenly. There was debris and garbage strewn near the entryway to the citadel. As simple-minded as the Phookas may have been, they were not the least bit wasteful.

He couldn't imagine the Twins had invaded. Surely Nelluc would have stopped them. Then he realized that if Nelluc believed he was not returning, his "nephew" would reach out to the Twins for salvation. How foolish of him, if he did that.

Walipreen landed at the entrance to the Kingdom. He instructed the Phookas to disperse and to find as many others as they could, and to bring them to the central hall. They were to surround the hall, but not to make an entrance until Walipreen instructed them.

Once they departed he strode into the Kingdom and into the central hall. He knew the Twins would be there. As he entered he saw them seated on thrones they had installed. In spite of the radical change to his features, the Twins recognized him.

They rose to greet him, moving away from each other and to opposite sides of Walipreen. They simultaneously began to cast spells on him to confine him. His power was immune to their efforts. He raised his arms and bellowed. Lightning flashed, the walls shook, and thunder boomed, echoing in the chamber.

The Twins, realizing they were outmatched, made an attempt to escape. That, too, was futile. Walipreen froze them both in place. With a flick of his wrist, he lifted them off the ground and their bodies floated up to him. He held them in the air, inches from his face. He peered into their eyes and filled them with fear.

They pleaded for their lives and he laughed. I mean you no harm, he told them. I expect you will make useful servants. They agreed to do whatever he asked. He told Rampool that he would return to the southern kingdom, with an assembly of Phookas. He would bend the Rebbercands to the will of Walipreen or they would be thrown into the seas.

He told Prine that he would govern the northern kingdom under the same rules. Once they were both situated and compliant with his orders, they would send armies of Rebbercands out to the villages of all the other peoples. They would follow the dictates of Walipreen or they would suffer the same fate as any Rebbercand who failed to commit himself to Walipreen – they would be cast into the seas.

The Twins eagerly agreed. They had little courage and the sorcerer knew that. When he was satisfied that they would submit to him, he asked where Nelluc was. They stuttered and stammered, finally saying that he was not in the Ice Kingdom; that he had ventured out with a small entourage.

What about the Phynnodderee, bellowed Walipreen. Yes, they told him. Nelluc had mentioned a Phynnodderee – a girl child with unusual powers. Walipreen demanded to know where she was. They told him that Nelluc had taken her somewhere, but that he failed to tell them where.

She's not here, Walipreen screamed. Where is she? The Twins cowered and cried. They didn't know where she was. They repeated that Nelluc hadn't told them. Then where did Nelluc go, he wanted to know. They again told him they had no idea where Nelluc had been. Walipreen pressed them. Where is he now?

Finally, they each feared the other would point the finger. They each feared the other would blame him for what happened to Nelluc. As a result, they both blurted out at the same time that Nelluc had been cast into the sea.

Walipreen couldn't believe what he was hearing. The Phynnodderee – the one person who could point to the weakness of the Boravak – was gone, hidden in some unidentified location. And the one person who knew of this location had been bound and thrown into the icy waters of the bay. Walipreen was outraged.

He spun on the Twins, his anger nearly out of control. You fools, he berated them. He grabbed Rampool, who happened to be only slightly closer. Whatever he was going to do was interrupted by Chardon. Walipreen's anger doubled when he saw that the Phooka had not waited outside the great hall as he had been directed.

Chardon explained that he could hear what had been going on. He reminded Walipreen that he was the one who had originally captured the Phynnodderee and brought her back to the Ice Kingdom. He suggested that it might be possible that the child got loose somehow and might have found her way back home.

Walipreen doubted that would happened but he was surprised that the Phooka had shown enough intelligence to have considered the possibility. He directed Chardon to take a small team to the Phynnodderee village and turn it upside down – make sure that if she was there, she was found. He ordered the Phooka to destroy anyone who got in his way.

"What happened to the village?" Aitch interrupted.

"No one really knows for certain, except for that Phooka and whoever he took with him," the Rebbercand answered.

"Didn't the Phooka tell anyone?" Aitch persisted.

"I don't know," barked the Rebbercand. "Who cares? It was just a bunch of worthless Phynnodderees."

Aitch fought the urge to stand up and strike the Rebbercand. He reminded himself that he needed to find out as much as he could about what had happened over the last fifteen years. He forced himself to chuckle as the Rebbercand's comment and mumble something about always enjoying stories about Phynnodderees being put in their place.

The Rebbercand refilled his cup, settled back, satisfied with his guest's response, and continued with his story.

Rampool returned to the south with the demands from Walipreen regarding the Rebbercands' allegiance. No opposition was launched. The story teller even admitted that the Rebbercands really have no allegiance except to themselves, so switching loyalty to Walipreen took little effort.

The hardest part had been becoming subservient to the Phookas. That had been the reward to the eleven who had remained faithful to Walipreen. They had been made regional governors, actually ruling the lands both north and south. The Twins were rulers in name only. No one was really sure why Walipreen kept the Twins around. They had been useless before he took over; there was no reason to believe they were any more useful now. However, no one was going to question Walipreen, the Supreme, as he had recently started calling himself.

Chardon returned several weeks later. The Phynnodderee village had been torn apart; no stone had been left unturned. The child was nowhere to be found. He did report one additional piece of information. It seems that this girl had a brother. He had disappeared as well. The parents, upon hearing that the girl had been taken by the Phookas pleaded to know if their son had also been kidnapped.

"What did he tell them?" Aitch asked. He couldn't control his curiosity.

"Who knows," the Rebbercand replied. "Whatever he told them it was probably a lie."

"What happened with the girl?" Aitch asked.

"The Phynnodderee?" the Rebbercand asked.

Aitch clenched his jaw to keep from screaming at the Rebbercand. Was he completely stupid, Aitch wondered. Who else have they been talking about? He took a deep breath and attributed his host's seeming lack of intelligence to a cup or two too many of ale.

"Yes," he answered. "The one who Walipreen seemed so desperate to find. Was she ever located?"

"No," said the Rebbercand. "There was no sign of her whatsoever. The Phookas who Nelluc used to take her wherever he took her never came back, either, so they weren't around to ask. It's as if they all vanished from the face of the earth. Weird, isn't it?"

Chapter eleven

Aitch sat there dumbstruck. He was so close, but now seemed to be at a dead end. He was sure the Phynnodderee that the Rebbercand had mentioned was his sister. But it looked like anyone who knew where she was had vanished. He watched as the ale that the Rebbercand had consumed took its toll and he dropped into a deep sleep.

"Summer," he whispered. "Where are you?"

She fluttered down from the tree and made herself visible to him.

"Did you hear all that?" he asked.

"Yes," she said. "I'm so sorry. I'm guessing the girl he was talking about was your sister."

"I think so, too," Aitch replied.

"Don't give up hope," she encouraged him. "I'm sure we'll find her. We're pretty good at figuring things out."

"I hope so," he said. "Go back and fill the others in on what we've learned. I'll go get the guys and meet up with you. I think we need to get away from here before this Rebbercand wakes up and starts asking questions I probably don't have answers for. Besides, I'd like to get back to my own body. This one feels creepy."

Summer darted up and away, easily finding Natalie, Stella, Solveig and Quinn well out of sight of the village. She related the story told by the Rebbercand, supplemented with moans of "Oh, no," from Quinn.

As soon as she disappeared from sight, Aitch crept out of the courtyard into the surrounding building. He looked around to see if anyone was present and as quietly as possible searched for the doorway through which he had initially entered.

I should have paid more attention when I first came in, he muttered to himself. He found a door that looked familiar, but it was locked. Did we come in from this direction or that, he asked himself, looking to the left and then to the right. He decided to go right until he came upon a split stairway – the left leading to a lower level and the right to an upper level.

This isn't right, he thought. He turned around and in a few yards came to a divide in the hallway. I don't remember this, he thought. How could I have missed it and which way do I go? He thought the left passage was correct and went that way. As soon as he came to a sharp turn, he realized he had taken the wrong one. He turned around and headed back.

He ended up back at the split stairway. What's going on, he asked himself. I should have come to the divide in the passages. I couldn't have missed it. Knowing, though, that he must have, he turned around and headed back once again. He walked much further than he had the first time he encountered the divide, but when he still hadn't come upon it, he began to wonder if he had somehow taken another wrong turn. His frustration was building.

"Where is the stupid door?" he hissed.

"What door would that be?" a voice behind him asked.

He jumped up in the air, barely able to keep a startled yell from escaping, and spun around. He found himself face to face with a Phooka. How long has he been watching me, was the first question that popped into his mind.

"Where did you come from?" he snapped.

"The cellar," the Phooka answered, gesturing vaguely to one of the many doors that lined the hall. "Are you looking for something?"

Aitch fought back his natural revulsion at the sight of the Phooka. He struggled to overcome his urge to grab the creature and demand that it tell him where is sister was. He controlled his breathing and cleared his throat.

"I'm looking for the way out," he said.

"Are you leaving so soon?" the Phooka asked.

Thinking quickly, Aitch answered, "I want to check on my prisoners."

"They have been properly secured," the Phooka told him.

This was not what he wanted to hear. He wanted to know how to get out of this nightmare, find the others and get well away from this village. What do I have to do to be free of this creature, he asked himself. Act like a Rebbercand, was the answer.

"I'll be the judge of that," he snapped. "Take me to them. Now!"

"Of course, sir," the Phooka answered. "As you wish."

He turned and led the way out of the building to the barn. All I had to do was act rude, thought Aitch. Who knew it could be as easy as that? The Phooka opened the door and allowed Aitch to enter first, and then followed immediately after him.

"As you requested," he said. "And as I described: they have been properly secured."

Aitch caught himself from saying thank you. Too polite, he cautioned himself. Be nasty, he thought.

"And as I said," he growled. "I'll be the judge of that. Go back about your business. If I have any other need of you, I'll summon you."

"Yes, sir," the Phooka replied.

He bowed and then backed out of the barn, leaving the door slightly ajar. Aitch waited a few seconds and then crept to the door and peeked out to see if the Phooka had gone. He saw the door to the main building shutting and felt a bit safer. He spun around and rushed over to the three sitting on the foul smelling straw. He pulled the dagger from his belt and was about to slice through the ropes.

"Not yet," cautioned Lochen. "We need to leave this village. Better to have prisoners in tow than strangers walking freely."

"Oh, yeah," Aitch replied. "I guess you're right. Come on, then. We need to get out of here quickly."

"What did you learn?" asked Liam.

"Did you bring any food?" asked Sean.

Everyone stopped and looked at him.

"What?" he asked. "I'm hungry. Is that a crime?"

"I'm sure there's an inn somewhere in town where we can stop for a bite to eat," said Liam.

"Really?" asked Sean. "That would be great."

"No, not really," said Liam. "Are you nuts?"

"Our continued presence in this place would not be advantageous," said Lochen. "At any time the three of us could be subject to the whims of any of several unstable individuals. The less attention we draw to ourselves the better off we will be."

"I think that's what I said," commented Aitch. "Only shorter."

"And I was merely concurring with your assessment," Lochen replied.

They had been carrying on this conversation in furtive whispers as they attempted to move stealthily from one structure to another.

"Why are we going this way?" asked Liam. "I thought you'd want to join up with the others."

"We do," said Lochen. "Isn't this the correct direction?"

"Only if you plan on completely circumnavigating the planet," replied Liam. "They're in the complete opposite direction."

"Why didn't you say something sooner?" asked Sean.

"I didn't know I was in charge," said Liam. "Besides, I thought we were trying to avoid something. Apparently not."

"This is terrible," said Aitch. "I'm completely lost."

"I'm not," said Liam. "Follow me."

"Wait," said Lochen. "You're supposed to be a prisoner. You can't be in front."

They hadn't considered this when they tied each other up before entering the village. Liam was at the end of the line of rope, Sean was in the middle, and Lochen was in front, being pulled along by Aitch.

"Why don't I just cut the ropes?" asked Aitch. "Wouldn't that be easier?"

"Yes, it would," said Lochen, "but we've already discussed this. If we're observed unbound we may be at greater risk."

"We need to get out of here," Sean reminded them. "Just leave him at the end of the line. He can whisper directions to me; I'll whisper them to Lochen and Lochen can whisper them to Aitch."

"It'll have to do," said Aitch.

Everyone got in line and Aitch started moving zigzag from house to house and building to building, keeping to the shadows to the extent he could.

"Left," Liam whispered when they came to an alleyway.

"Left," whispered Sean.

"Left" whispered Lochen.

A few yards later, Liam called for another turn.

"Right," he whispered.

"Right," whispered Sean.

"Right," whispered Lochen.

This continued for a few more minutes as the foursome wound their way from the wrong side of the village past the barn in which they had been held and the building in which Aitch was regaled by the Rebbercand on the history of Walipreen. They were close to the edge and freedom when Sean passed on the next command.

"Stop," the voice behind him whispered.

"Stop" whispered Sean.

"Stop," whispered Lochen.

Aitch stopped as did the others.

"Why are we stopping?" Aitch whispered.

"Why are we stopping?" Lochen whispered.

"Why are we stopping?" Sean whispered.

"Because I want to know what you are up to," said a voice from behind Liam.

They all turned around and saw another Rebbercand standing at the end of the line. He was much larger than Aitch's host had been and had a large ax in his hand. He walked up the line of supposed prisoners to where Aitch was standing and then turned towards him.

"What's going on?" he demanded.

"I'm taking these prisoners," said Aitch. "My prisoners. They're mine. I'm taking them."

"And where exactly are you taking them?" the Rebbercand growled.

He stepped closer towards Aitch, bending over him and sniffing.

"Who are you?" he snarled. "I don't recognize you, and you don't sound like you're from around here."

Recalling the misstated name he had been given earlier, Aitch replied, "I'm Umeruh, and I'm from...uh...the far west."

"Umeruh?" repeated the Rebbercand. "What kind of name is that? And where did these prisoners come from?"

"They were captured in a raid," said Aitch. "I'm taking them with me. They're mine. I found them. You know: finder's keepers."

"What are you blathering about?" snapped the Rebbercand. "Never mind. I don't want to know. Besides, if you're from the west, then why are you taking them east?"

"Uh...we...oh...well, we're,,, uh,,, we're going on a field trip."

It was the best Aitch could come up with under the circumstances. The Rebbercand was not convinced and decided that something in all this was not right. He grabbed Aitch's collar and pulled him close.

"I think you're lying," he hissed. "You and this lot are coming with me."

Before he could take a single step, Lochen raised his bound hands, opened his palm face down, extended his fingers and then lowered his hand slowly. The Rebbercand's eyes rolled back in his head, which lolled to one side. His knees buckled and he dropped to the ground like a sack of wet sand.

"What did you do to him?" asked Aitch.

"I cast a simple spell on him to put him to sleep," replied Lochen. "When he wakes up he'll have forgotten all about this little episode."

"You couldn't have done that sooner?" asked Sean.

"I was hoping it would not be necessary," said Lochen. "We're still too much out in the open and can be seen by anyone."

"Can I cut the ropes now?" asked Aitch.

"By all means," replied Lochen.

Aitch sliced through them quickly. Lochen swirled his index finger and the scattered pieces turned into squirrels and scampered away. Liam led the rest of the way out of the village and back to where the others were waiting for them.

"What took you so long?" asked Summer. "I thought you were close behind me."

"We decided to take the scenic route," said Liam.

"Well, what do we do now?" asked Natalie.

They had all been brought up to date on the information Summer and Aitch had obtained from the Rebbercand. They had a better picture of the world they were in now, but no answers as to how to get back to Aitch's time period or where his sister was.

"I think we need to continue moving east," said Lochen. "We need to find a place that Stella can use as a sanctorum. We need to get an even bigger picture of what's happened and what's about to happen."

"Why east?" asked Solveig. "Wasn't there something in that village that we could use?"

"No," Aitch, Lochen, Sean and Liam all said in unison.

"I'm afraid that due to the nature of our departure and the circumstances surrounding both our arrival and our visit, that would not be the most viable of solutions," said Lochen.

"I don't think that's a good idea," said Aitch.

"I believe that's what I just said," commented Lochen.

"I know," said Aitch. "Only I was shorter."

"OK, OK," interjected Summer. "We head east, but how far? Do we have a destination in mind?"

"Yes," said Lochen. "There is a deserted village about a day away, beyond the town we just fled. I'm certain there will be a suitable structure there."

"You're not thinking of where that Troll was, are you?" asked Quinn.

"Not exactly," said Lochen. "It was on the other side of the bridge under which he resided."

"Troll?" gasped Aitch. "Those are real? I've heard about them, but I thought they were only stories to scare us as kids."

"They're real," said Stella. "And the stories you were told were probably real, too.

"And you still want to go there?" he asked.

"Yes," said Natalie. "But this one is no longer there."

"How can you be sure?"

"We're sure," several of them responded at once.

"I don't like this one bit," said Quinn. "But if we're going to do this, then let's stop talking about it and get moving."

Without any further discussion, they skirted the village while it was still dark and headed west. Along the way, Sean and Quinn filled Aitch in on their experiences with trolls and the sentinels that the Alchemist had left in strategic locations when the eight of them were futilely trying to prevent the release of the Kelpies. They told him of their ongoing contact with the Rebbercand known as B'nair as he managed to stay one step ahead of them and freed one Kelpie after another.

Along the way, they came across a few more small towns that they gave a wide berth to. These towns hadn't been there when the eight had traveled this way before, and Aitch informed them that they hadn't existed to his recollection when he had been here only fifteen years earlier.

"Who are these people, then?" asked Liam. "And where did they come from?"

He couldn't help but notice that they were crossing what used to be the southern edge of the Swamp. There was no sign of the hazardous plants and animals that inhabited this area. Even though he knew where he was and where he was going, this all looked foreign to him.

Shortly before evening on the second day, they approached their destination. The stream that once existed was long gone. In its place was a dusty and rock-filled trench over which a bridge crossed, leading into an ancient walled city. It was the bridge under which the Troll, Sooli Vahn, had been residing.

They climbed across the trench so they could reach the bridge and the entry gates to the deserted town. The walls, which stretched high above them, were covered with dead and decayed vines. Shriveled black leaves still hung on the vines, covering and disguising many still treacherous thorns. Everyone stopped at the far side of the bridge.

Lochen looked closely at ruins and then strode purposefully forward. Stella was close by his side, and the others followed cautiously. Sean and Quinn peered over the side, looking for any sign of the Troll or his remains.

"Why are we going in there?" he asked.

"We may find a room constructed in a manner sufficient to serve as a Sanctorum," answered Lochen.

"I need a circular room of some kind so I can project images," Stella explained. "Given the age of this village, it's likely there will be something of that nature inside."

"This place gives me the creeps," Aitch said.

"Me, too," added Summer, Solveig, Sean and Quinn all at the same time.

"What's all the black dead junk crawling up the sides?" Aitch asked.

"Vines," said Liam. "Don't touch them. And especially avoid those thorns."

"Why?" asked Aitch. "What's the big deal about the thorns?"

Lochen stopped walking, turned around and said, "We don't have any potion to bring you back from the dead."

"Oh," Aitch gulped. "I didn't know there was such a potion."

"There isn't," said Stella. "So don't touch the thorns."

"I get it," he replied.

Just as they reached the gates, which were mysteriously open, they heard a noise from within. Sean wiggled his way up to the front, his slingshot loaded and ready. Liam had drawn a blade from his belt, and both Lochen and Stella stood poised to cast whatever spells would be needed. Aitch quickly shifted shape into a dragon fly and buzzed over the top of all of them.

"Let me go check it out," he whispered. "And I know, stay away from the thorns."

Without waiting for approval he darted past the gates and into the village. He could see nothing but derelict buildings and streets that were filled with debris – broken wagons, shattered pieces of furniture, remains of camp fires, and trash drifting all over the place. What a dump, he thought.

Off to his right, he saw an old Phooka sitting on a log, turned three quarters of the way away from him. Aitch couldn't tell what he was doing, so he flew up a little higher, now wishing he had transformed into something that didn't make quite so much of a buzzing noise when he flew.

When he thought he was high enough, he moved forward until he was directly over the Phooka and could look down on him. To the Phooka's side was an old, stained bucket. In front of him was a piece of wood on which he was cutting something up. The smell wafted up and was so foul that Aitch had to recoil. At the same instant he imagined a voice inside his head telling him to hurry up with the food.

He spun around trying to find the source, but could see nothing. This place is even weirder on the inside, he said to himself. Suddenly the voice he had imagined nearly shouted, "Who is that?" He looked down at the Phooka who hadn't changed position. Then he circled around once more looking for the source. Frightened, he darted out of the village and back to the others.

He flew downward and shifted shape back to his normal appearance as he was landing. Everyone could tell that something had happened. The color had drained from his face to a sickly green.

"That place is haunted," he gasped. "It's not safe. We should leave."

"What happened?" Natalie asked. "What did you see?"

"There's a Phooka in there," he said.

"Just one?" Sean asked. "You got scared by one Phooka?"

"One that I could see," Aitch explained. "But I heard a voice."

"Another Phooka?" asked Quinn.

"I couldn't tell where it was coming from," Aitch told him. "It felt like it was inside my head. Really, we need to leave."

"What did this voice say?" asked Solveig.

"What does it matter?" hissed Aitch. "It didn't say, 'Welcome to my village. Would you like to stay for dinner?' It...it...I don't know. It was creepy."

"Do you hear it now?" asked Lochen.

"No," answered Aitch.

"Listen closely," Lochen said.

"Nope," replied Aitch. "Nothing."

As Lochen was studying the walls and the dead vines, a movement over his shoulder caught Aitch's eye. He moved his head to one side to get a better look and became even more unsettled by what he saw. Coming towards them from the opposite side of the bridge was a small group of Phookas.

"Change into something else," said Summer.

"What?" asked Aitch.

"I don't know," she said. "Anything. They don't know who or what we are. We're not a threat to them. I'm guessing they know what you are and from what you've told us, they don't get along very well with your people. Get out of sight."

He shifted into a duck and waddled in circles on the bridge.

"Not something they might eat," gasped Stella. "Something else."

He quickly shifted into a shape that looked exactly like Stella, only with a faint greenish glow.

"What are you doing?" she asked.

"I don't do well under pressure," he snapped at her. "It was all I could come up with."

"Leave it," said Liam. "There's no time for you to be swirling around."

"Swirling?" objected Aitch. "I wasn't swirling."

"Enough," hissed Sean. He pulled back on his slingshot, ready for trouble.

The Phookas had not noticed the small group on the bridge. They were still several yards off when they turned to the left and instead of reaching the bridge, climbed down a well-worn path in the dried out stream to the other side and disappeared around the far edge of the village wall.

"That was strange," said Quinn. "Where did they go? Why didn't they enter the village?"

"I can go look," offered Aitch.

"No," said Lochen. "You stay here. Stella and I will approach them and see if we can keep this somewhat peaceful."

"I think Sean or I should come along," said Liam.

"No," insisted Lochen. "I don't want them to see any weapons or to perceive any kind of threat. If trouble arises, Stella and I can protect ourselves."

Lochen and Stella crossed back over the bridge and followed the same path down the stream bed and over to the other side. The carefully rounded the corner of the village wall and a few yards further came upon a camp site. It looked as if it had been there for some time. Instead of tents, there were well constructed lean-tos, a fire pit and what appeared to be storage caches similar to what Liam had scattered all over the Swamp.

"Hello," Lochen called. "We seem to have lost our way, and were wondering if you could provide some assistance."

There was no reaction from any of the Phookas. Strange, Lochen thought. He tried again; this time a little louder.

"Hello! Can you help us?"

Still nothing. At that moment, one of them turned and saw him. He immediately picked up a spear and tapped the one next to him. The second one spun around and upon seeing Lochen and Stella, picked up a club-like piece of wood, tapped the others on their shoulders and they all took defensive positions.

Lochen raised his hands to signify he came in peace, and said, "We mean you no harm. My friend and I seem to have taken a wrong turn. Can you help us?"

There was no reaction or response from the Phookas. The expressions on their faces still showed a look of suspicion.

"I don't think they can hear you," said Stella.

"Really?" asked Lochen. "I believe I was projecting sufficiently and enunciating clearly."

"It's not that," she told him. "I think they're deaf."

Lochen snapped his fingers and created a loud popping sound behind the staring Phookas. None of them reacted in any way.

"I think you're right," he said. "Well, then. That would seem to make an effort at communicating with them somewhat pointless, don't you think?"

Without waiting for an answer, he cast the same spell he had earlier and the Phookas, overcome with exhaustion, dropped to the ground in a deep sleep. Once they were clearly unconscious,

Lochen walked over and examined them. He looked closely in the ears of each one of them.

"What is it?" Stella asked.

"It's unusual for this many people to have the same affliction," he said. "Don't you think?"

"I suppose," she replied. "Do you think someone did this to them?"

"It certainly seems so," he said.

"How awful. Can we fix it?"

"That's what I was looking to see," Lochen told her. "I want to be careful, though. From what I see, this condition has lasted a long time. For them to suddenly regain their hearing could be more painful and disturbing that losing it."

He walked over to the wall around the village and studied the vines that had overgrown the stone and then died out. He reached up and carefully plucked one of the leaves.

"Uh, what are you doing?" Stella asked. "Aren't those still poisonous?"

"At full strength, yes, they are," he said. "But in a smaller dose, they can be quite a source for good."

He walked over to a bucket that contained water and scooped out a handful. With the other hand he pinched and rolled the leaf and then ground it into the water making a kind of paste. Then he went around to each of the Phookas, and using his little finger, smeared a tiny amount in each of their ears.

"That should do it," he said when he was done.

"Do you think the one inside the gates is deaf, too?" Stella asked.

"I do," he replied. "I've saved just enough for him."

"I hope they appreciate what you've done for them," she said as they headed back across the stream bed and back to the bridge.

"I hope they never find out," Lochen replied. "From what Aitch has told us, Phookas are not the most congenial of people."

When they met up with the others, Aitch informed them that nothing inside had changed, as far as he could tell. He had sifted back to his normal shape, much to Stella's relief. She told them all about the other Phookas – that they had been deafened some time ago, but that Lochen had given them something to change that while they were under a spell to keep them quiet for a while.

Aitch didn't say anything, but the look on his face made it clear that he thought Lochen's act of kindness was not warranted. These people had stolen his sister and he didn't think he could ever forgive them for that.

As soon as they crossed the gates, Lochen put the remaining Phooka to sleep before he even knew anyone was behind him. As with the others, Lochen smeared the remainder of the paste in the creature's ears and then wiped the residue from his hand. He motioned for everyone to move quietly in case there were any more Phookas within the walls.

Aitch, Solveig and Liam went off towards the right of the main road, looking for signs of other guards as well as a circular building. Quinn, Stella and Summer moved towards the left, and Lochen, Natalie and Sean continued moving forward.

Each of them recalled the history of this cursed village and could see signs of the damage the poisonous plants had done as the roots burrowed through the ground beneath the enclosure. There were rows of diseased and decayed vegetables in long dormant gardens. The well in the center of the village had been boarded up.

Along the ramparts around the top of the wall, they could see, even from the ground level, evidence of death and destruction. Aitch, Solveig and Liam found an old glass store. Inside, they could feel the hairs on the backs of their neck prickle. Something very powerful had been here at one time. They quickly backed out and headed towards the center of the village.

Quinn, Stella and Summer thought they had found a room that might be usable, only to discover that it had at one time been a prison. They found tiny cells with no windows and very small doors. The stench was overpowering. They bumped into each other as they got away as quickly as they could, also heading back towards the center of the village.

They met up with Aitch, Solveig and Liam, all of whom were looking around for the remaining three. Quinn saw Natalie waving towards them all, motioning for them to join her, Lochen and Sean. When they caught up to her, Lochen and Sean had already entered the building.

"This might be just what we need," she whispered to them. "We heard a noise inside in the lower level. Lochen and Sean went ahead to check it out."

"They should have waited," said Aitch.

Without any further comment, he shifted again; this time into a thick, heavy fog. He covered the stone floor at the threshold of the building and rolled across the ground and in. He could feel the walls as he moved over the remains of centuries of wreckage. To his right he could feel the floor drop away down an ancient stone stairway.

He could hear the voices of Lochen and Sean somewhere in the darkness at the bottom. He moved slowly forward.

"Who are you," another voice croaked.

"We come in peace," said Lochen. "We mean you no harm."

Aitch could hear the rattling of metal. When he reached the bottom, he rolled up closer to Lochen and Sean. Sensing no danger, he slowly shifted back into his normal shape. Once he did, and his eyes adjusted to the dimness, he saw a middle-aged woman sitting on the ground against the wall on the far side of a large circular room.

She was chained to a post that was driven into the ground. The chain was attached to a thick iron collar around her neck. Her hair was long and streaked with gray. Her clothes were thin and worn, but seemed relatively clean.

To one side of the room Aitch could see a pile of straw and bedding. Close to the staircase was a small fire. Next to the fire was a bucket that was attached to a rope that ran up to the ceiling and through a small hole. He heard the chain rattle as the old woman stood up.

She was staring at Aitch and slowly moving forward, pointing at him. He felt a strangeness creep over him that frightened him.

"Aitch," she croaked. "Is that you? It's me. It's Emm."

Chapter twelve

Emm had watched in disbelief as Nelluc climb up the stairs and out of the cell in which she was chained to the floor. Her head had been pressed against the stone while the Phooka kept his foot on the chain near her collar. She wanted to believe that this was some kind of punishment for not answering his questions and that he would be back soon.

Instead, the Phooka cut the ropes from her wrists, removed the gag from her mouth, and watched her for a few seconds before he left. She had started a fire to warm the dungeon and had the foresight to keep the torch in a safe place, lighting a candle before she extinguished it in order to preserve whatever fuel it had been soaked in.

She quickly learned to place her fire near the staircase instead of under the oculus in the center of the roof. In spite of her fear, she managed to sleep, although fitfully. Her thoughts as she drifted off were of Nelluc returning in the morning to grill her once again about things she really didn't know. She would make something up – anything, just to be taken away from here.

The next morning, she was awakened when another one of the Phookas arrived with a new bucket and what she assumed was meant to be breakfast. She overcame her revulsion and gagged down whatever it was, since she knew she needed to keep her strength up. She would be ready for Nelluc when he arrived. But he didn't arrive.

One day slipped into the next; weeks blended into more weeks. She found a chip of stone behind the staircase and began to scratch marks into the wall, keeping track of the passage of time. After two months she realized that Nelluc had probably returned to the Ice Kingdom and would not likely return immediately.

The Phookas rotated their custodial responsibilities. Most often they limited their contact with her by raising or lowering one bucket or the other. Every once in a while, one of them would bring down a load of fresh firewood or a new supply of candles.

Each time, she would try to speak with them, only to find that Nelluc had told her that one truth – they were all deaf. They were all immune to the sound of her voice and the commands she had been able to make them follow when they had first captured her. Now, even that was denied her. So she tried something else.

The next time one of them came down the staircase, she sat up against one of the walls, her arms wrapped around her legs, pulling them close to her body. She rested her chin on her knees and under lowered eyelids; she focused on the visitor and concentrated her thoughts.

Look at me, she said to herself. Look at me and nod. She repeated the command over and over again with no effect. Her eyes bored into him as he hauled in a load of firewood and deposited it a few feet from the base of the steps. Once he dumped it, he turned and climbed back up the stairs.

"AHHHHRRRR! LOOK AT ME, LOOK AT ME, LOOK AT ME," she screamed in frustration.

Get a hold of yourself, she thought. You didn't really expect it to work the first time, did you? She recalled what Nelluc had told her about the peculiar properties of this place – that some kind of hex shielded everything from spells. She wondered if that meant spells failed to work inside the village; that they couldn't penetrate from the outside to the inside; that they couldn't penetrate from the inside to the outside; or all of the above.

Her mind was spinning with all the possibilities, not that she had the capability of casting spells, regardless of what limitations may or may not actually exist. It was clear that whatever had caused these Phookas to lose their hearing was blocking her ability to control their actions with her verbal commands. She resolved to focus harder on trying to control them with her thoughts. After all, she reasoned, she didn't have anything else to do.

One after the other, any Phooka who ventured down into the pit, became the target of her mental commands to look at her and nod. By the marks she made on the wall, she had been confined more than five months when all of a sudden, one of them glanced in her direction and nodded. She was so startled that she jumped to her feet.

Her reaction startled the Phooka, who jumped back – not that he was anywhere near her, or the least bit in danger. It was the unexpected movement. He glared at her, confused by what had happened, and bolted back up the stairs. It didn't matter. Emm danced with joy, and laughed out loud. It was two weeks before another Phooka came down the stairs.

This was a different one. She wondered if they communicated with each other, and how. Had the first one told the others that she had done something to him? Would he even admit to it if he knew what had happened? This time, she controlled her excitement. She focused her eyes in the same manner and concentrated on the same command: look at me and nod.

The Phooka dropped the firewood, turned and headed towards the steps. At the last second, he turned in Emm's direction, looked her right in the eyes and nodded. She fought to keep her face from breaking into a smile and, instead, thought, nod again. He did, and then shook his head as if clearing out cobwebs. Confused, he moved slowly up the steps.

It worked, she beamed. Whatever "it" was, it worked. What now, she wondered. What should she think them to do? New bedding, she thought. Clean clothes. Better food. Escape. She tried to contain her excitement. Keep it simple, she thought. And don't expect too much, she warned herself. It was four days before she caught sight of another Phooka. When she did, she concentrated as hard as she could: get me fresh bedding; get me fresh bedding.

The Phooka stopped, glanced at her briefly, and then departed as if nothing had happened. It didn't work, she thought, immediately deflated. The next day, however, a blanket was tossed down from the floor above. It wasn't much cleaner, but that was beside the point. She could communicate commands with her mind.

The next command she gave was not as successful. She focused on the thought, "release me," but was only met with looks of confusion. She tried for several weeks to get this message across until it dawned on her that this was probably something they were incapable of doing. She guessed that Nelluc had anticipated something like this and took all the blacksmith tools with him when he left. She would never know for certain, but her assumption was correct.

After Nelluc had the collar fashioned and attached around her neck and to the chain secured to the rod that had been hammered into the floor, he packed up all of the tools and departed with them. He hadn't gone far before he tossed them in the nearest stream, but as far as the Phookas knew, they were all long gone. Emm's commands were impossible for them to comply with.

Resigning herself to this conclusion, she turned her thoughts in other directions. Over the next several months, she managed to secure fresh straw for the bedding, a clean change of clothes, and marginally better food. She was adjusting the best she could to her captivity. And then her first year went by.

When she counted the scratches she had made in the wall and discovered she had been a prisoner here for a year, she burst into tears. She was certain that something had happened to Nelluc. Surely, as cruel as he might be, even he couldn't leave her here this long unless something had prevented him from coming back for her.

Her family had no idea where she had been taken, and she had to assume that by now they would believe that she had died. Would Aitch believe that, too, she wondered. She didn't think so. Somehow, he would know she was alive and wouldn't rest until he found her. She kept that hope alive as long as she could.

In her anger, she thought about commanding the Phookas to kill each other, but then considered that should they do that, she would soon starve to death. She came to the realization that the Phookas were not only her jailers, they were her providers and her guardians. The futility of her situation drove her into a deep depression for the next several months.

As the depression covered her like a blanket, she stopped sending mental messages to the Phookas; she picked at her food; and she slept most of the time – on the stone floor, rather than on the fresh straw and bedding. Her lethargy became apparent to the Phookas, but there was nothing they could do, even if they understood what was happening.

Then one day, for no reason at all, she decided she had felt sorry for herself long enough. She still believed deep in her heart that Aitch would never give up looking for her. She held on to that thought and decided to be ready for him when that day came. She commanded the Phookas to bring her an additional bucket filled with water, so she could wash herself.

She eventually had them bring her a pot and some rocks so she could make a fire pit and begin preparing her own food. It took several tries for her to get them to bring her herbs and vegetables that were edible, but eventually she learned how to describe them so they understood.

Before long, the aroma of her cooking brought them to her in pairs. It had been so long since they had spoken to anyone, their ability to communicate verbally was greatly impaired. They croaked sounds they were unable to hear themselves; but it was enough for Emm to understand. At first she resented the fact that they asked her to share her food. They had stolen her from her home. But then she considered that they had never done her any harm and had been imprisoned here as much as she had been, chains or no chains.

Her heart softened towards them and she shared whatever she made. In spite of this she never saw more than two of them at one time. The lingering evil of the village kept them camped outside its walls. No words had to pass between them for them to each understand the danger that still lingered inside.

By the end of the second year, a silent truce evolved between the jailers and their prisoner. They found odds and ends that helped make Emm's life more tolerable. She had tried to convey the idea of a book to them, but it was beyond their comprehension. She longed for something to read – anything; but the idea was so foreign to them she was unable to make them understand.

She couldn't recall when it happened, but by the end of the third year, she had given them all names. She began to make up stories about them, creating wild and ridiculous histories for each one. At times she worried that she was losing her mind, but convinced herself that by making up these stories, she was keeping her mind sharp. And then the visions began.

It happened one day when several of the Phookas were out on a hunting party, and the others were huddled in their shelters out of the storm that had been pouring rain for the last two days. Enough water had come through the hole in the roof that a small puddle had formed in the center of Emm's cell. She was staring at the water as the drops falling from above caused overlapping ripples on the puddle's surface.

The monotony of the scene and her total boredom lulled her into a near trance-like state. She sat with her legs extended and her back against the wall, the stairway immediately behind her. She lifted her head back, resting it against the wall and stared at the opposite side.

Through the darkness she saw something shimmering. At first she dismissed it as a momentary illumination caused by the sun breaking through the clouds or a distant flash of lightning. But the shape remained and slowly became clearer. A head began to form. It was very large with long pointed ears.

Then it seemed to turn in her direction. At first a profile came into view. The lower jaw protruded far beyond the rest of the face, huge fangs poking upward past thick, leathery lips that were pulled back across smaller, jagged teeth. The nose was broad, but flat, the nostrils flared. The face continued to turn toward her.

She could see both eyes now. They were reptilian – a deep green with black oval around a center of blood red. The brow was wide and extended over the eyes giving the face an evil, brutish appearance. Then more came into view.

The head sat on a thick, squat neck atop massive, wide shoulders. The arms were short but extremely muscular, ending in large talons instead of hands and fingers. The skin was covered with what looked like blisters and boils that had hardened over. The legs were like the arms – short and thick with feet that were very wide; the nails long and broken.

Along the back there were ridges and stunted spikes. The spine extended into a split tail that looked like tentacles of a squid. The underside of the tails was covered with suckers, each of which had a razor sharp hook poking out of the center. The ends of the tails, though, looked more like stingers, with barbs and spikes covering the tip.

The image filled the wall on the other side of the pit. Emm was more intrigued than frightened. What was this image, she wondered. Where did it come from? What did it mean? She slowly got to her feet and moved closer. She was standing in the center of the room, oblivious to the rain falling on her head.

The creature raised its arms and large wings sprung from its back. The sudden motion made Emm take a step back. The rattling of her chain reminded her that she had no place to hide. She moved closer, slowly approaching the wall with her hand outstretched. Her fingers touched the image, but all she could fell was the stone.

She could see that more was being projected, so she took several steps back to take it all in. The ominous figure slowly fragmented into other, separate images. She could see mountains, volcanoes, jungles, deserts, and oceans. They did not seem to be connected, and then like the image before them, they, too fragmented into other images, spreading to the left and right, filling the wall until she was surrounded by the visions.

She turned around, her collar scraping her neck and collarbones. She could see armies of Phookas that merged and then blended into hoards of Rebbercands and then back again. She saw more creatures – a person that emerged from rocks, a giant squid, someone that looked to be made of molten lava, another that appeared to be a dragonfly, and others.

They sprung to the forefront and then were consumed in other images. The first one reappeared and then disappeared, only to reappear again. More creatures appeared, followed by an odd assortment of people – one in robes, another a giant, a woman with flowing red hair, a beautiful faerie, a creature from the forest, another that was oddly dressed and armed with daggers, a princess in green and blue veils, and the last a woman with a large pendant.

She had no idea who any of these people were or what the visions meant. She saw some of them running, and then engaged in a battle. She saw bursts of lightning, more strange creatures and then an old man in white. Then it all folded in on itself, compressing together into the shape of a giant tree. The last image was a fleeting one of Aitch as he transformed into a cloud of smoke. And then it was all gone.

Emm had no idea how long the visions appeared, but the rain had stopped. She reached up and felt her hair. It was dry. Her clothes were dry. How long have I been standing her, she asked herself. She wondered – not for the first time – if she was losing her mind. But something told her the visions were real. The sight of Aitch alone gave her strength.

Over the next several months she tried to conjure up the visions again, but without success. She studied her routine to try and recall what she could have done to prompt them, but drew a blank. My routine never changes, she told herself.

As time went by, Emm's visions returned. She saw images of the ancient Kelpies in a battle with eight strangers. She saw Meri Hocto when she was betrayed. She saw the Kelpies attempt to destroy one another in the Great War and the subsequent rise of Ena Ray and Tebaga. She saw Walipreen, Rampool and Prine. She saw Walipreen transform as he devoured the souls of the Kelpies.

She saw all of this, but understood none of it. She had no idea who these people were or what these images meant. She only knew that over the years they came more frequently and more vividly. And then they seemed to stop.

It had been months since she had seen the last image. She didn't know what was causing them, so she had no explanation for why they stopped. She felt certain that no more were coming. But then she had one more. Something about this one filled her with a sense of finality. It had been a very brief vision; probably the briefest of all of them.

She saw a cave with several ledges, and stairways carved into the sides. She could see eyes in the stone all around her following every move. She felt a sense of urgency that was so strong, it made her breath catch. The image fragmented, as the initial vision had, and was replaced by an enormous tree. Suddenly the tree split open, and the face of the monster that Walipreen had become filled its place, his eyes freezing her in their stare.

She could feel herself wrapped in cold. His gaze turning her to lead, filling her with fear. Aitch appeared, but only for an instant – off to one side – and then he was gone; swallowed by the arms of something unseen. And then the vision dissolved and she found herself staring at the stone wall.

"What good are these visions if I don't know what they mean?" she shouted.

Her voice echoed, heard by no one. She sat on the ground, her back against the wall, trying to recall all that she had seen. She sat there for hours lost in her own thoughts until she heard one of the Phookas somewhere in the village above her.

She realized she hadn't eaten for quite a while. Ever since she had been sharing her meals with them, they had all fallen into a pattern. They would catch and prepare whatever was available, including gathering nearby herbs and vegetables. When all was ready, they would lower it in a bucket and wait outside the village.

She would stoke her cooking fire, unload the bucket and mix the ingredients in her pot, allowing it to simmer until it was ready. She had no idea how they knew how long this took, but they did. When it was ready, one or two of them would shuffle down the steps. She would fill the bucket back up for them, and they would return to the others.

Even to this day, no more than two of them would enter the village or come into her cell. Once they were outside of the town gates, she had no sense of their presence or their location. Nelluc had been right. Whatever curse this village was under limited her abilities to control or even communicate with her captors.

Today she could tell there was only one inside the gate. He was cutting something up, but she couldn't tell what. She focused her thoughts to tell him to hurry up; she was hungry. Then she heard another sound – something different; something she hadn't heard before: a buzzing noise. She concentrated. In her mind, she asked, "Who's there?"

She hadn't had anyone to speak with for so long, she never thought of verbalizing her question. The thought flew through the air and then the sound disappeared. She strained to hear, but could detect nothing. All she could hear was the Phooka, preparing the food. She dismissed the sound as only her imagination, or simply to being tired.

Several minutes later, she could hear more noise. I knew I wasn't imagining things, she told herself. As quietly as she could, she got to her feet. Whatever it was, there was more than one, she thought. She heard the Phooka fall over and was surprised that her first reaction was that she hoped he hadn't been hurt.

Then she heard a voice. She couldn't make out what was said. Oh, no, she thought. What if it's Rebbercands, and they've killed the Phookas? A wave of panic flooded over her. She sat down again, curling up into a ball as if she could hide. She felt incredibly vulnerable and helpless.

"Who are you?" she croaked.

In addition to not having spoken in such a long time, her throat was dry and constricted with fear. Her question came out as a squeak and was barely heard. Then she saw a figure reach the bottom of the stairs. The hairs on the back of her neck stood out. This was one of the figures she had seen in the visions. And there was another she had seen right behind him.

"We come in peace," the figure told her. "We mean you no harm."

She had the same assurances from the Phookas when they stole her from her village. She scooted to her right, moving slightly towards the back of the stairway, closer to where her fire was. A burning piece of wood was the only weapon available to her, if she felt the need to protect herself.

As the two approached her slowly, a thick fog crept down the steps. Emm didn't notice it until it reached the bottom and curled around behind the two strangers. Her eyes darted from the stranger in front – the one in the robes – to the other stranger, to the fog and back again. It had been fifteen years since she had seen anyone other than her Phooka guards; now two unknown figures appeared, and she sensed there were more on the floor above.

Suddenly the fog stopped advancing and seemed to draw back and upward, like smoke. Emm was transfixed on it, while her conscious mind forced her to not be distracted from the other two. She forgot all about them when she saw the fog take the shape of a person. She gasped when the shape became solid and she could make out its features in the dim light. It looked exactly like Aitch.

It couldn't be, she told herself. It must be some kind of spell cast by one of the other two. Then the figure turned toward her, rubbing its eyes to quicken their adjustment to the dim light. She slowly got to her feet, her fear rapidly replaced by awe. She extended her hand and pointed her finger at the figure as she took tentative steps closer. Then she was sure.

"Aitch," she croaked. "Is that you? It's me. It's Emm."

Aitch recognized her voice in spite of how it had changed. He rushed forward and grabbed her in his arms, pulling her close and hugging her tightly.

"Emm," he said, his voice choked. "It's you. I can't believe it. I can't believe I found you."

She pressed him close as her eyes welled up with tears and she began to sob. Aitch could feel how thin she was beneath the frail rags she wore. Lochen and Sean stood by mutely, watching the reunion until Lochen cleared his throat, drawing their attention.

"I never gave up hope that you'd come," Emm said as she regained control. She then smacked him on the arm and took a step back. "What took you so long? I've been here..."

As she backed away to see his face, her words caught in her throat. She gazed at his face in disbelief. Once more she wondered if this was some kind of trick; but deep down inside, she knew this was her brother.

"You haven't aged," she gasped. "You are exactly the same. How is that possible?"

The reality of how long she had been imprisoned hit her with full force and her legs weakened. Aitch caught her before she could fall and gently lowered her to the floor. He squatted down in front of her, still holding her hands.

"I don't know how to explain it," he said. "It's complicated. But I'm here now and you're safe. There are others with me – friends – who will help, too."

Lochen turned to Sean and asked him to get the others and bring them down. He took a cautious step towards Emm and waited until she looked up at him.

"He's right," Lochen said. "It's complicated and we are here to help. Others will be joining us shortly and we can explain everything later. For now though, I think two things are in order. The first would be to release you from this chain."

He waited for his words to register with her. For a few seconds she stared blankly at him, still not comprehending what was happening. Then, once she realized what he said, she nodded. He placed one hand on the collar and with the other, tapped it twice. It popped open and he gently removed it from her neck.

She rubbed the skin as she got to her feet. After having worn the iron ring for fifteen years, its absence now felt strange. Lochen tossed the ring and chain to the side as five more people quickly came down the steps accompanied by a tiny faerie who flew over their heads and came to a stop just behind the one who had mysteriously removed her collar.

"Wow," Summer said. "How lucky is this? We were coming here to find a Sanctorum so we can find you and here you are."

"What..." Emm stammered. "I mean, who are you? Who are all of you?"

"There will be time for all that later," Lochen cut her off. "It would be wise not to tarry here longer than necessary. I have no doubt the spell I cast on the Phookas would have been adequate under normal circumstances, but I have no assurances that our circumstances are at all normal. In fact, I'm inclined to believe they are anything but that. We are still in a less than hospitable environment and it would be advantageous not to linger."

"What is he talking about?" Emm asked Aitch.

"He said we're still in danger and need to hurry up," Aitch explained.

"I believe that's exactly what I said," commented Lochen.

"Yeah," said Sean, "but he said it a lot shorter."

"This will do perfectly," said Stella, as she examined the shape of the room.

"Do for what?" asked Emm. "What's going on?

"Allow me to attempt to explain," said Lochen.

"We're from the other side of the Boravak," Sean cut him off. "Aitch came through looking for the Alchemist in order to find you. He got us instead. When we came back to this side, we were in a different time. We need to find a room like this so that she," he gestured to Stella, "can bring up images that will, hopefully tell us how to get back to where and when we belong?"

Emm stared at him in total confusion.

"That's precisely what I was about to say," Lochen said somewhat indignantly.

"Yes," said Solveig, "but it would have taken you about a million words more to do it."

"It doesn't make any sense, does it?" asked Quinn. "It's a mystery to me, too."

"This is a lot to take in," said Natalie. "We ask that you trust us, at least for now. If not us, trust your brother. He went to great lengths to find you."

Emm looked from Natalie to Aitch and nodded her understanding.

"OK," she said. "Wait, you said something about images. What kind of images?"

"They're visions, actually," said Stella. "Except they cross time and place. They're not in any particular order, and can show things that happened in the past, are happening now, or will happen in the future."

"We hope to identify some things that have been going on over here...inside the Boravak," Liam tried to explain, "you know...since we were here last."

"You mean in the last fifteen years?" Emm asked.

"Not exactly," said Summer. "More like two thousand years."

"I don't understand," said Emm. "I've been here for fifteen years. Aitch looks the same as the last day I saw him. How is that anything like two thousand years?"

Everyone was silent.

"The Boravak is not only a different place," said Liam.

"It's a different time," finished Quinn. "Trust me. Moving back and forth isn't as simple as it seems."

"When Aitch crossed over and came back," said Natalie, "fifteen years had gone by. That's why he looks the same to you. But for us, two thousand years passed. We all used to live in this world, but it's not the same as it was then. That's why we need to see what visions Stella can conjure."

"I see," Emm replied.

"You've seen visions, haven't you?" asked Stella. "Are you an Enchantress?"

"No," said Emm. "I don't think so. I don't know. What's an Enchantress?"

"I really must insist," Lochen interrupted. "There will be time to explore all this later. We need to engage in a greater sense of urgency."

Emm looked at him in confusion.

"We need to hurry up," clarified Summer.

"But if she's an Enchantress," Stella started to say.

"Later, please," Lochen urged. "I am uncomfortable staying in this place any longer than is absolutely necessary. The more we delay, the more difficult it will be to ensure our return to the correct time."

He motioned to the wall and added, "Stella. Please."

She nodded her agreement and moved to the center of the room. Her foot struck the top of the rod that had been driven there and to which the chain that had secured Emm for fifteen years was attached. Lochen thrust out his right hand, made a fist, and yanked the air. The rod slid out of the stone and flew across the room, the chain dragging after.

"I wish I had met you fifteen years ago," muttered Emm in amazement.

Stella stood over the spot where the stake had been and then grasped the pendant in her hand and closed her eyes. Within seconds, images began to flash up on the walls. Many were the same ones Emm had seen, although hers came unbidden.

"You can make them appear on your own?" she asked. "Mine just came whenever they wanted."

Stella turned to look at Emm, an expression of concern on her face. She turned to Lochen to say something, but he had moved closer to the wall to study the images. Emm turned slowly, looking at the shapes and scenes that filled the circle. She saw the masses of Rebbercands and equal numbers of Phookas. She also saw gargoyles and hobgoblins. It wasn't clear to her whose side they were on.

She saw a single, large Rebbercand holding an enormous axe in his hand and heard Sean gasp. She realized that he must have had an encounter with this one at some time. She was about to ask when she was distracted by the reaction the others had when the image of Walipreen appeared.

"What does all this mean?" asked Liam when images of the Kelpies flashed and quickly disappeared.

"These appear to be depictions of events," said Lochen.

"What kind of events?" asked Summer.

"I'm not sure," he said. "But they're not really relevant right now. What we're looking for is a specific location."

"The Boravak?" asked Solveig. "We already know where that is. Why do we need to see an image of it?"

"We know where it is now," Lochen said. "We need to know where it is fifteen years ago. Our first priority is to get Aitch back to his own time."

"What about us?" moaned Quinn. "I don't want to be here in the wrong time."

"As long as we all stay together," Lochen tried to explain, "when we are is less important. We can remedy that later. The key is where we are."

"Oh, yeah," said Sean. "That's as clear as mud."

"I don't understand," said Emm. "You just said you needed to know where this place is as well as when it is, so how can the 'when' be less important than the 'where?'"

"You're giving me a headache," complained Quinn.

"Don't try to make sense of it," Solveig told Emm. "None of this makes any sense."

"Aha!" shouted Lochen. "I think I've found it."

"Great," said Stella. "Now what?"

"I'll take us there immediately," he said.

"Hold on," said Natalie. "You said you THOUGHT you found it. Shouldn't you be a little more certain?"

"I am 80% confident that it's the right location and the right time," Lochen announced.

"Eighty percent?" questioned Solveig.

"Perhaps 78," he replied. "But that's within a standard deviation."

"And you trust this guy?" Emm asked.

Lochen turned to look at her and then to Aitch.

"I'm afraid you will have to leave," he told her.

"Leave?" she asked. "Where am I supposed to go?"

"She's not going anywhere," argued Aitch.

"It will all work out fine," said Lochen. "You must trust me on this. Please. Emm, you only need to go to the top of the stairs. And you must do it now. This image won't last much longer."

Sean made a move to escort Emm to the stairs, but Aitch blocked his way. He looked at Lochen and the others and realized he had no choice but to trust them. He turned and took Emm by the arm.

"I'll do it," he said. "Emm, I know this is hard, but I think we have to do what he says."

"Quickly, Aitch," advised Lochen. "And then come back, please."

She reluctantly let him lead her to the stairs and up to the main floor. As he backed down the stairs, he held her hand until their arms were outstretched and their fingers slid free of one another. He kept her in his sight until he reached the bottom and disappeared into the darkness.

When Lochen saw that he had rejoined them and that Emm was on the level above, he turned back to the wall and moved up to the image of the cave in which he and Stella had made a final stand against the Kelpies.

The image was the same as they had seen it upon their return from the other side. The only difference was that there was no sign of the clothes Aitch had left behind when he came through as a wisp of smoke. All at once, his image appeared.

"That's me," he exclaimed.

"Precisely," said Lochen. "Fifteen years ago at the moment before you crossed from one side of the Boravak to the other."

Emm stood anxiously at the top of the stairs. She looked at the room that she had lived under for fifteen years, but had never seen. She could catch glimpses of the dead and decayed village through the doorway. She could feel the evil that permeated this place.

She waited for something to happen, thinking about the last fifteen years, about how Aitch had come to find her. She decided that she would not be separated from him again. Not now; not this way. She ignored Lochen's request and tentatively moved down the first three steps. She stopped, gathering her courage.

"I spent fifteen years in that hole," she said to herself. "I can't believe I don't want to leave it now."

She looked up at the floor of the room above and the thought of being left alone again, especially after having just been found, was more than she could bear. A wave of fear washed over her and she ran down the remaining steps.

Lochen focused on the image of Aitch that was projected on the wall and placed his left hand on the spot where the tiny hole had been; the hole created by the single strand of hair that had been captured when Quinn was finally pulled free; the hole that Aitch, once transformed into nothing more than smoke, had squeezed through to reach the other side of the Boravak. He covered the spot with his left hand, murmured an incantation and then struck the wall with his right hand.

As soon as Emm reached the bottom of the steps, she saw Aitch's image on the wall not far from the bottom of the staircase. She heard him identify himself. She heard the stranger in the robes confirm that it was him, but that the image was fifteen years ago and just before he crossed the Boravak.

"Aitch," she gasped.

In the instant she said his name, in the instant Lochen struck the wall with his right hand, in the instant Lochen turned – distracted by the sound of Emm's voice – the room exploded. For several seconds they were all surrounded by a blinding light. They felt as if they were suspended in midair. As the light faded, their surroundings whirled around them furiously.

It was as if they were in the center of a tornado. People and object spun around them; any sounds muffled by the roaring wind. By the time they realized what had happened, they found themselves scattered across a field near the edge of a forest in the late afternoon.

"What happened?" several of them called out.

"Is everyone all right?" shouted Lochen.

They got to their feet, slightly dizzy, and ran towards each other.

"Where's Summer?" Stella shouted.

"I'm here," she replied, crawling out from under Liam.

They regrouped around Lochen, who was looking at the surrounding hills, his brow furrowed in thought.

"This isn't right," he said. "This isn't where we're supposed to be. I don't understand."

He turned to look at the others and to make sure that everyone was present and safe. That was when he noticed Emm.

"You're not supposed to be here," he said. "That's what threw things off. That's why we're not where we should be."

"I wasn't about to leave Aitch," she said defiantly. "Not after so long. Besides, what difference does it make? So what if we're not in that horrible place anymore?"

"Being away from the village is not the problem," he said. "The problem is that we're in the wrong time. We've gone back too far."

"How far is too far?" asked Aitch.

"We've gone back almost fifteen hundred years," he answered. "We're in the middle of the Great War."

Chapter thirteen

ochen's words seemed unreal to all of them. They looked around and saw nothing familiar. They weren't sure where they were, seeing no signs of the village of the Thumpers. There was also no sign of a war of any kind.

"I'm sorry; I'm so sorry," wailed Emm. "I just couldn't stay behind."

"It's all right," Aitch told her. "I'm sure we can figure something out."

"Liam, can you tell where we are?" asked Quinn.

He looked around, but before he could get his bearings, they all heard loud crashing noises coming from the forest. None of them could see anything, but the sound was definitely coming in their direction, and it didn't sound friendly.

"I think we should find some place to hide," Solveig shouted.

"Great idea," agreed Sean. "But where?"

"I think I know this place," shouted Aitch. "Follow me." He started running towards the forest.

"Wait," shouted Natalie. "Aren't you running towards the noise? Shouldn't we be going the other way?"

"Yes," he shouted back. "And no."

"Wonderful," grumbled Solveig. "He answers questions just like Lochen."

They had no choice but to follow them. Where they were was far too exposed. As they came over a low hill, they could see a narrow river that bordered the forest. Aitch jumped into the river and ran through the water.

"Wouldn't it be faster to run on the ground?" asked Summer as she flew over their heads.

"Yes," Aitch answered, "but I wouldn't find what I'm looking for."

"I hope you recall that we are in a time fifteen hundred years before you were born," called Lochen as he hiked his robe up to allow him to run faster. "Whatever you're looking for may not yet have been created."

"You might be right," Aitch answered. "But I hope not."

The river cut deeper into the land and the current quickened. Suddenly, it ended in a steep waterfall, dropping into a small lagoon. Aitch jumped out as far as he could and in midair transformed into a large swan. He spread his wings and soared out over the lagoon as the others behind him were unable to stop in time and shot out over the edge of the falls and into the water below.

"I don't think they're going to be happy with you," Summer said as she fluttered up beside Aitch.

"They'll get over it," he said.

Once he saw that they had all landed in the water, he dove downward and landed on the surface, quickly transforming back into himself.

"I will make you pay for this," grumbled Sean.

"Why?" Aitch asked. "Are you afraid of heights?"

"No," sputtered Sean. "It's water. I hate water."

"You'll get over it," laughed Summer.

"Follow me," Aitch called as he swam back towards the falls.

He swam to the right of the cascading water and then disappeared under the spray. Summer flew around the side and could see him come up onto a ledge that opened to a small cove hidden behind the falls. She pointed the way to the others, and soon they were huddled together, soaked but safe.

The sounds of the falls blocked out the sound of whatever was emerging from the forest, but the flashes of explosions broke through. There was no doubt that some kind of massive conflict was taking place not far from where they were hiding.

"This is your history, Aitch," said Natalie. "Not ours. We have no idea what's going on. Do you?"

"Uh, yeah. Sure," he muttered. "The Great War. It's the Great War. You know. Between those Kelpie guys."

"Oh," groaned Emm in frustration. "I knew you never paid attention."

"I did, too," he shot back. "I just don't remember any of that stuff."

"We're not sure what caused the Great War to start," explained Emm. "But it raged for centuries."

"I think we can make an educated guess at the spark that ignited it," said Lochen. "Perhaps you can fill us in on how it evolved."

"I'm sure you can," Emm replied, glancing over at the pendant around Stella's neck. "Once they discovered that they had been trapped inside the Boravak, and that the only other people in here besides them were Rebbercands, gargoyles and hobgoblins, they started blaming each other for everything that had gone wrong."

"Wait," said Sean. "We knew that our people had been transported out, but where did you come from and is there anybody else on this side?"

"We don't really know who was here before the Great Wars," answered Emm. "We've seen ancient artifacts that tell us there were several different civilizations, but nothing to tell us what happened to them."

"I know," said Aitch, excited that he knew something that Emm didn't.

"I do, too," she shot back at him, bursting his bubble. "I spent some time with the Alchemist, too. And I paid attention!"

She looked smugly at her brother, who folded his arms and frowned.

"As I was saying," she continued. "Very few people know who or what lived here before the Great Wars. The Phynnodderees, though, are descendants of a small group of people that you know as the sentinels."

"I thought they all...you know..." sputtered Sean. "Uh, crumbled and...disappeared?"

"Only the ones whose mission was completed," explained Emm. "There were several others that were never called on. It was these that survived and flourished. They are our ancestors. And because they posed no apparent threat to the Kelpies, they were ignored and left alone as the war between them carried on."

"What happened to the other two?" asked Liam. "The ones who weren't Kelpies – Tebaga and Ena Ray?"

"They were smart enough not to pick sides," said Emm. "They let the Kelpies eliminate each other one by one. It seems to have started with Akmen Milzu – the Mountain Kelpie. She wanted to remain at the source of the Boravak and rule those lands; but Pantano Izaki objected."

"I thought he was dead," interrupted Solveig. "I stabbed him with the dragon's tooth. He disappeared."

"He only went into a sort of suspended hibernation," said Aitch. "Evil never dies. He came back, and so did the others that had fallen."

"And when he came back," Emm continued, "he wanted to rule the Swamp again. That's when things started to get ugly. Akmen Milzu was supported by Neraka Ferr and Rovek. Pantano Izaki was supported by Angin Topan, Scirios and Saldeti."

"What about that thing from the ocean?" asked Natalie.

"Ollos Foscos," said Emm. "She wanted nothing to do with any of them, but she was considered a potential threat by some of the others, so she was lured from the sea, trapped and defeated."

"I thought Aitch said that evil never died," said Quinn.

"It doesn't," answered Emm. "But it can be contained. That's what happened to her. Her powers were reduced and contained and she went back to the ocean. Over time, Rovek turned on his two allies and defeated them with the help of the other four. Then Angin Topan tried to assert her authority and was quickly silenced. After that, Rovek joined forces with Scirios against Pantano Izaki and Saldeti. That was the state of things about fifteen hundred years ago...or, I guess that would be now."

"They really switched things around, didn't they?" commented Solveig.

"And the other two – Tebaga and Ena Ray – are still around, just watching?" asked Stella.

"Yes," said Aitch. "When it was all over, they were the only two survivors. Tebaga, who was a Rebbercand, became the leader of that people, and the hobgoblins went with Ena Ray. But some of the Rebbercands weren't happy with Tebaga and moved north to be under Ena Ray. They intermingled with the hobgoblins and that's where the Phookas came from."

"You mean they are all mixed together?" Summer asked, incredulously.

"Yes," said Aitch. "Weird, isn't it?"

"If I understand your estimate of history," Lochen tried to summarize, "then we are in the midst of a civil war, with Rovek and Scirios – southern Kelpies, if I recall correctly – engaged in battle with Pantano Izaki and Saldeti, with Tebaga and Ena Ray hovering on the side lines. Is that correct?"

"That about sums it up," said Aitch.

"Then there is no place that is really safe for us, is there?" asked Quinn.

"It sure doesn't look like there is," said Stella.

"This is worse than I thought," said Lochen.

"How is this different than before?" asked Solveig. "We had to deal with all of them and that maniac, B'nair as well."

"True," Lochen acknowledged.

"But we had help from the Alchemist," said Summer.

"And the sentinels," said Natalie. "Don't forget them."

"We still have the sentinels," exclaimed Sean. "This is fifteen hundred years ago, remember? The ones that didn't help us before are still here. They can help."

"Perhaps," said Lochen. "But if they are also the ancestors of Aitch and Emm."

"Then that would be all the more reason for them to help us," said Aitch.

"No," Lochen cut him off. "It wouldn't. We can't put any one of them in harm's way."

"Why not?" asked Liam. "I mean, I don't want anyone to get hurt, but don't you think they'd want to help?"

"I'm sure they would," said Lochen. "But that presents a dilemma, not so much for us..."

"But for them," continued Stella. "If something happened to one of them as a result of helping us, which wasn't a part of their history, it could alter the future."

"Exactly," said Lochen.

"So what?" asked Sean. "Don't you think it would be neat to know your great, great, great, great, great..."

"We get it," interrupted Quinn. "Finish the sentence."

"Grandfather," Sean concluded. "Or grandmother helped you out?"

"And if that ancestor was killed in doing so," added Lochen, "the end result could quite possibly be that Aitch and Emm never are born."

"Oh," said Sean. "Hadn't thought about that."

"There may be other complications as well," added Lochen, "that none of us have thought about or could even imagine. It is imperative that we get this sorted out. Somehow we have to get Emm back to her own time independent of the rest of us getting back to our own time."

"What do we need to do?" asked Aitch.

"The first step will be to find another structure that can suitably serve as a Sanctorum," answered Lochen. "Any suggestions?"

"How can we come up with suggestions if we don't even know where we are?" asked Sean.

"We know we're west of the village of the Thumpers," said Natalie. "That's a start."

"Wasn't there a forest between that village and the ocean?" asked Solveig.

"Yes," said Liam. "The one where we crashed the Wedgamaroon and where you got separated."

"Wedgamaroon?" asked Aitch. "What's a Wedgamaroon?"

"You don't want to know," said Quinn. "It was pretty scary."

"It got us where we needed to go," said Liam, defensively. "Sort of."

"Aitch," Stella said, "how far are we from the ocean?"

"It's on the other side of this forest," he said. "But it's not exactly close. These woods are huge."

"What do you have in mind, Solveig?" Lochen asked.

"The cottage of the sentinel that I ran into," she started.

"The one who turned you blue?" Sean pointed out.

"Blue?" asked Aitch.

"Yes, blue," said Solveig. "That one. Her cottage was circular. Couldn't that serve as a Sanctorum?"

"It should work just fine," said Stella. "But finding that one cottage in a forest that size would be nearly impossible."

"I could find it," said Liam.

"Even with the changes that have taken place since we were last here?" asked Natalie.

"I don't see why not," he answered.

"Then we should get going," said Stella.

"Wait," said Emm. "You plan on hiking through that forest for who knows how long in the middle of a war? You can't be serious."

"She's right," said Liam. "I can go by myself."

"And do what when you get there?" asked Stella. "No. I need to be the one to go."

"I'm going, too," said Aitch.

"Me, too," added several of the others.

"No," said Lochen. "Emm raises a good point. It would be imprudent for the ten of us to attempt to sneak through these woods in the midst of a battle and expect to remain unseen or unheard. The Kelpies have tremendous powers and while we have dealt with them before, we cannot assume we will be as fortunate in our endeavors this time."

"But we can't just do nothing," said Summer. "Can you use this place?" she asked Stella.

"No," she said. "The open end presents a problem and that's made worse by the falls. There's something about water that distorts everything."

"Emm. What about you?" asked Aitch. "You said you had visions."

"Yes," she said. "But I can't conjure them up. They come by themselves."

"Her skills haven't been developed, yet," said Stella.

"What skills?" she asked.

"You're an enchantress," Stella told her. "You need to be taught how to control and command those visions."

"I'm a what?" asked Emm, stunned by this revelation.

"You can explain more later," said Lochen. "We must focus on the issue immediately before us. I suggest that Liam venture forth and locate the cottage. Summer, if you are up to the task, you can accompany him. Once he's found it, you can return and lead us to it by the safest route."

"Awww, please don't say we're splitting up again," moaned Quinn. "That didn't work out so well the last time."

"We're not splitting up," said Liam. "Summer and I are just going first to find the safest route."

"I'm going, too," said Aitch.

"That's not necessary," said Lochen.

"He doesn't know the environment he'll be going through," argued Aitch. "He hasn't been here for more than five hundred years, remember?"

"Yes," said Lochen, "but you won't be here for fifteen hundred. How is that any more advantageous?"

"This is my history," he shot back. "And I did so pay attention," he commented to Emm. "I studied the battles. I have a better idea of where the greatest danger is. Besides, I can shape shift and go places none of the rest of you can go."

"I could use his help," said Liam. "With him and Summer keeping an eye on our surroundings, I can focus more on finding this place."

"It's settled, then," said Aitch.

Before anyone else could argue to go with them, the three slipped around the falls and climbed up the embankment, quickly disappearing out of sight. Liam led the way while Aitch shifted into a Blue Falcon to circle overhead and keep an eye out for either of the warring sides. Summer blended into the foliage and flew slightly above and behind Liam, watching his back.

Even with the two scouts, none of them saw the three Phookas that had burrowed in the ground over which he ran. Within seconds of passing over them, they surfaced. Liam's quick pace caught their immediate attention. After Aitch had circled twice, they noticed him as well. Summer, however, managed to remain invisible to them.

"Go back and see where he might have come from," their leader ordered one of them. "If you find that out, report to the masters and let them know we are following."

One of the Phookas dropped back and studied the trail to the point they first became aware of Liam. He searched the ground and was able to follow the tracks back to the falls. He tunneled down just below the surface and crawled closer until his head popped out of the embankment.

He could see figures moving behind the falls, but he couldn't see how many there were. He assumed they were Rebbercands who had either deserted or were planning some kind of sneak attack. He knew in either case he would be well rewarded for this information. He backed up through the tunnel and surfaced a safe distance away. Then he ran north to find Pantano Izaki and Saldeti.

The other two criss-crossed along the path behind Liam, keeping well hidden. They timed their moves when Aitch was at the furthest point of his circling pattern. They did not escape Summer's eye, however. She stayed as high as she could but moved slightly in front of Liam.

"We have company," she said. "Don't look around, there are two of them and they're behind us."

"Rebbercands?" he asked.

"No," she said. "It's those ugly goat-looking creeps. The same ones that were at the village of the Thumpers."

Liam kept his pace, but lowered one hand to a blade held in his belt. Summer saw his movement.

"No," she said. "Don't. We don't know anything about these creatures. They might hurt you. Let me tell Aitch. They're from his world. He'll know better how to deal with them."

She gently flapped her wings and rose higher and higher until she caught up with him. She let him know what she had seen and where the two were. He told her he'd make a wider circle and come up from behind them. He was fairly certain that the sight of an oncoming Blue Falcon would scare them off.

When he circled around, he fell back several hundred yards – far enough that they wouldn't see him coming. Then he dropped down lower and flew in between the trees. He spotted them both while he was still a ways back. It was by mere chance that one of them spotted him before he could surprise them. Instead of hiding, though, the Phooka pulled out a bow and arrow and prepared to take a shot.

"Oh, booger," said Aitch. "I hadn't thought about that."

He knew they were very accurate shots and he would not be able to avoid their arrows. He had to be something else. Blue Falcons were too tempting a target. He shifted into a hummingbird as the first arrow whizzed by him, missing him by a fraction of an inch.

"You dope," he said to himself. "They're not going to be too afraid of a hummingbird."

He hovered in midair and then darted to the left as a second arrow was dodged. Think, he berated himself. He quickly shifted into a dragon and went on the offensive. He was about to breathe fire, but then realized he didn't want to set the forest on fire. As a third arrow was heading towards him, he immediately shifted into a giant boulder.

He immediately dropped to the ground and rolled towards the Phooka that was firing at him. The arrow bounced off him and the Phooka dove into the ground. The other one, seeing what was happening, broke off chasing Liam, burrowed into the ground and tunneled off in another direction. When he was certain they were gone, he shifted back to himself and regrouped with Liam and Summer.

"Do you think they're gone for good?" Liam asked.

"Yeah," Aitch said. "They're tough fighters when they have the advantage, but otherwise they're pretty much cowards."

"Aren't you worried they'll tell somebody what they saw?" asked Summer.

"Not really," he said. "What would they say? That they were attacked by a Blue Falcon that turned into a really scary hummingbird? They'd be laughed at for the rest of their lives."

He was wrong. The two Phookas regrouped a safe distance away and commented on what had just happened. They confirmed that they were certain they had seen a shape shifter. Neither of them had ever encountered one before, but had heard about them. They considered this an important find and something that would be of interest to those they served – the two northern Kelpies currently battling with two southern Kelpies.

While they headed back to share what they had discovered, Liam, Aitch and Summer continued their search for the sentinel's cottage. In a few hours they came upon a large section of the forest that had suffered from an extensive fire. It stopped them cold.

"What happened here?" asked Summer, shocked at the devastation. "This is horrible."

They could see an area off to one side where it appeared there had once been a clearing of some sort with what had once been a circle of large and ancient trees. Liam recalled something Solveig had told them when they found her after the crash of the Wedgamaroon. She claimed to have found the elders of a village named Kalayaan. A Kelpie had cast a spell on them, changing them all into trees that awakened only once a month.

"I remember," said Summer. "We must be close now. Didn't we find her somewhere near here?"

"Yes," Liam said. "And she led us back to the cottage, but the sentinel was gone."

"Kalayaan?" asked Aitch. "I never heard of it. And you say a Kelpie changed them into trees? Why would he do that?"

"We never heard of it either," said Summer. "According to what Solveig said, these trees wake up once a month. She just happened to find them at the right time. They told her they had taken a stand against what the Kelpies were doing. As revenge, the Kelpies destroyed the village and turned the elders into trees. The village had been destroyed more than two thousand years ago."

"Two thousand years ago from now, or then?" asked Aitch.

"I don't think it really matters," said Liam. "Destroyed is destroyed. The point is, we're headed in the right direction and we're getting close."

Liam started to move further south, but Aitch couldn't help but take a closer look at the burned out trunks. Summer went with him, while Liam waited. He had seen too much of this kind of devastation when his Swamp had been poisoned. He couldn't bring himself to look more closely at the remains of a people cursed.

Aitch and Summer entered the circle. Even through the charred remains, the distorted faces, frozen in anguish, could be seen in the knots and twists of the trunks. Aitch reached out and touched one of the blackened stumps. He instantly felt a jolt and pulled his hand back.

"What happened?" asked Summer.

"I'm not sure," he said.

"Did you burn yourself?"

"No, it wasn't that."

He reached out and touched the side of the broken and burned trunk once more. This time, he kept his hand in place. After a few seconds, he moved to the next one. He turned to Summer with a look of astonishment on his face.

"What?" she asked.

"It's like I know what they felt," he said.

"You mean they're talking to you?"

"No. It's just a feeling. It's like...relief. That's the only way I can describe it."

He moved from one tree to the next, confirming the feelings as he went. When he had completed the entire circle, he sat down on the ground.

"What is it?" asked Liam.

He had watched as Aitch moved from tree to tree and came over to see what was happening.

"Solveig was right," he said. "These trees held the being...that's not the right word...the essence, I suppose, of the village elders. They had been held prisoners for centuries, not allowed to join the rest of their village. Until the same Kelpie set this whole area on fire."

"Rovek," said Liam.

"Yes," said Aitch. "That's right. Rovek. He thought he was punishing them even more, but he was wrong. The fire killed the trees and set the spirits of the elders free. That's the feeling I got when I touched the trunks. They felt free."

They stayed silent for a few minutes, sharing the sensations that Aitch had drawn from the burnt remains.

"We need to get going," said Liam.

"Yeah," Aitch acknowledged.

He got to his feet, immediately shifted into a Blue Falcon again and resumed his circling high above Liam, while Summer once more blended into the background and took her position. They continued on for a few more hours when Liam suddenly stopped. Summer fluttered down near his shoulder.

"What is it?" she asked. "More Phookas?"

"No," he said. "This is the place."

"Here?" Summer asked.

She looked around. Nothing looked familiar to her. The tree under which the sentinel's cottage stood was little more than a charred pinnacle, black and gray, pointing crookedly to the sky. The area around where the opening had been was covered with debris.

"Yes," said Liam. "Here. We need to clear this stuff away."

He and Aitch pushed the fallen branches, burnt shrubs and leaves off to one side. At the base of the tree an opening appeared.

"You're right," exclaimed Summer. "I remember. But it looks different."

"We were here five hundred years ago," Liam reminded her. "We're lucky to have found it."

They carefully climbed down into the hole. Summer fluttered behind the other two as they reached out to keep their balance. There were no steps. The ground was still solid, though and slanted downward. They passage of years had left bits of rubble along the way, and small clods of dirt rolled downward into the darkness.

Soon they were below the base of the tree. The cottage was larger than Aitch had expected. He could see that many of the larger roots had been cut off or broken away. Others twisted into one another forming a type of canopy roof. The floor was packed earth and a few woven reeds that had once served as rugs were covered with a thin layer of dust and dirt, and were rotted in places.

The only light came in through the opening, so Liam and Aitch moved to the sides as much as they could in order to keep from blocking it. As their eyes adjusted to the dimness, they could see that the place resembled a circular structure similar to Emm's cell. In one part they saw the remains of what Liam recalled was the fireplace.

Stones were stacked up and through the roof, making a chimney, but the hearth had long since crumbled. On the back side of the cove were a series of shelves. Most of them were the same as they had been so long ago, but others seemed to have eroded. Liam assumed that animals had discovered this place and had picked at the reeds, vines and twigs from which the shelves had been made.

There was still an aura of mysticism about the place. He was certain it was enough to keep these same animals from making this their home. He found a candle on one of the shelves and some flint and dried grass near the defunct fire place. He struck the flint until a spark caught in the grass and he put the flame to the candle.

With the additional light, they looked at the rest of the hut. There were still a few canisters on the shelves – pushed to the back and covered with dust. They included discarded bottles, broken jars, wooden bowls and boxes. Liam ran his finger across one of them and blew away the dust. He knew better than to open any of them.

To the right of the shelves was a small table. The top was covered with dust, but Liam could tell that it was an old sign from a pub or an inn. There were also two sections of tree trunks that appeared to have served as stools.

Finally, pushed up against the wall next to the table was a pile of rubble. Aitch bent down and poked his finger at it, expecting that some small animal might be hidden underneath. Nothing moved. He cleared away the dirt and discovered some bedding material that was so old and so rotten that it crumbled in his hands.

Aside from all this, there was nothing else to be found. There was no sign that anyone or anything had lived here for centuries. Liam studied the walls. They were packed earth, but relatively smooth, and the cave itself was circular – sort of.

"Do you think this will be good enough?" he asked Summer.

"What if it's not?" she asked back.

"I suppose we look for something else, but I can't think of where," he said.

"She's seen this place," said Summer. "I have to believe that if she thought her visions wouldn't work here, she would have said something before we left, don't you?"

"I suppose," he said.

"So is this it or do we have to look someplace else?" asked Aitch.

"This is it," Liam decided. "She'll have to make it work."

"Good," said Aitch. "What happens now? Do we all go back and get her?"

"No," said Liam. "It was risky enough for the three of us to make it through that forest. And it'll be even riskier for the rest of them to get here. We don't need to make matters more difficult by having all of us return to get them."

"I'll go," said Summer. "I can disappear in the trees – even the burnt ones – and bring them back."

"Are you sure you'll find this place on your own?" Liam asked.

"Of course," she assured him. "I was paying attention," she added, smirking at Aitch.

"Funny," he replied. "While you're gone, we can move some of the branches back over the opening just in case some prying eyes come around and decide to see what's down here."

"Good idea," said Liam.

With that Summer took off and within seconds disappeared out of sight. Liam and Aitch moved a few of the bigger pieces into place. Liam stayed on the inside and Aitch made sure they safely covered the opening. Once they were done, he had told Liam, he'd shift into smoke and seep through the opening.

"What are you doing up there?" Liam called to him when Aitch had moved things around for the third time.

"Just making a few adjustments," he replied. "It's not quite right."

"It doesn't have to be perfect," Liam reminded him.

"I KNOW!" snapped Aitch. "But I'd like it to be better than just good enough, if you don't mind. Besides, if someone finds it, we're kind of trapped in there."

"All right, all right. Whatever!"

Summer flew as fast as her wings would carry her, darting over the forest, past the clearing where the elders had once been imprisoned and beyond the charred remains of the fire. All along the way, she scanned the horizon in every direction, on the lookout for Rebbercands or Phookas.

She could hear random explosions and could see distant flashes of light, but nothing seemed to be nearby. She was thankful for that. She made it back to the falls in less than half the time it took the three of them to find the old sentinel's cottage.

She made a wide circle to make sure no one was watching. When she was satisfied it was safe, she dropped down and slipped behind the falls and into the cave. She immediately stopped, staring in stunned surprise. Everyone was gone.

Chapter fourteen

The Phooka that was sent back to report on what he saw arrived at the location where Pantano Izaki and Saldeti were planning their next attack on the other two Kelpies in their battle for dominance. Since the Phooka didn't understand the connection or the importance of the individuals he had seen, his Kelpie masters were barely interested.

"So what?" demanded Pantano Izaki. "You saw some strangers hiding in a cave behind a water fall while one of their lot ran off in another direction. They were probably deserters."

"Or they could be spies," interjected Saldeti, adding a note of caution.

"And what are they spying on?" snapped the Swamp Kelpie a bit too derisively. "The inside of a cave? If they were true spies wouldn't they be trying to infiltrate our forces?"

"Perhaps the one that was on his own was a scout," Saldeti suggested.

"But he was going the wrong way," argued Pantano. "That is if this Phooka's recollection is to be trusted."

"It is," sputtered the Phooka. "My partners followed the runner to see where he was going. I was instructed to return and report to you."

"And you've done that," said Pantano Izaki dismissively. "Now you can go. We have more important matters to attend to."

"Wait, my friend," Saldeti urged. "Don't be too hasty to send him away. Our former brethren can be very devious. Perhaps they have sent a team of spies to pose as deserters, hoping we may take them prisoner."

"But we're not taking them prisoner," Pantano growled. "We're not doing anything about them."

"Perhaps we should," Saldeti continued. He turned to the Phooka and added, "Where exactly is this waterfall?"

The Phooka described the location. It was not far away. He could easily show them where.

"Go if you like," Pantano told Saldeti. "It will be a waste of time."

Saldeti considered his options, but in the end he wasn't inclined to separate himself from the other Kelpie. He didn't completely trust him and was certain that, should they be successful in defeating the other two, he would find himself in conflict with his current partner. He gave in and told the Phooka to return to his duties. As the Phooka made ready to leave, two more appeared, breathless.

"Masters," they gasped. "We have information for you."

"About the deserters in the cave?" Pantano asked. "We already know."

"What deserters?" they asked.

The first Phooka explained that after they had parted, he followed the trail down which Liam had only recently come. He told them that he discovered the hiding place and could see others behind the falls.

"We followed the one that was running in the other direction," the second Phookas explained.

"Where did he go?" Pantano asked.

"We don't know," they said.

"Then what information do you have?" Pantano exploded. "Nothing! I should turn you into sand."

He raised his arm, about to cast a spell. The Phookas cowered with their hands raised in a futile attempt to protect themselves. Before the Kelpie could act, one of the Phookas spoke.

"There was a shape shifter," he cried. "We saw a shape shifter."

Pantano slowly lowered his hand and turned towards Saldeti. The Kelpies looked at each other in silence for several seconds. The Phookas realized they had been given a reprieve.

"Are you sure," Saldeti asked.

"Yes, master," the Phooka replied. "It was a Blue Falcon. It had been high in the sky and we hadn't noticed it when suddenly it swooped down on us from behind."

"You were startled by a Blue Falcon in attack mode? That's all?" Pantano sneered. "That's hardly evidence of a shape shifter."

"But we shot an arrow at it and it changed into a hummingbird," the Phooka continued.

"And then into a dragon," the other one added. "And when we shot at the dragon, it changed into a giant boulder."

The story was too unreal to be unreal, Pantano Izaki considered. The Phookas lacked the imagination to create such a story.

"Wait outside," he directed them.

When he and Saldeti were alone, he pulled his partner close and spoke in a low voice, even though there was no one else around to hear.

"If what they told us is true," he said, "this must be the work of the Alchemist."

"Do you think he's returned?" Saldeti asked.

"I was never certain he had ever left," replied Pantano.

"But then why wait so long to show himself? Could this be something conjured by Rovek or Scirios?"

"No," said the Swamp Kelpie. "Only Angin Topan had that ability and even so it was limited. This creature the Phookas encountered changed substance. It went from animal to rock. No one has the ability to do that. It was either an illusion or the work of someone whose powers far exceed our own."

"Could it have been an illusion, then?" Saldeti asked.

"I don't know," Pantano answered. "But now those hiding in the cave have suddenly become of more interest, don't you think?"

"I agree," Saldeti said.

They called the Phookas back and told them to assemble a team of twenty and to be ready to leave in ten minutes. The Phookas exited without a word and gathered the directed numbers and awaited the Kelpies.

The group departed and headed back to the falls. When they arrived, they moved to the base along the river bank and the Phookas were divided – half on one side and half on the other. The Kelpies had discussed what they planned to do and decided that they didn't need to capture anyone.

If those hidden were deserters or spies, they served no purpose to either Pantano Izaki or Saldeti. If, on the other hand, they were minions of the Alchemist, their destruction was even more necessary. When the two groups of Phookas were ready, Pantano gave the signal for them to fire a volley of arrows through the falls and into the cave.

- - - - - - - - - - - - - - - - - *** - - - - - - - - - - - - - - - - -

Shortly after Liam, Summer and Aitch left, Lochen asked Stella if she could conjure her images on the cave walls. She told him that the side open to the water made that impossible. He asked Emm about her visions and she again told him that they came unbidden. She had no control over them.

"What do you have in mind when Stella is able to generate her visions?" Solveig asked Lochen.

"First, we must all get back to the time in which we met Emm," he explained. "Then we must try to get back to the time when Aitch first left the Boravak – this time, leaving Emm behind."

"Sorry," she said for the hundredth time.

"You don't have to apologize," said Quinn. "It's understandable that you wouldn't want to be left behind where you had been held prisoner for fifteen years."

"That wouldn't have happened," Lochen commented.

"Of course it would," said Natalie.

"No," insisted Lochen. "We would have returned to Aitch's time and either rescued her or even prevented the kidnapping in the first place."

"But she didn't know that," piped up Sean.

"I assumed she could deduce that for herself," Lochen replied.

"It doesn't matter now," said Stella. "What's done is done. We need to find a way to fix things – for everyone."

"Agreed," said Lochen. "In the mean time we might as well all get some rest. There's no telling when we'll have the opportunity again. Find a way to get comfortable and try to get some sleep."

"It's the middle of the day," said Sean. "I can't sleep when it's light out."

"Me, neither," added Quinn.

"I can certainly fix that," said Lochen.

"NO!" they both shouted. "No spells. We'll fake it if we can't fall asleep."

They all curled up on the ground while Lochen sat at the front edge, close to the falling water where he could meditate. After a few minutes, he could see that the others were too wound up to sleep, so he surreptitiously wiggled his fingers and cast a very gentle sleeping spell on them. That was when he heard the arrival of the Phookas.

He reached over and tapped Sean's forehead, breaking the spell. Sean was instantly awake and discovered Lochen bending over him with one hand across Sean's mouth. With the other he was motioning for quiet. Sean nodded his understanding. He quietly sat up and readied his slingshot. Lochen motioned for him to wait.

"I believe we have been discovered," he whispered in Sean's ear.

"Was I asleep?" Sean asked. "Did you make that happen?"

"Yes and yes," Lochen replied. "You all needed some rest. Now you need to be awake."

"What about the others?"

"Wake them one at a time," Lochen said. "And be as careful and as quiet as you can."

Before Sean could start, a volley of arrows pierced the waterfalls and clattered against the walls of the cave. Because they had all been asleep on the ground, the arrows were too high and struck nothing. Before the next volley could be fired, Lochen waved his arm and the falls, although still appearing as water, became as hard as iron. The arrows bounced off, failing to penetrate.

The sudden change in the falls was immediately evident to the attackers. The Kelpies knew instantly that those who were inside were not mere deserters or spies. Saldeti cast a spell and the falls turned to ice, the intense cold crept into the rock of the cave and the air inside burned with frost.

Lochen snapped his fingers and the sleeping spell disappeared immediately. The others bolted up, aware of the imminent danger. Stella rushed to stand next to Lochen.

"What is it?" she asked.

"I had thought it was only a party of Phookas conducting some level of reconnaissance," he replied. "I appeared to have been in error. I believe they are accompanied by at least one of our former adversaries."

"Saldeti," she said, rubbing her arms to try to stay warm. "We need to counteract this spell quickly, or we'll all freeze."

Lochen stretched out his arms, and then brought his hands together, creating a ball of light between them. The light floated from his hands when he opened them and a wave of heat spread out in the small enclosure.

On the outside, the Kelpies could see the ball of light and heat through the frozen wall of water. Saldeti waved his hand again and the spell Lochen had cast on the falls shattered.

"Fire again," he ordered the Phookas.

Another volley of arrows shot through the water. Stella reacted quickly and threw her hand in the air, changing the arrows into bubbles that floated to the ceiling of the cave and popped as they contacted the rock. More arrows came and were converted to bubbles; and still more came. Stella was struggling to keep up.

Pantano Izaki pressed his hands together and raised them straight out in front of him. Then he parted them, and as he did so, the falls separated like a curtain.

"There are your targets," he called to the Phookas. "See if you can hit them this time."

Seeing they were now exposed, Natalie thrust her arm forward and created a bubble, sealing the cave entrance. Although they could still be seen, the bubble protected them from the arrows. But it could not protect them from the spells of the Kelpies.

"It's them," shouted Saldeti once the water had parted and he could see inside the cave.

"How is that possible?" exclaimed Pantano Izaki in disbelief.

His eyes fixed first on Stella and the pendant around her neck. Then his gaze shifted to Solveig – the one who had driven the dragon's tooth into his body and sent him into nothingness.

"The pendant," he shouted. "We must capture the pendant."

Saldeti threw a blast of icy air into the cave, but Lochen deflected it. The burst was so powerful, though, that it threw him back against the cave wall and to the ground. Pantano Izaki snapped his fingers and the rock walls and ceiling slowly began to crumble. Natalie expanded the bubble to keep them safe from any cave-in, but the cave and her bubble began to fill with sand.

"We need to get out of here," shouted Quinn. "We're sitting ducks."

"I am certainly open to suggestions," replied Lochen as he struggled to his feet.

"I don't have any," Quinn shouted again.

Sean tried shooting back, but the bubble that had protected them from the incoming arrows only served to bounce the stones he was firing straight back at them.

"Stop shooting," shouted Solveig to Sean. "They're bouncing off the bubble and hitting us."

"Sorry," he shouted back. "But we can't just sit here."

"If we don't do something soon," said Natalie, "we're going to be buried alive or frozen to death."

As they were arguing, the three walls of the cave suddenly came alive with wild and disjointed images.

"I thought you couldn't project visions on three walls," Lochen said to Stella.

"It's not me," she said.

They turned and saw Emm standing in the center of the cave in a trance-like pose, her eyes rolled back in her head and her arms outstretched.

"Can you make this work?" shouted Quinn.

"I don't know," said Lochen. "I can't tell what these images mean. They're from Emm's time. They don't have any relationship to us."

"So what?" shouted Sean. "In case you hadn't noticed, I've got news for you. We're getting our butts kicked."

"I'm well aware of the dire circumstances that have surrounded us," Lochen answered, "but that's no excuse for acting in a haphazard manner."

"Would you prefer trying to breathe sand?" Sean asked.

"Good point," Lochen replied.

He struggled to wade through the sand that was now over their knees. He studied the images in the walls until he spotted something that looked vaguely familiar.

"I think I see something I recognize," he announced. "However, I have only a minimal degree of certainty of success in arriving..."

"Just do it," shouted Solveig.

"As you wish," he replied.

He located the image he had previously identified and covered the spot with his left hand, murmured an incantation and then struck the wall with his right hand. The inside of the cave exploded. For several seconds they were all surrounded by a blinding light – the same light they had seen in Emm's cell. Once more they felt as if they were suspended in midair. As the light faded, their surroundings whirled around them furiously.

It was as if they were in the center of another tornado. People and object spun around them; any sounds muffled by the roaring wind. As suddenly as it had all started, it stopped. They found themselves in a forest on the edge of the sea. There was no sign of the cave, the waterfall, the Phookas or the Kelpies.

"Where are we?" asked Quinn. "This place doesn't look the least bit familiar to me. Does it look familiar to anyone else?"

They all looked around and saw nothing to indicate where they were – or <u>when</u> they were.

"I thought you said you saw something familiar," Sean said to Lochen. "Can you give the rest of us a clue as to what that might have been?"

"I made no guarantees," replied Lochen. "In fact I was quite clear that I had only a marginal degree of confidence. I only said I <u>thought</u> I saw something I recognized."

"OK," interjected Solveig. "Enough with the disclaimers. Where are we?"

"At the risk of stating the obvious," said Lochen, "we're in a forest near the sea."

"You think?" snapped Solveig. "I figured that much out for myself."

"Wait," said Sean. "I know this place. At least I think I do."

He looked around for several seconds, and then crept towards the sea. The water was a brilliant blue. They were located near a long beach. To their left as they faced the water, off in the distance, there was a cliff wall. High on the face of the cliff, several feet from the top was a dark spot – a cave.

"Well?" asked Quinn. "Are you going to fill the rest of us in?"

"I'm not certain," Sean answered.

"Take a guess, then," suggested Natalie. "Anything is better than nothing."

"I think this is my forest," he said.

"Your forest?" asked Emm. "How can anyone own a forest?"

"No," he clarified. "I don't mean my own personal forest. I think this is the forest where my Lodge is located – was located. Whatever. But it doesn't look quite right."

"I believe you might be more accurate if you said this is the forest where your Lodge will be located," said Lochen.

"What?" asked Natalie. "I don't understand."

"I think we've gone back a bit too far," said Lochen.

"How could that happen?" demanded Solveig.

"Well, it's not an exact science," snapped Lochen. "I told you I wasn't exactly positive about what I saw in the images on that cave wall."

"What about Aitch?" Emm asked, her voice carrying an edge of panic. "Where's Aitch?"

"I'm afraid Aitch, Liam and Summer are still where we left them," Lochen told her.

"Great," said Natalie. "How do we get back to them?"

"We need to find a sanctorum," Lochen said. "Someplace where Stella can project images that are a bit more defined."

"I'm sorry," said Emm. "I couldn't control the visions."

"It's not your fault," said Stella. "It's no one's fault. If we had stayed where we were, there's no telling what would have happened to us. At least we're out of danger. We found you, Emm. We'll figure out a way back. The important thing is that we're safe and can do this the right way this time."

As she was speaking several figures had moved silently and unobserved through the thickets. They had formed an arc around the seven travelers, enclosing them between the sea and their line. Sean sensed their presence first.

"I think you might have spoken too soon," he whispered.

"What do you mean?" asked Solveig.

"I believe he's referring to the individuals who have encompassed us as we were debating our current predicament," said Lochen.

Quinn spun around, pointed at the hidden figures, and shouted, "Oh, poop. Who are those guys?"

"Well, there goes the element of surprise," muttered Sean.

Before anyone could react, one of the figures casually walked towards the shore and up to the group. He was bigger than

Quinn, dressed in black material that looked like some kind of leather, and looked disturbingly familiar.

"Greetings," he called as he got closer. "Allow me to introduce myself. My name is Lenod. I am the leader of this...ah...exploratory group. And who do I have the pleasure of speaking with?"

He was a Rebbercand. Everyone stood, staring at him with their mouths open, unsure of how to respond. There was something oddly familiar about him, but his dress and appearance were different in some way.

"We're...ah...we..." stammered Solveig. "We're from the mountains."

"The mountains?" Lenod asked as he looked around, not seeing any mountains in any direction. He ignored the fact that she hadn't really answered his question. "You must be far from home, then."

"Yes," said Stella. "We're from the mountains, and yes, we're far from home. We've been...traveling."

"Interesting," said Lenod. "You are ALL from the mountains?"

He looked closely at Quinn, examining his blond hair and his clothing; and then he looked at Emm – tiny and green. Then he turned to Sean and then back to Stella.

"Yes," she said. "That's correct. We're all from the mountains."

"And which mountains would that be?" he asked.

"The...those...far away mountains," Stella tried to explain.

"The mountains far to the north of here," inserted Sean, pointing to his left.

"I believe the mountains are in the other direction," said Lenod.

"Oh, yes," said Sean, motioning to his right. "The other mountains. In the other direction. Those mountains."

Being this close to a Rebbercand made Sean's skin crawl. None of them felt comfortable. None of them had anything but a history of bad experiences with Rebbercands. They all knew how treacherous they could be. They knew that the smooth talking and gentle manner of Lenod was only a façade.

Lochen inched closer to Stella and tried to get her attention without Lenod noticing. He knew this Rebbercand was not alone; that there were several others hidden from view in the woods — probably in a circle around them, pinning them between a well-armed force and the sea. He realized they had been foolish to be taken in by the apparent tranquility of their surroundings.

He nudged Stella, gently trying to push her behind Quinn to block Lenod's view of them.

"What are you doing?" she muttered to him. "I can't see."

"I'm trying to block his view of us so I can discuss our options without being observed," he mumbled out of the side of his mouth.

"And why would you want me not to observe you?" Lenod asked.

"Uh...oh...you see...I...ah...no reason," stammered Lochen. "I just didn't want to interrupt your conversation with my colleague."

"How kind of you," said Lenod.

His voice oozed with false sincerity. He bent forward from the waist, his head looming over Lochen as he spoke. The smile on his face belying the sinister glint in his eyes. Lochen wanted to cast a spell on him to turn him to stone, but knew that those hidden in the woods would immediately pounce on them. He knew they were there, but he couldn't determine their exact location or their number. He decided on a different approach.

"Not at all," he said in response to Lenod's comment.

He took a step towards the Rebbercand and reached out, taking Lenod's large hand in his own and shaking it vigorously.

"I must apologize," Lochen continued. "You asked us who we are, not where we are from. Your arrival took us by surprise. Please forgive our lack of manners. My name is Lochen. These are my associates."

He introduced them one by one, stepping in front of each of them as he did, momentarily blocking Lenod's view. When he stepped in front of Stella, he carefully motioned for her to hide her pendant. She gracefully tucked it under her tunic with one hand as she stepped around Lochen and grabbed Lenod's hand with the other and shook it as vigorously as Lochen had.

"I'm pleased to meet you," she said.

Lenod was taken off guard by the sudden outburst of friendly greetings. This had never happened to him and he was at a loss as to how to react. He was stunned even further by Stella's next words.

"I see you are not alone," she said, gesturing broadly to the hidden figures in the woods. "You have nothing to fear from us. Please invite your friends to join us."

Lenod realized he had been outmaneuvered. He clenched his jaw in anger, but bit back his words. He glared at Stella for a second and then grinned widely. Without turning away from her, he reached out his arm and snapped his fingers. Then he motioned for the others to come out from hiding. Still staring at Stella he slowly straightened up to his full height – more than three times her size – in an attempt to intimidate her.

As he did this, twelve other Rebbercands emerged from the woods. Lochen's assumption had been right. The Rebbercands had formed a very strategic circle around them, were well-armed and had their weapons at the ready.

"Were you expecting some kind of trouble?" asked Solveig as she studied the armaments the Rebbercands held.

"Not really," said Lenod. "We just like to be prepared for any eventuality."

Sean leaned as close to Lochen as he could without attracting attention, which was impossible. Everyone else was standing still but him and he was leaning at an awkward angle.

"Can't you...do something...like...you know...cast something...like a...you know...spell?" he asked.

Lenod looked at him, astonished that he was asking this question and assuming that he was not being seen or heard. He shifted his gaze to Lochen.

"You can cast spells?" he asked. "Are you a wizard of some kind?

Lochen bristled at the term. Wizards were a myth — a comical joke that amused children. He was a sorcerer and proud of his position. He resisted the temptation to react to the comment. He believed Lenod knew what he was saying and was trying to gain information. Lochen thought it might be more advantageous to keep this Rebbercand in the dark, at least for the time being.

He also considered Sean's comment. He had been trying to get Stella's attention in an effort to have her cast a spell to hold off the Rebbercands that had been hidden in the woods, while he cast something on Lenod. That had not worked. Now the Rebbercands were alerted and any attempt to initiate something would be met with a quick and very damaging response. He couldn't risk putting the others in that kind of danger.

"No," he answered Lenod. "I have no idea what my friend is talking about. We have been traveling for a long time. He's obviously tired and hungry and this has affected his mind."

Sean frowned at Lochen, and was about to object.

"He's really not very bright, either," added Natalie, understanding the danger they were in and what Lochen was doing. "He lives in a fantasy world, always making things up. We usually just ignore him."

Lenod seemed to be deliberating on what Lochen and Natalie had said. He wasn't sure what to believe. He turned to face Sean, studying him. He had very few encounters with Forest Creatures.

"Yes," he said, finally. "I can see what you mean. He does look rather simple-minded."

Sean opened his mouth to respond, but saw the look on Lochen's face and understood that he should keep quiet. He turned back to Lenod and grinned as widely as he could.

"We won't detain you any longer from whatever it was that you were doing," said Lochen. "We'll just be on our way, then."

"Impossible," objected Lenod. "You must allow me to take you back to our camp to give you some food and drink, and a place to rest."

"That's not necessary," said Solveig.

"Nonsense," replied Lenod. "I insist."

He said it with such force it was clear that he was not going to let them just leave.

"How can we refuse your hospitality, then?" asked Lochen. "We would be glad to join you, but only for a short while."

"Of course," said Lenod. "We won't keep you very long."

His words did little to comfort anyone. He turned and led the way along the beach for a while and then into the woods. The rest of the Rebbercands fell into positions on either side of and behind the "guests" preventing any chance of escape or attack.

As they were walking, Lochen was able to whisper some words to Stella.

"I believe they mean to do us harm," he said.

"You think?" Stella whispered back, incredulously.

"We need to assess our situation once we get to their camp. We may be in a better position to act then," he continued, ignoring her sarcasm. "For now we are at a clear disadvantage. I don't think we could all escape without injury."

At the same time, Quinn had mumbled to Natalie asking if she couldn't just cast a protective bubble around all of them, or maybe over the Rebbercands. She managed to whisper to him that covering themselves would only keep them trapped, and the Rebbercands were too scattered to be covered in a single bubble. It was just too dangerous.

As they were led through the woods, Emm had been concentrating with all her strength. She had been sending messages to Lenod, planting thoughts to let them go and forget he had ever seen them. For some reason, there was no sign that her efforts were having any effect. She wondered if she had lost her power.

After several minutes, they arrived at a camp site. It looked like a military fort. A large stockade wall had been constructed. Defensive positions were established high on the inside of the wall with guards stationed in strategic locations, allowing for intersecting fields of observation in a complete circle around the camp. Trenches had been dug outside of the wall and there were signs of traps in various locations.

What were they preparing for, Solveig wondered. It looked like they were expecting a serious armed attack. She was a master at military strategy and begrudgingly had to admire the Rebbercand's defenses. She hated to admit it, but she couldn't have done better herself.

As they entered the compound through a large wooden door, all eyes were focused on them. Not one of those eyes showed any sign of welcome. Inside the compound there were several structures that had been erected. It looked more like the beginnings of a village rather than a camp.

At the far end, in the direction they appeared to be heading, stood a stone enclosure. There were small openings along the walls of the enclosure, but they were long and thin. It looked more like a prison than anything else. Before they reached the building, a small Rebbercand came running up to Lenod.

"Have you captured more prisoners, father," he exclaimed.

"Prisoners?" Lenod asked. "No, of course not. These are our guests."

"Guests?" the child asked. "What are guests?"

The little Rebbercand was identical to Lenod; only in miniature. It was clear that this child was Lenod's son. In spite of this, there seemed to be no warmth between them. The child had expressed no excitement at seeing his father, and Lenod showed no signs of affection or pride in the child. He did, however, introduce him.

"This is the boy's first excursion," he said. "He has a lot to learn."

"Your son, I take it," said Lochen.

"Yes," said Lenod. "His name is B'nair."

Chapter fifteen

Summer wondered at first if she had found the right waterfall and the right cave. She flew behind the water and zoomed around in circles inside the small cavern. There was no sign that anyone had ever been there, but she was certain she was at the right place. Where could they have gone? Why didn't they leave some kind of clue?

She flew back to where Liam and Aitch were waiting for them and reported what she found – or, more specifically, what she had NOT found.

"What do you mean they're gone?" demanded Aitch.

"I mean they're gone," she repeated. "I don't know how else to explain it. They're not there. They're absent. They've disappeared. There is no sign of them. What more do you want me to say?"

"OK, OK," he said. "I get the picture. Any idea where they could have gone?"

Summer hovered in the air, inches from his face, her hands on her hips as she glared at him.

"Sorry," he said. "Stupid question."

"We should have anticipated something like this," said Liam. "We should have agreed upon a meeting place in case we got separated or something happened."

"What kind of meeting place?" Summer asked in frustration. "Everything is different. A lot of places don't exist anymore...or not yet – whatever. This is all making my head hurt."

"There are a few places that are still around," Liam said. "Like the village of the Thumpers."

"Not exactly a place I'd like to go back to," shot Summer.

"It was only an example," he said, defensively.

"Well," she said. "You have any OTHER examples?"

They thought a minute and then at the same time looked up and at each other.

"Virkio!" they both shouted.

"Who's Virkio?" asked Aitch.

"It's not a who," said Liam. "It's a what. It's the five towers of the Alchemist."

"I thought you said he trained you," said Summer.

"He did," replied Aitch. "But it wasn't inside the Boravak."

"Still, didn't he ever mention his castle and the five towers?" she asked.

"He mentioned some place that sounded kind of creepy," Aitch replied. "Is this Virkio place creepy?"

"You could say that," said Liam.

"But he didn't call it Virkio," Aitch went on. "He called it Calabuko."

"Calabuko?" asked Summer. "What kind of name is that?"

"Wait," said Liam. "I know that word. It's from some ancient language."

"What ancient languages do YOU know?" Summer challenged. "Just when we need Lochen most, he's not here."

"I don't know any languages," said Liam. "But remember when Lochen was speaking all those strange words?"

"That doesn't help me," said Aitch. "I find most of what he says is strange."

"No," said Summer. "This was different. He was speaking a foreign language. No one knew what it was, and then, all of a sudden he stopped. What's that got to do with this?"

"After we left the Boravak," explained Liam, "he and I spent some time together. He found this old library and some documents that had been written in the language he had been speaking. He recognized a lot of the words. It was all mumbo-jumbo to me, but then he started translating it."

"What did he find out?" asked Summer.

"Not much," said Liam. "The documents were incomplete, but they told of stories that went back way before the Kelpies; maybe even before the Alchemist."

"So what about Calabuko?" asked Aitch.

"It was a dungeon, if I recall correctly," Liam told them. "And it was pretty nasty."

"That doesn't sound like something the Alchemist would use as a castle," said Summer.

"It wasn't," said Liam. "It was what he built his castle on top of."

"This is all interesting, but what's it have to do with our situation now?" asked Aitch.

"We don't know where the others are and they don't know where we are, right?" said Liam.

Summer and Liam nodded their heads.

"What do you think they'll do when they realize they can't find us?"

"They'll try to think of some place to meet," announced Summer, "just like we did!"

"Right," said Liam. "And Virkio is probably the first place that will pop into their minds."

"What if it's not?" asked Aitch. "I wouldn't think of this Virkio place. I never heard of it before. I doubt that Emm knows anything about it. Why wouldn't they come up with some other place – like that Thumper village?"

"Because they would have the same reaction we did," explained Summer. "They'd look for some place they would consider safe."

"But there have to be hundreds of places like that," argued Aitch.

"Yes," Liam agreed. "But not hundreds that would exist two thousand years ago as well as two thousand years from now. Look at this place, where the sentinel lived. It's nearly buried in decay and dust. Our homes are all gone. No. They'll think of Virkio. I'm sure of it. Besides, we can't do nothing and Virkio is as good a place as any."

Aitch was not as convinced as Liam and Summer, but he could not come up with any alternative ideas. They had considered going back to the falls to wait, but then decided that if the others had left voluntarily – which seemed highly unlikely – they would have found some way to leave a message. They decided that they had been forced to leave, which meant they had either been captured by the Kelpies or that Stella had somehow managed to generate images on the cave walls and they were someplace entirely different – and, perhaps, some time different.

"How far away is this place?" Aitch asked.

"Too far to walk," said Liam. "Can you shift into something that can fly and carry us?"

"How about a dragon?" Aitch asked. "That should scare off any potential threats."

"Not a dragon," said Summer. "That wouldn't be the best idea, considering where we're headed. How about something a little bit smaller?"

In a flash, Aitch shifted into a large, winged, green horse.

"How's this?" he asked.

"Perfect," said Liam as he climbed on Aitch's back and Summer sat on Liam's shoulder.

Aitch rose high into the air, above the trees, and then turned west, following Liam's directions towards Virkio.

------------------ *** ------------------

Sean was speechless to find himself face to face with B'nair. The fact that his nemesis – he couldn't work out if it's his future or past nemesis – was only a child didn't seem to matter. Quinn had to pull him back before he did anything rash. As Lenod guided them to the "guest quarters," B'nair kept staring at these new visitors. He had never seen strangers like this before.

"You all really look strange," he announced.

"We're from different....ah...worlds," Lochen responded. "We come from different cultures and backgrounds. That's what makes us all unique."

"You should be the same as us," B'nair declared. "The same is better."

"Wouldn't that be boring?" asked Solveig.

"No," B'nair shot back. "Things should be the same; things should never change. Change is bad; different is bad."

"But we're all different," countered Quinn. "And we've seen a lot of change lately. I know that sometimes it's scary, but it can be exciting, too."

"No," argued B'nair. "It's stupid. You are stupid. All of you."

"Now, now, B'nair," interjected Lenod. "That's not the way to talk to our guests."

"Well, they are," he continued.

"Maybe I should just shoot him in the eye now," muttered Sean, "and get it over with early."

"No," Natalie whispered back. "Don't do anything."

Emm tried to keep out of direct sight as much as possible, hiding behind Quinn to avoid B'nair's attention. If the child thought the others were different, her green coloring would only be an unwelcome target. As they walked, Lochen and Stella were making careful mental notes of their surroundings. They were still closely guarded and knew that any attempt at casting spells would be disastrous.

When they reached their destination, Lenod opened a heavy wooden door. The interior of the room was dark. Once the door was opened, he stepped aside and motioned his guests inside. Lochen poked his head in and could see that they were being placed in a dungeon. He turned back and saw Lenod and the guards blocking any escape. He raised his arms into the air.

"Thank you for your hospitality," he announced. "You have been far too gracious."

As he brought his arms down, he snapped his fingers. The guards visibly tensed, but made no aggressive move. Lenod gently nudged B'nair behind him, clearly expecting some kind of trick. Instead, Lochen ducked inside and was quickly followed by the others. Lenod pushed the door shut with a slam.

"Can I lock them in, father?" B'nair shouted, almost with glee. "Please. Let me do it."

Quinn bent down and pressed his face against the small, barred window.

"Hey, kid," he called. "If someone gives you an axe, hold on to it real tight."

"An axe?" he replied. "Father, can I have an axe? Are you going to give me an axe?"

Lenod looked curiously at Quinn and without responding to B'nair's questions, moved away from the dungeon, leaving the guard detail behind.

"Why couldn't I shoot him in the eye?" groused Sean once they were alone.

"Because you can't do anything to change the future," Natalie told him.

"But I wasn't going to change the future," argued Sean. "I was going to shoot him in the same eye he's going to lose after he

338

falls into the lava. I was just going to make sure he lost that eye sooner rather than later."

"And if you did that," Natalie explained, "you'd change the future."

"I don't see how," said Sean.

"By blinding him in one eye at this time in his life," said Solveig, "he might not become a leader and he might not ever lead that mining operation."

"So how is that a bad thing?" asked Quinn. "I'm with Sean. Poke him in the eye now."

"No," said Stella. "They're right. We can't change the future no matter how much it appeals to us. There's no telling what other changes could happen. We may never meet up; we may never defeat the Kelpies."

"We may never end up here," said Sean. "And that would be a real tragedy. We'd miss out on these wonderful accommodations. What's that smell, by the way? It's really bad."

"Oh, man," moaned Quinn. "You're right. It smells like raw sewage."

"Raw sewage?" asked Emm. "I don't understand. Do you cook sewage where you come from?"

"NO!" shouted Quinn. "Of course not. It's just...uh...I don't know. Raw sewage just sounds worse than plain ordinary sewage."

"Does it smell any better?" asked Emm.

"How would I know?" asked Quinn. "It's just a figure of speech."

"Can we talk about something else?" asked Solveig. "Like how we're going to get out of here? And why neither one of you cast a spell on those clowns?"

"It was too dangerous," said Stella. "We were too well guarded."

"I managed to sneak one in," said Lochen.

"What?" asked Solveig. "You mean you took a chance and put us at risk?"

"Yes and no," he replied.

"I don't understand," said Emm. "Which is it? How can it be both? You're very confusing to listen to."

"Get used to it," said Sean. "I still don't understand half of what he says."

"Yes, I took a chance," explained Lochen, "and no, I didn't put us at risk. Once I looked into this dungeon, I saw that it would easily serve as a sanctorum upon which Stella could project images sufficient to allow us to escape."

"So what was all that nonsense about them being so gracious?" asked Quinn. "We're you hoping for an extra serving of slop for dinner?"

"Are they serving slop again?" asked Sean. "I can hardly wait."

"You mean you really like slop?" asked Emm.

"No," Sean recoiled. "Of course I don't like slop."

340

"But you said..." Emm was confused. "I don't understand any of you."

"To answer your question," Lochen interjected. "I was not really thanking them for their hospitality – and as a footnote, I don't believe they plan on feeding us at all: slop or no slop. That was when I cast the spell."

"But nothing happened," said Natalie. "What kind of spell is that – where nothing happens?"

"I delayed the effectiveness of the spell until after we've departed," Lochen explained.

"You're turning them into snails, right?" asked Sean.

"No," Lochen clarified. "I've only erased any recollection of us from their memories."

"What good will that do?" complained Quinn. "We'll be gone. Who cares if they remember or not? I'm with Sean. You should turn them into snails. Or gnats."

"Because," Lochen answered. "As Natalie and Solveig have already indicated, we must do as little as possible to alter the future – no matter how far off that may be. Our presence here has already done that. If, for example, B'nair were to remember having met us as a child, he may decide when he encounters us as an adult to take a different course of action. That could have unexpected and severe consequences. This way, he won't recall us at all."

"That's all fine," said Emm. "But how do we find Aitch?"

"And don't forget Summer and Liam," added Solveig.

"Can you take us back to their time?" asked Quinn.

"You mean forward to their time," said Stella. "At least I think they're forward. I'm losing track."

"Yes," said Lochen. "They are in our future. Quite a bit in the distant future."

"Can we get to their location?" asked Natalie.

"That may be more difficult," said Lochen. "The Boravak seems to be in a constant state of change. Time and place are swirling in random and complicated patterns. I have been able to identify certain times or locations in Stella's images, but have yet to master the ability to transport us with any accuracy to either. The key now is to get us out of here."

"How are we going to find the others?" asked Natalie.

"We should focus on a location," said Stella. "If we can land in a place we know – some place relatively safe – then maybe we can stay there and try to focus on getting to the right time."

"That's sounds like a good idea," said Quinn. "But what place?"

"Where would any of you go if we were separated and needed to settle on a meeting place?" asked Solveig.

"Virkio," said Natalie.

"The hole in the Boravak," said Sean at the same time.

"You'd go to the hole?" asked Solveig, incredulously. "That was a cave with all those Kythauls hiding in the walls, and the roots that attacked us, and where the Kelpies nearly destroyed all of us. That's what you think of as a safe place?"

"Well, when you put it like that," said Sean. "It's just that when we came through that hole, it was sort of safe. At least in the time we came through it was."

"But what if we come through in the middle of when the Kelpies were attacking us," asked Quinn. "Hey! Would we meet ourselves? That would be weird."

"I think Virkio makes the most sense," said Lochen. "It was the Alchemist's castle.

"But it was almost impossible to get through," said Sean. "All those bridges – and don't forget that dragon."

"A dragon?" asked Emm. "There's a dragon there? That doesn't sound like a safe place to me."

"Solveig has a knack with dragons," said Lochen dismissively.

"Only when I'm blue," she countered. "I agree with Emm. I'm not sure that's the safest place, although between that and the cave, I suppose Virkio is only slightly better."

"If Lochen can get us to the roof of the fifth tower," Stella started to say.

"Where the dragon is," Solveig reminded her.

"Yes, where the dragon is," continued Stella, "we can avoid all the other towers and the traps inside them."

"Traps?" moaned Emm. "There are traps? What kind of place is this?"

"It's a place where the other three will most likely try to get to," said Lochen. "It's the place where we have the best chance of reconnecting with them, in spite of what perils may exist there."

Stella pulled the pendant from under her tunic. She then moved to the center of the room and closed her eyes, concentrating.

"Wait," said Quinn. "Have we decided that we're going to Virkio?"

"It seems to make the most sense," said Lochen.

"Shouldn't we make Solveig blue?" he asked. "Just in case?"

"Thanks," she said. "But I'll take my chances just the way I am."

"Besides," said Sean. "We've got Emm."

"She's green," said Quinn. "That's not the same thing."

Stella shook her head and glanced at Lochen. He nodded his understanding. This discussion could go on interminably. They needed to get away from where they were. Stella ignored the jabbering in the background. The pendant flashed briefly and the images sprang forth onto the walls.

Lochen stepped closer to the wall. He located the image of the five towers of Virkio. He turned back towards Stella and without waiting to be asked, she concentrated on this particular image, increasing its size on the wall until the fifth tower became clearly visible. Lochen covered the spot with his left hand, murmured an incantation and then struck the wall with his right hand. The inside of the dungeon exploded. For several seconds they were all surrounded by the same blinding light they had seen before as they experienced the same moment of weightlessness.

As the light faded, their surroundings once again whirled around them furiously. People and objects spun around them; any sounds muffled by the roaring wind. As suddenly as it had all started, it stopped.

Outside the dungeon, B'nair's attention was captured by the sudden blast of light from behind the door. He ran to look inside. By the time he got to the door, the inside of the dungeon was empty. He had a fleeting thought that his father's prisoners had disappeared. Just as suddenly, he had no recollection of any such prisoners, and he wondered why he was looking inside the small, dank room.

He turned around and saw the guards standing there. After a few seconds, they looked at each other, not recalling what they were doing. One by one, they moved away and went about their business. B'nair had a moment where he knew he had forgotten something, but couldn't bring forth the thought. Then that, too, faded away.

------------------ *** ------------------

Walipreen spent several months searching for anyone who had any idea or clue as to where Nelluc had taken the Phynnodderee child, or who had any information about her brother. Every once in a while he would come across someone who had seen the entourage during its travels, but no one could tell him of the final destination, and no one knew anything of a brother.

And then, one day, he discovered a small group of Phookas near a dried out river that bordered an ancient village. He had almost dismissed them, but something piqued his curiosity. The story was that they had been deaf and one point and then mysteriously regained their hearing. He found them in a camp on the outside of a walled town long deserted.

His unexpected arrival startled them and they fled in fear. Walipreen swiped his large hand in an arc through the air. The spell scooped up each of the fleeing Phookas in an invisible net and dragged them back to the feet of the sorcerer. They pleaded for mercy.

"Silence," he demanded. "You won't be harmed, as long as you answer my questions truthfully."

They all spoke at once, agreeing to tell him whatever he wanted to know, still pleading for mercy. He pointed to one of them and told him to speak for the others, and demanded that the rest of them remain quiet. He had thought about simply stealing their memories, but was concerned that their dull wits would diminish the powers he had taken from the Kelpies. So instead, he settled for questioning them.

"Why are you here?" he wanted to know.

"We serve the sorcerer, Walipreen," the spokesman replied.

I AM THE SORCERER, WALIPREEN," Walipreen screamed.

His features had changed so drastically over the time he had been absorbing the memories of the Kelpies that he was completely unrecognizable to those who had not seen him during this transformation. The Phooka was shocked into silence. Enraged, Walipreen grabbed his head, lifted him into the air and threw him into the village ruins.

"You," he shouted, pointing to another. "Explain to me why you are here, and do it quickly, or you'll suffer a worse fate."

The new spokesman sputtered, but managed to explain that they were directed by Nelluc to accompany him to this place;

that they had the Phynnodderee child with them at the time. She had been chained to the ground in a room inside the village. He explained that before they left the Ice Kingdom, they had been given a potion by Nelluc that took from them their hearing.

"Why would he do that?" demanded Walipreen.

"She talked to us," the Phooka said. "But when she talked, she controlled our minds. She could make us do things, just by telling us. Nelluc took our hearing so that she couldn't do this anymore."

Walipreen realized that he had found the Phynnodderee he had been searching for.

"But you can hear now," he said. "How did that happen? Did the potion wear off?"

"No, master," said the Phooka. "We don't know how it happened; only that it happened after the strangers appeared."

"Strangers?" Walipreen asked. "What strangers?"

"We don't know who they were," the Phooka continued. "They appeared one day. They must have hexed us. None of us knows what happened after they first appeared. We were..."

He was afraid to say they had fallen asleep.

"They made us sleep," he said, waiting for Walipreen's' wrath to descend upon them. He quickly continued. "When we awoke, they were gone."

"And what of the Phynnodderee?"

"She was gone, too," he answered. "There was no sign of where they went."

"And why have you remained here?" asked the sorcerer.

"Nelluc ordered us to stay until he returned," the Phooka said proudly.

"You stayed here even though your prisoner was gone?" Walipreen asked.

"Nelluc has not yet returned," the Phooka reiterated. "We were ordered to stay until he returned."

Walipreen could feel his rage rising. He was tempted to destroy each one of them, but controlled his anger. He had gotten so close, only to discover that he was, in reality, no closer at all.

"Show me where she was held," he ordered.

The Phooka led Walipreen through the village gates. They walked down the central road. The body of the Phooka that the sorcerer had thrown lay broken on the side of the road. The guide stared nervously at the remains of his former comrade. Walipreen kicked the body out of the way has he passed. When they reached the mill, the Phooka gestured to the building.

"In there," he said. "She was chained to the floor on the lower level. We passed food and water in buckets through the hole in the roof."

"Wait here," Walipreen ordered.

He entered the mill and walked down the stone steps to the cell in which Emm had lived for fifteen years. He saw the straw mat that had served as her bed. He saw the buckets that had transferred food and waste to her keepers. He saw the small fire place, now dead. Finally, he saw the chain and the broken collar that held her prisoner.

He bent down and picked up the collar. He could feel the power of another sorcerer's magic in the broken neckpiece. He could feel the presence of the Phynnodderee. But he could feel nothing that would tell him where they had gone.

He climbed up out of the cell, frustrated and angry, pondering his options. As he left the mill, something caught his attention: a feeling more than anything. He looked up and down the street at the different shops and buildings. To his left he saw a shop with barrels of small glass pieces inside. He felt drawn to it.

The Phooka watched as his master entered the strange, small building. He thought about running away, but Walipreen quickly turned and looked at him, fixing the Phooka in his gaze. The Phooka stayed where he was as the sorcerer entered the store.

Walipreen closed his eyes to block out distractions. Something was here, he told himself. He stretched out his right hand and was drawn towards the back of the shop. He stopped at a bin of various sized polished pieces of glass. He opened his eyes and stared down at the crystals, and then lowered his hand.

The Pendant, he gasped. A piece of it was hidden here. The memories of the Kelpies – memories that were now his, intertwined with his own – came flooding forward. The pendant had been broken into four pieces. One of those pieces had been hidden here. At the instant he touched the pieces of glass, his mind exploded with images.

Everything the Kelpies had known about the pendant, the Enchantress, and the Alchemist flashed through his mind. Then he stretched his memory – the memory that he had stolen and that was now his. The Twins' memories filled in some of the gaps.

He saw images from his ancestors – actually the ancestors of the others. He saw their battle with the Alchemist and the Enchantress. He saw the Kelpies. He saw the strangers who had defeated the Kelpies. He saw Yokais and dragons. He saw sentinels and Rebbercands. He saw the village of the Thumpers before it became the ruins it was today. He saw much more.

He emerged from the building with a fire in his eyes. He still did not know where the Phynnodderee child was, but he had an idea where she might go. He strode past the Phooka and ordered him to follow. Outside the village, he returned to the other Phookas. He ordered them to return to the Ice Kingdom.

"Do you no longer need us to guard this village?" the Phooka asked.

Walipreen turned to the walled town. He raised his arms high above him and then made a sweeping circle, bringing his hands together before him. The walls surrounding the ancient town crumbled inward with a roar. They folded in on top of the ruins. Dust shot up into the air and outward in a circle, covering the Phookas and the feet of Walipreen.

He turned his palms downward and pressed the air. The walls of the destroyed village flattened, crushing everything inside. He pressed down even more and the walls drove themselves and every sign of the village into the ground. Within minutes, the town was completely leveled. All signs of it disappeared as the ground swallowed up what was left.

When the dust settled, the dirt spread out over the dead village like a grave cover. The Phookas had backed away in fear. The only vestige of the town was the bridge that crossed the dried out river bed. Nothing else was left.

"What village?" Walipreen asked.

Seeing that the Phookas had no answer, he amended his order for them to return to the Ice Kingdom. He split the group in two and sent half of them back to the Ice Kingdom to instruct Prine to bring an army of Phookas to the location where Walipreen would be going next. He sent the other half to the south to deliver the same instructions to Rampool.

He told them they were not to stop until they reached the Twins and to instruct the Twins to summon the Yokais. He expected them to meet with him without delay. The Phooka who had asked about guarding the village was about to ask if the sorcerer needed to be accompanied, but looked back at the missing town and kept his mouth shut.

Walipreen watched as the Phookas broke their camp, leaving much of their home for the last fifteen years behind them. They divided up as ordered, and half headed north while the other half headed south. Not once did either group look back at their master. When they were out of sight, Walipreen looked towards the west. He opened his enormous wings and rose in the air, heading for the location of the last image he had seen in the glass shop: the image of Virkio.

Chapter sixteen

As Liam, Aitch and Summer headed west, they found themselves in the middle of an all out battle between the warring Kelpies. Aitch flew higher and then lower, doubled back and tried to dodge the spells and attacks that the warriors launched at one another.

"This is crazy," cried Summer. "We're liable to get hit with something and we're not even the target."

"We need to think of something else," said Aitch. "I haven't shifted for this long of a time before. I don't know how much longer I can sustain it. I'm getting exhausted."

"Can you land someplace out of the way and get some rest?" asked Liam.

"If you can find such a place," Aitch answered.

"I think we should turn back," said Summer.

They each had been thinking the same thing, but were reluctant to suggest it. Going to Virkio seemed like the answer to their current dilemma. They realized, though, that it really didn't solve anything. Virkio was no better of a choice than anyplace else.

"We need to think of another place the others might go," said Liam. "Virkio was the first thing that came to our minds, but it might not be the first thing they would have thought of. What would be your second choice?"

"Where we came through the Boravak," said Aitch. "It seems like a logical starting point."

"I agree," said Summer. "It's as good a choice as anything else. And it's away from here."

"Can you make it that far?" asked Liam.

"We'll soon find out," replied Aitch.

He reared up, spun around and changed course. Liam pointed the way and Aitch put every effort into flying as fast as he could. By the time they were close to their goal, it was clear that he was losing strength. Liam suggested that they land so that Aitch could change back to his natural form. They could walk the rest of the way.

"Thanks," said Aitch. "I wasn't sure I was going to be able to go much further. Sorry I couldn't take us all the way."

"No," said Liam. "Don't apologize. We never could have come this far without you."

"Where are we, exactly," Aitch asked.

"This forest looks familiar," said Summer.

"How can you tell?" asked Aitch. "They all look the same to me."

"Summer's right," said Liam. "This is the Navedi Forest. Look at the trees. They're different than any we've encountered before. They don't grow anyplace else."

Aitch studied the trees. His attention was drawn to the branches which extended as far as he could see, like long fingers stretching out from very long arms. The trunks were very wide. They would have to be in order to support such long branches. Their color, however, added to the darkness. They were covered with bark that was black as night.

The limbs, also covered in the same black bark, were thin and covered with dense leaves that were also black. Aitch realized the Liam was right. He had never seen trees like this before. Soon the sky was completely blocked from view and they were walking under a impenetrable canopy.

"Are we safe here?" he asked.

"We were the last time we were here," said Liam.

"But that was a long time ago," Summer pointed out.

"Does anything live in here?" asked Aitch.

"Yes," said Liam. "Maybe not. I don't know. There was a tribe that lived here in our time, but I can't be sure they're still here."

"I don't see any signs of any people in here," said Aitch. "I was thinking more of animals."

"If the Navedis are here," said Summer, "we won't know until they're ready for us to know."

Aitch jerked his head in her direction, unsure whether she was being serious or merely trying to scare him. As soon as he saw her face, he realized she was serious. She was fluttering close to Liam's shoulder, her eyes searching intently, as was Liam.

"Why don't you take out one of those daggers you are carrying?" Aitch asked. "You could give one to me, too. I'd like to be a little bit more prepared."

"That would be the worst thing we could do," said Liam. "If the Navedi are here, they're already watching us. If we reveal weapons, they'll take that as a threat."

"Won't that scare them away?" Aitch asked.

Liam stopped walking and turned to Aitch. Summer fluttered a few feet ahead and, when she realized the other two had stopped, she spun around and rejoined them.

"They are expert hunters," said Liam. "They don't scare."

"OK," said Aitch. "I get it. So we just walk into a trap."

"I don't think they'll harm us," said Summer. "And it may be already too late for us to leave the forest. Let me scout ahead. If there is any sign of danger, we can take our chances on trying to get out of here before we've gone too far."

"Now's a fine time to think of that," said Liam.

"Better late than never," Summer shot back at him.

She faded into near invisibility and floated up to the canopy. Even though Aitch had watched her the entire time, he could no longer see her or any sign of her.

"She's really good at that," he said.

"Yeah," said Liam. "That's come in handy a few times."

They waited in silence, still studying their surroundings. Summer moved as silently as she could deeper into the forest. She didn't want to get too far away, since there was no path and no real landmarks by which she would be able to find her way back. Still, she needed to go far enough to see if there were any signs of the camp that she and the others had visited so long ago. Or was that some time in the future?

All this bouncing back and forth made her lose track of when they were. Future, she reminded herself. The Kelpies are trying to eliminate each other. We're in the future. She took a deep breath and continued on. After a few minutes, she decided she had gone far enough and turned around.

A wave of panic swept over her. She could see nothing familiar. The darkness of the forest was so pervasive that she had no sense of her location. She turned around again to look in the direction she had initially been traveling and even that seemed to have changed. She spun to her left and then to her right and then to the back. Or was it the front? She was confused.

Her throat tightened and she was on the verge of tears. She was lost. She wanted to call out, but then thought if the Navedi were around they may take her shouting as a threat. What have I done, she screamed at herself. Get a grip, she thought. Think.

She tried to imagine what the others would do. Then she thought of Sean. She remembered how he maneuvered through the forest with Aitch back on the other side of the Boravak. He made spirals. That's what I'll do, she thought.

She started with small circles, keeping her eyes fixed on some specific point as she made her loop. Then she widened the circle. She did this several more times until she saw Aitch and Liam in the distance. She immediately made a bee-line for them.

"Where have you been?" asked Liam. "You were gone so long, we got worried."

"I was making a thorough sweep of the forest," she said.

Her breath was still coming fast and the tightness in her throat, which had not yet eased, caused her voice to come out in a somewhat squeaky fashion. Aitch looked at her strangely.

"You got lost," said Liam.

"I did NOT!" Summer snapped.

"Yes, you did," he replied, a smile creeping onto his face. "I can tell by your voice."

"Well, maybe," she admitted. "Just a little. But I'm back and I didn't see any signs of the camp or of any people."

"They were probably driven out by the war," Liam said.

"That's a good thing, then?" asked Aitch.

"I'm not sure," said Liam. "But we can probably move a little faster since it's not likely we'll be viewed as invaders by anyone."

Liam stepped up the pace and before nightfall they reached the other side of the forest. They were on the bank of the river that separated the Navedi Forest from the Swamp. The evening sky made it difficult to see much. He wondered if all the work he had done removing the toxic environment in the Swamp had survived his absence.

When they had emerged from the other side of the Boravak the first time, they had discovered themselves in a world that was centuries into the future. They hadn't ventured too far from the edge of the Swamp, and Liam hadn't really paid much attention to the environment. Still, it would be wise to be cautious.

They made camp for the night on the edge of the Forest, but not too close to the water. Even though they had seen no signs of any other people or animals, they decided to keep a guard. They spelled each other every two hours until dawn, passing an uneventful night.

The next morning they stayed on the Forest side of the river until they reached the location of the burial place of the Swamp Kelpie and the site of the cave that led to the opening in the Boravak. Aitch shifted into the form of the winged horse once again, to carry Liam across the river to the other side.

There was no sign that anything had changed or that anyone had been there since Aitch brought all the others back into his world. They scoured their surroundings for any possible watching eyes, and seeing none, climbed down into the cave. They moved deeper inside to the steps, climbed down and then Aitch shifted into a bridge so Liam could cross to the ledge where the opening was.

"OK," he said. "We're here. Now what?"

Aitch shifted into a gnat and moved close to the hole. He could feel a slight puff of air coming through – so faint that anything larger than the size he was now would not notice it. The opening was still there. He shifted back to himself.

"The hole is still there," he reported. "I can feel air coming through it. If you put your hand there, you can feel it."

"Just barely," said Liam after he did as Aitch had suggested.

"What if we crossed over and came back?" Aitch asked. "We came back in a different time then, why not now?"

"Because there's no guarantee that we'll come back in the same time as the others," said Summer. "It's too dangerous."

"So we just wait here for them?" he asked. "How long?"

"Let's give it a day," suggested Liam.

"Why only a day?" asked Summer. "Don't you think it may take them longer to find us?"

"It won't matter how long it takes them," answered Liam. "Once they shift in time, they'll either be here or they won't. A day will give us time for Aitch to rest, since we will need him to change shape again and give us another ride."

"Fine with me," said Aitch, "but a ride where?"

"Virkio," said Liam. "If this place doesn't work, I think we need to try once more to get to Virkio. If the others can shift to a location, I'm sure they'll pick one of these two."

"What if they're at Virkio now, and then after we leave, they come here to find us?" asked Summer.

"We can leave them some kind of note or message," said Liam. "Something that won't get moved, taken or erased by anyone else who finds it. Something only they will understand."

"Like a code?" asked Aitch.

"Like a riddle," said Summer.

"That's a good idea," said Liam. "We can carve it into the stone and make it look like it's been here for ages."

"What will we say?" asked Aitch.

They were silent for a while trying to think of what message they could leave. One after the other they started something only to decide it wasn't satisfactory. After a while, their thoughts were interrupted by sounds from the opening of the cave.

"Shhh," whispered Aitch. "Do you hear that?"

"Yes," Liam whispered back. "Keep as quiet as you can, but let's move back as much into the shadows as possible."

Without waiting, Summer blended into the stone background and fluttered up towards the opening. She kept close to the ceiling as she silently worked her way to the entrance. She stopped a little more than halfway and began backing up. Dozens of Rebbercands were sneaking into the cave. She raced back to Liam and Aitch.

"Rebbercands," she whispered. "Dozens of them. They're coming down here."

"We have to hide," said Aitch.

"Where?" asked Liam. "We're exposed no matter where we go."

"I could shift into a rock," Aitch suggested. "You could hide behind me."

"And what if they make camp here/?" asked Liam. "You can't stay like that for days."

"What choice do we have?" asked Summer.

"You can get out," said Liam. "Make yourself invisible and get out of here."

"And go where?" she shot back. "Besides, I'm not leaving you – either of you."

"I can hear them getting closer," said Aitch. "I think they're coming down here. Whatever we're going to do, we need to do it fast."

Liam looked around and then turned to the hole in the Boravak. He pulled out his narrowest dagger, felt around with his free hand until he could feel the thin wisp of air coming through, and then drove the dagger into it.

"What are you doing?" asked Summer.

He didn't answer. He pushed the blade in with all his strength and then wiggled it around in circles, making the opening wider. When he pulled the dagger back, the blade was gone. He bent down to see if it had come off in the hole, but there was no sign of it.

"What are you doing?" Summer repeated.

"It's big enough for the two of you to fit through," he said.

"I'm not going through that," she told him.

"And I'm not going back alone," said Aitch.

"Both of you go," Liam insisted. "If we all get captured, there's no telling what will happen to us. Someone needs to find the others and tell them. With a little bit of luck, you'll find them and come back to get me before any of this happens."

"With a little bit of luck?" Summer hissed. "Are you mental? Look how hard it's been to find the others – how hard it's been to stay in one time together. We'll never find you."

"And if you don't find the others, then they'll keep searching and they could end up here forever, not knowing where we are or what happened to us," Liam shot back. "Someone has to get word to them."

"He's right," said Aitch. "I hate it, too, but he's right."

"Go, now," Liam insisted. "Before it's too late. And put a stone in the hole on the other side. Leave it there for a day. That way the Rebbercands won't find it."

"This is not right," moaned Summer.

Aitch shifted into the same smoke he had changed into the first time he crossed over. He hung in the air watching until Summer resigned herself to the fact that Liam was right. Reluctantly, she ducked into the hole, compressing her wings tightly against her body as she wiggled through the narrow passage. Aitch followed immediately after. Once on the other side, they did as Liam asked and plugged the hole with a small pebble.

Liam bent down and peered through the hole, making sure they had plugged it. Then he took some dirt from the ground and filled in the hole from the other side, making sure not to pack it down too tightly. He was about to turn away when he noticed a pile of clothing. Aitch was going to be surprised when he shifted back to himself on the other side, Liam thought.

He quickly folded the clothing, tucked it in the corner formed by the wall and the floor and scattered a little bit of dirt over it to make it as inconspicuous as possible. No sooner had he done that when he heard the voices of the Rebbercands behind him.

"What have we here?" one of them shouted. "A spy?"

""I'm no spy," Liam said. "I'm merely a traveler passing through."

"Is that so?" the Rebbercand said.

"And who would you be loyal to, traveler?" the second one asked.

Liam hesitated. Which Kelpies did the Rebbercands side with, he wondered. In his time they were all together. He wasn't even sure of which Kelpies had joined each other. There was no safe answer to this question.

"I have no stake in this war," he said, opting for neutrality. "I am from another land," he added, hoping to ensure his position, or lack of position.

The third Rebbercand came down the steps and jumped across the ravine to the landing with Liam. He then grabbed Liam by the arm and tossed him up to the others as if he was nothing more than a turnip. He jumped back across and came up the steps.

"Another land?" the first one asked. "Where?"

"Uh...it's..." Liam hadn't expected this question.

"It's what?" the second one asked. "Nowhere?"

"Yes," said Liam. "I mean no."

"What it is?" roared the third one.

"It's somewhere," said Liam. "It's not near here."

"Oh, that clears up everything," said the first one.

"Then, if it's all right with you, I'll be on my way," said Liam.

"Of course," said the second one. "Have a safe trip."

"Uh...well...OK, thanks," replied Liam.

He hadn't expected it to be that easy. He turned to leave, but the third one cut him off.

"Just one question, though, before you go," said the first one.

"Sure," said Liam.

"What were you doing down there?"

"I...uh...I was...sleeping," Liam stammered. "I had been traveling and needed a place that was safe from...you know...uh...predators. So I found this cave and just went down to that...the...uh...that ledge."

"That sounds reasonable," the third one said to the others.

"I agree," said the first one. "It sounds completely reasonable."

"There you have it, then," said the second one, gesturing to Liam. "We won't delay you any further."

Liam looked from one to the other, expecting some kind of trick. They looked back at him, smiling. He nodded to them and turned to leave.

"Wait," said the third one. "I have a question, if it's not too much trouble."

Liam turned back. They were still standing there, smiling at him.

"No trouble at all," he said.

"How did you get onto that shelf?" the third one asked.

"The shelf?" asked Liam.

"Yes," said the Rebbercand. "The shelf. You know. The one we found you on. How did you get on it?"

"I...uh...I...I jumped," Liam gulped.

"He jumped," the third one said to the others.

"Of course," the first one said. "He jumped. That makes sense."

"Thank you," said the third one.

Liam looked at them, waiting for another question or a comment. He nodded again. They nodded back, still smiling at him. He turned to leave.

"Can you show me?" asked the second one.

"Can I show you what?" asked Liam as he turned back to them.

"You said you jumped," the second one said. "Can you show me how you did it?"

"You want me to show you?" asked Liam.

"Yes," the Rebbercand said. "It must have been an amazing feat. My friend here who went down there and tossed you back up is much bigger than you, so it wasn't such a accomplishment for him. But, you? You're much smaller, and that ravine is very wide. You must be an amazing jumper. I'd really like to see you do that."

"Jump across?" Liam asked again. "You want to see me jump."

They all nodded at him. He swallowed hard, and took tentative steps down the old stone staircase to the bottom. He moved to the edge as close to the opposite side as he could. Looking at the expanse now, he wondered how he would have crossed it if the Rebbercands hadn't found him. I should have thought of that before, he told himself.

He looked back at his audience. They were still at the top of the steps, smiling at him. He turned back to the shelf, swung his arms for momentum, and rocked back and forth. Then he turned back to the Rebbercands.

"I didn't jump," he admitted. "I...I...uh...I was left there by...by...by a sorcerer."

"A sorcerer?" asked the first one. "And which sorcerer would that be?"

"Lochen," Liam blurted out.

"Lochen?" asked the second one. "Never heard of him."

"Me, neither," the other two chimed in.

"That's because he's...he's...he's not from around here," Liam explained, making things up furiously as he went. "He's from...from...Crabatoonia."

Crabatoonia, Liam thought. Where did that come from? He wished he had paid more attention to the names of the planets that Lochen had always gone on about.

"Crabatoonia?" asked the first one.

"I know," said Liam, anticipating the question. "I had never heard of it either. He came here with plans to take over everything. He's really evil...and...and powerful. Really, really powerful."

"Then why didn't he just turn you into a plum?" asked the third one.

"A plum?" questioned the first one. "Why a plum?"

"I don't know; I just like plums," the third one answered.

"Not me," said the second one. "I prefer prunes."

"Prunes?" said the first one. "Those are the same thing, just dried up."

"No," said the second one. "You're thinking of raisins."

"You're wrong," said the third one. "Raisins are dried up grapes."

"Are you sure?" asked the first one. "I don't like grapes."

While they were having this discussion, Liam stealthily crept back up the stairs and inched his way behind them towards the opening. The debate was still going on when he felt a hand on his collar, pulling him back.

"How could you leave such a stimulating conversation?" asked the first one.

"I didn't want to interrupt," Liam said.

"Of course you didn't," the Rebbercand said. "But I think you were on your way back to your masters to report our little scouting party, and we can't have that, now. Can we?"

"I told you before," said Liam. "I don't support anybody in this war."

"I'd like to believe you," the first one said. "Really, I would; but I just can't."

"What are you going to do with me?" Liam asked.

"I think we'll tie you up and throw you in the river," the Rebbercand said. "Attached to some large rocks to make sure you don't come back to the surface."

Liam's stomach rolled. He couldn't believe his time would end so close to his home, but so far away in time. He thought about the others and that they would never know what happened to him. He wished he could find a way to leave them some kind of message. That was not to be.

He was hauled to the top of the cave and out the opening. He passed by the other Rebbercands that Summer had seen when they first approached. He could see that they were heavily armed, but were traveling without any supplies. The Rebbercand had told the truth about their purpose. They were a scouting party for one side or the other.

He was dragged outside of the cave where one of the Rebbercands was preparing the rope while another was gathering some large rocks. He looked around, gazing for the last time on his home. He could see that the toxic plants had taken back much of the land and marsh, but there were still large areas where beneficial plants and shrubs were growing.

His hands were bound behind him, and then the rope was wound around his body with the rocks bound in the wrapping. One of the Rebbercands picked him up and moved to the bank of the river, looking for the deepest section.

"Wait," said Liam.

"I suppose you want to say some last words," the Rebbercand said. "Why not? Go ahead."

"Actually," Liam said, an idea coming into his head. "I just wanted to thank you."

"Thank me?" the Rebbercand asked. "Thank me for what."

"Not just you," said Liam. "All of you; well, at least the one who made the decision to throw me in the river. Was it you? Or was it one of the others? I didn't really see."

"Yes it was me. You want to thank me for throwing you in the river?" the Rebbercand asked.

His curiosity had been piqued. He put Liam down on the ground to look at him.

"And why do you want to thank me for throwing you in the river?"

"Well," said Liam. "It'll be quick. Won't it?"

"I suppose," said the Rebbercand. "I don't know. I've never been drown before."

"It's got to be better than being poisoned by plants or eaten by them," Liam continued. "That would really be nasty. You wouldn't do something like that. You're too civilized."

"What are you talking about?" the Rebbercand demanded.

"That's the Venomous Swamp right over there," Liam said motioning with his head. "That place is really scary. It's filled with all sorts of dangerous, man-eating plants."

The Rebbercand looked over at the Swamp. He furrowed his brow, deep in thought.

"I've heard of that place," he said, somewhat to himself.

"Who hasn't heard of it?" asked Liam. "Only a cold-blooded, hard-hearted down-right dirty...guy...would tie somebody up and leave them there. So I wanted to thank you for not being such a tough guy. It's clear that you are kind-hearted; that you want me to have a quick end."

"Thanks for pointing that out to me," said the Rebbercand. "Now that I think of it, leaving your body for everyone to see might send a better message."

"But you can't do that," argued Liam.

"DON'T tell me what I can and can't do," shouted the Rebbercand. "I'll do whatever pleases me. And it pleases me to leave you to the plants."

"Awwww," wailed Liam. "I should have never told you about the Swamp."

"Yeah," said the Rebbercand. "That was your mistake."

"It's a good thing I didn't say anything about the worst plants being those bright yellow ones on the high ground."

Liam had identified the safest section in an area at the far horizon. He also knew that he had one of his supply caches near that rise. At least it had been there when he use to live in the Swamp. He hoped it was still there. The Rebbercand picked him up, tucked him under one arm and began trekking through the brush, up the hill to the field of bright yellow flowers.

As he walked, he thrashed through plants that Liam knew carried infectious insects in them. He knew that if the Rebbercands camped in that cave tonight, by the morning they would be infested with the tiny mites. Two days after that, their eggs would have been planted beneath the skin of their hosts and two days after that, the Rebbercands would be covered from head to toe with a minute, very hungry and very nasty blight.

When they reached the top of the rise, the Rebbercand loosened the ropes, threw away the rocks and tied Liam to a nearby tree.

"Please don't do this," Liam begged. "This is way too cruel. What will people think when they hear about this? Have you given that any thought?"

"Yes, I have," the Rebbercand answered. "They'll think twice about dealing with me."

When he was done tying Liam to the tree, he turned and left without another word. Liam watched as he departed, making a few feeble calls to keep up the pretense. Once the Rebbercand was out of sight, Liam wiggled one hand free enough to unsheathe a small dagger and he cut the ropes.

"They truly are as stupid as they look," he said once he was free. He picked his way through the plants, careful not to leave a trail and headed for his supply cache. He had recalled exactly where it was. He moved away the camouflage and opened the access way.

This had been one of his larger storage areas because it was so far away from his home base. He found a lantern and lit it for light, closing the door behind him so he could take stock in privacy. He found all sorts of things and immediately went to work.

There were containers of water as well as stores of food. The water was still good, but the food had hardened to the consistency of rock. I think I'll save my teeth and see if I can find some edible plants outside, he told himself.

He spent the rest of the day and worked into the night, assembling the materials that he had stored here so long ago. Long after darkness had fallen, he was done. He carefully opened to door to the hideaway and poked his head out.

This area had been crawling with gargoyles when the Swamp had been his home. He had no idea where they had gone, and no interest in finding out. Still, he knew he had to be cautions. There were Rebbercands nearby, and the opposition probably had Phooka spies sneaking around as well. He didn't need to be recaptured. He was certain he would not be able to fool anyone again with his "please don't leave me in the Swamp" routine.

He could detect no sign of anyone or anything near. He looked up at the sky and saw no moon. That would help a lot. He then ducked back inside and moved several pieces out of the storage area. Outside he finished his assembly. It wasn't much, but he hoped it would do.

"It'll have to do," he said to no one.

He climbed into a small seat and fitted his feet into a pair of pedals. At first the vines that served as belts moved slowly, but then he picked up speed. Gears turned a long pole that rose up behind his seat to a fan-like apparatus over his head. As the fan turned the contraption rose into the air.

A few seconds later, he was above the treetops. He then pulled a lever next to him. Nothing happened. He leaned over the side and saw that one of the vines had slipped. Still pedaling, he awkwardly reached down, tilting slightly to one side. He tried to keep his balance and at the same time, re-situate the vine.

He had dropped down a few feet, but then regained altitude. Once more he shifted the lever. The pedaling became more strenuous, but now he had forward motion. He turned his make-shift helicopter to the west and made his way for his destination. He was headed to Virkio.

Chapter seventeen

Everyone spun wildly; much more so than before. Lochen reached out for whoever was closest and grabbed Natalie's hand on one side and Quinn's on the other. He shouted to them to try to reach the others. They felt their bodies being pulled, feeling like they were stretched out of shape.

Quinn was able to touch Stella's fingers and tugged them towards him until he could grasp her hand. As she spun around, she reached out and captured Solveig's arm. Sean was tumbling head over heels and zoomed past Natalie. She missed his hand, but he whirled around like an orbiting planet and she caught him during his second passing. He had Emm wrapped in his free arm.

They shot through a dark tunnel into the daylight and slid across the flat roof of the fifth tower, skidding into the crenellated wall on the far side, piling up on top of one another. Dazed and bruised, they slowly caught their breath before sitting up and taking notice of where they were.

"What was that all about?" asked Sean. "That didn't happen before."

"It must have something to do with where we landed," said Stella.

"This place looks different in the daylight," said Quinn. "It's still scary, but different. Anyone see the dragon?"

"What dragon?" squeaked Emm.

"I don't think there's any dragon here," said Solveig. "Is everyone all right?"

Once they all took stock, they acknowledged that they were fine. Lochen had already started walking around the perimeter, periodically glancing over the side of the wall to the mountains and valleys below.

"Are you looking for the dragon?" asked Emm.

"No," he called back to her from the other side of the tower. "I don't believe the dragon resides here, although I can't tell if it doesn't reside here any longer or it doesn't reside here yet."

"What's he talking about?" she asked the others, totally confused.

"I think he means he can't tell what time we are," said Solveig.

"You understood that?" Emm asked.

"I speak Lochen," Solveig replied, rolling her eyes.

"I think we should see about moving inside the tower," he said when he rejoined the others.

"Why?" asked Sean. "As I recall, it's not real safe on the inside."

"Why isn't it safe?" asked Emm. "Is that where the dragon is?"

"There is no dragon," said Lochen.

"How can you be sure?" asked Quinn. "You just said you didn't know what time this is. Maybe we came back when the dragon was here. You don't know that."

"I am certain now that we have arrived in the future," said Lochen. "What I can't determine is how far in the future. I know that it's long after we were here before, but I don't know how much after that time."

"You're making this up," said Sean. "There's no way you can know that."

"I never make things up," declared Lochen. "Well, almost never. I made this determination based on the evidence."

"What evidence?" Sean persisted.

"Come here," Lochen directed, moving over to one side of the roof. "Look," he said pointing to the floor.

Sean moved closer, unsure of what he was supposed to see. The others huddled close to and moved with him.

"I'm looking," said Sean. "What am I looking at?"

"This stain," said Lochen with a sigh.

Everyone looked down at the stone floor. There were minute flecks of silver in some of the blocks.

"What stain?" asked Sean. "All I see is some glitter."

"That glitter is dragon's blood," said Lochen. "This is the location of the dragon that had been killed here."

"Someone killed the dragon?" asked Emm, looking at the area of glittering stone. "This is its blood stain? It must have been huge."

"It was the dragon's child," said Solveig. "The mother was much bigger."

"There was a mother?" gasped Emm. "What if it comes back? He's right. We need to get off this place."

"I have no reason to believe the dragon will return," said Lochen. "However, I agree that we should get inside. We're far too exposed out here and there are limited avenues of escape should we encounter anyone who would do us harm."

"Not so fast," said Sean. "How do you know we'll be safer inside than outside? Have you forgotten all the booby traps in this place?"

"Booby traps?" asked Emm. "What kind of booby traps? What kind of place did you bring us to? How is Aitch ever going to find this place?"

"This is the fortress of the Alchemist," Lochen explained. "He placed several...safeguards in each of the towers. If he, Liam and Summer are able to deduce the most likely place to meet up with us, they will arrive at the same conclusion we did. Aitch was trained by the Alchemist. He will understand how to avoid the false illusions and Liam and Summer, having been here before, will help him."

"Don't worry, Emm," said Natalie. "Your brother is in good hands."

"Now I must insist," continued Lochen. "We need to get inside."

"I'm not moving," complained Sean. "Not until you can convince me that it will be safer inside that maze than it is here on the roof."

"I expect that would require very little on my part," said Lochen.

He didn't say anything further, but, instead, studied the floor, apparently looking for something.

"What's that supposed to mean?" asked Sean. "And what are you looking for?"

"I think he's lost it," said Quinn.

"Me, too," replied Sean. "Big time."

"What did he lose?" asked Emm. "Maybe we can help him find it."

"I think they mean he's lost his mind," explained Solveig. "He gets like this sometimes."

"Get's like what?" Emm asked. "I don't understand."

Lochen straightened up, glanced at the sky and then turned to the others.

"I'm looking for the doorway into this tower," he said. "It must be somewhere on the floor. There must be an access to the interior. If you recall, we never went inside this part of the fortress. We came across on the bridge, which, in case you hadn't noticed, is no longer in one piece. We have no other way off this tower, other than going into it. And we must do that rather quickly."

"Maybe there's no way inside," said Natalie. "Did you ever think of that?"

"That's certainly a possibility," Lochen answered, his attention focused back on the ancient stone floor. "But should that be true, then we are most likely doomed."

"Isn't that a bit of an exaggeration?" asked Stella. "I know this wouldn't be the ideal place to spend some time, but doomed? Really?"

"Really," said Lochen, glancing once more at the sky.

"What do you keep looking at?" asked Sean.

He turned around and looked up at the sky in the direction that Lochen had been glancing. He saw a dark object in the distance. At first he thought it was a bird crossing the horizon. But as he watched, he could see it was coming in their direction. He squinted. Then he jerked back in surprise.

"Oh, poop!" he exclaimed. "What is that?"

The others turned to look as well. They were all watching in rapt silence as the figure got larger and larger.

"Whatever it is," said Quinn, "it's moving really fast."

"And it's heading this way," said Solveig.

"And it probably means to do us harm," added Lochen. "So staying here is no longer an option."

With that, he found what he was looking for. It was a small stone, wedged in the seam between two large blocks near the side of the tower roof. He pressed on it and the surrounding stones rumbled and lowered, forming a spiral staircase into the fortress.

"Now," said Lochen. "If you would exercise a bit of alacrity, I think our chances of survival may rise exponentially."

"What did he say?" asked Emm.

"He said we should move our butts or we're going to end up dead," said Sean. "I'm convinced."

He pulled his slingshot and placed a pellet he pulled from a pouch at his belt in the firing patch. Then he nodded to the others to go ahead of him.

"I fear that will be of little use," said Lochen, motioning him down the steps.

They all quickly dropped out of sight and as soon as they reached the bottom, the steps rose back up towards the ceiling and out of sight.

- - - - - - - - - - - - - - - - - *** - - - - - - - - - - - - - - - - - -

Summer wiggled until she popped through to the other side. As soon as she was out she turned around to see a cloud of green smoke come through after her. She backed away, at first startled and then realized that Aitch had shifted into this form. Once he was through, he shifted back into himself.

"Awww, dude," moaned Summer. "What's with you and the clothes?"

He looked down at himself and saw that once again, his clothes had not made the transition with him. He covered himself with his hands and arms, at the same time picking up a small stone to temporarily plug the opening.

"I don't understand," he wailed. "You saw me shift on the other side. This doesn't happen there. It's something about this place."

He tossed the stone away and looked for another one.

"What was wrong with that one?" Summer asked about the pebble he had rejected.

"It wasn't the right kind," he said.

"What kind do you need?"

"It has to fit just right," said Aitch. "Otherwise if someone on the other side looks at it, they'll see they can just push it out."

He picked up another and rejected it. At the same time, he continued to try to cover himself with one arm.

"Can you find a stone later?" Summer asked. "You really need to find some kind of...covering. I can see way too much of you."

"Then don't look!" he snapped as he threw away another stone.

"By the time you find the right stone, an entire army is going to come through that hole," Summer said.

"All right, all right," Aitch nearly shouted. "I can see you're willing to accept 'just good enough.'"

He picked up a smooth round stone and plugged the hole. Unbeknownst to him, what had taken him several minutes to do, took only seconds on the other side. By now, Liam was placing the dirt in the hole on his side.

"Finally!" exclaimed Summer. "Now, can you please cover up?"

"This never happened to me when the Alchemist was teaching me how to shape shift," complained Aitch.

"Maybe it's a little trick on the part of the Alchemist," she suggested. "Did you ever think of that?"

"Why would he do something like this to me?" asked Aitch.

"To keep you from bouncing back and forth from one side to the other, maybe?" she answered. "In the meantime, for the last time, PLEASE go find some cover."

"Forget it," he said. "This is ridiculous. I'm going back."

"How do you know enough time has passed?" Summer asked.

"I don't care," he replied. "Coming over here was a bad idea. This isn't where I belong. Stay here if you want, but I'm going back."

"I'm not staying here by myself," she argued. "But think for a minute. What if we return in the middle of a bunch of Rebbercands?"

"Then that's what happens," he said.

He reached up and tried to remove the stone. It was too smooth for him to get a grip on it. His fingers pinched at it, but only managed to push it further in.

"Oh, oh," he said.

"What, oh-oh?" snapped Summer. "I don't like the sound of that."

"I can't get a hold on the stone," he said. "Can you pull it out?"

She tried to wedge her hands into the opening, but only one would fit. There was not enough space on the other side of the pebble to get her fingers in between it and the hole. She was unable to get any kind of leverage or grip.

"No," she said. "All I'm doing is pushing it further in. Nice job. Did you try to find the smoothest stone possible?"

"I was looking a stone that would fit perfectly," he argued.

"Well you found one that fit TOO perfectly," she countered.

"I could have found a better one if I hadn't been rushed," he responded.

"Oh, so now it's my fault?"

"Hey, if the shoe fits – oh, wait a minute. You aren't wearing shoes!"

"What's that supposed to mean?"

She swooped down and hovered inches from his face, her chin thrust forward, her hands on her hips. He was startled by her confrontational stance and backed up a step or two. She pressed forward, backing him up even further until he fell over on his back and thrust out his arms to break his fall.

"Oh, gross," Summer cried, turning away. "Look. If you're intent on going back, turn into that smoke stuff again, squeeze into the hole and push the stone out. Do you think you can do that?"

Aitch sat up, an idea springing into his head.

"I can do better," he said.

He shifted into the cloud of smoke and pushed his way into the hole until he made contact with the dirt Liam had packed in the other side. Once he was nestled between the stone and the dirt, he shifted into water so suddenly that the expansion blew the stone out on one side and the dirt out the other.

The stone shot by Summer, missing her by inches and Aitch allowed himself to seep to the ground in a puddle on the inside of the Boravak. Summer poked her head in the hole and then wormed her body the rest of the way. She quickly broke through to the other side as Aitch was putting on the clothes that Liam had neatly folded and covered with dirt.

"What happened?" asked Summer.

"I forced the stone out of the hole," said Aitch.

"Not that," said Summer. "I meant with your clothes. Look at them. They look really dirty."

"Liam must have covered them to hide them after we crossed over," Aitch said.

"No," said Summer. "It's more than that."

She sniffed them and then jerked back.

"They're moldy!" she declared.

Aitch smelled them, too and had the same reaction.

"They're old," he said. "We've come back to a different time."

"But we weren't gone that long," moaned Summer. "How can that be? How much time? Can you tell?"

"I don't know," said Aitch. "Obviously it's later. The clothes were folded, so it had to be after I crossed over the first time. When I came back with the rest of you, they were just in a pile."

"This is horrible," Summer cried. "Liam is somewhere all by himself. How are we ever going to find him?"

"We will," insisted Aitch. "I don't know how, but we will. I promise. Right now we need to see if we can find out what time we're in and how we find the others."

"We need to go to Virkio," said Summer.

"Are you sure? How do you know that's where everyone will go?"

"I don't," Summer answered. "I just feel that's where we need to be. You'll have to trust me."

"OK," said Aitch. "I do. Then that's where we're going. Do you know how to get there?"

"I...uh...well...Liam was the Pathfinder," she said weakly.

"Oh, great," groused Aitch. "We're going someplace neither one of us knows how to get to."

"I'll find it," Summer said bravely. "No matter what it takes, I'll find it."

"And I suppose I have to trust you on this, too," said Aitch.

"You don't have any choice."

"Right. OK, then. Let's go."

"Wait," she said. "We have to leave a message. In case the others come here."

"What kind of message?" asked Aitch.

"Uh...I don't know. No. Wait. We can draw a picture," she decided. "Grab a stone. Scratch a picture of the towers in the wall near the hole."

"Good idea," he said. "What do they look like?"

"Towers," she said. "They look like towers. Five of them."

"I got that," he answered. "But what kind of towers. What do they LOOK like?"

"How many kinds of towers are there?" she demanded. "They're towers. Does it matter? Just draw five towers."

"But what if they don't look like the towers at Virkio?" he argued. "If the others come here see this so-called message, but it doesn't look like the towers at Virkio, how will they know which towers to go to?"

"You are in serious need of help," she said shaking her head. "They'll know because there will be five of them."

He looked at her for a few seconds, considering her comment and debating with himself if it would be worthwhile to pursue the matter.

"Right," he finally conceded. "Good point."

He began scratching an image of the first tower into the wall. He drew one side, and then stepped back to look at his work. Then he drew the other side and stepped back. He went back to the first line and made it a little longer, standing next to it and measuring its height against his body and then comparing it to the second line. He then made the second line a little longer.

"What are you doing?" asked Summer.

"I'm making sure they're even," he said. "I don't want them to look lopsided."

"You're not creating art," she nearly screamed. "Just draw the freaking towers. I can feel my arteries hardening, you're taking so long!"

"What – is – it – with – you – people?" he growled through clenched teeth. "Doesn't anyone appreciate a job well done?"

"Are you sure your sister wants you to find her? Maybe she faked being kidnapped just to get away from you."

"That's just hurtful," he shot back. "But I get it. I'll hurry up."

He hastily scratched the rest of the first tower and then the other four. He was still trying to make adjustments to the drawing and Summer was ready to bang her head against the wall. When he was finally finished they carefully exited the cave, discovering that there was no one around on the surface.

"What's the fastest creature you can turn yourself into?" she asked.

"Blue Falcons are pretty fast," he said.

That thought caused Summer to shiver.

"How about a dragon?" she asked. "That might be as fast and it will be more intimidating. We need to make sure anything we run into thinks twice about trying to stop or capture us."

"I can do that," he said. "Of course, you know, I won't be able to breathe fire."

"You know nothing, do you?" she smiled. "They don't breathe fire. They breathe ice."

"Yeah, right," he said, unsure if she was teasing him or not.

She was not. She had very vivid memories of the dragon mother on the roof of the fifth tower of Virkio, when she covered that tower with a breath of ice. She and the others were riding on the back of the gigantic beast as she circled the place where her child had been slaughtered by the Rebbercand, the same place where Solveig had discovered the tooth that she used to dispatch some of the Kelpies.

As the dragon dropped over the tower, a blast of flame surged from her gigantic jaws. Summer had expected an explosion of fire. Instead, the dragon breathed streams of blue and white that crystallized everything in her path. In two quick passes, she had coated the towers with a thick layer of ice. Summer doubted Aitch would believe her if she told him this story. She hoped, though, that he wouldn't find out first hand.

No sooner had Aitch shifted shape into the form of a dragon – large and a deep emerald green – Summer flew back and forth over him, sprinkling him with faerie dust.

"What's that for?" he asked.

"It will make you lighter and even faster," she said. "I don't think we want to waste any more time than we already have."

"You're assuming that we haven't already missed whatever has happened...or will happen...or is happening now. This is all too confusing."

He was right, Summer thought. When they had left the Boravak, leaving Liam behind, they were in the middle of the Great War – a time somewhere between when they had all escaped the Kelpies and when Walipreen, Rampool and Prine had come to power. When she and Aitch had returned, that had all changed – again. She knew they were in a period later than when they left, but she couldn't tell how much later. Judging from the condition of Aitch's clothes, it was clear that a considerable amount of time had passed. She only hoped that whatever time it was, it coincided with the same "when" as the others

She flew up to sit on Aitch's shoulder, and he spread his enormous wings, lifting them both high into the air. He pushed them downward and flicked his tail, rocketing them forward.

The ground below them was little more than a blur. The wind nearly pushed Summer from her perch on Aitch's shoulder.

"This is a blast," he said. "I'll have to try this again some time."

"If you can see that river below us," she shouted, "follow it to the sea and then we can turn north."

"Isn't there a more direct route?" he asked.

"Yes," she said. "But I'm not Liam. I can't point us to the exact spot. All I know is that it's north of where this river meets the sea."

As night fell, Aitch dove closer to the ground to keep the river in sight. Summer supposed that they would be nearly invisible in the darkness and would, therefore, be safe from anyone or anything on the ground. She was glad to see the first signs of dawn a few hours later as the sun rose behind them.

"Get higher," she cautioned him.

"Why?" he asked. "Who's going to try to shoot at a dragon?"

"A sorcerer," she reminded him. "A really nasty sorcerer."

"Oh, yeah," he replied.

Aitch raised his nose and soared nearly straight up into the clouds. Then he leveled out until around midday when they reached the Viridian Ocean. At that point, he turned right and followed the coast. By late afternoon, the five towers came into view.

"Change your shape," Summer told him.

"To what?" he asked.

"Something smaller," she answered. "And less conspicuous."

"Why? Why not stay this way until we reach the towers?"

"There might be another dragon there," she told him. "And that one would be real. It might not like someone trespassing on its territory."

Without arguing, he shrunk into a Blue Falcon. The sudden change caused Summer to fly from her perch and tumble in the air. She righted herself as Aitch circled around, coasted underneath her and then rose into the air. He positioned himself so that she was seated on his back immediately behind his head and he flew lower to the ground towards the towers.

At Summer's direction, he made a wide circle around them as they searched for any sign of the others, the sorcerers or the dragon. She could see the broken bridge that connected tower four to tower five. The scorch marks caused by the fire that Lochen had set had faded, but were still visible.

"Put down on the last tower," she told Aitch.

"I thought you said that these towers had been destroyed in a fire," Aitch said once they had landed and he had shifted back to his normal form.

"They had," she said. "I saw it myself. It started with the fourth tower. Lochen had us pour this vat of dragon's breath across the bridge. When it ignited, the flames ran down the bridge to the tower. It lit up like a torch and exploded."

"I can see the bridge is gone, but that fourth tower looks OK to me," he said. "I mean it looks pretty frightening, but other than that it looks fine."

"It does, doesn't it," replied Summer. "They all do, although all the bridges seem to be gone."

"Do you think the Alchemist rebuilt them?" Aitch asked.

"No," she said. "What I really think is that they were never destroyed in the first place; that it was all a trick, or that whatever spells the Alchemist had cast only made it look like they were destroyed."

She kept looking back over her shoulder up at the sky as she was speaking.

"Looking for that dragon?" he asked.

"That, and anything else that may be out there," she answered. "We need to go inside."

"I thought you said this whole place was a bunch of traps and mazes," he said.

"It is...or it was," she said. "It probably still is. I'm sure that hasn't changed. But we can't stay up here."

"Won't the others come to this tower?"

"I don't know," Summer answered. "It seems like the most logical choice, but I don't know if they can get up here the same way we did. If not, then they'll have to enter from the bottom."

"Why don't we do that, then?"

"I don't know," she said.

"What kind of answer is that?" wondered Aitch.

"I mean I can't say why, but I think we should start at this end."

"Fine," said Aitch. "But how do we get in? When we were circling this place, I noticed there were no windows. The only doors I saw were the ones at the ends of the bridges that are no longer here. I'll bet the doors are locked, so unless you have a key…"

"There has to be a way in," she said. "Look around."

"Look around where?" he mumbled.

Summer didn't answer. Instead she began hovering close to the stone floor and searching for anything that would look like an entrance. She flew over a small pebble imbedded in the seam between two flagstones and then jerked back.

"Come here," she shouted. "I think I found something."

Aitch rushed over and looked where she was pointing.

"Step on it," she ordered.

He did as she directed and the floor gave way to a descending stone staircase. They exchanged glances and then Aitch stepped cautiously downward. Summer followed, fluttering over his shoulder as they dropped into the darkness.

Chapter eighteen

Walipreen rose high into the sky, his broad wings blocking out the sun. He could see the Phookas racing to the north and the south to carry out his orders. Satisfied, he turned towards the west and fixed his mind on the ancient towers of Virkio.

He could picture the pendant, believing he had seen it at some point in his life. The memories of the Kelpies were indistinguishable from his own. He had lost that ability and was also losing his sense of reality. He was certain he was about to do battle with the Alchemist and the Enchantress. He believed the Twins were his allies and would help him defeat the sorcerer and the witch.

His mind wandered, reliving the experiences he was certain were his. After more than two days he was ranting to himself, unable to separate the several lines of recollections; unable to separate the real from the perceived – regardless of whose perception he was drawing on.

He looked down and saw a river – one he was certain he had been following. He swooped down closer and saw a sandbar. In the sand he could see a number of holes.

"He's back," Walipreen growled in anger.

He dropped to the ground and lowered his head, staring into one of the holes.

"I know you're in there, Gulper," he shouted. "They're just holes. It doesn't matter if it's half a hole or a whole hole. They're all the same. Come out and face me!"

He had been recalling a circular discussion Scirios had with the sentinel, Gulper. He had no recollection that the sentinel, after having completed his mission, dissolved into the sand in which he had dug the holes.

His anger and frustration mounted. In the end, he clenched his fist, raised the level of the river until the holes all filled with water and then turned it all to stone. He stood there breathing heavily – not from the exertion, but from the aggravation of not being able to see the sentinel to ensure his destruction.

Slowly Walipreen regained his composure, shook his head and reminded himself of his goal. He rose into the air and continued to the west. Within a few hours he reached the deserted seaport of Satamakau. He searched for the long departed entertainer, the Amazing Artabarat.

He found no trace of the decrepit acrobat, his gaudily colored wagon or his crate of hats. They had disappeared centuries ago in another lifetime, in another world. Walipreen looked along the harbor, seeing the wall that had protected the town against the tidal bore. The events of the past were blurring together. In addition to losing his ability to separate the memories he had stolen, he was losing his ability to recall when things happened.

His fury was mounting. His head broke out with beads of perspiration and he found himself muttering aloud to no one.

"Get a grip on yourself," he demanded, failing to realize that this, too, was spoken aloud to no one but himself.

He jerked his head back and forth, looking for something; his aggravation escalating with his failure to understand what it was. Then the single item reclaimed the center of his attention: the pendant.

He rose into the air and followed the coast line. He repeated the name of the towers, over and over again as a mantra. Virkio, Virkio, Virkio – burning the name and its image into his consciousness. Finally, the towers appeared in the foreground.

They were much bigger than he had recalled; than the memories of the Kelpies had revealed to him. He circled them several times far above the complex of towers, seeing the broken bridges, the absence of any windows, the doors near the defunct bridges. Something drew him to the fifth tower and he veered back towards it.

He sensed before he could see the tiny figures on the roof of the fifth tower. He felt a surge of power and increased his speed. He knew that by now the Twins were on their way and should arrive shortly, and was certain they hadn't arrived before he had. Then he saw more clearly the figures on the top of the tower the moment they disappeared inside. As they had been moving into the interior of the fortress, the sun had glinted on an object carried by one of them.

The reflection shot a beam of light directly at him. In that instant, all the memories he had stolen stirred. A single image flooded his mind: the Pendant. He had been searching for the strange Phynnodderee child, but this prize was much more valuable. It had nearly been in his grasp at one time. A piece of it had been held by the Rebbercand that had traveled with him.

These recollections were not his, but his mind was now so twisted with the strands of memories he had taken from the Kelpies that he could no longer make any distinction. He caught a final glimpse of the bodies scurrying from the roof into an opening of some sort. He eye caught sight of another flash – this one was a blur of green.

The Phynnodderee, he gasped in astonishment. He would have both – the power of this child and the Pendant. His mind reeled at the thought, except that the Phynnodderee looked much older than the child he had seen in the Ice Kingdom. Could this be the other one? When he finally reached the tower, he was enraged to see no sign of how they had escaped. He roared in frustration. He saw the glitter on the floor and knew it was the blood of a dragon – a dragon slain by the Rebbercand, B'nair. He knew it as if he had been there himself.

He moved to the side of the tower and looked back at the other four pinnacles. He could see the remains of the thin strand that connected the fourth tower to the fifth. He knew how it had been destroyed: the inferno created by the dragon's breath that had been ignited.

He paced back and forth on the tower roof in a state of high agitation, his mind racing. He raised his arms, clenched his fists, and brought them down forcefully, casting a spell to shatter the tower. The air around him rippled with the energy that extended from him, and the air exploded with a thunderous crash. But the tower remained unchanged.

The memories of the Kelpies told him that his spells would not be effective over the power of the Alchemist. He knew the hexes the ancient sorcerer had encased this fortress in would protect it. He began searching for the opening into which the others had disappeared.

As he was doing this, the sky above him darkened and he sensed the presence of others. He spun around and looked up to see thousands of riders on thousand of Yokais. He raised his arms, preparing to cast a spell when two riders lowered their beasts to the tower roof and dismounted.

Rampool and Prine landed on the roof top, leaving their armies aloft and approached Walipreen. He looked at them suspiciously. Why are they here, he wondered. Did they arrive because I willed them to come? He watched them closely for any signs of treachery.

"You summoned us, master," they both said.

He stared at them without any comprehension until his brain matched what they said to what it could recall. Understanding settled in slowly.

"Yes," he said. "I did."

"How can we serve you?" they asked.

"I believe what I am searching for is hidden inside these towers," he said. "Rampool, take your army to the lowest of the towers and guard the exit. Make sure nothing leaves without my direction."

"Yes, master," Rampool replied.

Without waiting for further instructions, the sorcerer climbed back on the Yokai, motioned to half the assembly and moved to the ground across the ravine from the first tower. Once there, Rampool could see the remains of the bridge. What was left still appeared to be solid. However, the tower to which it ran was about a hundred feet away and the chasm that separated him and his men from the tower was filled with dozens of pinnacles, jagged and pointed, like bristles on a porcupine.

He looked up at the tower, which blocked out some of the ones that rose behind it. Walipreen was keeping something from them, he knew. His lifelong animosity towards Walipreen was not as easily snuffed out as his enemy had thought. Rampool felt a glimmer of defiance rise up inside him. There was something inside those towers that was important. Rampool decided he wasn't going to let it slip away from him.

His defiance, however, was shrouded in cowardice. What if Walipreen discovered what he was doing? How would he explain his actions? He would just tell the master that he decided not to wait on the off chance that someone would emerge from the nearby tower and find no way across. What point was there for him and his army to wait here and do nothing?

Once he convinced himself that this sounded like a reasonable explanation, he ordered his men to find timbers to reconstruct the bridge. There was a seemingly endless supply of vines to secure long sections of trees to the remnants of the old stone bridge. The timbers could be suspended from the Yokais until the sections were lashed together. It didn't take long, and soon the repairs were complete.

Rampool led a small group across and found a landing that led to stone steps on the right. To the left were cantilevered beams with nothing attached to them. He moved to the right. He quickly discovered himself back where he had begun and realized the true path was the one that appeared more hazardous.

He climbed up the bare supports and found himself suddenly inside the tower. His initial bravado evaporated. The unexpected access through what had appeared to be solid stone, combined with his fear of Walipreen forced him to exit the tower, cross the bridge back to the rest of his army.

He was covered in a cold sweat, trying to hide his fear from the Rebbercands that surrounded him. He puffed up his chest and told them that there was nothing to fear. He ordered a large portion of the Rebbercands to accompany him into the tower, letting them take the lead. He would guide them from the back.

Meanwhile, back on the roof of tower five, Walipreen had given instructions to Prine to bring his army to the roof and guard that end in the event someone attempted to escape in that direction.

"And where will you be, master?" Prine asked.

"There must be a way into this tower," he said. "Once I find it, I will go in search of what brought me here."

Walipreen told Prine to stay where he was and to bring his men to the roof only after the entryway had been discovered and

Walipreen had begun his search. He made it clear that no one was to follow him unless directed. He then turned his attention to the battlements and the floor.

His frustration grew as his search revealed nothing. When he at last reached the glittering, but faded, stain of the blood of the dragon, he sensed he was near. He got down on his hands and knees to study the stone more closely until his hand pressed the pebble and the floor opened up to expose the spiral descending staircase.

Walipreen motioned to Prine to bring his army to the roof as he squeezed his bulk through the opening. No sooner had he disappeared than the staircase closed itself, leaving Prine and his army alone on the surface. Prine sensed the moment of defiance on the part of his twin brother; and in the next instance knew what Rampool was doing. This understanding came not from anything magical, but only from the bonds between the twins. He smiled inwardly, realizing that they could trap Walipreen between them when he least expected it. He waited several minutes before opening the stairwell and taking a large force with him into the tower.

------------------ *** ------------------

Liam had no idea what to expect. He had flown on his contraption for three days, stopping and hiding during the day and traveling at night. In spite of the raging war between the Kelpies, he saw no sign of the battles. He also found no sign of any villages or people. He thought they may all be in hiding or have fled to safer locations.

Under the cover of darkness at the end of the fourth day, he saw the towers in the light of the moon on the distant horizon. Even at this distance, they seemed incredibly tall. The fourth and fifth towers were hidden in the darkness and the mist. Shortly before dawn, he was close enough to circle them, searching for an opening.

He saw the damaged bridges and large wooden and metal doors, but nothing that presented evidence of any access. He circled higher and higher encountering steadily increasing winds. A strong gust pushed him dangerously close to the middle of the fifth tower and then an updraft propelled him skyward.

He felt several seconds of weightlessness as the wind lifted him high above the top of the tower. He had difficulty regaining control and lowering to the roof. Another gust spun him around and onto his side, tossing him over the parapet. Pedaling frantically, he was able to straighten up and rise up over the rooftop.

"You better get this thing on something solid," he told himself.

He made a nosedive for the top of the tower. As soon as his craft touched down, he hopped off and hugged the stone floor. He was hit with another blast of wind. It was as if a giant was trying to blow him off the roof. His flying machine was lifted into the air, slammed against the wall and hurled over the side. Several seconds later, he heard the faint sounds, thousands of feet below, of his machine crashing on the rocks below.

"Looks like I'm not going anywhere for a while," he muttered.

He crawled across the floor, searching for a way into the tower. He had dragged himself to the edge where the bridge had been. What little was left was scorched. He curled up into a ball and squeezed himself into the corner between the wall and the floor as another blast of wind battered the tower.

When he looked up across the expanse of the roof, he saw the stain of dragon's blood glimmer in the moonlight. He thought there may be some kind of access in that direction and, keeping as close to the floor as he could, he crawled in that direction. The wind was getting even fiercer. He lowered his head and pulled himself along with his hands and arms.

Stretching out one hand, he felt something hard and round protruding from one of the seams between the flagstones. Pulling himself forward, he inadvertently pressed down on the object and felt the floor beneath him give way. He had found the pebble and had opened the staircase. Unfortunately, he was stretched across the staircase when it opened.

He dropped through the opening, and tumbled down the stone steps, landing at the bottom and hitting his head on the stone. He saw flashes of brilliant light and then everything went black. He woke up some time later. He couldn't tell how long he had been unconscious and wasn't sure it mattered. He was certain he was still in a time zone far away from all the others.

He got to his feet and found himself in a wide hallway. He looked to his left and saw the stone floor, stone walls and stone ceiling disappear more than a hundred yards off as it curved away to the right. He looked to his right and saw an identical image curve away to the left. The inside of this circular tower looked much bigger than the outside, he thought.

He looked around for the source of the light, but could not discover where it was coming from. It was as if the hall had been lit by hundreds of torches, but not a single torch was in sight. Liam felt the floor and the walls. They were cool to the touch, and felt like ordinary slate. More of the Alchemist's trickery, he considered.

Which way should he go? Did it make any difference? Probably not, he thought. He decided to go to his left and started walking along the hall. After about a hundred feet or so, he came upon an archway that opened to the center. Inside was nothing but darkness. He considered stepping through the arch. The problem was that inside the archway and into the interior itself was complete black.

In spite of the amount of light in the hallway, nothing penetrated through the arch into the darkness. He stretched his arm into the opening and couldn't see his own hand. He wasn't sure going through was such a good idea, and he continued walking. He came upon another archway in another hundred feet. The same blanket of darkness was here. He continued walking.

It felt like he had been walking for several minutes and he was certain that he had made a complete circle. The problem was that everything looked the same and he couldn't be positive that he was back where he started. He pulled a dagger from his belt and scratched a mark in the stone on the edge of the archway.

"I should have thought of this when I started," he said out loud.

He wrinkled his brow. Something didn't sound right. He repeated what he had just said, expecting some kind of echo. There was nothing. In fact, the sounds seemed muffled. In spite of the stone all around him, it was as if his voice was absorbed into the air. Or like I'm underwater, he thought. He took a deep breath.

"If I'm under water," he said, his voice still muffled, "then I must be breathing like a fish."

Giving it no more thought, he resumed walking around the hall. When he reached the next archway, he thought he'd count them to see how many there were. He gave up on that idea when he looked down and saw the scratch mark exactly where he had placed it on the last archway.

"That can't be right," he said.

He looked back the way he had come. He moved to the opposite side of the hall as far from the arch as he could and looked back. He could see the edges of the previous arch. What kind of place IS this? He made a second scratch mark in the second arch and moved on to the next one. When he got there, he found both marks on the stone.

"Wonderful," he said. "I've lost my mind."

When he looked through the arch into the darkness, he was startled to see openings at regular intervals in a large circle to his left and right. He could see evenly spaced duplicate archways, all opening to the central blackness.

"Those weren't there before," he said. "Yes, I'm sure. Oh, great. Now I'm not only talking to myself, I'm answering myself. The next thing you know, I'll be arguing with myself. At least I know I'll win."

He stretched his arm out through the archway again, and again his hand disappeared into the black. He slowly brought it back and couldn't see it until it cleared the arch. He did it again with the same result. As he was moving his hand back and forth, watching it disappear and reappear, a sudden movement on the opposite side caught his attention.

He jerked away from the portico, and flattened against the wall. He crouched down and poked his head carefully around the stone corner and took another look. He was focused on the opening directly across from him, when he saw movement to his right out of the corner of his eye. He jerked back again, trying to avoid being seen.

He tightened his grip on the dagger and pulled a short sword from his belt with the other hand. Then he stood up and looked back through the opening. This time he decided he would stand his ground. He scanned several of the distant openings. This time he saw a figure pass by one of the openings moving from his left to his right. It was Quinn.

Liam's heart flew to his throat. Where did he come from, he wondered. He was so excited to see his friend he almost stepped into the darkness. Keep your head, he told himself.

"Quinn," he shouted. "Quinn. It's me. It's Liam. I'm over here."

Quinn had passed the opening and was gone from sight. Liam didn't wait for him to reappear at the next opening. Instead, he turned towards the direction Quinn was heading and began to run. He ran like a mad man, passing one doorway after another. He was positive he should have reached his friend by now.

He stopped to catch his breath and looked across the darkness. As he did, Quinn passed by, directly opposite him. This time he was followed by Solveig.

"Quinn," he shouted again. "Solveig. It's Liam."

They were moving in the same direction Quinn had been moving before. Liam turned towards them and ran to meet them once more. He ran and ran and ran; certain he had made the complete circle more than once, but found no sign of them.

- - - - - - - - - - - - - - - - - *** - - - - - - - - - - - - - - - - - -

Almost immediately after Aitch and Summer reached the bottom of the stone staircase, it rumbled shut, enclosing them in darkness. Neither of them moved or made a sound for several seconds.

"Are you still there?" Summer whispered.

"Where else would I be?" Aitch whispered back. "I can't see a thing. I can't even see myself – any part of me. I have my hand up against my nose and I can't see it. I don't think this was one of your best ideas. We probably should have stayed on the roof."

"If you had seen that dragon, you wouldn't be so sure about staying up there," Summer replied.

"Fine; but what do we do now? We can't go back and I'm not about to start walking around without knowing what's in front of me."

"Can you feel anything?" Summer asked.

"Like what?' Aitch asked back. "I can feel the floor under my feet. That's about it."

"Move your toe forward," she told him. "See if there's any kind of drop-off."

"Drop-off?" he said, raising his voice.

"Shhhh," she hushed him. "We don't know if we're alone."

"Is anybody out there?" he shouted.

"What are you doing?" Summer demanded, hissing at him.

"I'm finding out if we're alone," he said loudly. "Are we alone?" he shouted again. "It doesn't seem like anyone's there."

"Or maybe they don't want us to know they're there!" Summer shot back at him. "Did you ever think of that?"

"So what?" he asked. "If someone is out there, they can't see any more than we can."

"You don't know that," Summer said. "I've run into things that see just fine in the dark."

"Oh, poop," sighed Aitch. "Where do you people come from?" he whispered.

"I don't think you need to whisper now," she complained loudly. "If anyone's in here, they've already heard you," she shouted.

They were both silent for several more seconds.

"Can you see anything, yet?" Aitch asked.

"No," Summer answered. "What about..."

Before she could finish her sentence, a dull light appeared in the distance. It looked like a doorway. A few seconds later, two more arches appeared at equal distances on either side of the first one.

"Do you see that?" Summer whispered.

"Yes," whispered Aitch. "What is it?"

"A doorway" she whispered back.

"I can see that," whispered Aitch. "But to what? And why are we whispering?"

"Oh," said Summer in surprise. "I don't know."

"You don't know what?" asked Aitch. "You don't know what it leads to or why we're whispering?"

"Both," said Summer in her normal voice. "Look!"

As they were speaking two more arches appeared, also at equal distances from the other three. They watched as more of the porticos appeared, pair by pair, in a large circle around them. When it seemed as if they all were now visible, they discovered they were in the center of a very large circular room, but they were still in complete darkness.

"What does this mean?" asked Aitch.

"I have no idea," said Summer.

"I thought you said you had been here before," he said.

"I have, but I didn't see anything like this before. Besides, I think the interiors change every time someone comes into the towers."

"Great," moaned Aitch. "How are we supposed to find Emm and the others?"

"Can you move your foot around to see if the floor extends further?" she asked. "Be careful, though. We could be standing on some kind of pedestal and there's no telling how far down the bottom could be."

"You keep making this better every time you say something," he muttered sarcastically.

He leaned back to keep his weight on his left leg while he stretched out his right toe and felt the floor immediately in front of him. When he didn't feel any edge or drop-off, he moved his toe to the right. Still feeling a solid floor, he swung his foot to the left.

"It seems like the floor is at least a foot or so around us," he said.

He took a tentative step forward. As he did, the darkness began to slowly evaporate. The room they were in gradually became awash in an eerie glow. They looked around for the source of the light, but could find nothing. Above them they expected to see a low ceiling and some sign of the stairway down which they had come. Instead, they saw a huge domed ceiling.

"How is that possible?" asked Aitch. "Where's the stair case? Where's the ceiling that it came through?"

"I told you this place was like nothing you'd ever seen before," Summer said.

She was equally awed by what she saw. She was tempted to fly upward to the top of the dome, but was afraid that this might cause another change in the room and that she might get separated from Aitch. He could imagine what was going through her mind.

"Don't even think about it," he said.

"About what?" she asked, her eyes still fixed on the dome.

"Going up there," he said as he, too, stared in disbelief.

The walls of the room rose high above them before they gently curved toward the center. There was no molding; no carvings; nothing but smooth stone squares that had first looked a dull gray but turned to a light golden color and then to a soft white. As the walls curved inward, the square blocks became trapezoidal until the last row where they were triangular; the points all converging in the center.

"It's beautiful," said Aitch.

"Yeah," said Summer. "Which really makes me nervous."

"Why?"

"Because this place is full of traps," she said. "I have to think this is just one more of those traps."

She stopped staring at the ceiling and looked at the walls. The arches, which had initially been filled with a low level glow of light, were now completely darkened.

"See what I mean?" she asked, pointing to them.

When Aitch didn't respond, she turned to face him. He was still staring at the dome. She flew in front of his face, placed her hands on either side of his chin and pulled his head downward and to one side, aiming him towards the porticos.

"See what I mean?" she repeated.

"Oh, yeah," he mumbled.

He looked down at the floor. It was the same large square blocks of the soft white stone as the walls. It extended all the way in every direction to the wall.

"At least we're not on some kind of pinnacle surrounded by some deep chasm," he said.

"Don't be so sure," she cautioned. "This whole room could be that pinnacle and the chasm could be through those doorways."

"You are such a buzz-kill," he groaned.

In that instance a flicker of motion in one of the archways caught his attention.

"Did you see that?" he shouted, pointing to the archway that was still dark.

"See what?" Summer asked.

"I don't know," he answered. "I saw something move."

In the next archway to the right his eye was caught by another image.

"There it is again," he said, pointing to the next portico. "It's moving. Watch the next one."

They focused their attention on the next opening in line. In a few seconds, they both saw a figure pass by the archway.

"I saw it," she gasped with a mixture of fear and shock. "What was it?"

"I'm not sure," Aitch said. "Watch the next opening."

They fixed their eyes on the next doorway. This time the image was clearer.

"Emm," Aitch shouted. "That was Emm. I saw her. Did you see her? Emm! Emm! It's me. It's Aitch!"

"Yes," exclaimed Summer. "I saw it."

"It was Emm," said Aitch.

He started running for the next opening to which she seemed to be headed. Summer watched in panic as he ran off. She darted ahead of him, swung around and dropped down immediately before his face, both arms extended.

"Wait," she shouted. "Stop."

"Stop?" Aitch asked, pulling up short, and leaning to look around her. "Why? That was Emm. We have to catch up with her."

"It LOOKS like Emm," cautioned Summer. "That doesn't mean it IS Emm."

He was still several yards from the opening. He waited as Summer had asked, but leaned to look past her at the doorway. Once more, Emm's figure strode by. This time Aitch could see another figure next to her, somewhat hidden in the darkness.

"That was Sean," he shouted. "He's with her. I know it. Didn't you see him?"

"Sean?" asked Summer. "No. I didn't see. I was watching you."

"Look, then," said Aitch excitedly. "Watch the next opening. He was walking on the other side of her."

They fixed their eyes on the next portico. In a few seconds, the image of Emm walked by and a second image was apparent next to her.

"See?" shouted Aitch. "That was Sean."

"I saw something," said Summer, "but I'm not sure it was Sean."

"Come on," shouted Aitch. "Before we're too late. Before they get away."

He side stepped Summer and ran towards the opening that was next in line.

"No," shouted Summer. "Wait. It might be a trick."

"It's not a trick," Aitch shouted back, oblivious to her warning.

"Then why can't they hear us?" Summer shouted, chasing after him.

"Who know?" Aitch responded. "You said yourself that nothing in this place is normal. Maybe they can't hear us because they're on the outside of this room."

"Or they can't hear us because they're not really there," Summer called out. "Please, Aitch. Please wait."

He slowed down to a walk, considering her warning. He watched the next opening and then once more saw Emm walk by. He concentrated on the figure next to her and was certain it was Sean. Then he saw another figure behind them. There was no mistaking the size. It was Quinn.

"It's not a trick," Aitch shouted.

He ran to the opening, not waiting to go to the next one, hoping to fall in right behind his sister and the others. Summer rolled her head back in despair. She couldn't let them get separated. Against her better judgment, she darted after him.

They burst through the portico at the same time. Instead of finding themselves in a darkened passageway close on the heels of the others, they discovered themselves in a long, straight hallway. Aitch stopped dead in his tracks.

"What...how...where are they?" he stammered.

He turned around and behind him all he could see was a hallway that stretched straight back the other way. It was the same soft white stone, but the ceiling was at normal height and curve above them from one wall of the hallway to the other. There were no doors or windows or openings of any kind.

He turned back the way he had thought his sister had gone and saw exactly the same thing: a hallway that seemed to have no end. There were no doors or windows or openings of any kind. And there was no sign of any other living person.

"They were never here," said Summer.

"That can't be," said Aitch. "I saw them. They were here."

"Then why didn't they answer?" she repeated her earlier question.

"I don't know!" he snapped in frustration. "But it was Emm. I know that much. It wasn't any kind of a trick."

They both looked up and down the hallway once more, coming to the realization that there was no point in trying to follow the elusive images, regardless of whether they were real or not.

"What now?" asked Aitch. "What do you think we should do?"

There seemed to be only one option. The single break in the entire wall, at least as far as they could see, was the doorway through which they had just come.

"I don't see any choice," said Summer. "I think we should go back where we started. Maybe we should try going through one of the other doorways."

"I thought you said we shouldn't do that," remarked Aitch.

"I said we shouldn't chase after images that didn't answer us," she corrected. "We have to be careful, though, and not run through openings when we don't know for sure what's on the other side. Agreed?"

"Agree," he replied.

They turned back to the portico, glanced at each other, and looked closely into the opening which was now as dark as it had been when they first arrived.

"When did this happen?" asked Aitch.

"Apparently when we weren't looking," replied Summer.

Aitch stepped up to the edge of the arch. He put his hand through and it disappeared into the darkness. He turned to look at Summer with uncertainty. She moved closer and sat on his shoulder.

"I'm right with you," she said. "Whenever you're ready."

He took a deep breath and stepped across the threshold into the darkness. However, instead of entering the blackness, he found himself facing another wall. He looked left and right and discovered they had stepped into another hallway. This one was almost identical to the one they had just left, except that it clearly curved. Aitch looked to the right and he could see the hall curve to the right. He turned to his left and saw the hall curve to the left.

"It's a circle," he said, turning around to face the portico through which they had just stepped.

"This looks like the hall that circled the room we were in at the beginning," said Summer. "Look."

She was pointing through the archway towards the hall they had exited. The hall was gone. In its place was a large black room with archways dimly lit at regular intervals in a circle ending with the one at which they were standing.

"Isn't that where we started?" she asked.

"Summer?" a familiar voice sounded. "Is that you?"

"What was that?" asked Aitch. "Tell me you heard it."

"I heard," said Summer. "That wasn't you?"

"No it wasn't me," said Aitch.

"Aitch?" asked the voice. "Are you there, too?"

"This is not funny," Aitch shouted. "Whoever you are – show yourself!"

"Where are you?" asked the voice. "I can't see you."

"Never mind where we are," shouted Summer. Then she whispered to Aitch, "This may be a trap. Don't say anything about where we are."

"That won't be a problem," Aitch whispered back. "I have no idea where we are."

"We're not telling you anything," Summer shouted to the voice. "Who are you?"

She rose up slightly from Aitch's shoulder, looking left and right down the hall, although she was certain the voice was coming from the darkness.

"Who are you?" she repeated.

"It's me," the voice answered. "Liam."

Chapter nineteen

ochen followed the others down the steps into the darkness. As soon as he reached the bottom, the steps rose up towards the ceiling and disappeared. He blinked his eyes, trying to adjust to the total absence of light, but his efforts were pointless. He could see nothing.

"Is everyone here?" he asked.

In reply he heard several voices at once. Then he called to each of them separately until he was satisfied that they were all together.

"What kind of place is this?" asked Emm.

"It belonged to the Alchemist," said Natalie. "It's really strange."

"And we thought it was a good idea to come here?" Emm asked.

"Yeah," agreed Sean. "Why DID we come here?"

"The spells that the Alchemist has layered over these towers," explained Lochen, "should offer ample protection to us from the Kelpies or the sorcerers that have taken their place. At the same time, it is the logical location for the other to come."

"But if they're in a different time, isn't it possible they're already here?" asked Emm.

"I suppose," said Lochen.

"And if they are in a time that's earlier than we are," she continued, "and they came here, how long do you expect they will stay?"

"Uh...I'm...ah...not sure," Lochen stammered.

"I only ask because if they're...what...maybe a hundred years? Two hundred years? A thousand years in our past, and they came here, I doubt they would wait around all that time waiting for us to show up and find that they've aged – even assuming they're still alive. Does that about sum it up?" Emm asked.

"Hmmm," Lochen pondered. "I hadn't quite thought of that."

"What?" exclaimed Quinn. "You mean she thought of something that YOU didn't?"

"I can't be expected to think of everything," Lochen said, defensively.

"Maybe not," said Solveig. "But that seems to be a pretty big thing not to think of."

"I'm not concerned about that," said Lochen.

"Maybe you should be," said Sean. "I sure hope we don't come across a bunch of bones."

"If you're not concerned about that," asked Natalie, "what exactly ARE you concerned about?"

"The rather large and evil looking figure that was approaching the towers as we were making our decent," Lochen answered.

"What?" shouted Solveig.

"You're only telling us that now?" asked Sean.

"If you recall," Lochen replied, "I was preoccupied with responding to questions about our apparent inability to locate the others in light of the dimensional shift in time that we've encountered."

"What did he say?" asked Emm.

"It's not worth explaining," said Stella. "The important thing is we can't stay here. Potential danger is right behind us."

"We can't get very far if we can't see where we're going," said Quinn.

"Let me see if I can shed some light," said Solveig.

She made a fist and thrust her arm forward, letting loose with a bolt of lightning.

"No," shouted Lochen, too late. "Don't...."

It was too late. The bolt escaped Solveig's hand before he could stop her. Instead of opening into a burst of light and illuminating their location, the ball of energy struck something in the darkness, ricocheted off whatever it was and bounced off in another direction, striking something else and ricocheting over and over again. They all dropped to the floor to avoid being struck, unable to do anything until the ball of lightning burned itself out several seconds later.

"...release a burst of lightning," Lochen finished his warning.

"Sorry about that," Solveig said. "That's never happened before."

"I'm afraid our magic might not work in here the same way it does on the outside," said Lochen.

"It was worth a try," said Natalie. "We can't sit here in the dark and hope that whatever is up on the roof doesn't find its way down here."

"Let me try something," said Stella.

"Just be careful," cautioned Sean. "I nearly wet myself."

"Oh, dude," moaned Quinn. "I didn't need to hear that."

Stella felt around for the pendant, grasped it in her hand and raised it above her head. The glow inside the stone began to churn. It slowly grew brighter and stronger until it flashed. When it did, the walls around them brightened.

"Wow," said Emm. "How did you do that?"

"It belonged to the Enchantress," said Stella. "I thought if anything could penetrate the Alchemist's spells, it would be her pendant."

"Wonderful," said Sean. "But where are we?"

They all looked around. They were in a wide hall, but unlike the ones in which their missing friends had found themselves, these were straight and not very long. In fact, they saw that they were in the center of an intersection.

One of the paths went straight for about ten yards and then seemed to bend to the left. The next one went straight for about half that distance and turned to the right. The third one went straight for more than twenty yards and turned left, and the last one went straight for only a few feet before turning right.

"Those turns should be running into each other," observed Emm.

"Yeah," said Natalie, "you would think. But not in this place."

"Should we split up and check them all out?" Emm asked.

"NO!" they all shouted.

"That's not the best idea," said Stella. "We tried that once before without much success."

"She's right," said Quinn. "We need to stay together, no matter what."

"Whatever," she said. "But how do we know which one to take?"

"I suppose any one of them is as good as another," said Sean. "Let's start there."

He pointed to the passage that was the shortest. No one could find a reason to disagree, so they allowed him to lead the way.

They quickly reached the first turn, which they made. Ahead of them the passage stretched out into the distance.

"Great choice," smirked Quinn.

"Like you could have done better," said Sean.

They followed the hall for several yards and came upon a split. One part continued straight and the other presented another right turn.

"Which way now?" asked Emm.

"Right," said Lochen. "We should always go to the right."

"Why right?" asked Natalie.

"Because our first turn was right," Lochen answered. "By making all our turns to the right, we have a better chance of retracing our steps should the need arise."

"You mean we may have to go back?" asked Emm.

"That's entirely possible," answered Lochen. "This appears to be a maze. If that's correct, then it's very probably that some of these paths will be dead ends."

"Arrrr," growled Emm. "We're never going to find Aitch."

"He's in good hands," said Natalie.

"Yeah," said Sean. "As long as he sticks with Liam, he'll never get lost."

"And Summer will stick by him, too," said Stella.

"I hope so," said Emm. "Let's keep going. I don't want to waste any time."

They continued along for several minutes before coming to another intersection. They turned right once more. Emm was expecting that they'd end up back where they started, but there was no sign that this had happened. Then it dawned on her that the walls all looked the same. They could find themselves back at the beginning and not ever realize it. She voiced this thought to the others.

"That's a very real possibility," said Lochen.

"How do we know it hasn't happened already?" asked Emm.

"Because we haven't run into an intersection," said Sean. "Remember? Where we started was a four-way intersection. We haven't seen anything like that."

"But we could," said Emm. "And how would we know if it was the same one?"

"Why don't we leave some kind of mark or sign?" suggested Quinn.

"That's a great idea," said Natalie. "But how?"

Sean plucked one of the small stones he carried in a pouch at this belt to use with his slingshot. He held it up for them to see and then scratched a mark in the stone at the bottom of the corner.

"How's that?" he asked.

"Better," said Emm.

They continued on until they came to another intersection. This time the passage made one turn to the right and one directly across from it to the left. They all started to turn to the right as previously planned until Quinn looked down at the bottom stone and saw a scratch mark on it.

"Hey," he called to the others. "Someone else has been here and had the same idea we had," he added and he pointed to the mark on the stone.

"That looks exactly the same," said Solveig. "It IS the same. How is that possible?"

"Maybe it's just a coincidence," said Natalie. "Let's keep going and see what happens."

After a few more minutes they came to an intersection where the passage went straight or turned to the left. Turning right was not an option, but on the far left corner of the left-turn passage there was a scratch mark on the bottom stone. It was in the exact place it would have been made if they had come from the opposite direction.

"This is too freaky," said Emm.

"And it would seem pointless," added Lochen. "Something in the spells placed on the towers has made such markings ineffective."

"And they don't work, either," said Sean.

Lochen rolled his eyes and suggested that they trust their instincts. They should continue onward as they had originally planned. When they reached the next split in the passages, there was no mark on any of the stones. They weren't sure they should be glad about that or not.

Eventually, the hallway changed. It began to curve to the right. They came across no more intersections. Instead, they approached an archway on their right. Emm stopped before they reached the archway, a look of stunned surprise on her face.

"What is it?" asked Solveig. "What's wrong?"

"Aitch," she said. "He's here."

"Where?" asked Natalie.

"I don't know exactly," Emm replied. "But I know he's close by."

They moved on. When they came to the archway, Lochen stopped them from turning into it. Instead of a well-lighted hall, there was nothing but darkness inside the portico.

"Shouldn't we turn right?" asked Quinn. "Like all the other times?"

"No," said Emm.

Everyone had expected Lochen to answer the question. All eyes turned to Emm. She answered the question so forcefully, they waited for some explanation. She looked from one to the other before continuing.

"Something else is here," she said. "Some powerful evil. Can't you feel it?"

They all indicated that they could notice nothing different. They had felt uncomfortable from the moment they entered the interior of the tower. Other than that, they could detect no additional danger.

"I can feel it gripping my throat," Emm said. "It feels like it's strangling me."

"I think it might be a heightened level of anxiety at being separated from your brother," suggested Lochen. "I feel no such threat, although I wouldn't expect to. However, nothing in these towers is normal. I trust your judgment in this. Let's continue along the hall."

They passed several more archways. Each one was as dark and foreboding as the first one. However, each time they passed an opening, Emm had an overwhelming sensation of Aitch's presence. That was immediately followed by the feeling of the presence of unimaginable power and evil.

"We need to get out of here," she finally said.

"But where?" asked Solveig.

"Back the way we came," she said. "I don't care, just as long as it's not the way ahead. My sensations are getting stronger. I'm afraid we're headed straight for something very dangerous. Please. Let's go back."

They started winding their way back the way they had come, turning left at every opportunity. Emm's anxiety rising with every step. She was becoming frantic.

"No," she finally said. "This isn't right. That feeling of danger is growing stronger."

"Are you saying we should go back the way we had originally been going?" asked Quinn.

"No," she said. "There's something in that direction as well."

They had stopped at another of the intersections. They would have otherwise turned to the left, but the hall that continued straight ahead ran for a few yards before ending in a "T." She looked down that passage skeptically, turned to look the way they had come and then towards the direction they were supposed to turn.

"We need to go that way," she said.

"We're going to get seriously lost," objected Sean.

"I'm afraid he's right," added Lochen. "This maze is very complex. As you have seen, we are unable to leave any markings that would prevent us from losing our way."

"I don't care," she nearly screamed. "We're in danger."

Before she could explain any further, a dark shadow filled the hallway behind them. Emm saw the figure first and backed away in horror. The others spun around to see what had frightened her and came face to face with Walipreen. He had to bend over to fit into the corridor, and his shoulders were so wide that his movements were inhibited. It was that obstacle to his mobility that gave them all a split second to react.

"Run," shouted Sean as he fired his slingshot in a futile attempt to gain a few precious seconds.

They scattered blindly. Sean, Quinn, Lochen and Solveig flew down the passage to the left, back towards the original starting point, while Stella and Natalie ran towards the T intersection. As soon as they reached it, they started to separate, going in opposite directions. At the last second, Natalie grabbed Stella's arm and pulled her along.

"Keep to the right," she hissed. "That's the only way we won't completely lose the others."

In the pandemonium, Emm did the unthinkable. She ran right towards the giant sorcerer and dove between his legs, coming up behind him. She ran down the hall and turned to the right where she stopped to listen.

Walipreen had been surprised and slightly distracted by Sean's shot. He hadn't seen Emm shoot by him. He ignored the two that had run to the right and went after the four that were in front of him. Before they reached the next juncture in the maze he had them within his sights. He pointed a finger at them and froze them in place.

Lochen tried to turn and counter the spell, but his arms felt like lead. He was able to look back, but he couldn't raise his arms. Walipreen made a circular motion with his hand and turned them all to face him. He looked them over as he slowly moved closer to them.

"I can see that none of you is the Phynnodderee," he growled. "Which of you has the pendant?"

When no one responded, he clenched a fist. Solveig started gasping, struggling for air.

"Speak, or this one will stop breathing forever," he snarled.

"Leave her alone," barked Lochen. "None of us has the pendant. You chose poorly."

"Then none of you are of any value to me," Walipreen said as he glared at Lochen. "And you," he added, leaning in even more closely towards Sean, "you were the one who threw that stone at me, aren't you? No respect for your superiors, I see."

"The only thing you're superior at," said Sean "is being really ugly."

A sneer crept across Walipreen's face. He had released his grip on Solveig and was now much closer, leaning over the four of them. As he was speaking, his eyes became distant. He seemed to falter for a few seconds.

Around the corner from him, Emm had crept up, hugging the wall, her heart hammering in her chest. She had seen Walipreen go after the four, leaving Stella and Natalie free for the moment. She focused her attention on the sorcerer and allowed her mind to enter his thoughts. When she had controlled the minds of the Phookas, she had encountered images that were relatively simple.

This time, she was staggered by the chaos. She could sense overlapping images and memories. Her head was spinning and she fought to concentrate her energy. I can't do this, she thought, panic rising. She inched closer and tried harder. She found a thread she believed was the actual Walipreen. She had to plant a thought and get out quickly. She needed to find Stella and Natalie.

"I'll come back later for you," Walipreen said.

His eyes lost their glazed look, but something was different. The sorcerer stepped back and waved his hand. The four were pushed back into the wall and became part of it. Their bodies were absorbed into the stone, only the faintest outline of their features bled through.

Emm could feel the change in Walipreen and broke off the limited control of his mind. She ran   down the hall to the T intersection and stopped. There was no sign of Stella or Natalie. Which way, she wondered. Right, it came to her in a flash. They would have gone to the right. She turned and ran.

Stella and Natalie discovered quickly that they were not being chased. They decided to turn back to see if they could rescue the others. Within a few yards, they ran into Emm. Emm's eyes were immediately drawn to the pendant.

"I understand," she said pointing to it.

"Understand what?" asked Natalie.

"The pendant," said Emm. "I would read that beast's mind. That's Walipreen, the sorcerer of the north. He's changed. I could feel the memories of several others – Kelpies. He has somehow stolen their history and their power. He can't catch us. He can't get his hands on that pendant."

Emm grabbed their hands and pulled them along, running down the hall, and turning right at every opportunity.

"Where are the others?" asked Stella.

"They're safe – for now," gasped Emm. "But they won't be if he catches us. He's insane. Once he has the pendant – and me..."

She understood for the first time that she, too, was a target. This realization came as a shock to her. She could detect that Walipreen didn't fully understand why he wanted to capture her; only that he would steal her power the same way he had stolen the powers of the Kelpies.

"He means to destroy the Boravak," she blurted out. "He has absorbed the powers of the Kelpies and he wants to steal mine. But I don't have any powers. Not really."

"I think you do," said Stella. "You're an enchantress. The potential is there; it just hasn't been realized yet. If he comes after you, he'll probably come after me as well; and not only for the pendant. We have to prevent this at all costs."

"What about the others?" asked Natalie. "We can't leave them behind."

"We'll have to come back to them," said Stella.

"How are we going to find them?" demanded Natalie. "We don't even know where we are. How can we ever expect to locate them?"

"We can't worry about that now," said Stella.

"She's right," said Emm. "If we're captured, he'll have no use for them; and I don't think I can control his mind enough to prevent him from destroying them."

"You won't be able to," confirmed Stella. "Once he has us, you're powers will be his."

They could hear him roaring as he struggled to turn around. He was unable cast any spells to break the walls down and his frustration was growing rapidly. Natalie pointed to the next turn in the maze, but Emm stopped her.

"No," she whispered. "Not that way."

"But Walipreen is back behind us," said Stella.

"Something else is that way," said Emm. "Something almost as bad as Walipreen. We need to go to the left."

Natalie hesitated for a second, realizing they may never find their way back – or out, for that matter. Trusting in Emm, she turned left and led the way.

------------------ *** ------------------

Liam was certain he was losing his mind. He had seen images of Quinn and Solveig. They were in the same circular corridor that he was. He assumed that they hadn't stepped into the black center room, but could find no explanation for his inability to catch up to them. He approached one of the archways and stuck his toe through.

It was immediately engulfed in the darkness. He leaned forward, holding on to the stone doorway and tried to feel the floor with his foot. There seemed to be nothing inside the circle. He got down on his hands and knees and felt around blindly. Nothing.

He thought it was a good thing he hadn't tried to cross. It was probably some kind of abyss. He wondered if it was the same at every access. He moved to the next one and tested it. Like the first one, there was nothing of substance on the other side of the threshold. One after another, he felt around finding nothing solid beyond the arch.

He sat on the floor, uncertain of what to do next. That was when he heard a voice. At first it was muffled and he wasn't sure he had actually heard it. He looked up at the ceiling and then to the left and the right. He thought he had only imagined it. Then he heard another one. This one was different. Were there two people talking? Where was it coming from? He rolled over onto his knees and strained to hear.

"I'm...you...ready."

He couldn't make out everything, but he was positive he understood those words. They seemed to be coming from inside the darkness. He ran around what he thought might be about a quarter of the circle.

"...circle..."

The voice was the same, but still muffled. And it didn't seem any closer. He ran around further. Then he heard the second voice.

"...looks...hall...room...at the beginning."

He still couldn't make out what was being said, but the few words that came through were distinctive enough that he could tell there were two of them. Then he heard a complete sentence.

"Isn't that where we started?"

He knew that voice. It was coming from the center of the black room, but it was as if it's owner was only a few yards away.

"Summer?" he called. "Is that you?"

There was silence for a few seconds. Then he heard the first voice again, but not as clearly.

"What...heard..."

The voices faded a bit. Liam could hear them talking back and forth. Then he heard a full sentence again and recognized the speaker.

"No, it wasn't me."

Liam stood up and leaned into the darkness, holding tightly to the edge of the archway.

"Aitch?" he asked. "Are you there, too?"

"This is not funny," Aitch shouted. "Whoever you are – show yourself!"

"Where are you?" asked Liam. "I can't see you."

"Never mind where we are," shouted Summer.

What was wrong, wondered Liam. Why would she be so nasty to him? He could hear them talking to one another in low voices. He couldn't make out what they were saying. Then Summer shouted back.

"We're not telling you anything," Summer shouted. "Who are you?"

Liam was surprised by the question. He assumed they had recognized his voice. Then he wondered if it really was Summer and Aitch. Maybe it was some kind of trap. What if some sorcerer had captured them and was imitating their voices?

"Who are you?" Summer repeated.

Liam decided he had to take a chance. He readied himself to run in case something evil jumped out of the darkness.

"It's me," he answered. "Liam."

His words were met with silence. He waited for a few seconds. When he still heard nothing, he called out again.

"Are you still there?" he asked. "Can you tell me where you are? All I see is darkness. Is it dark where you are?"

His words were absorbed in the blackness. He wasn't sure if they could hear him anymore. He shouted more loudly this time. Then he repeated his call to them, but still received no response. What if something happened to them, he asked himself. I need to help them.

He thought for a few seconds and considered his options. He had gone round and round this hall. He had seen images of Quinn and Solveig, but he had no idea if these were real or merely his imagination. He had carried on a conversation with Aitch and Summer, brief though it was. But they had answered him.

There was nothing more he could do in this corridor. He saw no other options. He took a deep breath, let go of the archway and took a long step forward into the darkness. Too late he tried to pull back, when he felt himself falling forward and not stopping. Great, he said out loud. My last thought will be that this was an abyss after all, and I should have stayed put.

He could tell he was falling fast. His arms stretched outward in a feeble attempt to fly or to at least slow his descent. He was surprised when it seemed to be working. His fall slowed down for no apparent reason. Then he felt himself turning and tossing, like he was being buffeted by the wind.

He saw a light off in the distance and saw that he was moving in that direction. Except, he didn't feel like he was falling in that direction; instead, it felt like he was being gently moved that way. Although his drop – now his apparent sideways motion – had slowed down, the light was still coming at him at a very fast speed.

He lunged to his right to find something to grasp to stop him. There was nothing there. He lunged to the left with the same result. He started flapping his arms, but nothing would stop him. Finally, he stretched his arms out in front of him to brace himself as he burst through the opening and slid across a long, stone floor.

When he stopped sliding and spinning, he found himself in a hallway of some kind. Smooth, soft white stone covered the walls, the floor and the ceiling. He turned back the way he had entered and saw nothing but a solid wall. He seemed to be at the end of the hall. He turned around and began walking.

Soon he came to an intersection. He turned to the left where the hall ended with an abrupt right turn. He walked down the hall a few feet and passed some peculiar marks on one side. He barely gave them a glance, but stopped and went back to them.

Wow, he thought. It almost looks like the pattern of the stone has created faces in it. He saw four of them and they looked remarkably like Quinn, Sean, Lochen and Solveig. He dismissed the vision, thinking that he was seeing things that weren't there. He missed his friends too much.

Then he heard noises. In fact, he was sure he had heard a scream. He ran in the direction of the sound, rounded another corner and almost ran into an enormous gray-black creature with a hideous tail. At the sound of his approach, the beast turned to look at him, struggling to turn around.

"What's this?" roared Walipreen. "Another insect to crush?"

"Oh, poop," cried Liam.

He pulled a dagger from his belt and flung it at the sorcerer. Walipreen was able to free his left arm as he fought to turn around, and batted the blade away like it was nothing. Liam didn't wait to try again. He slipped and scrambled as he ran back the way he had come, trying to remember which way that was. He didn't want to find himself in a dead end with that thing chasing him.

He turned to the left and then to the right. He ran by what he thought was the dead end and kept weaving in and out of the turns. He was looking back over his shoulder to see if he was being followed, only glancing forward to watch where he was going. As he rounded another corner and turned his face forward, he skidded to a stop.

His feet flew out from under him and he slid along the floor, kicking to get a foothold and to slow his progress. In front of him was another creature. This one was not as big, almost as ugly, and as surprised to see Liam as Liam was surprised to see him.

"Oh, double poop," muttered Liam.

He rolled over onto his stomach as he was slowing down and got to his feet. He pulled another dagger – this one from the other side of his belt – and flung it without really looking over his shoulder.

Prine had heard something coming toward him and half expected to find himself confronted with Walipreen. He was about to turn back the other way, hoping to find his way out of this nightmare of a maze, when an odd little figure came around the corner, slid across the floor, scampered to his feet, threw a knife at him, and disappeared back the way he had come.

The dagger had been thrown haphazardly and Prine watched as it bounced off one of the walls and fell to the floor. It hadn't come close to hitting him, but was enough of a distraction to slow him down. By the time he gathered his wits, Liam had fled out of sight.

What kind of mess did I get myself into, Liam wondered. He was running blindly now. He knew where Walipreen was when he last saw the sorcerer. He hoped he was taking paths that would put more distance between them. He also wondered if there was a way back to the circular hallway, thinking that place didn't seem so bad now.

He was once again looking back over his shoulder as he rounded another corner and came up short when he nearly ran into some more figures. He was about to reverse direction thinking that this place was far too crowded when he saw that he had run into Natalie, Stella and Emm. All four of them screamed in fright and then nearly started laughing in relief.

"Where did you come from?" asked Natalie.

"It's a long story," said Liam. "And I'm sorry, but now's not the time to tell it. There are two really big and really ugly guys in this maze. We need to get away from them."

"Walipreen and one of the Twins," said Emm. "I could feel their presence, but we only saw Walipreen."

"What about Lochen, Quinn, Sean and Solveig?" asked Stella. "Did you see them?"

"No," said Liam. Then he realized what he had seen. "Wait! Yes, I think I did. But that Walrussy guy…"

"Walipreen," interjected Emm.

"Yeah," said Liam. "That guy. He's between us and them."

"Can you find a way to get to them?" asked Natalie.

Liam looked at the walls. He looked down one corridor, and then the other. He seemed to be giving her question some thought.

"I think so," he said. "But not if Walipoop…"

"Walipreen," said Emm.

"Whatever," said Liam. "That guy. Not if he's still where he was."

"I have an idea," said Stella.

Chapter twenty

Walipreen was furious that the little creature who had suddenly appeared and thrown a knife at him had escaped. His anger mounted when he sensed the presence of Prine nearby. He knew both the pendant and the Phynnodderee were close, but he was lost in this cursed maze. The walls were so narrow and the ceiling so low that he had difficulty moving and felt wedged in place when he tried to turn around.

His ire was so great that he thought about returning to the place he had imbedded those four into the wall and attempt to squeeze information from them. Maybe if the ones who had escaped heard the screams of their friends, they'd give up what he was looking for. He moved towards an intersection to make turning around easier.

That was when he could feel a thought come into his mind. It was like a voice calling to him and only he could hear it. The witch with the pendant and the Phynnodderee were going to try to slip by him and release the ones encased in stone.

He sensed a trap, but then he changed his mind. He was too powerful to be fooled by this enchantress. He shook his head, trying to clear his mind. It seemed that every thought he had that encouraged caution was dismissed.

"It's a trap," he shouted out loud.

"Shut up," he told himself. "You are Walipreen. You can control this witch. She is no match for you."

He argued with himself, his voice roaring through the halls. In another area of the maze, his voice was heard by Stella, Emm, Natalie and Liam.

"Who is he talking to?" asked Natalie.

"Himself," said Emm. "Well, actually, he's talking to me, but he doesn't know that. I've gotten inside his head."

"Remind me never to get on your bad side," said Liam.

"What's he thinking?" asked Stella.

"He received the thought about you and me trying to find the others," answered Emm. "He can't find his way through the maze to get to them, though. He's lost. He also thinks this is a trap. I can convince him it's worth the risk, but I can't get him there."

"Can you tell where he is?" asked Liam. "If you can, I can tell you how to get to the others."

"No," said Emm. "I can only read his thoughts. If he's lost, then so am I."

"But you can tell if he's close or not, can't you?" asked Stella.

"Yes, but what good would that do?" replied Emm.

"Because I can get us to the others, and if you can sense where he is, then we can lead him to us," said Liam.

"That's a long shot," said Emm.

"It may be the only one we have," said Natalie. "But we have to get there before him so Liam and I can hide. This won't work if he sees us."

They agreed on the plan and Liam started to lead them towards the stone images he had passed earlier. He was hardly paying any attention to the twists and turns, taking one after the other, only asking if they were getting too close to Walipreen. He hadn't thought to ask about Prine. The turned a corner and came up behind him.

He had been completely turned around and was searching frantically for the way out. He hadn't noticed them approach, but when he heard them stop and gasp at the sight of him, he spun around, shocked to see them.

"Get me out of here," he pleaded.

Regaining his composure, he raised his hand to cast a spell, but was quickly blocked by Stella. She shot a blast of energy at him, knocking him off his feet. Emm's concentration on Walipreen was momentarily interrupted, and he could sense a change.

Through Emm's connection, he realized that Prine was no longer on the tower roof.

"Prine," he bellowed. "I gave you an order. You disobeyed it and you will pay."

Prine was flat on his back, dazed by the blast Stella had delivered. She and the other three quickly changed direction and put several intersecting corridors between them and him. Once they were certain they were safe, Emm once again concentrated her energy on controlling Walipreen's mind.

She had difficulty instilling a sense of reason. She was distracted by the madness that had taken over his mind. At the same time Liam was directing them in a wide loop around both him and Prine.

"I hope no one else is in here," said Natalie.

The words were no sooner out of her mouth than they ran into Rampool. He had entered through tower one with most of his army. Now he was alone – alone and clearly disheveled. His eyes were bulging, he was panting, his clothing was torn and his hair had apparently been burned from his head.

"Please," he begged. "Get me out of here."

They backed away from him, but he fell to his knees and crawled towards them, pleading.

"Everyone I entered this accursed place with – each one of my soldiers – has disappeared, turned to stone, been covered in ice or lava, or suffered some other demise," he moaned. "I have nowhere to turn; no one to help me. I beg of you. Show me how to escape."

His eyes fixed on Emm and he lunged at her.

"You," he shouted. "You have the power. You have to help me."

"Let go," she shouted, pulling her shirt sleeve free. "I don't know what you're talking about."

Stella stepped in front of her and Liam pulled a small knife from his boot. Rampool scrambled forward, oblivious of their defensive postures.

"Take me to my brother," he demanded. "Do that at least."

"He's that way," said Liam, pointed down an adjacent corridor.

Rampool turned his head in the direction Liam had indicated. He wasn't sure whether or not to believe what he was being told until he heard his brother's shout. He then jumped to his feet and ran down the hall.

"Is Prine really down that hall?" asked Emm. "Having them join forces isn't going to help us."

"No," said Liam. "I'm pretty sure he's in the opposite direction."

Emm looked at him curiously, trying to decide if he had purposely sent Rampool in the wrong direction. Without any further discussion, Liam continued to lead them through the maze. After several minutes and so many turns to the left and right and back again, Liam discovered the corridor in which the four were encased. Emm could feel that Walipreen was not very far away.

"Can't you cast some kind of spell to get them out?" Natalie asked Stella.

"I don't think so," she said. "That's more of Lochen's area of expertise, not mine; and he's not in any position to help."

"I wish there was another way to do this," said Liam. "I'm not confident this is going to work."

"It has to work," said Stella. "Emm, which direction is Walipreen?"

She thought for a few seconds and then pointed to the right.

"That way, I think."

"You think?" asked Natalie. "I hope you're sure."

"I told you before that I can't tell exactly," she said. "It's more of a feeling."

"Let's just do this," said Liam. "We'll go around that corner and wait," he added pointing to the left.

Once they were out of sight, Emm stood behind Stella and concentrated on Walipreen. She whispered to Liam the paths the sorcerer was taking as much as she could. He whispered back changes in direction, and she planted those thoughts in Walipreen's mind. He soon believed he could tell where he was going and started moving faster.

"He's getting confident now," Emm told Stella. "He thinks he's outwitted whoever created this maze. He thinks he knows exactly where he's going. He hasn't even given any thought to why we would be here. He's not rational."

"That's what I'm counting on," said Stella.

After several painfully slow minutes, the sorcerer rounded the corner, coming from the right as Emm had hoped. He saw them and at first took a few quick steps towards them. Then he slowed down, exercising more caution. He raised his hand, ready to cast a spell, but stopped when he saw Stella look directly at him.

"Please," she said and then lowered her head. "Please show us mercy. I will give you this pendant, if you would please release my friends."

She had removed the pendant from around her neck and held it in her extended hand. He glanced down at the gem, then at Stella, and then to Emm, searching for some kind of trick. Emm stood cowering behind Stella, clearly frightened. He waited. Stella kept the offering held out to him, waiting for him to take it. Then he did.

He snatched it from her hand. He missed the slight flicker of her finger as she released it to his grip. He held the pendant tightly, the gossamer thread that had held it around Stella's neck, dangled. He studied the gem and could feel its power coursing up his arm and into his body. Then he eyed Emm.

"And her," he growled, motioning with his other hand towards Emm. "I will have the Phynnodderee, too."

Stella jerked her head up in surprise.

"No," she objected. "Please. You don't need her. She knows nothing. She has no power. I have given you all the power you need. Release my friends and let us leave."

"You are in no position to make demands!" he roared back at her. "Not now; not ever."

"Forgive me," begged Stella. "I did not mean to presume. I implore you, because of your power, to allow us to leave. We will be forever in your service. Just spare us. All of us."

Walipreen was reveling in his control over this so-called enchantress. The recollections of the Kelpies had led him to believe that she was a challenge equal to them – equal to him, he thought, unable to make the distinction. He leaned over her to further intimidate her.

As he did, he was oblivious to the thread that now grew from the pendant like a spider's web, wrapping around his arm, extending to the other arm, and entrapping him. Unaware, he had lowered the arm that held the pendant, and the filament crawled around and around his body like a cocoon. Faster and faster it moved, winding downward, spinning from one leg to the other.

It wasn't until Walipreen tried to take a step closer towards Stella that he realized he was ensnared. He began to teeter, losing his balance, unable to spread his feet to maintain himself. As he crashed to the floor, the pendant was dislodged from his hand and slid across the stone with the original length of thread, back to its rightful owner.

He bellowed in outrage, screaming and cursing, shouting threats at Stella and Emm. He ranted and raved, foaming at the mouth in fury. Emm backed away from him. Even though he was incapable of striking out or casting a spell, his anger was so venomous, it frightened her.

At the same time, Stella placed the pendant against the wall and murmured an incantation. Very slowly, the markings in the stone wall began to move. The faces re-formed and the bodies gradually followed. One by one, Quinn, Lochen, Sean and

Solveig emerged from the prison in which Walipreen had held them.

"Oh, poop," said Quinn when he saw Walipreen writhing on the floor. "I thought for sure we were stuck there forever."

"I surmise that you effected a very clever ruse," said Lochen.

"What did he say?" asked Emm.

"He said he guessed you played a pretty good trick on him," said Solveig.

"Thanks for the translation," replied Emm.

"Where did you come from?" asked Sean, noticing Liam for the first time as he and Natalie came from around the corner.

"It's a long story," he said. "I'll fill you in later. Right now we need to find a way out of here."

"Wait," said Solveig. "Where are Aitch and Summer?"

"I don't know," said Liam. "We were separated back where we all came into the Boravak."

"What were you doing there?" asked Lochen. "Please tell me you didn't attempt to go back and forth."

"All right," said Liam. "I won't tell you, but we did. They did. I didn't. Anyway, that's when we got separated."

"We need to find them," said Sean.

"We will," said Liam. "But we have to get out of here. It's not safe."

"He looks like he's trussed up pretty good," said Quinn, motioning to Walipreen.

He had been shouting at them the entire time and trashing in an attempt to loosen his bonds.

"That won't last," said Stella. "Besides, there are two more in here somewhere."

"The Twins," said Emm. "Liam sent one of them off on a wild goose chase, but neither of them is very far away, and I don't think it will be long before they find each other."

"Then making our escape seems paramount," said Lochen. "Liam, I presume you can show us the way out of this maze."

"I think so," he said. "But after that, I'm not sure where we can exit the towers."

"If you can get us to a circular room," said Lochen, "a place where Stella can project her images, I believe I can deliver us to a safer place."

"I can do that all right," Liam said. "I was stuck near a room just like that."

He led them through one turn after another, periodically asking Emm if she could sense or in some way connect with Prine to ensure they didn't run into him. She assured him he was lost somewhere in the distance. After several minutes he approached an archway that led to complete darkness.

"We're not going in there, are we?" moaned Quinn. "There's no light in there."

"Sorry, but that's the way out," said Liam. "Just stay close everybody."

He had expected to experience the reverse or perhaps even the same as he had when he initially stepped into the blackness. He was certain they would feel a falling sensation. Instead, he was taken aback when they burst through and found themselves in another hallway, but one that was completely different.

"What happened to all that darkness?" asked Sean.

"It appears that we are in a corridor surrounding it," said Lochen, motioning to their left.

Liam was still in the lead. Quinn was staying close by his side. Lochen, Natalie and Stella were following them, with Solveig a few steps back. Behind her was Emm and she was followed by Sean, who kept looking back over his shoulder for any signs of danger.

The corridor curved to the left, and before long it was evident they were moving in a large circle. Archways slowly emerged through the darkened center, visible on the opposite side. Liam kept walking, hesitant to suggest stepping into the darkness, even though he had been in this place before.

"Can't we just go through the middle?" asked Natalie.

"No," said Liam, as he continued walking at a quick pace. "It's a vortex of some kind. That's how I ended up in the maze."

"How is that possible?" asked Lochen. "You, Summer and Aitch were in a different time. When we were behind the falls, we came under attack. Emm was able to project a vision sufficient enough for me to transport us, but as before, it was to a different time as well as a different place. You and the others were left behind. How could you get to the same time and location as we were?"

"I guessed," Liam started to explain. "That is, we guessed you all would either go to the hole in the Boravak or come here. I got separated from Aitch and Summer. When I did, I came here. I saw you...well, two of you. I saw Quinn and Solveig."

"Why didn't you call out to us?" asked Solveig, trying to keep up with Liam.

"I did," he replied. "You couldn't hear me."

"We were in a different time," said Lochen. "That makes sense."

"Is he serious?" Emm asked Sean. She had to run every few steps. "I don't find anything in this place that makes sense."

"He's kind of weird that way," said Sean. "He sees sense in things none of the rest of us do. After a while, we just learned to live with it."

"But I also heard voices," Liam added. "I heard Aitch and Summer."

"That means they're here, too," said Emm, excitedly. "Where?" she called to Liam. "Where did you hear them?"

"It sounded like they were coming from inside the center of this room," Liam said.

As they were quickly circumnavigating the central room, a flash caught Emm's eye. She glanced to her left, worried that either Prine or Rampool had discovered them. She slowed down and studied the archways on the opposite side. Sean nearly bumped into her.

"Don't stop," he cautioned. "They'll get too far ahead of us."

She quickened her pace again and he glanced behind them. At that moment, Emm saw the image of Aitch flash by one of the arches.

"Aitch," she shouted. "Aitch. Over here. It's me. It's Emm."

On the opposite side, Aitch stopped and looked towards the sound.

"Emm," he shouted back and waved.

Without thinking; without regard for the possible danger, Emm stepped through the archway before Sean could stop her.

"No," he shouted.

"Emm!" Aitch shouted.

He was about to go into the room after her when Summer spun around and, as before, hovered immediately in his line of vision and stopped him.

"NO!" she shouted into his face. "Don't go in there."

"But that was Emm," he objected.

"Don't trust anything you see," she warned him. "Nothing in this place is what it seems."

On the opposite side of the circle, the others had rushed back when they heard Emm and Sean's shouts.

"What happened?" asked Solveig.

"Emm," said Sean. "She...she just stepped into the darkness. I couldn't stop her. It happened too quickly."

"Why did she do that?" asked Natalie.

"She shouted her brother's name and then just went in," said Sean.

They all looked into the blackness and saw nothing. The arches on the opposite side had disappeared.

"What do we do?" asked Quinn. "Shouldn't we go in after her?"

"No," said Liam. "There's no telling where that will lead or if whoever goes in after her will find her. We could end up losing each other completely."

"We can't just do nothing," said Sean.

"The best thing we can do," said Lochen, "is to find our way out, reunite with Aitch and Summer, and leave this place and time. The security of the Boravak is more important than any one of us. That must be our priority."

As they were talking, the large area surrounded by the corridor gradually lightened. A single archway appeared on the opposite side of the room. Sean was the first to see.

"Summer," he shouted. "Aitch. It's us."

Summer turned when she heard her name. She saw the others on the opposite side of a large circular room that was beginning to glow.

"Stay there," she shouted. "Don't go in the...darkness? Where did it go? Where did this come from?"

The central room that was becoming more and more visible was open at only two sides. Summer and Aitch were on one side and the others were on the other side. The inside of the room was the same smooth, soft white stone. The walls rose to a domed ceiling.

"It's a sanctorum," said Stella.

"Is it safe?" asked Quinn.

She turned to smile at him.

"They've always been safe," she said, stepping into the room.

Everyone watched as she walked calmly to the center, gazing at the ceiling. She extended her arms and spun in a circle, basking in comfort.

"This is the safest place of all," she said to them.

Slowly, the others stepped into the room. Then Sean ran towards Summer and was quickly followed by the others. Aitch stepped in last, looking at the walls and the floor, wondering what had become of his sister.

Back in the maze, Rampool and Prine managed to find each other. Their fear was quickly replaced by anger. They agreed that those who had left them in this trap would be made to suffer. They concentrated their efforts on finding the way out. Along the way, they discovered Walipreen.

"Should we release him?" Rampool asked.

"If you don't free me from these bonds," screamed Walipreen, "I will make you regret ever being born."

"That doesn't sound encouraging to me," said Prine. "Leave him."

They didn't bother casting another glance back at him as they disappeared around the next corner.

"Come back," shouted Walipreen. "I command you to come back."

He wrenched his body one way and then another. He could feel the ties loosening, but not quickly enough. He vowed to himself that once he was free, he would hunt the Twins down and destroy them. Then he would find the enchantress who did this to him and make her pay dearly.

Meanwhile, back in the sanctorum, Stella sensed that the Twins were getting close and that Walipreen was nearly untangled.

"Can you project an image of these towers?" Lochen asked Stella.

"In this place, I can project anything you want," she answered. "Tell me quickly what you need. We don't have much time."

The pendant around her neck was radiating brightly.

"Can you find a similar room in one of the other towers?" he asked.

"Why would you want to go to another tower?" asked Natalie.

"Is that where Emm is?" Aitch asked hopefully.

"No," said Lochen. "I am fairly certain we can do nothing for Emm. At least not here. We need to tie up loose ends in this world and then get back to our own world."

"So that's it, then?" snapped Aitch. "You're going to leave my sister some place in here. What? For the rest of her life? If that's your plan, then leave me behind. I'll find her and I'll find my own way out."

"That's not our intention," said Lochen.

He reached up to put his hand on Aitch's shoulder to console him. Aitch shoved it off and stepped back.

"Don't," he said. "Don't lie to me. You just want to get out of here. Well, I'm not going. Not without Emm."

"I'm afraid you are," said Lochen.

He swiped his hand in a downward motion in front of Aitch's eyes before the Phynnodderee could react and before he knew what hit him. In an instant he was in a deep sleep and fell to the floor like a sack of potatoes.

"Quinn," Lochen said. "Could I prevail upon you to carry him?"

"Sure," answered Quinn as he bent over, picked up the lifeless form and slung it over his shoulder.

"Now," continued Lochen. "Stella, if you would; project an image of the room in tower four that is as close to this as possible. It wouldn't by any chance be near the roof, would it? With an easy access?"

"Actually," she said, "I think it's directly below the roof."

She stretched out her arms and the walls burst with light. It was as if a map of tower four appeared before their eyes.

"And, yes," she said. "It seems there's a stairway to the roof."

"Good," said Lochen.

He stepped to the image and looking over his shoulder, motioned for the others to come closer. He then covered the base of the staircase with his left hand, murmured an incantation and then struck the wall with his right hand, but very gently this time. The inside of the sanctorum shook slightly and the light flared, but wasn't blinding.

They felt the ground beneath them disappear and their stomachs rolled. By the time they realized this, they were on solid ground once again. They had a slight spinning sensation and the walls spun around them, blurring from the soft white to a dull gray. As suddenly as it started, it stopped.

They were in a room nearly identical to the one they had left, except that the stone was older and dingier, and instead of arches at opposite sides of the room, there were staircases: one leading up to the roof and one down to the lower levels of the tower and who knew what dangers.

"Natalie," said Lochen. "Would you please join me on the roof? The rest of you can stay here. We won't be long."

They all looked at her with puzzled expressions as she followed Lochen to the roof. They walked to the edge and could see tower five and the remains of the narrow ice bridge that they had destroyed in another time.

"Can you cast a bubble around the entire tower?" Lochen asked.

"I suppose," she said. "Why would you want to do that?"

"To bring this matter to an end once and for all," he told her.

"OK," she said.

She took a deep breath, flung her arm forward and covered the tower from front to back, from top to bottom in a giant bubble. Lochen nodded his approval and told her she could join the others. He'd be down in a few seconds.

When he came down the stairs a few seconds later, he had a devious smile on his face, but told no one why. Instead he asked Stella if he could cast an image of the town of Satamakau.

"Satamakau?" she asked. "What for?"

"Because I believe that will be the optimum location for the conclusion of our mission," he told her.

"Whatever," she said.

She stood in the center of the room and concentrated on her memories of the ancient port town. In front of her was the sea wall that held the periodic tidal bores that struck the town. To her right in the distance was the edge of the town where they had encountered the Amazing Artabarat.

Behind her was the river down which they traveled on the makeshift raft. To her left was an extensive forest. That was the location Lochen chose. He gestured to the others and they huddled around him. He focused on a clearing deep in the woods and covered this spot with his left hand.

He murmured an incantation and then struck the wall with his right hand; this time much harder than the last time. The inside of the old gray sanctorum exploded. Once again they were surrounded by a blinding light and felt as if they were suspended in midair. As the light faded, their surroundings whirled around them, as if they were in the center of a tornado.

People and objects spun around them; any sounds muffled by the roaring wind. As suddenly as it had all started, it stopped. They found themselves in the clearing in the forest exactly as it appeared in the image on the wall. Once the dizziness subsided, Lochen waved his hand in front of Aitch's eyes and woke him up.

"What did you do to me?" he sputtered angrily.

"I couldn't leave you in the towers," Lochen said.

"But you didn't have any problems deserting my sister," he shouted. "Take me back. Take me back right now."

"I will," Lochen replied. "If that's what you want, I'll do as you ask."

"What are you talking about?" interrupted Solveig. "You can't go back there."

"And if you do," interjected Sean, "it won't be without us."

"I don't believe that will be necessary," Lochen told them. "Aitch. I ask that you trust me. Allow me one day." He looked at the sky and judged the position of the sun. "The rest of this day. If by nightfall, you still want to return to the towers, I will take you there myself and I will stay with you until we locate Emm."

"What kind of trick is this?" Aitch demanded. "One of your sorcerer tricks?"

"I certainly hope so," smile Lochen. "One day?"

Aitch thought it over. He didn't really have much choice. He had no idea how to get to the towers from here and no clue as to how to get in. Finally he agreed.

"All right," he said begrudgingly. "One day. And I'm going to hold you to your promise."

"Agreed," said Lochen.

He turned and began heading through the woods.

"Where are we going?" asked Liam. "Do you need me to find the way?"

"Thank you, but no," said Lochen. "I'm quite certain I know the way."

After a few hours, Sean started paying more attention to where they were.

"I must be losing it," he said. "This place looks really familiar."

"Familiar how?" asked Natalie.

"If I didn't know better, I could swear I've hunted near here."

"Lochen," called Natalie. "Do you know what time we're in? Did you take us back too far?"

"Time is irrelevant," was all he said.

A little while later the woods began to thin out. They could see mountains to their left – to the north.

"Oh, wow," said Solveig. "You're right, Sean. This really looks familiar. Those look like our mountains. Look! That one that rises higher than the others: it's purple."

"Where are we?" demanded Aitch. "If this all looks familiar to them, it's way before my time. I want to know…"

He stopped mid-sentence. He could see his village through the trees.

"How?" he asked.

As they got closer, several of the Phynnodderees saw them approaching and waved in welcome. Then through the onlookers, a small girl burst through.

"Aitch" she shouted. "You're back. Who are your friends?"

"Emm?" he asked.

"What do you mean, 'Emm?' like you don't know me?" his sister asked. "You haven't been gone that long: only a couple of days."

He turned to look at Lochen. He didn't know what to say. Stella asked the question for him.

"This all looks like it was when this was our home," she said. "Sean recognized the woods, Solveig recognized the mountains, which, if I recall correctly, had been destroyed. How is this possible?"

"When we left the tower," Lochen explained, "the Boravak collapsed."

"What?" Quinn nearly shouted. "You mean we have to do this all over again?"

"No," said Lochen. "I didn't express it correctly. The Boravak that separated us from Aitch's world – that Boravak collapsed, and time was compressed as well. This is our time. It's his as well, but it's ours, too. Sean, your Lodge is deeper in the woods. Your people and the Phynnodderees are very close allies; not that there are any real enemies. Natalie and Stella, your people are well established along the shore, as they had been before it was necessary to create that bubble on the ocean floor."

"And the faeries?" asked Summer.

"Right where they always were," he answered. "I will enjoy spending time with them when we travel back that way. And, yes, Solveig. Our castle is still at the top of the mountain, but there's a cable system that transports us back and forth. Liam, your people live in a wonderful garden and Quinn, your family is still to the north."

"I'm sorry I got in your face," said Aitch.

"I understand," said Lochen. "I wasn't certain all this had happened until just now. I assumed it would work out this way, but I wasn't positive."

"But what about the Kelpies?" asked Natalie.

"Ancient history," said Lochen. "Of course, that same ancient history speaks of eight strangers who to this day are unidentified, but who battled and defeated the Kelpies."

"What about Walipreen and the Twins?" asked Aitch.

"Ah, yes," said Lochen. "I had almost forgotten."

He reached into an inner pocket and pulled out a glass ball the size of a grapefruit. He handed it to Aitch.

"A gift for Emm," he said.

Aitch drew the ball closely and peered at it. Inside the glass was a tiny, stone tower. It bore an uncanny resemblance to tower five at Virkio.

"For me?" Emm asked. "It's a bit creepy looking. But beautiful at the same time. How interesting."

"What did you do?" asked Natalie.

She moved up and looked over Emm's shoulder at the orb. The others' interests were now piqued as well.

"That looks like tower five," said Sean.

"It is," said Lochen. "After Natalie cast the bubble I requested, and left to join the others, I...well...I thought..." He seemed uncertain of how to explain.

"I shrunk it down to a more manageable size and then proceeded to cast several complicated and obscure spells over it. It hardened quite well."

He reached over and knocked on the top of the ball.

"In fact, it's now made of the hardest substance in the universe. Nothing will shatter or open it," he declared.

"Why did you make is so strong?" asked Summer.

"I wanted to make sure it would protect the contents," he replied.

"The fortress?" asked Stella.

"That, too," Lochen answered.

He looked at their confused faces.

"And what's inside that particular tower," he explained. "On the inside are Walipreen and the Twins, captured in the mazes and mysteries of tower five."

Everyone looked at him, not sure what he was saying. He smiled, rather pleased with himself, and spelled it out for them.

"They are tucked away nice and neatly in their own separate Boravak."

Quest of Eight Addendum: The Other Side of the Boravak

Richard Reda

ABOUT THE AUTHOR

Richard Reda spent most of his life working for various agencies and Departments in the Federal Government. He believes this gave him a solid foundation for writing fantasy and fiction, so much so that he was encouraged to return after retirement to write some more. He lives with his wife in Manassas, Virginia, where he retired – the first time.

The *Quest of Eight* series originated as bedtime stories for his grandchildren. As the grandchildren got older and the bedtime stories got longer, it was suggested to him that he write them down. So he did. One, however, was not enough. The eight stories have been a true labor of love.

Quest of Eight Addendum: The Other Side of the Boravak

Richard Reda

E. DE MÉNORVAL

PARIS

DEPUIS SES ORIGINES JUSQU'A NOS JOURS

TROISIÈME PARTIE

DEPUIS L'AVÉNEMENT DE HENRI IV, LE 2 AOUT 1589
JUSQU'A LA MORT DE LOUIS XIV, EN 1715

OUVRAGE ILLUSTRÉ D'UN PLAN EN COULEURS

MAISON DIDOT

FIRMIN-DIDOT ET Cⁱᵉ ÉDITEURS

IMPRIMEURS DE L'INSTITUT,
RUE JACOB, 56, PARIS